The Best
AMERICAN
SHORT
STORIES
2015

GUEST EDITORS OF
THE BEST AMERICAN SHORT STORIES

The Best AMERICAN SHORT STORIES® 2015

Selected from
U.S. and Canadian Magazines
by T. C. BOYLE
with HEIDI PITLOR

With an Introduction by T. C. Boyle

HOUGHTON MIFFLIN HARCOURT
BOSTON • NEW YORK 2015

ISSN 0067-6233
ISBN 978-0-547-93940-7
ISBN 978-0-547-93941-4 (pbk.)

Printed in the United States of America
DOC 10 9 8 7 6 5 4 3 2 1

Contents

Foreword

THIS IS THE hundredth volume of *The Best American Short Stories*. Over the past century, series editors have provided early support and exposure to such writers as Ring Lardner, Willa Cather, William Faulkner, Dorothy Parker, Thomas Wolfe, Richard Wright, Saul Bellow, Delmore Schwartz, Robert Coover, John Updike, Shirley Jackson, and Raymond Carver, among countless others. I am deeply honored to be the editor of this esteemed, long-lasting series and to have been for the past nine years. For more about the series, its history, and a sampling of the gems that have appeared in its pages, see *100 Years of The Best American Short Stories*, edited by Lorrie Moore, coedited by yours truly.

When I think back over some of the characters from this series that have stayed with me most, I think of Sarah Shun-Lien Bynum's Ms. Hempel, the bewildered and imperfect schoolteacher from "Yurt," which appeared in the 2009 volume. I think of the lapsed recovering alcoholic therapist, Elliot, from Robert Stone's story "Helping," featured in the 1988 volume, and in 1982, the narrator of Raymond Carver's "Cathedral," whose discomfort with his blind guest is palpable. I think of all the tough-as-nails mothers: Mabel, in Bobby Ann Mason's "Shiloh"; the bigoted woman known only as Julian's mother in Flannery O'Connor's "Everything That Rises Must Converge." I think of writers like Mary Gaitskill and Ann Beattie and Joyce Carol Oates and John Cheever and Ernest Hemingway and Sherwood Anderson, writers whose characters are complex, whose conflicts are often internal and unspoken, and whose decisions some people might deem "unlikable."

Lately I've been mulling over the idea of likability of fictional characters. The topic received a burst of attention a couple of years ago, after the writer Claire Messud was asked about the protagonist of her novel *The Woman Upstairs,* "I wouldn't want to be friends with [her], would you? Her outlook is almost unbearably grim." Messud famously responded to the interviewer, "Would you want to be friends with Humbert Humbert? Would you want to be friends with Mickey Sabbath? Saleem Sinai? Hamlet? Krapp? Oedipus? Oscar Wao? Antigone? Raskolnikov? Any of the characters in *The Corrections?* Any of the characters in *Infinite Jest?* Any of the characters in anything Pynchon has ever written? Or Martin Amis? Or Orhan Pamuk? Or Alice Munro, for that matter? If you're reading to find friends, you're in deep trouble. We read to find life, in all its possibilities. The relevant question isn't 'Is this a potential friend for me?' but 'Is this character alive?'" Messud's answer ignited both readers and writers, many glad for her illumination of a troubling but increasingly prominent trend in how readers talk about fiction.

Soon after, *The New Yorker* interviewed a group of fiction writers about the issue. Donald Antrim said, "Reading into persona is a waste of time and life; our empathy will not be engaged but our narcissism might, and our experience will likely come without deeper emotional and spiritual recognitions and awakenings. The author maneuvering for love is commonplace and ordinary, and the work of fiction that seductively asserts the brilliance or importance or easy affability of its creator is an insubstantial thing. I have no problem with liking a character. But if that's the reason I'm reading, I'll put the book down." And Margaret Atwood answered, "I myself have been idiotically told that I write 'awful' books because the people in them are unpleasant. Intelligent readers do not confuse the quality of a book with the moral rectitude of the characters. For those who want goodigoodiness, there are some Victorian good-girl religious novels that would suit them fine."

And yet in the couple of years since then, I still somewhat regularly encounter reviews that attack a character's or even a writer's likability. To like a story or a novel is still, it seems, to like its characters. One female protagonist was just last week labeled a "morose, insufferable American narcissist" in a major Sunday book review. Another renowned book review laments that in a well-received debut novel, one character "isn't much of a heroine. She's annoying,

self-centered and tragically naive." The female narrator of one of
my favorite novels of last year was called "irritatingly self-obsessed"
by yet another major newspaper. Dip a toe into the reviews of fiction on GoodReads or Amazon, and you'll find the question of likability everywhere. I'd hazard a guess that more female characters
written by female writers are deemed unlikable than male characters or really any characters written by men. Hopefully VIDA,
the organization that studies women in the literary arts, and other
similar groups will research this question.

In this year's volume of *The Best American Short Stories,* we are
treated to characters like Kavitha, the emotionally numb wife who
comes alive only in the face of violence, in Shobha Rao's gorgeous
story, "Kavitha and Mustafa." We meet a desperate absentee father
in Justin Bigos's devastating "Fingerprints" and an emasculated
man who sells dental equipment in the hilarious and profound
"Unsafe at Any Speed," by Laura Lee Smith. And Joe Carstairs, a
ruthless champion speedboat racer and oil heiress in Megan Mayhew Bergman's unforgettable "The Siege at Whale Cay." Here are
living, breathing people who screw up terribly and want and need
and think uneasy thoughts. Did I like these characters? I very much
liked reading their stories, as did T. C. Boyle. I liked the honesty of
the portrayals, and their poetry and humor and surprise. Would I
want to be friends with these characters? Who cares? To me, that
question is tantamount to asking someone at an art exhibit if she
would like to be friends with the color green, or someone listening
to music if he would care to befriend a drum.

To readers who tend to think primarily in terms of liking or
disliking characters: these people are fictional. They do not stand
before us asking to be liked. They stand before us asking to be
read. They ask to be seen and heard and maybe even understood,
or at least for their motives to be understood, if that is what the
author is after. But, for the sake of argument, let's pretend these
characters are in fact real, that they are human beings standing
before us. Let us open up at least a little to those we might not
like—in their presence, we might experience something new. To
me, facing those we might not want to face is crucial to living in a
diverse world. To echo Donald Antrim, when we instinctively turn
away from something different or uncomfortable or what we deem
"incapable of being liked," we shortchange ourselves. Maybe we
unwittingly dislike characters who do or say what we ourselves can-

not or simply, for whatever reason, do not. As the fiction writer and critic Roxane Gay wrote, "Perhaps, then, unlikable characters, the ones who are the most human, are also the ones who are the most alive. Perhaps this intimacy makes us uncomfortable because we don't dare be so alive." If reading fiction has the power to enlarge our understanding of others and enliven ourselves, let us try to no longer shrink from these things.

What an honor it has been to work with T. C. Boyle, whose own stories have appeared in this series many times. He came at the job of guest editorship with the deep knowledge and experience of a master. He chose twenty thrillingly diverse and stellar stories by established and exciting new writers.

The stories chosen for this anthology were originally published between January 2013 and January 2014. The qualifications for selection are (1) original publication in nationally distributed American or Canadian periodicals; (2) publication in English by writers who are American or Canadian, or who have made the United States their home; (3) original publication as short stories (excerpts of novels are not considered). A list of magazines consulted for this volume appears at the back of the book. Editors who wish for their short fiction to be considered for next year's edition should send their publications or hard copies of online publications to Heidi Pitlor, c/o *The Best American Short Stories*, 222 Berkeley Street, Boston, MA 02116.

HEIDI PITLOR

Introduction

BACK IN THE 1970S, when I was a student at the Iowa Writers' Workshop, I went one evening to hear Stanley Elkin read from his latest novel. Stanley was a magnetic performer, fully invested in his role, and we students knew enough from previous encounters to avoid the first three rows, where the audience was at risk of being sprayed with flying spittle as he worked himself into an actor's rage. This was performance at its highest level, as was the Q&A that followed. The first question was from a student who was as hopefully dedicated to the short story form as I was: "Mr. Elkin, you've written one great book of stories, why don't you write another?" Stanley's response: "No money in it. Next question."

Was he joking? Was his cynicism part of the act? I don't know. But in our time the literary marketplace has certainly favored the novel over the short story, and anyone seeking to make a living off stories, as Fitzgerald did in the 1930s, would have to have been transported in time. Either that, or gone off his meds. And it's interesting to note that aside from a late collection of early pieces, Stanley did publish only that one collection. As did James Joyce and Philip Roth and so many others, who through temperament, ambition, or calculation went on to publish exclusively in longer form.

A hundred years ago, when Edward O'Brien inaugurated this annual volume in celebration of the short story, things were both different and the same. Different, in that O'Brien's principal motivation in making his selection of the year's twenty best stories was to distinguish the artists from the commercial hacks, the original from the conventional. "There are many signs," he wrote in his introduction, "that literature in America stands at a parting of ways. The technical-commercial method has been fully exploited, and, I think, found wanting in essential results" and was responsible for "the pitiful gray shabbiness of American fiction." It's difficult to grasp just what he's militating against here, unless we consider how the function of short stories on the page was co-opted first by radio serials and films, then television, and more recently the Internet, with its panoply of blogs, tweets, and postings. That there *was* a commercial short story to denigrate is fairly astonishing in itself, like learning that a new Dead Sea scroll has been unearthed. O'Brien can rest assured that we no longer have to worry about the commercialization of the short story for the obvious reason that there is no commerce to speak of. Our stories—and the stories in this volume stand as a representative sample—are conceived and composed solely for the numinous pleasure artistic creation imbues us with, the out-of-body experience writer and reader share alike.

Still, then as now, the short story was considered inferior to the novel, a mere stepping-stone to higher things, and the less dedicated (less addicted? less fou?) could find their métier in writing longer works, or better yet, writing for the screen. This was great good news for O'Brien: "The commercialized short story writer has less enthusiasm in writing for editors nowadays. The 'movies' have captured him. Why write stories when scenarios are not only much less exhausting, but actually more remunerative?" So much for the money-grubbers. Let them stand out there in the blaze of Hollywood sun, at the beck and call of actors, directors, producers, and their mothers, while the serious practitioners of the form rise up to take their rightful place in the popular and literary magazines.

An evangelist of the literary story, O'Brien went beyond praising the individual writers he'd chosen for the inaugural volume to applaud and promote the magazines that met his standards as well, including *The Bellman,* in which the top story of the year appeared ("Zelig," by Benjamin Rosenblatt), and a new monthly, *Midland,* which though it published but ten stories that year, found its writers displaying "the most vital interpretation in fiction of our national life that many years have been able to show." And more: "Since the most brilliant days of the New England men of letters, no such group of writers has defined its position with such assurance and modesty." Hyperbole? Yes, of course, when viewed from the far end of the long tunnel of a hundred years' time, but hyperbole in a good cause. He also singled out stories by writers like Stacy Aumonier, Maxwell Struthers Burt, and Wilbur Daniel as achieving the highest honor he could bestow, that of being of lasting value—and if he was wrong, carried away in his enthusiasm, give him credit here too. After all, who can say with any certainty what literature will endure and what will die with the generation that produced it? Make no mistake about it, O'Brien was on a mission to cultivate the taste of the reading public and champion the homegrown story, and he was feisty over it too, singling out British critics like James Stephens, who, in his estimation, insufficiently appreciated the American novel and seemed barely aware of the achievement of the American story.

But what of the stories themselves, the selection from 1915 that included pieces from Fannie Hurst and Ben Hecht (the only names I recognized, both of whom would, traitorously, go on to careers in film)? I'd like to report that there are hidden gems here, works equal in depth and color to Joyce's *Dubliners* stories or Conrad's "Youth" or Chekhov's "Peasants," but that's not the case. The stories are rudimentary—character studies, anecdotes, tales that exist only to deliver a surprise or the mild glimmer of irony. And they are short, for the most part, more like scenes that might have been contained in the longer narratives of this volume. The shortest of them, what would be called "flash fiction" today, at just 152 words, is by Mary Boyle O'Reilly. It's called "In Berlin," and I find it fascinating in its historical context (two years before America entered the First World War) and the way in which the author so nakedly attempts to extract the pathos from her episode set aboard a German passenger train. The scenario: "The train crawling out of Berlin was filled with women and children, hardly an able-bodied man. In one compartment a gray-haired Landsturm soldier sat beside an elderly woman who seemed weak and ill." The woman, lost in her thoughts—dazed—kept repeating "One, two, three" aloud, which prompted titters from the pair of girls seated across from her. The old soldier leaned in: "'Fräulein,' he said gravely, 'you will perhaps cease laughing when I tell you that this poor lady is my wife. We have just lost our three sons in battle. Before leaving for

the front myself I must take their mother to an insane asylum.'"
Paragraph. "It became terribly quiet in the compartment."

All right. I'm sorry. But if that penultimate line doesn't make
you burst into laughter, you'd better check your pulse. O'Brien
read 2,200 stories that year (by contrast, Heidi Pitlor, who, as series
editor, does the heavy lifting here, considered 3,000), and his aim
was to define the literary story and elevate it above the expected,
the maudlin, the pat and declamatory. To give him credit (he is, after all, one of the first to have recognized Hemingway's talent, including "My Old Man" in the 1923 volume, even though it hadn't
yet been published, and in subsequent editions he recognized the
work of Sherwood Anderson, Edna Ferber, J. P. Marquand, Dorothy Parker, F. Scott Fitzgerald, and Josephine Herbst, among many
others), he can play only the hand he's been dealt, as is the case
with all editors of best-of anthologies. "Zelig," the story he singled
out above all the rest, does show elements of modern sensibility in
terms of its milieu—Zelig is a working man, a Russian Jew come to
America reluctantly because his immigrant son is stricken ill—and
in its representation of the protagonist's consciousness, which
moves toward the close third-person on display in a number of
stories in the current volume, like "The Fugue," by Arna Bontemps
Hemenway, or Victor Lodato's grimly hilarious "Jack, July." Still,
Zelig is cut in the mold of Silas Marner, a miser and nothing more,
and it's his lack of dimension that artificially dominates the story
and propels the reader toward the expected (and yes, maudlin)
denouement. I can only imagine what the "technical-commercial"
fiction must have been like that year.

The Model T gave way to the Model A and to the Ferrari and
the Prius, the biplane of the First World War to the jet of the Second, modernism to postmodernism and post-postmodernism. We
advance. We progress. We move on. But we are part of a tradition
and this is what makes O'Brien's achievement so special—and so
humbling for us writers bent over our keyboards in our own soon-
to-be-superseded age. *The Best American Short Stories* series still follows his template and his aesthetic too, seeking to identify and
collect some of the best short fiction published in the preceding
year. O'Brien listed 93 stories in his Roll of Honor for 1914–15
and 37 periodicals from which the selections were made. In addition, he included an alphabetical listing of the authors of all
the noteworthy stories he'd come across, replete with asterisks

for the ones deserving of readers' special attention. In the same spirit, the editors of the 2015 volume list the 100 Distinguished Stories of the year and some 277 magazines. (In a wonderfully fussy way—and by way of encouraging competition—O'Brien also produced a graph of all the magazines, showing how many stories each periodical published and figuring the percentage of those he considered exceptional.) Finally, O'Brien made no apologies. The stories he presented were the best of the year by his lights—and his lights were the only ones that mattered.

I have to confess that I came to my role as guest editor this year with just a tad less assurance. This was my show, yes, but those hundred years of history—that tunnel of time—was daunting. Ultimately, though, what I was looking for wasn't much different from what O'Brien was: stories that grabbed me in any number of ways, stories that stood out from the merely earnest and competent, that revealed some core truth I hadn't suspected when I picked them up. Another editor might have chosen another lineup altogether from the 120 finalists, but that only speaks to the subjectivity each reader brings to his or her encounter with any work of art. If I expected anything, I expected to be surprised, because surprise is what the best fiction offers, and there was no shortage of such in this year's selections.

For one thing, I was struck by the intricate narrative development and length of many of these stories, some of which, like the two powerful missing-child stories that appear back-to-back here due to the happy accident of the alphabetical listing O'Brien ordained at the outset (Colum McCann's "Sh'khol" and Elizabeth McCracken's "Thunderstruck"), seem like compressed novels in the richness of their characterization and their steady, careful development. So too with Megan Mayhew Bergman's elegant historical piece, "The Siege at Whale Cay," which presents a deeply plumbed love triangle involving the young protagonist, her mannish lover, and, convincingly, touchingly, the cinema star Marlene Dietrich. (What *did* Marlene do on vacation during those grim war years? Where did she go? Who was she? It's testimony to Bergman's imagination that such a familiar real-life figure can seem so naturally integrated into the world she creates that we're never pulled out of the story.) Likewise, Diane Cook's feminist fable, "Moving On," with its dark shades of Kafka, Atwood, and Orwellian control, develops with the pace and power of a much longer work, as does

Julia Elliott's delicious and wickedly funny examination of the ascetic versus the sensual in the convent that provides the setting for "Bride." Long stories all. Very long stories.

Which begs the question, eternally batted about by critics, theorists, and editors of anthologies like this one: what, exactly, constitutes a short story? Is it solely length (the 20,000-word maximum that the how-to manuals prescribe)? Is it intention? Is it a building beyond the single scene of the anecdote or vignette but stopping short of the shuffled complexity of the novel? Lorrie Moore, in her introduction to the 2004 edition of this series, quipped, "A short story is a love affair; a novel is a marriage." And: "A short story is a photograph; a novel is a film." Yes, true enough, and best to get at any sense of definition metaphorically rather than try to pin down the form with word and page limits. For my part, I like to keep it simple, as in Norman Friedman's reductive assertion that a short story "is a short fictional narrative in prose." Of course, that brings us back to the question of what, exactly, constitutes "short." Poe's criterion, which gives us a little more meat on the bones, is that a story, in contrast to a novel, should be of a length to be read in one sitting, an hour's entertainment, without the interruption that the novel almost invariably must give way to: "In the brief tale . . . the author is enabled to carry out the fullness of his intention . . . During the hour of perusal the soul of the reader is at the writer's control."

There's an undeniable logic to that—and a mighty power too. What writer wouldn't want the reader's soul held captive for any space of time? But Poe, for all his perspicacity, couldn't have foreseen how shrunken and desiccated that hour has become in the age of the 24/7 news cycle and the smartphone. We can only hope to reconstitute it. Ultimately, though, beyond definitions or limits, I put my trust in the writer and the writer's intention. If the writer tells me that this is a short story and if it's longer than a sentence and shorter than, say, *The Brothers Karamazov,* then I'm on for the ride. I have never had the experience of expanding a short story to the dimensions of a novel or shrinking a novel to the confines of a short story. I sit down, quite consciously, to write a story or to write a novel and allow the material to shape itself. "The more you write," as Flannery O'Connor pointed out, "the more you will realize that the form is organic, that it is something that grows out of the material, that the form of each story is unique."

Certainly the most formally unique piece included here is Denis Johnson's "The Largesse of the Sea Maiden," a story about stories, about how we're composed of them and how they comprise our personal mythologies. Johnson builds a portrait of his distressed narrator through the stories he tells and absorbs. At one point, the narrator picks up the phone to hear one of his ex-wives, through a very poor connection, telling him that she's dying and wants to rid herself of any lingering bitterness she still has for him. He summons up his sins, murmurs apologies, but at some point realizes that he may in fact be talking not to his first wife, Ginny, but to his second, Jenny, and yet, in a high comic moment of collateral acceptance, realizes that the stories are one and the same and that the sins are too. In a similar way, Sarah Kokernot's "M & L" switches point of view midway through the story to provide two versions of events, both in the present and the past, which makes the final shimmering image all the more powerful and powerfully sensual. And Justin Bigos's "Fingerprints" employs a fractured assemblage of scenes to deepen the emotional charge of the unease the protagonist feels over the stealthy presence of his estranged father, who haunts the crucial moments of his life.

There are others I'd like to flag for you too, but since this is merely the preliminary to the main event, I'll be brief. Kevin Canty's "Happy Endings" gives us McHenry, a man widowed, retired, freed from convention, who is only now coming to terms with that freedom in a way that makes luminous what goes on in the back room of a massage parlor, while Laura Lee Smith's "Unsafe at Any Speed" plays the same theme to a different melody, pushing her middle-aged protagonist out onto the wild edge of things just to see if he'll give in or not. Smith plays for humor and poignancy both, as does Louise Erdrich in "The Big Cat." Edrich's story came to me as a breath of fresh air, the rare comic piece that seems content to keep it light while at the same time opening a window on the experience of love and containment. In contrast, Thomas McGuane's "Motherlode" presents us with a grimmer sort of comedy and a cast of country folk as resolutely odd as any of Flannery O'Connor's.

There's a whole multiplicity of effects on display here, which is as it should be, each of the best stories being best in its own way. Shobha Rao's "Kavitha and Mustafa" is a riveting, pulse-pounding narrative that allies two strangers, an unhappily married young woman and a resourceful boy, during a brutal train robbery in Pakistan, while Aria Beth Sloss's "North" unfolds as a lyrical meditation on a life in nature and what it means to explore the known and unknown both. In "About My Aunt," Joan Silber contrasts two women of different generations who insist on living their own lives in their own unconventional ways and yet, for all their kinship, both temperamental and familial, cannot finally approve of each other. Ben Fowlkes's "You'll Apologize If You Have To" was one of my immediate first-round choices, an utterly convincing tough-guy story that wouldn't have been out of place in Hemingway's canon and ends not in violence but in a moment of grace. So too was Jess Walter's "Mr. Voice," a story about what it means to be family, with one extraordinary character at the center of it and a last line that punched me right in the place where my emotions go to hide. Which brings me to the most moving story here, Maile Meloy's "Madame Lazarus." I read this one outdoors, with a view at my command, but the view vanished so entirely I might as well have been enclosed in a box, and when it came back, I found myself in the mortifying position of sitting there exposed and sobbing in public. An old man, the death of a dog, Paris. What Meloy has accomplished here is no easy thing, evoking true emotion, *tristesse,* soul-break, over the ties that bind us to the things of this world and the way they're ineluctably broken, cruelly and forever, and no going back.

We've come a long way from the forced effects of Benjamin Rosenblatt's "Zelig" and Mary Boyle O'Reilly's hammer and anvil pounding out the lesson of "In Berlin." I can only imagine that this series' founding editor, Edward J. O'Brien, would be both amazed and deeply gratified.

T. C. BOYLE

The Best
AMERICAN
SHORT
STORIES
2015

The Siege at Whale Cay

FROM *The Kenyon Review*

GEORGIE WOKE UP in bed alone. She slipped into a swimsuit and wandered out to a soft stretch of white sand Joe called Femme Beach. The Caribbean sky was cloudless, the air already hot. Georgie waded into the ocean, and as soon as the clear water reached her knees she dove into a small wave, with expert form.

She scanned the balcony of the pink stucco mansion for the familiar silhouette, the muscular woman in a monogrammed polo shirt, chewing a cigar. Joe liked to drink her morning coffee and watch Georgie swim.

But not today.

Curious, Georgie toweled off, tossed a sundress over her suit, and walked the dirt path toward the general store, sand coating her ankles, shells crackling underneath her bare feet. The path was covered in lush, leafy overhang and stopped in front of a cinder-block building with a thatched roof.

Georgie looked at the sun overhead. She lost track of time on the island. Time didn't matter on Whale Cay. You did what Joe wanted to do, when Joe wanted to do it. That was all.

She heard laughter and found the villagers preparing a conch stew. They were dancing, drinking dark rum and home-brewed beer from chipped porcelain jugs and tin cans. Some turned to nod at her, stepping over skinny chickens and children to refill their cans. The women threw chopped onions, potatoes, and hunks of raw fish into steaming cauldrons, the insides of which were yellowed with spices. Joe's lead servant, Hannah, was frying johnnycakes on a pan over a fire, popping pigeon peas into her mouth. Everything smelled of fried fish, blistered peppers, and garlic.

"You're making a big show," Georgie said.

"We always make a big show when Marlene comes," Hannah said in her low, hoarse voice. Her white hair was wrapped. She spoke matter-of-factly, slapping the johnnycakes between the palms of her hands.

"Who's Marlene?" Georgie asked, leaning over to stick a finger in the stew. Hannah waved her off.

Hannah nodded toward a section of the island invisible through the dense brush, toward the usually empty stone house covered in hot pink blossoms. Joe had never explained the house. Now Georgie knew why.

She felt an unmistakable pang of jealousy, cut short by the roar of Joe pulling up behind them on her motorcycle. As Joe worked the brakes, the bike fishtailed in the sand, and the women were enveloped in a cloud of white dust. As the dust settled, Georgie turned to find Joe grinning, a cigar gripped between her teeth. She wore a salmon-pink short-sleeved silk blouse and denim cut-offs. Her copper-colored hair was cropped short, her forearms covered in crude indigo-colored tattoos. "When the fastest woman on water has a six-hundred-horsepower engine to test out, she does," she'd explained to Georgie. "And then she gets roaring drunk with her mechanic in Havana and comes home with stars and dragons on her arms."

"I've never had that kind of night," Georgie said.

"You will," Joe said, laughing. "I'm a terrible influence."

Joe planted her black-and-white saddle shoes firmly on the dirt path to steady herself as she cut the engine and dismounted.

"Didn't mean to get sand in your stew," Joe said, smiling at Hannah.

"Guess it's your stew anyway," Hannah said flatly.

Joe slung an arm around Georgie's shoulders and kissed her hard on the cheek. "Think they'll get too drunk?" she asked, nodding toward the islanders. "Is a fifty-five-gallon drum of wine too much? Should I stop them from drinking?"

"You only make rules when you're bored," Georgie said, her lithe body becoming tense under Joe's arm. "Or trying to show off."

"Don't be smart, love," Joe said, popping her bathing-suit strap. The elastic snapped across Georgie's shoulder.

"Hannah," Joe shouted, walking backward, tugging Georgie toward the bike with one hand. "Make some of those conch fritters too. And get the music going about four, or when you see the boat dock at the pier, OK? Like we talked about. Loud. Festive."

Georgie could smell fresh fish in the hot air, butter burning in Hannah's pan. She wrapped her arms around Joe's waist and rested her chin on her shoulder, resigned. It was like this with Joe. Her authority on the island was absolute. She would always do what she wanted to do; that was the idea behind owning Whale Cay. You could go along for the ride or go home.

Hannah nodded at Joe, her wrinkled skin closing in around her eyes as she smiled what Georgie thought was a false smile. She waved them off with floured fingers.

"Four p.m.," Joe said, twisting the bike's throttle. "Don't forget."

At quarter to five, from the balcony of her suite, Joe and Georgie watched the *Mise-en-scène*, an eighty-eight-foot yacht with white paneling and wood siding, dock. Georgie felt a sense of dread as the boat glided to a stop against the wooden pier and lines were tossed to waiting villagers. The wind rustled the palms and the visitors on the boat deck clutched their hats with one hand and waved with the other.

Every few weeks there was another boatload of beautiful, rich people—actresses and politicians—piling onto Joe's yacht in Fort Lauderdale, eager to escape wartime America for Whale Cay, and willing to cross 150 miles of U-boat-infested waters to do it. "Eight hundred and fifty acres, the shape of a whale's tail," Joe had said as she brought Georgie to the island. "And it's all mine."

Georgie scanned the deck for Marlene and did not see her. She felt defensive and childish, but also starstruck. She'd seen at least ten of Marlene's movies and had always liked the actress. She seemed gritty and in control. That was fine onscreen. But in person—who in their right mind wanted to compete with a movie star? Not Georgie. It wasn't that she wasn't competitive; she was. Back in Florida she'd swum against the boys in pools and open water. But a good competitor always knows when she's outmatched, and that's how Georgie felt, watching the beautiful people in their beautiful clothes squinting in the sun onboard the *Mise-en-scène*.

Joe stayed on the balcony, waving madly. Georgie flopped across the bed. Her tanned body was stark against the white sheets.

"Let's send a round of cocktails to the boat," Joe said, coming into the room, a large, tiled bedroom with enormous windows, a hand-carved king bed sheathed in a mosquito net. Long curtains made of bleached muslin framed the doors and windows, which were nearly always open, letting in the hot air and lizards.

"I'm going to shower first," Georgie said, annoyed by Joe's enthusiasm.

Joe ducked into the bathroom before heading down, and Georgie could see her through the door, greasing up her arms and décolletage with baby oil.

"Preening?" she asked.

"Don't be jealous," Joe said, never taking her eyes off herself in the mirror. "It's a waste of time and you're above it."

Georgie rolled over onto her back and stretched her legs, pointing her painted toes to the ceiling. She could feel the slight sting of sunburn on her nose and shoulders.

"My advice," Joe called from the bathroom, "is to slip on a dress, grab a stiff drink, and slap a smile on that sour face of yours."

Georgie blew a kiss to Joe and rolled over in bed. It wasn't clear to her if they were joking or serious, but Georgie knew it was one of those nights when Joe would be loud and boastful, hard on the servants. Maybe even hard on her.

The yacht's horn blew. Joe flew down the stairs, saddle shoes slapping the Spanish tile. Hannah must have given the signal to the village, Georgie thought, because the steel drums started, sounding like the *plink plink* of hard rain on a tin roof. It was hard to tell if it was a real party or not. Joe liked to control the atmosphere. She liked theatrics.

"Hot damn," she heard Joe call out as she jogged toward the boat. "You all look *beautiful*. Welcome to Whale Cay. Have a drink, already! Have two."

Georgie finally caught sight of Marlene, as Joe helped her onto the dock. She wore all white and a wide-brimmed straw hat. Even from yards away, she was breathtaking.

My family wouldn't believe this, Georgie thought, realizing that she could never share the details of this experience, that it was hers alone. Her God-fearing parents thought she was teaching swimming lessons on a private island. They didn't know she'd spent the past three months shacked up with a forty-year-old womanizing heiress who stalked around her own private island wearing a machete across her chest, chasing shrimp cocktails with magnums of champagne every night. A woman who entered into a sham marriage to secure her inheritance, annulling it shortly thereafter. A woman who raced expensive boats, who kept a cache of weapons and maps from the First World War in her own private museum, a cylindrical tower on the east side of the island.

"They'd disown me if they knew," Georgie told Joe when she first came to Whale Cay.

"My parents are dead and I didn't like them when they were alive," Joe said, shrugging. "Worrying about parents is a waste of time. It's your life. Let's have a martini."

That evening, as she listened to the sounds of guests fawning over the mansion downstairs, Georgie had trouble picking out a dress. Joe had ordered two custom dresses and a tailored suit for her when she realized Georgie's duffel bag was full of bathing suits. Georgie chose the light blue tea-length dress that Joe said would look good against her eyes; the silk crepe felt crisp against her skin. She pulled her hair up, using two tortoiseshell combs she'd found in the closet, and ran bright Tangee lipstick across her mouth, all leftovers from other girlfriends, the photos of whom were pinned to a corkboard in Joe's closet. Georgie stared at them sometimes, the glossy black-and-white photographs of beautiful women. Horsewomen straddling thoroughbreds, actresses in leopard-print scarves and fur coats, writers hunched artfully over typewriters, maybe daughters of rich men who did nothing at all. She couldn't help but compare herself to them, and always felt as if she came up short.

"What I like about you," Joe had told her on their first date, over lobster, "is that you're just so *American*. You're cherry pie and lemonade. You're a ticker-tape parade."

She loved the way Joe's lavish attention made her feel: exceptional. And she'd pretty much felt that way until Marlene put one well-heeled foot onto the island.

Georgie wandered into Joe's closet and looked at the pictures of Joe's old girlfriends, their perfect teeth and coiffed hair, looping inky signatures. *For Darling Joe, Love Forever.* How did they do their hair? How big did they smile?

And did it matter? Life with Joe never lasts, she thought, scanning the corkboard. The realization filled her with both sadness and relief.

On the way downstairs to meet Marlene, Georgie realized the lipstick was a mistake. Too much. She wiped it off with the back of her hand as she descended the stairs, then bolted past Joe and into the kitchen, squeezing in among the servants to wash it off. Everyone was sweating, yelling. The scent of cut onions made Georgie's eyes well up. Outside the door she could hear Joe and Marlene talking.

"Another one of your girls, darling? Where's she from? What does she do?"

"I plucked her from the mermaid tank in Sarasota."

"That's too much."

"She's a helluva swimmer," Joe said. "And does catalog work."

"Catalog work, you say. Isn't that dear."

Georgie pressed her hands to the kitchen door, waiting for the blush to drain from her face before she walked out. She took her seat next to Joe, who clapped her heartily on the back.

The dining room was chic but simply furnished—whitewashed walls and heavy Indonesian teak furniture. The lighting was low and the flicker of tea lights and large votives caught on the well-shined silver. The air smelled of freshly baked rolls and warm butter. Nothing, Georgie knew, was ever an accident at Joe's dinner table—not the color of the wine, the temperature of the meat, and certainly not the seating arrangement.

She'd been placed on Joe's right at the center of the table. Marlene, dressed in white slacks and a blue linen shirt unbuttoned low enough to catch attention, was across from Joe. Marlene slid a candle aside.

"I want to see your face, darling," she said, settling her eyes on Joe's. Georgie thought of the ways she'd heard Marlene's eyes described in magazines: *Dreamy. Cat-shaped. Smoldering. Bedroom eyes.*

Joe snorted but Georgie knew she liked the attention. Joe was incredibly vain; though she didn't wear makeup, she spent time carefully crafting her appearance. She liked anything that made her look tough: bowie knives, tattoos, a necklace made of shark's teeth.

"This is Marlene," Joe said, introducing Georgie.

"Pleased to make your acquaintance," Georgie said softly, nodding her head.

"I'm sure," Marlene purred. "I just love the way she talks," she said to Joe, laughing as if Georgie wasn't at the table. "I learned to talk like that once, for a movie."

Georgie silently fumed. But what good was starting a scene? If I'm patient, she thought, I'll have Joe to myself in a matter of days.

"I'm sure Joe mentioned this," Marlene said, leaning forward, "but I ask for no photographs or reports to the press."

"She has to keep a little mystery," Joe explained, turning to Georgie.

"Is that what you call it?" Marlene asked, exhaling. "I might say sanity."

"I respect your privacy," Georgie said, annoyed at the reverence she could hear in her own voice.

"To re-invention," Joe said, tilting her glass toward Marlene.

"It's exhausting," Marlene said, finishing her glass.

Aside from Marlene, there were eight other guests at dinner—including Phillip, the priest Joe kept on the island, a Yale-educated drunk, the only other white full-time inhabitant of the island. There were also the guests from the boat: Clark, a flamboyant director; two financiers and their well-dressed wives, who spoke only to one another; Richard, a married state senator from California; and Miguel, Richard's much younger, mustachioed companion of Cuban descent. Georgie noticed immediately that no one spoke directly to her or Miguel.

They think I don't have anything worth saying, she thought. She turned the napkin over and over in her hands, as if wringing it out.

Before Joe, she'd never been around people with money. Back home, money was the local doctor or dentist, someone who could afford to send a child to private school.

Hannah, dressed in a simple black uniform, brought out fish chowder and stuffed lobster tail. The guests smoked between courses. Occasionally, Joe got up and made the rounds with the wine, topping off the long-stemmed crystal glasses she'd imported from France. After the entrées had been served, Hannah set rounds of roasted pineapple in front of each guest.

"How many people live here?" Clark asked Joe, mouth open, juice running down his chin.

"About two hundred and fifty," she said, leaning back in her chair, an imperial grin on her face. "But they're always reproducing, no matter how many condoms I hand out. There's one due to give birth any day now. What's her name, Hannah?"

"Celia."

"Will she go to the hospital?" Clark asked.

"I run a free clinic," Joe said.

"You have a doctor here?"

"I'm the doctor," Joe said, grinning. "I'm the doctor and the king and the policeman. I'm the factory boss, the mechanic too. I'm the everything here. I give out acetaminophen and mosquito nets and I sell rum. I sell more rum than anything."

"Well, more rum then!" Clark said, laughing.

Joe stood up, grabbed an etched decanter full of amber-colored liquor, unscrewed the top, and took a swig. She passed it down the table, and everyone but the financiers' wives did the same. Georgie kept her eyes on Marlene, who seemed unimpressed, distracted. She removed a compact mirror from her bag and ran her index finger along her forehead, as if rubbing out the faint wrinkles.

When she wasn't speaking, Marlene let her cigarette dangle out of one side of her mouth, or held it with her hand at her forehead, resting her forehead on her wrist as if she was tired of the world. She smoked Lucky Strikes, Joe said, because the company sent them to her by the carton for free.

"How does she do it?" Georgie whispered to Joe, hoping for a laugh. "How does her cigarette never go out?"

Joe ignored her, leaning instead to Marlene. "Tell me about your next film," she said, drumming her fingers on the white tablecloth.

"We'll start filming in the Soviet Occupation Zone," Marlene said, exhaling.

"No western?"

"Soon. You like girls with guns, don't you, Joe?"

"And your part?" Joe asked.

"A cabaret girl," Marlene said. "But the cold-hearted kind. My character is a Nazi collaborator."

Joe raised her eyebrows.

"Despicable," Marlene said in her husky voice, "isn't it? Compelling, though, I promise."

"You always are," Joe said.

Georgie sighed and stabbed a piece of pineapple with her fork. The rum came to Marlene and she turned the bottle up with one manicured hand. She even knew how to drink beautifully, Georgie thought.

Joe moved her fingers to Georgie's thigh and squeezed. It was almost a fatherly gesture, Georgie felt. A we-will-talk-about-this-later gesture. When the last sip of rum came to Georgie, she finished it off, coughing a little as the liquor burned her throat.

"More rum?" Joe asked the table, glancing at the empty decanter.

"Champagne, if you have it," Marlene said.

"Of course," Joe said. She pushed her chair back and went to discuss the order with a servant in the kitchen.

Georgie shifted uncomfortably in her chair, anxious at the thought of being left alone with Marlene. Next to her she could see Miguel stroking the senator's hand underneath the dinner table while the senator carried on a conversation about the war with the financiers.

"And you," Marlene said to Georgie. "Do you plan on returning to Florida soon? Pick up where you left off with that mermaid act?"

Georgie felt herself blushing even though she willed her body not to betray her.

"It's no picture show," Georgie said, smiling sweetly. "But I suppose I'll go back one of these days."

"I suppose you will," Marlene said, staring hard at her for a minute. Then she flicked the ashes from her cigarette onto the side of her saucer and stood up, her plate of food untouched. Georgie watched her walk across the room. Marlene had a confident walk, her hips thrust forward and her shoulders held back as if she knew everyone was watching, and from what Georgie could tell, scanning the table, they were.

Marlene slipped into the kitchen. Georgie imagined her arms around Joe, a bottle of champagne on the counter. Bedroom eyes.

Georgie took what was left in Joe's wineglass and decided to get drunk, very drunk. The stem of the glass felt like something she could break, and the Chardonnay tasted like vinegar in her mouth.

When Joe and Marlene didn't return after a half-hour, Georgie excused herself, embarrassed. She climbed the long staircase to her room, took off her dress, and stood on the balcony, the hot air on her skin, watching the dark ocean meet the night sky, listening to the water crash gently onto the island.

Some days it scared her to be on the small island. When storms blew in you could watch them approaching for miles, and when they came down it felt as if the ocean could wash right over Whale Cay.

I could always leave, Georgie thought. I could always go back home when I've had enough, and maybe I've had enough.

She sat down at Joe's desk, an antique secretary still full of pencils and rubberbands Joe once said she'd collected as a child, and began to write a letter home. Then she realized she had nothing to say.

She pictured her house, a small white-sided square her father had built with the help of his brothers, within walking distance from the natural springs. Alligators often sunned themselves on the lawn or found the shade of her mother's forsythia. Down the road there were boys running glass-bottom boats in the springs and girls with frosted hair and bronzed legs just waiting to be discovered, or if that didn't work, married.

And could she go back to it now? Georgie wondered. The bucktoothed boys pressing their faces up against the aquarium glass to get a better look at her legs and breasts? The harsh plastic of the fake mermaid tail? Her mother's biscuits and her father's old car and egg salad on Sundays?

She knew she couldn't stay at Whale Cay forever. But she sure as hell didn't want to go home.

In the early hours of morning, just as the sun was casting an orange wedge of light across the water, Joe climbed into bed, reeking of alcohol and cigarette smoke. She put her arms around Georgie and whispered, "I'm sorry."

Georgie didn't answer, and although she hadn't planned on responding, began to cry, with Joe's rough arms across her heaving chest. They fell asleep.

She dreamed of Sarasota.

There was the cinder-block changing room that smelled of bleach and brine. On the door hung a blue star, as if to suggest that the showgirls could claim such status. A bucket of lipsticks sat on the counter, soon to be whisked away to the refrigerator to keep them from melting.

Georgie pulled on her mermaid tail and slipped into the tank, letting herself fall through the brackish water, down, down to the performance arena. She smiled through the green salty water and pretended to take a sip of Coca-Cola as customers pressed their noses to the glass walls of the tank. She flipped her rubber fishtail and sucked air from a plastic hose as elegantly as she could, filling her lungs with oxygen until they hurt. A few minnows flitted by, glinting in the hot Florida sun that hung over the water, warming the show tank like a pot of soup.

Letting the hose drift for just a moment, Georgie executed a series of graceful flips, arching her taut swimmer's body until it made a circle. She could see the audience clapping and decided she had enough air to flip again. Breathing through the tricks was hard, but a few months into the season, muscle memory took over.

Next Georgie pretended to brush her long blond hair underwater while one of Sarasota's many church groups looked on, licking cones of vanilla ice cream, pointing at her.

How does she use the bathroom? Can she walk in that thing? Hey, Sunshine, can I get your number?

That afternoon, as the sun crested in the cloudless sky, Marlene, Georgie, and Joe had lunch on Femme Beach. Marlene wore an enormous hat and sunglasses and reclined, topless, in a chair. She pushed aside her plate of blackened fish. Joe, after eating her share and some of Marlene's, kicked off her shoes and joined Georgie in the water, dampening her khaki shorts. Neither of them spoke for a moment.

"Marlene needs a place where she can be herself," Joe said eventually. "She needs one person she can count on and I'm that person."

"Oh," Georgie said, placing a palm on top of the calm water. "Is it hard being a movie star?"

Joe sighed. "She's been out pushing war bonds, and she's exhausted. She's more delicate than she looks. She drinks too much."

"You're worried?"

"Sometimes she's not allowed to eat. It's hard on her nerves."

"Is this why the other girls left?" Georgie asked, looking out onto the long stretch of water. "You could have mentioned her, you know. You could have told me."

"Try to be open-minded, darling."

"I'll try," Georgie said, diving into the water, swimming out as far as she ever had, leaving Joe standing knee-deep behind her.

Maybe Joe would worry, she thought, but when she looked back, Joe was in a chair, one hand on Marlene's arm, and their heads were tipped toward each other, oblivious to anything else.

What exhausted Georgie about Joe's guests is that they were all important. And important people made you feel not normal, but unimportant.

That night the other guests went on a dinner cruise on the *Mise-en-scène*, while Joe entertained Marlene, Georgie, and Phillip. They were seated at a small table on one of the mansion's many balconies, candles and torches flickering, bugs biting the backs of their necks, wineglasses filled and refilled.

"How do you like Whale Cay?" Phillip asked Marlene.

"I prefer the drag balls in Berlin," she said, in a voice that belied her boredom. "But you know I've been coming here longer than you've been around?"

Marlene leaned over her bowl of steamed mussels, inspecting the plate. She pushed them around in the broth with her fork. "Tell me how you got to the island?" she asked Phillip, who, to Georgie, always seemed to be sweating and had a knack for showing up when Joe had her best liquor out.

"After Yale Divinity School—"

"He sailed up drunk in a dugout canoe. I threatened to kill him," Joe interrupted. "Then I built him his own church," she said proudly, pointing to a small stone temple perched on a cliff, just visible through the brush. It had two rustic windows with pointed arches, almost gothic, as if it belonged to another century.

"He sleeps in there," Joe said.

"I talk to God," Phillip said, indignant, spectacles sliding down his nose. He slurped his wine.

"Is that what you call it?" Joe said, rolling her eyes.

"What do you have to say about all this?" Marlene asked Georgie.

"About what?"

"God."

"Why would you ask me?" Georgie felt her face get hot.

"Why not?"

Georgie remembered the way sitting in church made her feel pretty, her mother's hand over hers. She could recall the smell of her mother, the same two dresses she wore to church, her thrifty beauty and dime-store lipstick and rough hands and slow speech and way of life that women like Joe and Marlene didn't know. Despite Phillip, the church still had holiness, she thought. Just last week Hannah had sung "His Eye Is on the Sparrow" after Phillip's sermon, and it had brought tears to her eyes and taken her to a place past where she used to go in her hometown church, something past God as she understood Him, something attainable only when living away from everyone and everything she had ever known. That even if He wasn't a certain thing, He could be a feeling, and maybe she'd felt Him here. That day she'd realized she was happier on Whale Cay than she'd ever been anywhere else. She'd been waiting all her life for something big to happen, and maybe Joe was it.

"I suppose I don't know anything about God," she said. "Nothing I can put into words."

"You aren't old enough to know much yet, are you? You haven't been pushed to your limits. And you, Joe?" Marlene asked. "What do you know?"

Joe was quiet. She shook her head, coughed.

"I guess I had what you'd call a crisis of faith," she said. "When I drove an ambulance during the First War. I saw things there I didn't know were possible. I saw—"

Marlene cupped her hand over Joe's. "Exactly," she said. "Those of us that have seen the war firsthand—how can you feel another way?"

Firsthand, Georgie thought. What was firsthand about seeing a war with a posh hotel room and security detail, cooing to soldiers from a stage? Firsthand was her brother Hank, sixteen months dead, who'd been found malnourished and shot on the beach in Tarawa.

"That's exactly when you need to let Him in," Phillip said, glassy-eyed.

"You have a convenient type of righteousness," Joe said.

"Perhaps."

"I don't see how a priest can lack commitment in these times," Marlene said, scratching the back of her neck, eyes flashing.

Phillip rose, flustered. "If you'll excuse me, one of our native women is in labor," he said, "and I must attend." He turned to Joe. "Celia's been going for hours now."

"Her body knows what to do," Joe said, lighting a cigarette.

Joe and Marlene smoked. Georgie poured herself another glass of wine, finding the silence excruciating. Nearby a pea hen screamed from a roost in one of the small trees that flanked the balcony. The island had been a bird sanctuary before Joe bought it, and exotic birds still fished from the shore.

"Grab a sweater," Joe instructed, standing up, stamping out her cigarette. "I want to take you girls racing."

The water was shiny and black as Joe pulled Marlene and Georgie onto a small boat shaped like a torpedo. It sat low on the water and had room for only two, but Georgie and Marlene were thin and the three women pressed together across the leather bench seat.

"Leave your drinks on the dock," Joe warned. "It's not that kind of joy ride."

Not five minutes later they were ripping through the water, Georgie's hair blown straight back, spit flying from her mouth, her blue eyes watering. At first she was petrified. She felt as if the wind was exploring her body, inflating the fabric of her dress, tunneling through her nostrils, throat, and chest. A small sound escaped her mouth but was thrown backward, lost, muted. She looked down and saw Marlene's jaw set into a tight line, her knuckles white as her long fingers gripped the edge of the seat. Joe pressed on, speeding through the blackness until it looked like nothingness, and Georgie's fear became a rush.

The bottom of the boat slapped the water, skipped over it, cut through it, and it felt as though it might capsize, flip over, skid across the surface, dumping them, breaking their bodies. Georgie's teeth began to hurt and she bit her tongue by mistake. The taste of blood filled her mouth but she felt nothing but bliss, jarred into another state of being, of forgetting, a kind of high.

"Enough," Marlene yelled, grabbing Joe's shoulder. "Enough! Stop."

"Keep going," Georgie yelled. "Don't stop."

Joe laughed and slowed the boat, cutting the engine until there was silence, only the liquid sound of the water lapping against the side of the craft.

"Take me back to the island," Marlene snapped.

Georgie stood up, nearly losing her balance.

"What are you doing?" Joe demanded.

"Going for a swim," Georgie said.

Georgie kicked off her sandals, unbuttoned her sundress, leaving it in a pool on the deck of the boat. She dove into the black water, felt her body cut through it like a missile.

"We're a mile off shore! Get back in the boat!" Joe shouted.

Joe cranked the engine and circled the boat, looking for Georgie, but everything was dark and Georgie stayed still so as not to be found, swimming underwater, splashless, until Joe gave up and headed for shore.

Georgie oriented herself, looking up occasionally at the faint lights on the island, the only thing that kept her from swimming out into the open sea. It felt good to scare Joe. To do what she wanted to do. To scare herself. To risk death. To do the one thing she was good at, to dull all of her thoughts with the mechanics of swimming, the motion of kicking her feet, rotating her arms, cutting through the water, dipping her face into the warm sea and coming up for air, exerting herself, exhausting her body, giving everything over to heart, blood, muscle, bone.

That night, Georgie crept into the bedroom, feeling a little less helpless than she had the night before. The bed was empty, as she expected it might be. Even if Joe was with Marlene, she would still be worried, and Georgie liked the idea of keeping Joe up at night.

She went to the bathroom to comb her hair before bed. She stared at herself in the mirror. The overhead light was too bright. Her eyes looked hollow. She should eat more, drink less, she thought. As she reached for the comb, she heard whimpering in the walk-in closet. Her heart began to beat quickly. She tiptoed to the closet and opened the door to find Joe sitting with her back against the wall, silk blouse soaked in sweat, a cache of guns and knives at her feet. She was breathing quickly, chest heaving. She looked up at Georgie with glistening, scared brown eyes.

"Go away," she said, her voice hoarse. "Don't look at me like this."

Georgie stood in the doorway, tan legs peeking out from underneath the white-cotton gauze gown Joe had bought for her, unsure of what to say. "Are you OK?" she asked. "Are you sick?"

"I said go away."

But Georgie sensed hesitation in Joe's voice and kneeled down beside her, sliding two guns away, bringing Joe to her chest. Joe gave in, sweating and sobbing against Georgie's skin.

"You can't begin to understand what I saw," Joe whispered. "There were bombs whistling overhead, dropping in front of me as I drove. There were men without heads, arms without bodies, the smell of gangrene we had to wash from the ambulance—every day, that smell. There were the boys who died. I heard them dying. Their faces were burned off. They were not human anymore. I can still see them."

"Shh," Georgie said. "That was a long time ago and you're here. You're safe."

"Why did you leave me like that?"

"I just wanted to swim."

"I thought you were dead."

"Where's Marlene?"

"Asleep. In the stone house."

Georgie kissed Joe tenderly on the forehead, cheeks, and finally her mouth, and eventually they moved to the bed. Georgie had never been the aggressor, but she pushed Joe onto her back and pinned her wrists down, straddling her, biting her neck and shoulders.

That night, as they lay quietly on the bed, they could hear the faint sounds of a woman screaming, not in anger but in pain. Celia, Georgie thought, wincing.

When morning came, Joe acted as if nothing had happened, and Georgie found her standing naked on the patio, newsboy cap over her short hair, her toned and broad body sunned and confident, big white American teeth clenching a cigar from which she never inhaled.

"Shall we have breakfast with Marlene?" she said.

"I just thought—"

"Don't think. Don't ever make the mistake of thinking here."

Georgie came to the dinner table that night with a renewed sense of entitlement. She belonged there. She sat down, considered her posture, and took a long drink of white wine, peering at the guests over the rim of her glass.

Marlene came into the dining room like a bull. She plowed past the rest of the company, ignored Georgie, and reached for Joe's hand across the table.

Hannah set shrimp cocktails and sliced lemons in front of each guest.

Phillip and Joe were in an argument about using the boat to take Celia to the hospital in Nassau.

"Just put her on the goddamn boat," Phillip said, ignoring his food. "She's been in labor for two days."

"What did they do before I was here?" Joe asked, exasperated, letting her fork hit the plate in disgust. "Tell her to just do that."

"Darling, have another glass of wine," Marlene said. "Don't get worked up."

"Have you seen her?" Phillip demanded. "Have you *heard* her? She's suffering. She's dying. What don't you understand?"

"I've seen suffering," Joe said. "Real suffering."

"Oh, don't pull out your old war stories now," Phillip scoffed, tossing his greasy, unwashed hair to the side.

"Joe—" Georgie began.

"It's not your place," Marlene hissed.

"Just put her on the boat and let's go," Phillip interrupted. "Let's go now. She's going to die. I'm going to get a stretcher and we'll put her on the boat."

"You'll do what I tell you to do," Joe snapped, solemn and intimidating. "For starters, you can shower and sober up before you come to my dinner table." Georgie looked down at her plate, at once ashamed of Joe's savage authority and in awe of it.

"Do you want to go outside with me?" she whispered, lightly touching Joe's shoulder. "Walk this off, think about it?"

Joe ignored her.

Phillip stood up from the table, foggy spectacles sliding off his nose in the wet heat. "Sober up? Please. You're so regal, aren't you? The villagers hate you. You punish them for infidelity and you've got a different woman here every month. You walk around with a machete strapped to your chest like you're just waiting for an uprising. Maybe you'll get what you want," he said.

"They're talking about it, you know," he said. "Maybe we'll just take the boat."

Joe stood up and leered at Phillip, practically spitting across the table. "They can hate me all they want. They need me. Why don't you get back on that goddamn canoe you came in on? Yale degree, my ass. You're a deserter. Don't think I don't know it."

"You don't know anything about me," Phillip spat back, storming out of the dining room. Georgie could hear him shouting as he marched away in the still air. "Blessed is the one who does not walk in step with the wicked!"

"I think we should take her to Nassau," Georgie said, turning to Joe.

"Oh please," Marlene said, rolling her eyes. "It isn't the time to interfere."

"It's the right thing to do."

"What do you know?" Marlene snapped.

"A little rum will make us all feel better," Joe said, forcing a smile. "Hannah?"

"It doesn't make *me* feel better at all," Georgie said quietly. She had been determined to hold her own tonight, to look Marlene in the eye, to prove to her that she and Joe were a worthy couple. But she quickly sensed a loss of control, of confidence.

"It's all about you, is it?" Marlene asked. "You're lucky to be here, darling, you know that?"

"We need to get the hell out of this room," Joe announced, knocking over her chair as she stood up.

Joe gathered her guests in the living room, which was full of plush sofas and polished tables covered in crystal ashtrays. Mounted swordfish and a cheetah skin decorated the whitewashed walls.

Joe put on a Les Brown record and opened a cigar box. She clamped down on a cigar and carried around a decanter of Scotch in the other, topping off her guests' drinks.

"No restraint," she said. "Drink as much as you want. It's early."

Georgie leaned against a window, gulped down her drink, and stared out at the black sea. Joe pulled her away and into a corner.

"Are you having a good enough time?" she asked. "Are you angry?"

"What do you think?" Georgie said.

"You're drunk," Joe said.

"What?" Georgie asked, voice falsely sweet. "I'm the only one who's not allowed to have a big night?"

"It's just unusual for you," Joe said.

"We should take the boat to Nassau," Georgie said.

"You're slurring," Joe said. "And besides, I've said no. If I go, I'll lose authority."

"You might lose it anyway."

Joe was silent and turned to refresh her drink, pausing to talk with the financiers. Georgie stayed at the window. She could hear the islanders' voices outside. She couldn't understand what they were saying, but they were loud and animated. Hannah, who was making the rounds with a box of cigars, lingered by the window, a worried expression on her face.

Would the native islanders riot? Or worse, attack the house and guests? Maybe. But what weighed most heavily on Georgie was the sense of being complicit in Celia's suffering.

Marlene approached, locking eyes with her. She topped off Georgie's glass with straight rum and lit another cigarette.

"Got ugly in there, didn't it?" she said, exhaling.

Georgie nodded.

"Bet you don't see that every day in the mermaid tank," Marlene said. "But Joe can handle it. Even if you can't. Those of us that have been to the war—"

Georgie held up a hand, stopping Marlene. She felt claustrophobic, drunk. She knew she wasn't thinking clearly. Her body was warm from the rum and wine and she felt anxious, as if she needed to move.

"Tell Joe I'm off for a walk. To think about things."

"Stay out awhile," Marlene said, calling after her.

Georgie left the house through the kitchen and walked away from the group of islanders who had clustered near the dock. She wanted to tell them that they were right, that they should take the boat, but she was too ashamed to look them in the eyes, too afraid to speak against Joe. She wanted to talk to Phillip, so she followed the path of crushed oysters and sand north toward the simple silhouette of the small stone church.

Georgie recalled the hymn her mother liked to sing—"O God, Our Help in Ages Past." She was tone-deaf but couldn't help herself from singing. As the words came, her tongue felt too big for her mouth, but still the sound of her voice filled her with unexpected serenity. She took another drink from the crystal tumbler she'd taken from the house and sang the first verse again, and then again, until she could feel her mother's nails on her back, calming her down, loving her to sleep.

She found Phillip passed out on a wooden bench in front of the church.

"Phillip," she said, gently rocking him with her hands. He was shirtless and his skin was warm. A single silver cross Joe had given him hung around his neck and across his chest.

"Phillip," she said. He stirred but didn't open his eyes. She pinched the skin above his hip bone.

"What?" he said, opening his eyes into slits.

"Take the boat. Just take it."

"I'm in no shape to drive a boat."

"You have to. Someone has to."

"I like you, Georgie," Phillip said. "But you have to leave me the hell alone now." He waved her off with one hand, the other tucked underneath his head.

"But you said—"

"I give up. You should too." He rolled away from her, turning his face toward the back of the bench.

She took another sip of her drink while waiting for him to roll back over. When he didn't, she walked to the place where the sandy island broke off into high cliffs and began to walk the rim of the island, staring at the water below.

Looking down at the waves from the cliffs, she remembered Florida. She remembered sipping on the air hose and drinking Coca-Cola while tourists watched her through thick glass at the aquarium show. Sometimes Georgie had to remind herself that she could not, in fact, breathe underwater.

"Whatever you do," the aquarium owner had said, "be pretty."

And so the girls always pointed their toes and ignored the charley horses in their calves or the way their eyes began to sting in the brackish water. Georgie recalled the feeling of her hands on the arch of another swimmer's back as they performed an underwater adagio, the fatigue in her body after the back-to-back Fourth of July shows. She remembered a time when she felt good about herself.

She thought of Joe, and her arm around Marlene's back. She thought of the stone house, and for a minute, she wanted to leave Whale Cay and return home. But home would never be the same.

In days the yacht would pull away and Joe would wake her up with coffee in bed. Hannah would make her eggs, runny and heaped on a slice of white toast with fruit on the side. She would take her morning swims and read a book underneath the shade of a palm. And would that be enough?

They had a rock in the yard back home. Her father used to lift the copperheads out of the garden shed with his hoe and slice them open with the metal edge, their poisonous bodies writhing without heads for a moment on top of the rock. The spring ritual had horrified and intrigued Georgie, and it was what she pictured now, standing above the sea, swaying, the feeling of rocks underneath her feet.

But she might never see that rock again, she thought.

It was dark and she couldn't see well. There was shouting in the distance. She felt bewildered, hysterical.

She set down her glass and took off her sandals. She would feel better in the water, stronger.

With casual elegance, she brought her hands in front of her body and over her head and dove off the cliff. As she began to fall toward the water, falling beautifully, toes pointed, she wondered if she'd gotten mixed up and picked the wrong place to dive.

She was falling into the tank again, the brackish water in her eyes, but no one was watching.

She was cherry pie.

She was a ticker-tape parade.

Her hands hit the water first. The water rushed over her ears, deafening her. Her limbs went numb, adrenaline moving through her until she was upright again, gulping air.

She treaded water, fingers moving against the dark sea, pushing it away to keep herself afloat. There were rocks jutting out from the water, a near miss. There were strange birds nesting in the tall grass, a native woman bleeding on a straw mattress in a hut on the south shore, a stone house strangled by fig trees.

JUSTIN BIGOS

Fingerprints

FROM *McSweeney's Quarterly*

A STORY: A man, once a wealthy banker but now anonymous in rags, retired, richer than ever, wandered the streets of our city. He dug through trash, ate trash, slept on sidewalks, walked with a slight limp, as if he had years before suffered a minor stroke, or a terrible beating. Years before, in fact, his wife and children had died on a highway. After drinking away a decade of his life, the man quit alcohol, quit his job, quit his life. He became someone else. Do we still think it possible? To become someone else? We know this is just a story, so: He wandered the streets of our city and he smiled at anyone who met his eyes. And to those who then returned his smile with their own, he would speak: "Excuse me, ma'am," or "Sir, just a moment," and he would fake-limp with all his dignity—they could see this now, the ones who looked—and he would reach out a hand. Those who took it—very few, very few, God save us all—would find he had pressed into their palm a hundred-dollar bill. And was already walking away.

Another story: Sometime in your teens, in high school, around the time your father started showing up again, your house was robbed. In the night, the family asleep. No one awoke, no one was hurt. In the morning: "Mom, where's the car?" The slow realization: missing VCR, missing jewelry, missing wallets and purses. Also missing: a baseball cap from your bedroom, a Cabbage Patch doll from your sister's. "Are you sure, are you sure it's gone?" said your mother, your sister crying. "Why would someone steal a doll?" Your stepfather silent, raging. The police found the car a few blocks away, in the projects, a man asleep, passed out, high as a kite, behind the wheel. It took weeks to get the smell out.

Your father didn't show up again until a few days after the robbery. Sitting at the table, shaking for alcohol: "It's horrible, son. You should have an alarm system." He comes, as if by magic, only when your mother and stepfather are not home. "Just pour me one drink, son."

This man you cannot say you love, cannot say you don't. He is the mystery man, the question mark. After a few weeks of his visits, always at night, the house empty, your sister asleep, he stopped showing up. The last visit you knocked him to the ground. He limped to the door, faking it a little, maybe, it was impossible to know, and he said something deliciously cruel. But you have never been able to remember what it was.

He said, *Your eyes are like two sapphires in a window in Chinatown on the kind of day that makes a man want to get down on one knee.* That was the first date, your mother tells you. Talked like that for a few months, then they got married. Her second marriage, his first. Marie had introduced her to him, the Italian guy who owned the deli across the street. He had noticed her walking by one day and asked Marie who she was. On the first date he wore about six gold chains around his neck, paid for everything with a fat wad of hundred-dollar bills. They did cocaine and drank beer, and he whipped out the line about the sapphires. Smooth customer, she says. Look at him.

And you look, you remember: white T-shirt, two gold chains, pressed slacks, black loafers. He dresses like his brothers, his friends. Cooking calamari and clams casino on the deck, working at the deli all day, asking you why you want to date a nigger or kissing your mother behind the ear, he has looked the same since the day you met him, when you were four years old. Your mother wanted at least a father for you and your sister. She got a man, twenty-one years older, who worshipped her—even if he eventually lost the words for it. On the first date, she tells you, I had no idea he'd been living with another woman and her daughter for almost ten years. An entirely different family. I told him, Look, you make a decision. And he left me. Next morning, there he is, at the door with a suitcase, cigarette in his lips. She smiles. That fucker, you should have seen the look on his face.

But she hadn't yet told him she was separated from her hus-band—that he had tried to kill her and was still trying to find her and his children. Like the new man she knew she would marry, she had an unshakable sense of timing.

Your father at the table in jacket and tie. Have you ever seen him not in jacket and tie? Raised a Jehovah's Witness, he learned early that one must represent God as His witness, and when you knock on someone's door it can't hurt to have pressed your slacks. He downs a glass of gin like milk.

Last week you saw him on a corner begging for change. There was a cut above one eyebrow, like a boxer's cut, swabbed with Vase-line. He smiled drunkenly at those who passed, his smile widening for those who laughed at him. You hid behind a bus stop, back-pack slung over your shoulder. When the bus came you hopped on, and from the back you seemed to catch his eyes. Your father, the village idiot, the fallen preacher, his own cut man, a sad clown smiling in a dirty suit. But he was already looking away.

He drinks a rocks glass of vodka. He drinks a plastic cup of Scotch. He drinks a Dixie Cup of ouzo, a beer stein of sherry, a mug of warm Chardonnay, he drinks handful after handful of wa-ter from the kitchen sink, combs his hair with his fingers. He has stopped shaking. You are just getting started.

The thief had come in through the kitchen window that led to the deck. The deck had been under construction but abandoned by the time we bought the house. The previous owner, a cop, lost his job and a couple years later lost the mortgage. At auction in 1983 my stepfather got the house for just over forty thousand dollars. It was on a dead-end street overlooking Bunnell's Pond, five blocks from Beardsley Terrace, one of the city's eight housing projects. The house was filled with empty tallboy beer cans and nudie maga-zines filled with black women. There were posters of naked black women—their skin greased, hair curled and wet, lips parted—on the walls of the bedroom, bathroom, living room, kitchen. The ceil-ings were painted brown, the carpet was dark chocolate shag. One wall was cocktail-olive green, another cat-tongue pink, another flaking, cheap gold wallpaper. On the first day we arrived, armed with garbage bags, disinfectant, sponges, and rubber gloves, we noticed again the deck jutting out from the back of the house. We walked up the steps, my stepfather, mother, sister, and I, and saw the deck half-built, the wood nailed down two years before now blond and raw in the sun. One of us peered through the kitchen window, a hand visored over our eyes. Inside, for whoever looked first: a florid signature of defeat.

A story about Bermuda. A father visits his two children through a window. Legally he is allowed to see them through a window, and the window must not be open more than four inches, court's order. He brings candy, toys small enough to pass through. He holds their small fingers in his hand, their faces shimmering behind glass. One day the mother is blow-drying her hair, or running toward burned toast, or yelling at a girlfriend or boss over the phone—and he convinces the boy, the smart one, the one who watches everything, to open the window wider. Not with the promise of candy or baseball cards, but with—we forget. But the boy is now being pulled through the window by his arms and his mother is screaming as she pulls him by the legs, and to make sure the scene doesn't get too comical the boy starts to cry in silence.

The father wins.

When he is arrested, twenty-two minutes later, at the train station in New Haven, the police ask him what in the hell he was thinking. "We were going to go live in Bermuda," he says.

Some nights he would bring paperbacks. I'd pour him a drink and he would flip through dime-store books on nutrition or the paranormal. Books on Los Alamos and the Lindbergh baby. The Salem witch trials and the Connecticut witch trials. The Pequot graveyards that, he said, protected my great-great-great-grandmother. Cancer cures buried by the government. The Ouija board in the trunk of JFK's limo. Coenzyme Q10 and how to live on only water, honey, and cayenne pepper.

Once he brought three different books on the Bermuda Triangle. It was not something to scoff at, he said. The disappearances and ghost blips on NASA radar were not coincidence or fantasy. It was our Atlantis, he said, trying to speak to us.

Also missing: two slices of bread, half a pound of deli turkey, a handful of lettuce, a fat slice of tomato, and lots of mayonnaise, scooped out with fingers. The thief had left the dregs of his late-

night snack on the kitchen table, along with a rusty knife. The
knife was nearly brown, and looked like something someone
might use hiking or hunting, who knew. No one hiked or hunted
around here. And there was mayonnaise everywhere, oily mayonnaise fingerprints all over the house. On the jewelry box: fingerprints. On the coffee pot: fingerprints. On the toilet flush (but
he didn't flush): fingerprints. On the photo of my father and me
on the desk (the father clearly drunk, the boy on his shoulders
screaming, but look, maybe in joy, in delight, and the father, let's
face it, the father is happy): fingerprints. The cops dusted it all,
didn't need any of it. Asleep at the wheel. High as a kite.

Marie is combing the green glob of jelly into her niece's hair.
She holds the comb in one hand and the jelly is stuck to the
palm of the other. She dabs from the glob every few seconds, wiping different parts of her niece's head, then combing until the
green disappears. Her other niece is the one you like, but you
can't remember her name. You sit on the floor playing a game
called Connect 4. Her eyes are green, her skin brown. Her hair is
braided tightly and close to her head, with yellow and pink butterfly barrettes, like your sister's. You beat her every time, but she
doesn't seem to care. Marie makes chicken and rice for dinner.
She puts you to bed on the couch, tells you your mother will be
back in a few days. You think that you have never slept so high in
the air. The sixteenth floor. You might be in the clouds, but it is
too dark to see.

Father Panic Village was torn down a few years ago. It was one of
the remaining housing projects in Bridgeport. When my father
grew up there, it was called Yellow Mill Apartments. My neighborhood, where I lived with my mother, stepfather, and sister, had
once been called Whiskey Hill. It was where the Irish mobsters
distilled and hid their whiskey during Prohibition. My father knew
the city in a way I never would. Each street, building, and patch
of grass he could describe in terms of its former self. He knew the
story of Thomas Beardsley, the man who donated acres of park to
the city under the condition that it never charge citizens admis-
sion. My father always sneaked us in through torn fences or secret
dirt pathways off the interstate. He refused to pay dirty American
money to enjoy the land that Beardsley had promised him. Beards-

ley's statue was once stolen, when I was in grade school—then, mysteriously, the next day, put back in its spot. This was not coincidence, my father said.

In the park we hid in places where security would not find us. We brought hot dogs and bags of whole-wheat bread. He taught me how to build fires without matches. He told me the Pequot names of plants. He ripped sassafras from the ground by its long roots and later, in his apartment, he would boil these roots and pour me a mug of hot unsweetened root beer. He would not allow me sugar, the white man's poison. He gave me a quarter for each apricot pit I ate. He explained the qualities of laetrile: a compound of two sugar molecules, one of them cyanide, which detaches when—and only when—confronted with the enzymes released by cancerous cells. He gave me baggies of apricot pits to take home to my mother and sister.

He drank while he drove me home, a forty-ounce bottle in a bag between his legs. He tipped his chauffeur's cap to police officers, who sat studying us at red lights.

Your mother tells you the story of your stepfather: Out of prison, he finds his way back east, gets a basement apartment in Brooklyn, finds a job busing tables at a Greek joint, just something to hold him over till he figures things out, gets his head straight—talks to some guys from the old neighborhood, sees what's cooking. And a month and a half later, after having robbed two jewelry stores, three homes, and a delivery van, he's headed west again, back to California, sunny California, 1958, walking the highway with his thumb out, his broken thumb, snapped by Fat Frannie—your stepfather, just a twenty-eight-year-old hood, convicted felon, about to get caught again, spend, this time, twelve years in prison. Fat Frannie takes his thumb in his hand and snaps it, clean with indifference. "Tomorrow. The rest of the money tomorrow, you fuck. Just like your old man."

Your stepfather in slacks and a jacket, maybe a hat, a fedora, dark brown with a black feather, with his broken thumb in the wind, just needs to get back to California, Frisco maybe, there's that one girl made him breakfast, eggs and ham and coffee, orange juice, California orange juice, no one ever made him breakfast like that ever, the nuns in the orphanage would've said it was a sin, California itself a sin, the rising sun of the devil, and a woman in a chemise, that's what he thought it was called, a chemise the color of peaches, cooking him breakfast after they had made love with the curtains open. But what does he do? He leaves her for New York. And now what does he do?

He gets into a truck, the only vehicle to pull over for the forty-nine miles he's walked, somewhere now in New Jersey, on windy 78. He steps up into the truck and before he even looks at the driver, the gun is in his lap. "Out of the truck, friend. It's my truck now," he says. Twenty-eight years old, driving a Nabisco truck to California, a day, almost exactly, until he's caught. He gets out of the can when he's forty.

There was the time he crashed into a girder on I-95, his ridiculous Cadillac suddenly in front of her Cutlass. I swerved, she says, and I don't know how, there was traffic all around us, but I got over to the edge of the highway and pulled over. I saw his car totally wrecked. I couldn't move. The police came and your father, he's sitting there covered in blood, the steering wheel was split in half from his chest, you know your father, he's big but back then he was huge, and both his eyes black and blue, and his leg, the right one, we found out later, broken. But he was awake, and he kept looking at me. The cops are trying to get him to say something, what day is it, who's the president, how many fingers, you know, and he's sitting there in all this blood, looking right at me. The whole highway was blocked off and I was standing right in the middle of it. Can you imagine? Right in the middle of I-95 in broad daylight, all these ambulance and police lights, just standing right there. Do you know what he did? When they cut off the door and get him onto a stretcher, he's looking at me again, and right before they put him in the ambulance, he grins. She pauses. I had just left him that morning. We were going to his mother's so I could get you and your sister. I told him it was over. Do you understand what I'm saying? She finishes her cigarette. Your father, she says, the way she has always said it.

A rocks glass of Scotch. A plastic cup of vodka.

The difference between your mother and me, he says, is my demons are real. Satan's angels. They visit me, son. Last night, he says, then stops. These angels, he says. They once walked the earth. God had already expelled Lucifer from His Kingdom, and Lucifer, listen, son, bitter, angry, proud, had begun his reign on earth. He sent these angels to breed with Woman. The offspring were the Nephilim. They were giants, demigods. They stole land, beat their neighbors, raped their own daughters. Listen. In the beginning of the Old Testament, right there in Genesis, he says, the tale of these human demons is there for anyone who wants to see. Look around, he says. They never left.

After he falls to the ground, you tower over him, and that is when he gets back up and takes off his clown nose. Flattens it like a silver dollar and slips it into a pocket of his oversized trousers. Takes off his dented stovepipe hat, his enormous bow tie, wipes each cheek stippled with gray grease paint, and says something through his lips smeared white. Before he leaves, he says: When you were a baby I gave you a bath but I didn't know how hot the water was. I couldn't tell your mother, explain; she just kept screaming. She was in her nurse's aide uniform, she just got home. In the ambulance I prayed to Jehovah, first time in years, I was praying and your skin, it looked so red and you, I can't remember if you were still screaming. I had never bathed you before. I was your father. I was off booze. Driving a cab and making good money—this is what, 1977, 1978? Jimmy Carter. Your mother took me back. Maybe it was. A mistake. I can still hear your voice, screaming to me, when we were up in the sky. The circus when you were two or three. You wanted to get down, but the ride was broke, we were stuck up there for what. Over an hour. I could see the ocean, and, across the Sound, Long Island. I could see the whole circus below us, in miniature, just like at the Barnum Museum. Do you remember? All the little tightrope walkers and clowns and weightlifters, all the wild animals, the cotton candy. The music.

Then, limping toward the door, his voice slurred with whiskey, victorious in its cruelty, the last thing he ever said to me: We could see all the way to Bermuda.

Over twenty years later, walking early one morning into the private country club where I tended bar: the lock on the bar's refrigerator busted, two empty bottles of Burgundy in the trash, the maître d's tie slung over the bar's mirror. As if all he had wanted was to finally catch himself in the act.

*

You dream of waking in the night, or half-waking, or less, but there is something there. You cannot see anything except your desk, your homework from the night before lit up a little by the streetlight outside. Your pencil. Your baseball cap. Then, more faintly, the television to the left, resting on a small bookshelf. A poster of Larry Bird above it, his green Converse almost black. Out the window the streetlight is hidden, but its light sifts through at an angle, and on the right side of your room, right in front of your bed, is a darkness. And it moves, like a muscle, like a heartbeat, before you wake up.

Another story: this one true. A married couple wanders the streets of the city for years. Everyone has grown used to their presence. They never ask for money. They sleep together, spooning, in a house made of cardboard and blankets. Their faces are ruddy and without expression, and when not asleep they are always in motion, always searching through garbage for survival.

The first time you see them you do not know any of this. You are with your father, holding his hand, and you are walking just to walk, a stroll through downtown on a Sunday afternoon. He is humming a song, maybe about rain but it is sunny, and he hums so loudly you can feel it in the palm of your hand. He begins to swing your hand with his, slightly, as if in a wind. Then you see them, ahead. The man is digging through a mesh trashcan on a corner, his arm buried to the shoulder, and he is looking at you. The woman stands beside him, looking inside one of many shopping bags hung from her shoulders. The man does not take his eyes off you and you cannot look away. Your father stops. He looks at you. He kneels. Son, he says, it is rude to stare. Some people have very hard lives, and it is hard to understand for many of us why they live this way. But they are human beings, and Jehovah made them the same way he made you, me, your mother, your sister. I want you to say you are sorry. I am right here. Go say you are sorry to that man and woman, and I will be right here waiting for you.

But you can't. You begin to cry. Your father says it is OK. To just wait here.

You watch him as he walks, in his long, slow strides, in a suit and tie, toward the man and woman. He is wearing a new hat, and you remember that was the reason you came downtown, so your father could buy a new hat. He stops just a couple steps from the man and woman and they look at him. The man's arm remains in the trash but is now still. After a few seconds, the man looks at your father's hand, which is held out to him. The man looks at the woman briefly, then he takes something from your father, looks at it, then puts it into his pocket. He goes back to rifling through the trash and the woman begins to yell at your father. She begins to scream, her face turning even redder, you cannot hear or understand what she is saying but you know she hates your father, hates you, hates many, many people. You want to help your father, the man who has only recently come back into your life, clean-shaven and speaking of God, you want to run toward him and defend him, protect him, but now he is holding out his hand to the man again, he has taken off his hat and is holding it out toward the man. The woman is now silent. The man takes the hat, a brand-new fedora with a feather, and puts it on his head. And looks at you, as if for the first time.

Happy Endings

FROM *New Ohio Review*

ALL HIS LIFE McHenry had lived with someone watching him: a mother, a father, a wife, a daughter, his customers. He dug wells for a living and his customers were cattle ranchers and wheat farmers, which meant they were always about to go broke, except when they were rich. They didn't make a show of watching him but they did. *Assholes and elbows:* a thing he learned in high school, doing pick-and-shovel work on an extra gang for the Milwaukee Railroad. It didn't matter how much you got done or how many mistakes you made or how smart you were. The only thing was to look like you were working when Sorenson, the straw boss, came by. *I just want to see assholes and elbows.*

So he learned to look like he was working when he worked. He learned to act like a father when his daughter was around, to look like a husband when Marnie needed a husband. He did what people expected him to or maybe a little more. He always tried for more. McHenry had a brisk practical manner, plastic glasses, and a crewcut that turned gray early, an all-purpose character that didn't change. He got along with people. It was a way through.

He wasn't expecting to find himself with nobody watching, but here he was, age fifty-nine. Marnie had gone five years before, a pancreatic cancer that burned so swiftly through her that McHenry never felt it until she was buried. Still sometimes it felt to him that the death had never happened, an unreal, ugly dream. Then Carolyn, their daughter, had ended up in Guangzhou, China. This too felt unlikely. She had gone off to Missoula and ended up as a dual major in Chinese and business and now she was importing Chinese

balers and hay rakes and making crazy money. They Skyped each
other every few weeks but it was nothing like having her around,
just a picture on a computer screen. McHenry talked about how
busy he was and how things were going fine and so on. He was still
her father, even if she was on the other side of the world. Plus the
time was impossible for him to figure out. He would call her on
Sunday afternoon and it would be Monday morning where she was.

McHenry approved on principle. If you were going to get the
hell out of Harlow, you might as well just keep going. And he liked
the fact that she was good with money. He felt like he had given
her that.

Still it was just him and Missy, the little papillon dog that Marnie
had gotten just before they found out. It seemed like a dirty trick.
Claws skittering on the wood floors.

And then these two kids down out of Billings talked one of their
dads into bankrolling a brand-new computer-controlled Japanese
drilling rig. McHenry did the math. They were losing money every
time they took a job from him. They had to be. But he couldn't
underbid them, despite the fact that his rig was paid for. McHenry
knew better than to expect his customers to turn down a low bid.
These were men who would drive ninety miles to the Sam's Club
to save a nickel on toilet paper.

McHenry could have waited them out. But one afternoon, when
he got off the phone with Gib Gustafson, a wheat farmer McHenry
had known since kindergarten, a millionaire, telling him that they
weren't going to be able to do business—after he got that call,
McHenry just got angry. If Marnie had been there, if Carolyn. But
they weren't. By five that afternoon he was out of the business, rig
sold, trucks sold, FOR RENT sign on the shop.

Was this a mistake? Maybe. He had all the money he was going
to need, from savings along the way and from Marnie's life insurance. The house was paid for and so was the shop. Even if nobody
rented it, and nobody was able to stay in business in Harlow anymore, it was still worth five or six times what he had paid for it, the
year after the railroad left town. He had a couple of rentals, and
no crew, by then, that was depending on him.

But the quiet.

The phone just didn't ring.

And if he didn't get laid pretty soon he was going to go out of
his mind. He hated to think like this. He was not a crude man, not

naturally. But this was the simple fact of the matter. McHenry was not an old man, not yet, and whatever had switched off when Marnie got sick had gotten switched back on again somehow. He remembered one of his crew—an extra guy, a friend of somebody's, not one of the regulars—talking about his day off, going to a massage place in Billings. He shut up about it when he saw McHenry was listening. But it stuck in his mind. You could just pay for it. And nobody was watching.

McHenry lived with these thoughts for two or three months and then decided he needed to go to Billings to see what the truth of the matter was. It took him another few weeks to gather his nerve. It was April before he made it.

Spring has a good reputation, he thought, driving south through spitting snow, but it maybe shouldn't. Not Montana spring, anyway. Just a hard season. Easter Sunday with Marnie in her flowery dresses and the freezing rain just pounding down.

He found the Bangkok Sunshine out by the Interstate, alone and kind of forlorn-looking in a giant gravel parking lot behind the truck wash. His pickup was the only car in the lot. A pink building with the word MASSAGE in red neon, a white door. Momentum carried him inside where a young, not-quite-pretty Asian girl in a swimsuit top and a piece of flowery cloth for a skirt sat reading a magazine in a language McHenry didn't recognize.

"Thirty or sixty minutes?" she asked.

"I don't know," said McHenry. "Sixty, I guess."

"That's a hundred," she said, and McHenry was shocked. He didn't know what he was expecting but this was somehow a substantial amount of money. But it seemed too late to back out now, and it was just this once. He could afford it.

"I don't see you much," said the girl.

"This is my first time."

"Are you a cop?"

"No."

"Okay. Room two. And people usually tip."

It was a room with a bed and a poster of a beach. The door he had come in and another door and a third he guessed was a closet. No windows. Linoleum floors, everything easy to clean, like a veterinarian's exam room. McHenry sat on the bed and waited. It was taller and narrower than a regular bed and he could feel plastic under the sheet. It was a room without any music, he thought, too many people passing through and nobody staying long. The sadness came back to him. PHUKET, said the poster. He didn't know where that was. It looked beautiful, in a faceless way. Palm trees and blue skies.

Then the far door opened and another Asian girl walked in, smiling—a little shorter and rounder than the girl at the desk but dressed the same, her breasts spilling out of the swimsuit top. Her hair was long and bound at the back with a red ribbon. She was barefoot.

"You have to take your clothes off!" she said, laughing. "Otherwise it doesn't work."

McHenry had allowed himself to forget this part. He had not had his clothes off in front of anybody for a long while, anybody but doctors and Marnie. An urge to flee arose, was suppressed by an act of will. She opened the closet. He took his shoes off, then his pants. Then he hesitated.

"Come on," she said. But lightly, playfully. She was alive if the room was not. He went the rest of the way naked and then lay facedown on the bed. Cold plastic under a thin sheet. She covered his ass with a towel and bent to look him sideways in the face.

"What's your name?" she asked.

"Bill," he lied.

"I'm Tracy," she said. "Relax."

McHenry tried to make himself relax. But the body doesn't lie, and he tensed at the touch of her hand on his shoulder.

"OK, OK," she said. "It's going to be OK." She turned the lights down quite low, and music seeped in from the corners. He smelled something complicated like herbs or hay but pleasant and then she touched him again with warm oil on her hands and he lay still this time. It was like getting a haircut, the way he knew where her body was around him, the accidental brush of her breasts on his skin as she bent over him. Small as she was, she had a firm hand and surprising strength and after a few minutes he understood that she knew what she was doing. Her breasts were everywhere but he wasn't even thinking about that now or maybe thinking about that from a different direction, because it was just very nice. He didn't know till now how many troubles he was carrying in his body. They just kind of stopped being there after a while. He felt light and free.

She massaged his feet, which was something that had never happened to McHenry before and although he liked it, he felt the pressure on unexpected places, as if his liver and his testicles and even his eyes were all connected somehow to places in his feet and he had not known this. Then she worked her way up his legs. It was pleasant but he felt vulnerable. Her hand just grazed his scrotum. Something woke up then and stayed awake as she worked on his back, his neck.

McHenry hoped he was in the right place.

He let go for a while. Time passed, he wasn't sure how much. It wasn't important. All touch, all her hands and music of a kind he generally hated and dim lights and the scent of the oil. Then when he had basically turned into a puddle of goo she rolled him over on his back. The towel came off. Tracy put it back on after half a minute but she must have noticed.

She did his feet again from another angle and then his face and then his chest. All this was absolutely new to McHenry and surprising. Also, her breasts, just touching, spilling out of her top, and the feel of her small strong hands and the scent of her perfume mixed with the scented oil. This should have been relaxing but McHenry got more and more agitated in his need. Did he need to ask? How would he go about asking? What were the words, what was the code? She must see. She must know.

In the end, he didn't need to know anything. Tracy worked his calves and then his thighs and then leaned down toward him, her breasts dangling, and whispered in his ear: "Happy ending?"

"Please," said McHenry.

"Twenty extra."

"Please," he said.

She laughed, but pleasantly, dropped the towel to the floor, and got him off with her strong little hands. It didn't take much. McHenry kept his eyes closed, all touch and scent. If he kept his eyes closed, this moment would never end. It was magic.

"OK," said Tracy. "See you next time. Shower's right outside that door."

McHenry opened his eyes. He was naked in a room with a stranger. The lights were still dim but the magic was gone. Tracy smiled at him and was pleasant. He unfolded his pants, found his wallet, gave her a twenty and then another. He would have stood there handing her twenties all night if she had wanted him to. He had made a fool of himself. He understood that much.

*

He made it two weeks before he was back. The girl at the front desk didn't like him any better this time. She said that Tracy was busy but she could get one of the other girls to take care of him. Either that or he could wait.

McHenry waited. Nobody else came through, just him and the bored girl, reading a magazine in what he assumed was Thai or Vietnamese. *Remember what you're doing,* he told himself. *That girl is with somebody else in the next room. It's what she does. It's her job.*

Still he felt the excitation, like bees or butterflies, at the thought of seeing Tracy. It wasn't love. He was almost sure. But it was some-thing like it. Not even the sight of a trucker in a ball cap coming out of the back could deter him. He had noticed the eighteen-wheeler in the parking lot. It was hard not to.

She was shorter than he remembered, but prettier.

"That girl out front," he said. "I don't think she likes me."

"She's a bitch," Tracy said. "She doesn't like anybody."

This time McHenry let himself watch her, at least at first. Tracy was brisk, professional, exact in her movements, the way she cupped her hand to take the oil from the bottle, for instance. She held it there to warm before she let it rain onto his back. Beneath the cloth skirt—was it a sarong?—she wore lime-green striped un-derpants, like a kid would wear. She was clothed and he was naked. She was at work, in charge, she knew where she was and what she was doing. While McHenry was way out past the safe shallows. This made no sense to him, the fact that he was here.

And then it didn't need to make sense, he was just all body again, all goo and drool. At least at first. He went down again into and then back up with the nearness of her, the body. When she rolled him over this time, she didn't bother with the towel. In fact she touched him there, a little, just lightly, then went on with the massage. When she went from his face to his feet, she touched him again, as if she were befriending it; and when she had worked her way up his thighs, when it was time for the happy ending, she moved so easily and automatically from one thing to the other that it was not like they were two things at all but just one movement.

She left. He lay empty and adrift, on his back on the bed. They must change the sheets, he thought, between each one of us.

What if this was not wrong? He turned the thought around on the drive home in the dark, a white crust of ice at the edge of the headlights. He knew he'd never do a thing like Tracy if he had to explain it to anybody. If Marnie were alive, if Carolyn were around. He wasn't a cheater. But just in himself, he couldn't figure out what was wrong with it. He wasn't stealing tenderness from anybody or spending someone else's money. On the other hand, he knew he wouldn't want to get caught doing this. So that was something. But he couldn't figure out who was being hurt. Tracy herself seemed cheerful enough.

Then came this other thought, which McHenry didn't want in his head but which wouldn't leave. That thought was this: What if this was something beautiful that he had shut himself off from his whole life? What if they were wrong, the watchers? Maybe there was really nothing bad with this. Had he been mistaken his whole life? Until now, near the end. Something sad here. Even with Marnie there was something furtive, always in the dark. That one time they went to Mexico, just the two of them. It was a glimpse of something. But they could never quite bring it home. *Fucking,* he thought. He had been using the word his whole life as a curse. What if it instead turned out to be a blessing?

Not a thought he wanted to have. But McHenry could not put it away.

He wound up in a Christian Singles group, run by the church where they used to spend Christmas and Easter. He could not be trusted by himself. This was McHenry's conclusion. He needed minding.

The Christian Singles mixed in the lobby of the Graves Hotel on the first Friday evening of each month. Although this month was May, it was still cold out; men and women both arrived in Carhartt brown. The Graves had a coffee shop off one side of the lobby and a bar off the other so you could go one way or the other. McHenry opted for drink. It was looking like a long night.

"Look at you," said Tom LaFrance. "Come to meet us on a Friday night. I was wondering if you might join the group."

"Just putting a toe in," said McHenry.

"Nice bunch. Good to get some new blood in, though, I'll tell you." He leaned closer to McHenry, inside the bloom of his whiskey breath. "The same old faces. After a while you've made the rounds."

"It's a small town," said McHenry.

"In the middle of nowhere," said LaFrance. "Oh, well."

They left the bar and joined the group: about a dozen altogether, with only four men. Some of them were people McHenry had known (and in LaFrance's case, disliked) since high school. The women especially had made an effort, red lipstick and pretty skirts and city shoes, but in every one of their faces were the marks of weather, of a life lived outdoors in a place where the wind hurried and the snow flew. The men were dressed Western in boots and sport coats. They looked at home in these clothes, while some of the women looked like an impersonation, a costume. These were widows, most of them, and had the short hair and hard practical faces of Montana wives, their girlishness erased by weather and work. They didn't look at home in their pretty dresses.

All but Lydia Tennant. She was ten years younger than the rest of them and dressed for a ski resort in sporty, bright colors. She had married into the Maclays, an old ranching family, and had somehow stuck it out after her husband, Tom, was killed in an avalanche, three or four years ago. She had two kids, both boys, McHenry thought. He had never considered her as a possibility. But here she was, presenting herself as a single, smiling, making small talk, looking tan and pretty in the lobby of the Graves Hotel. This was interesting, at least.

But before he could make his way to her, he was sidelined by Adele Baker, one of Marnie's good friends, an English teacher at the high school. She was plump, energetic, dry.

"Are we moving forward or giving up?" she asked him.

"I've no idea," McHenry said. He was wary of her; she thought before she said things, and you were likely to get yourself in trouble if you just said the first thing that came into your head. He asked, "What do you think?"

"I gave up several years ago," she said. "I'm just here to get out of the house."

"Oh, me too. Getting the shack nasties."

He looked over to see where Lydia was in the room—the far side, by the bar door, with Tom LaFrance standing at her elbow—and Adele caught the glance and laughed.

"No fair," she said.

"What's not?"

"You and she are the only two new faces since last summer. I believe that almost everybody else has dated almost everybody else. And by dated I don't mean *dated*. Don't be shocked."

"I thought these were the Christian Singles."

"We're all Christian and we're all single, but we're not always both at the same time."

"You've been saving that one up."

"Maybe," Adele said. "It's a long winter. Come buy me a drink and I'll tell you all our secrets."

That Saturday they went birdwatching, or birding, as it was now called. Adele wanted to go to Freezeout and McHenry hadn't been there in decades so they went, three hours each way and iffy weather but they went. They left at seven in the morning, which was early for Adele on a weekend, she said so. McHenry had been up for two hours.

It wasn't a date, they agreed on that. They didn't have another name.

Adele drove her Honda, which only made sense—McHenry still had the Expedition from his drilling days, which smelled of dirt and petroleum and got eleven miles to the gallon. But he hadn't been a passenger in a while and it was strange, filling her go-cup from the thermos and watching the weather. It really had been quite a while. Marnie never drove when they went places together unless she was driving him to the hospital, which had happened a couple of times. But just sitting back and relaxing and watching the snow fall on the far hills—this was like something out of his childhood, a distant memory, watching the telephone wires loop by in their rhythm of rise and fall.

"You miss her," Adele said. "Hell, I miss her and I wasn't married to her."

"It's been a while," McHenry said.

"Feel any better?"

"I don't know. I mean, sure, better than that first few months. It took a while to see the point of keeping things going. It helped having the girl around but she wasn't around that much except summers. It was kind of happening to both of us at the same time, you know? I do miss that."

"But she's doing well."

"I know she is. I'm not talking about her, I'm talking about me." McHenry laughed. "Carolyn's perfectly all right. I'm the one that's messed up."

"You're all right," Adele said.

"Maybe," said McHenry. In fact he didn't know. It felt like he was telling a story and it was a true story but it wasn't who he was. Wasn't where he lived. He looked at Adele, who drove with great concentration, slightly hunched forward over the wheel, and knew her for part of that story—he had known her, never well, for thirty years at least—and yet the known, the familiar, seemed strange to him, and only the thought of Tracy seemed his own. This felt mysterious. He felt like he didn't know himself.

The snowstorm drifted down off the hills and onto the road and Adele flipped the wipers on and leaned even farther forward. She seemed like a comic character from this new distance. McHenry felt, small, upholstered, flowery. Though this was underestimating her. She was a serious person, intelligent, and she had been very good to Marnie in her last year. It just seemed impossible to think of her in bed. That sadness, again, that waste of years that should have been joyful.

"You were married," McHenry said.

"I still am," she said, blinking into the storm.

"How does that work?"

"His family was Catholic," she said. "He developed mental problems after we were together. I mean, I guess he had them all along. But they pretty much took over after a while and he lost control of his life."

"I'm sorry," McHenry said. "I didn't know that."

"Really?" A quick glance over, to see that he wasn't lying. "I thought everybody knew. A town the size of Harlow. I talked about it with Marnie, I remember."

The sadness again, at the secrecy and fear that had kept them from bright life. It was too late for Marnie. McHenry thought it was too late for him too, and maybe for Adele too. This had meant something. Marnie had known but never told him.

"Where is he now? Your husband, I mean."

"He's in Seattle," she said. "Kaiser, a long-term-care place. They tried to make him better but they wrecked his mind from trying, all the different drugs and treatments. He had a very beautiful mind."

"I'm sorry," McHenry said again.

"It was a long time ago," she said. "I'm sure I could find a lawyer to straighten it out, if there was ever any need. It's just never come up."

She shrugged. It wasn't a hint. Nothing was going to happen between the two of them. The deep elemental strangeness of another life, even one as familiar as Adele's, and McHenry naked and alive inside. It was just such a strange world.

They got to Freezeout a little after ten—a couple of cars and pickups—blue skies and a cold breeze but shoots of raw green in the grass. Spring was coming after all. They bundled up and carried folding chairs and binoculars and in Adele's case a bird book and a life list. McHenry had an old, heavy pair of Leupolds that had been kicking around in the glove compartment of the Expedition for years but Adele had an immaculate medium-sized Leica pair. She was going to add a few to her list today. Only then did McHenry realize how boring this day would be. He could look at birds for about ten minutes.

They walked over the last rise. There was the lake and on the lake were geese and swans beyond counting, tens of thousands of them, teeming. As they watched, some invisible impulse ran through the flock at the far edge and they rose in one movement and circled through the air, blocking out half the sky in white movement, black wing tips. Okay, McHenry thought. This was worth it. All this beautiful life, this excess, generosity.

"Don't say it," Adele said.

"Don't say what?"

"The joke," she said. "Whatever it is. About how they mate for life."

"I'm not really a joke-type person," McHenry said. Which was true.

And then the next morning, back at the Bangkok Sunshine. Sunday morning! And his truck parked right out front for all the world to see.

A different and much friendlier girl up front. But heart-stopping beautiful. McHenry could barely talk to her, she was so perfect, so nice and lovely and young. Sunday morning, he thought: celebrate a life so full of amazing things as this. Just lately it felt like the world was full of gifts.

But Tracy wasn't there; he should have known as much. Would he like one of the other girls? A test of some kind, McHenry thought. Not what he was supposed to want, or what somebody else would like him to want—he wasn't trying to please anybody but himself. So what did he want himself? Nobody was watching.

"Why not?" he said. And went into room number two and stripped and folded his clothes neatly on the shelf provided for that and lay facedown and naked and asked the question again: why not? There must be a reason why not. He still couldn't sort any of this out. What would Adele have thought? But he knew as he asked the question that she would have disliked him for it. It was just a rule. But who made the rule?

A girl came into the room barefoot, in the same outfit as the others, but this one had an unhappy look to her, even an angry look, as if she had just been woken up, which maybe she had. She said her name was Flower and he said his name was Bill. She was, if anything, stronger and more expert than Tracy had been; he found himself spiraling down into that same pure moment of feeling, of being in his body and not thinking and not even being present in the room. He didn't even think of himself, of his nakedness. He was in the moment of her touch and nowhere else. Until she turned him over, covered him with the towel. Then he began to wonder again, whether the rules were the same, whether he had to do something that he didn't know how to do.

The feet. The face. The legs.

And then the whisper: "Happy ending?"

"Sure."

"Twenty extra."

"Sure," he said.

And then he was standing, blinking in the warm sunlight, alone in an acre of gravel parking lot. While he was inside, spring had come. It was actually warm. McHenry took his jacket off and threw it in the back seat of the Expedition. The smell of old petroleum grease filled the cab, released by the new heat. He didn't want that, not just yet. He lay back on the hood of his truck and closed his eyes and felt the sunlight pouring down on his skin, another gift in a world of gifts. Somebody might come by, Lydia Tennant or LaFrance or any of the Christian Singles. Somebody might see him. It didn't matter. His life was about to change.

DIANE COOK

Moving On

FROM *Tin House*

THEY LET ME tend to my husband's burial and settle his affairs.
Which means I can stay in my house, pretend he is away on business while I stand in the closet and smell his clothes. I can cook
dinner for two and throw the rest away, or overeat, depending on
my mood. Or make a time capsule full of pictures I won't be allowed to keep. I could bury it in the yard for a new family to discover.

But once that work is done, the Placement Team orders me to
pack two bags of essentials, good for any climate. They take the
keys to our house, our car. A crew will come in, price it all; a sale
will be advertised; all the neighbors will come. I won't be there
for any of this, but I've seen it happen to others. The money will
go into my dowry, and then someday, hopefully, another man will
marry me.

I have a good shot at getting chosen, since I'm a good decorator
and we have some pretty nice stuff to sell off and so my dowry will
likely be enticing. And the car is pretty new, and in the last year I
was the only one who could drive it and I kept it clean. It's a nice
car with leather seats and lots of extras. It was my husband's pro-
motion gift to himself, though he drove it for only a few months
before illness swept him into his bed. It's also a big family car,
which will appeal to the neighbors, who all have big families. We
hadn't started our own yet. We were fretting over money, being
practical. I'm lucky we didn't. Burdened women are more difficult to place, I'm told. They separate mothers from children. I've
heard it can be very hard on everyone. The children are like phan-

tom limbs that ache on a mother's body. I wouldn't know, but I'm good at imagining.

They drive me away from our house, and I see all the leaves that fell while I was too busy burying my husband and worrying what will become of me. The leaves, glossy and red, pile in airy circles around the tree trunks like Christmas-tree skirts. I see the rake propped against the rainspout. The least I could have done is rake the yard one last time. I had told my husband I would.

I am taken to a women's shelter on a road that leads out to the interstate. They don't let us go beyond the compound's fence, because the land is ragged and wild. The night skies are overwhelmed with stars, and animals howl far off. Sometimes hiding men ambush the women scurrying from the bus to the gate, and the guards, women themselves, don't always intervene. Sometimes they even help. As with all things, there is a black market for left-behind women, most often widowed, though, rarely, irreconcilable differences can land one in a shelter. A men's shelter is across the road. It is smaller, and mainly for widowers who are poor or who cannot look after themselves. My father ended up in one of these shelters in Florida. A wealthy woman who had put her career first chose him. Older now, she wanted a mate. They sent him to her, somewhere in Texas. I lost track of him. The nearest children's shelter is in a different county.

My room has a sealed window that faces the road and when I turn off my light I can see men like black stars in their bright rooms. I watch them move in their small spaces. I wonder what my new husband will be like.

There are so many handouts and packets. We have been given schedules and rules and also suggestions for improving our lives and looks. It's like a spa facility on lockdown. We are encouraged to take cooking classes, sewing classes, knitting classes, gardening classes, conceiving classes, child-rearing classes, body-bounce-back-from-pregnancy classes, feminine-assertiveness classes, jogging classes, nutrition classes, home economics. There are bedroom-technique potlucks and mandatory "Moving On" seminars.

In my first "Moving On for Widows" seminar we are given a manual of helpful exercises and visualizations. For one, I'm to re-member seeing my husband for the first time—we met at a new hires lunch—and then imagine the moment happening differently. So, for example, rather than sitting next to him and knocking his water onto his welcome packet, I should visualize walking right by him and sitting alone. Or, if I let myself sit down and spill his water, instead of him laughing and our hands tangling in the nervous cleanup, I should picture him yelling at me for my clumsiness. I'm supposed to pretend our wedding day was lonely, and that rather than love and happiness, I felt doubt, dread. It's all very hard.

But, they say, it's helpful in getting placed. What I find funny is that since my husband died, as he was dying, really, I hadn't thought about the possibility that this would be hard. I thought it was just the next step. My Case Manager says this is normal and that the feeling of detachment comes from shock. She says that if I can hold on to it and skip over the bewildering grief that follows, I'll be better off. The grief-stricken spend more time here. Years, in some cases. *Practice, practice, practice,* she always says.

We're each given a framed picture of a man, some model, and I take it back to my cell and put it by my bed as instructed. I'm supposed to replace my husband's face in my memory with this man's face while being careful not to get too attached; the man in the photo won't be my new husband. The man is too smooth; his teeth are very straight and white, and there is a glistening in his hair from gel that has hardened. I can tell he probably uses a brand of soap I would hate the smell of. He looks as if he doesn't need to shave every day. My husband had a beard. But, I remind myself, that doesn't matter now. What I prefer is no longer of concern.

We are allowed outside for an hour each day, into a fenced pen off the north wing. It is full of plastic lawn chairs and the women who have been here awhile push to get chairs in the sun. They undress down to their underwear and work on their tans. Other women join an aerobics class in the far north corner. The fences are topped with barbed wire. Guards sit in booths and observe. So far I've just walked the inside border and looked through the chain. The land beyond is razed save for the occasional toppled rooty stump. Weeds, thorny bushes grow everywhere. This is a newer facility. Decades from now, perhaps young trees will shade it, which, I think, would make it cozier. Far off, the forest is visible; a shaky line of green from the swaying trees. Though coyotes prowl the barren tract, it is the forest that, to me, seems most menacing. It is so unknown.

On my walks I often need to step around a huddle of women from another floor (the floors mostly keep together, socially); they form a human shield around a woman on her knees. She is digging into the ground with a serving spoon from the cafeteria. It is bent, almost folded, but still she scrapes at the pebbly soil. I can't imagine the guards don't know what is going on. There are runners who try to escape at night. They think they will fare better on their own. I don't think I could do it. I'm too domestic for that kind of thing.

Four weeks in, and I have gotten to be friends with the women on my floor. It turns out we're all bakers. Just a hobby. Each night one of us whips up some new cookie or cake from a recipe in one of the old women's magazines lying around the compound, and we sample it, drink tea, chat. It is lovely to be with women. In many ways, this is a humane shelter. We are women with very little to do and no certain future. Aside from the daily work of bettering ourselves, we are mostly left alone. I like the women on my floor. They are down-to-earth, calm, not particularly jealous. I suspect we are lucky. I've heard fights in the night on other floors. Solitary, in the basement, is always full. As is the infirmary. A woman on floor five who had just been chosen was attacked while she slept. Slashed across the cheek with a razor blade. The story goes that when the Placement Team contacted the husband-to-be with the news, he rejected her. There she was, all packed and about to begin a new life. When she returned from the infirmary with tidy stitches to minimize the scarring, she had to unpack and crawl into the same bed where her blood still stained the sheets. If she had been on our floor I would have changed the sheets for her. And I know the others would have too. That's what I mean about feeling lucky.

Last week, our girl Marybeth was chosen and sent to a farm near Spokane. We stood in a circle embracing, laying our heads on each other's shoulders, and Marybeth did not want to leave. We made her a care package; in our best handwriting we'd written out recipes on index cards of the things we'd baked together so she could always remember her time here if she chose to. She cried when we handed it to her. "I'm not ready," she whimpered. "I still miss him." A couple of us encouraged her. "Just do your best." When, eventually, the guard led her away we heard her trying to catch her breath until the elevator doors closed.

A window has blinked to life across the road. A man is awake, like me. He pads around his small room in pajamas—hospital blue, like ours. I want to be seen, so I stand in my window. He sees me, steps to his window, and offers a quiet wave. I wave back. We are opposing floats in a parade.

If we had been poor and I had died, my husband would be over there now, waiting for someone to want him. How strange to worry about someone wanting you when we had been wanted by each other so confidently. Most people reach the age of exemption before their partner dies, and they are allowed to simply live alone. Who would want them, anyway? Ideally, you marry the man you love and get to stay with him forever, through everything you can think to put each other through, because you chose to go through it together.

But I had not prepared for something like this. Had he? Had my husband kept some part of himself separate so he could give it to someone else if he needed to? Was it possible I too had managed to withhold something of myself without even realizing it? I hoped so.

I look around my small cinder-block room, painted a half-hearted pink, the desk too large for the unread library book on it. I had a picture of us hidden under my mattress. It was one of those pictures couples take when they are alone in a special place, at a moment they want to remember. We smooshed our heads together and my husband held the camera out and snapped the picture. We look distorted, ecstatic. One night, I fell asleep while looking at it; it fell to the floor, was found at wake-up, and was confiscated. I still can't believe I was so careless.

In bed, I imagine my husband lying beside me, warming the rubber-coated mattress, beneath the thin sheet so many women have slept under before me. My scalp tingles as I think of him scratching it. We rub feet. Then I have to picture him dissolving into the air like in a science-fiction movie, vaporized to another planet, grainy, muted, then gone. The sheet holds his shape for a moment before deflating to the bed. I practice not feeling a thing.

*

A few women on other floors have been chosen and will leave tomorrow. I can smell snow in the air pushing through the small crack where the window insulation has peeled away. Late fall is now winter. When it is too cold, we aren't let outside for activities in the pen. I would give anything to run through a field and not stop. I have never been the running-through-fields type.

From what I can tell, being chosen is bittersweet. I imagine many of us wouldn't mind living out our days at the shelter in the company of women like ourselves. But then again, it wouldn't always be us. Marybeth's replacement was cruel and tried to start fights between us. She told me my muffins were dry. She squeezed one in my face; it crumbled between her fingers. She crept into sweet Laura's room and cut a chunk of her long shiny hair with safety scissors. Laura was forced into a bob that didn't suit her. Luckily, this woman was very beautiful and was chosen after only four days. We're waiting for her replacement. Even though there is uncertainty in being chosen, it seems more uncertain to remain among the women, a sentiment I've also seen expressed in the manual.

Something very special has happened. I met my window friend. He came over with the other men from the men's shelter for bingo. This happens occasionally. It keeps everyone socially agile.

Even though we wave across the road, when he walked in I recognized him instantly—the darkness of his hair and the general line of his brow. The nights we wave have become important to me. It's nice to be seen by a man.

My window friend spotted me too, stopped in the doorway, and waved. I waved back and then we laughed. A tiny, forgotten thrill bubbled up in me.

He sat next to me. Close up I found him handsome. He clowned around, pushed the bingo chips off my board whenever I wasn't looking. He was nervous.

He said, "I'm going to tell you ten bad jokes in a row," and he did, counting on his fingers, not pausing for my laughter, which made me laugh through the whole thing. A guard watched us disapprovingly. We looked to be having too much fun. I guess it goes without saying that relations between shelter dwellers are prohibited. I mean, how could we survive together in the world if we have both ended up in a place like this?

At the end of the evening a whistle blew and the men began to shuffle out. Again my window friend stood in front of me and waved and I did the same. But this time he touched his open hand to mine and we pressed them together and smiled. I felt us quake like small animals that have been discovered somewhere they shouldn't be and have no time to run, or place to run to.

The next night, after we waved quietly, I undressed in the window, the lights bright behind me. He placed his hands against the glass as if to get closer and watched.

Tonight, his light isn't on and so we don't wave, but still, I undress in front of my lit window. I can't know if he's watching from the darkness, or who else is watching, for that matter. I loved my husband. I mourn his tenderness. I have to believe that someone out there is feeling a kind of tenderness for me. I'll take it any way I can.

I've been moved to another floor. Someone from the men's shelter reported me, and my Case Manager thought it best for me to occupy a room in the back of the building. Now I look out over the pen.

For days, I feign illness and stay in bed. I hear the groups of women doing their outside activities. It is a cyclical drone of laughing, arguing, calisthenic counting, and loaded silence.

When I do go outside to the pen, the women from my old floor give generous hugs and we try to talk, like the old days, but it's different. There are new women. A couple of friends have been chosen and are gone. A new woman replaced me; she lives in my room and has a view across the road to the men's shelter and my window friend. Her name is even close to mine. She told me that the women sometimes slip and call her by my name. She told me this to comfort me, with a sympathetic pat on my arm. But it doesn't help. Is there any difference between us beyond a few letters in our names?

The women on my new floor are mostly concerned with escape. They are bullish. Their desire scares me. But there are two nice women. They don't try to escape, or not that I've heard about. Our way out of here is to get chosen. So we swap tips from the different pamphlets we've read.

We don't bake. Sometimes my old girls send down cookies, but they come a couple of days after their baking parties and so they are crumbly, stale; nothing like the warm, fresh treats I was so fond of. I've started throwing them away, but I won't say anything, because I like it that they still think of me.

The alarm sounds.

It sounds when someone runs.

Floodlights sweep over the field, then through my window. I hear the far-off yowling of dogs as they smell their way through the night, tracking some woman. Curiously, I find myself rooting for her. Perhaps I'm half-asleep but, peering out my window, I think I can see her. When the lights pan the wasteland between the pen and the forest, something like a shadow moves swiftly, with what seems like hair whipping behind, barely able to keep up with the body it belongs to.

There's nowhere to hide before the forest line. The runner needs a good head start. I doubt she got it. They never do. And yet they always try. What are they looking for? Out there, it's dark and cold. No guarantee of food or money or comfort or love. And even if you have someone waiting for you, still it seems such a slippery thing to depend on. Say my window friend and I ran. Would he love me outside of here? Could I ever be sure? I barely know him.

I picture myself running. My nightgown billowing behind me, my hair loosening from a braid as I speed along. Finally it comes undone and free. I hear the dogs behind me. I see the forest darkness in front of me. From across the field a figure races toward me. But I'm not scared. It's him. My friend. We planned it. We're running so that when we reach the woods we can be together. I feel hopeful to be running across this field, and then I suddenly know why they do it. They are running toward what they believe is best for them, not what the manual claims is best. It should be the same thing but it isn't.

I find at the end of this fantasy I am weeping and so I write it down in a letter to my friend. I write it as a proposition, though I'm not sure it is one. I just want to know if he would agree to it. It's another way of asking, if we weren't both poor wretches, would he choose me? I don't know why, but it's important to me. Maybe I've changed. The manual says that in order to move forward we must change. But this change feels more like a collapse. And that is not how the manual says it will feel.

I open my window and the wind pinks my cheeks. I like it. The wind brings the smell from the field and even from the trees. It smells good out there, past where I can see. The dogs are silent now. The runner might have made it. I shake my head at the night. I know it's not true.

My window friend is gone.

At bingo I search for him. I want to explain my absence, tell him I was moved, while discreetly slipping the letter into his pocket. I can't find him. Another man follows me around trying to grab my hand; he whispers that he has secret riches no one knows about. Finally a guard from the men's shelter intervenes, takes the man by the arm. I ask about my friend and it turns out he was chosen. The guard says he left a few days ago. I ask how many exactly. "Just two," he says a little sheepishly. I'm destroyed. I say, "Two is not a few," and return to my room. It is painted a buzzing shade of yellow and I hate it. The desk is even bigger and emptier now that I've stopped pretending to read. The floodlights from the pen shine in my window at all hours.

The next day I slog to lunch, but I can't eat. I stare at my crowded tray until the cafeteria empties. My Case Manager calls me in. Her eyebrows are raised, imploring. She opens a file and in it is the letter I wrote to my window friend. I can't even muster surprise. Of course they would find it.

"I wasn't really going to run," I say. "It was just a fantasy."

"I know."

She pushes the letter to me.

I read it. My handwriting is looped and sleepy. The pages are worn. I wrote a lot, and reread it obsessively to make it right. Reading it now makes me blush. In the letter, I am begging. My tone near hysterics. I promise that we'll find a house, unoccupied in the woods, abandoned years ago. That we'll forage for our food, but that eventually we'll find work, even though all the jobs are spoken for. I insist we'll be the lucky ones. We'll have a family, a house with a yard. He'll have a nice car, and I'll have nice things. We'll have friends over to dinner. We'll have a vacation each year even if it is a simple one and we'll never put anything off if we really want to do it. And we'll never wait for something we want now, like children. We'll never fight over silly things. I won't hold a grudge and he'll say what he's feeling instead of shrugging it away. I won't be irresponsible anymore. I won't buy bedding we can't afford. And

I'll be more fun. I'll be game. I won't insist he tell me where we're going when all he really wants to do is surprise me. I'll never cook him things he doesn't like because I think he should like them. I won't forget to do small things like pick up the dry cleaning or rake the leaves in our yard.

Of course, I'm writing to my husband.

It reads as if we're fighting and he's stormed out, is staying on a friend's couch. Here is my love letter, my apology: please come home.

I look up.

"Be sensible," my Case Manager says, not without some kindness. "I can't put your name on any list until you've shown you're moving on."

"But when do I grieve?"

"Now," she says, as though I have asked what day it is.

I think of the man from across the road, my window friend. But I can't even remember what he looks like. I try to picture him in his room, but all I see is my husband, waiting, in his plaid pajamas and wooly slippers. He shakes a ghostly little wave. I can tell from his shoulders he is sad enough for the both of us.

For a couple of weeks I allow myself a little moment. I scrape other women's leftovers onto my plate. I eat the treats my old floor still sends, even though I don't like them. I barter for snacks with some rougher women who somehow had it in them to set up a secret supply business. Now my pants don't fit. My Case Manager finally intervenes and tells me to cut it out. She says even though we live in a progressive time it's probably not a good idea to let myself go. She gives me some handouts and a new exercise to do that is, literally, exercise. "Get that heart rate up," she says, pinching the flesh above my hip.

I know she's right. We all deal with things differently. At night, some women cry. Other women are bullies. Others bake. Some live one life while dreaming of another. And some women run.

Each night a new alarm sounds, the dogs, the lights. In the morning I'll see who looks ragged, as if she spent a futile few hours flying across the barren tract to the forest, only to be recaptured. I'll also look to see if anyone is missing. I still secretly hope she, whoever she was, made it, and I feel twinges of curiosity at the thought of that life. But they're just twinges. Not motivation. What

I want, I can't have. My husband is gone. So my future will be something much quieter. It won't be some dramatic feeling in the wild unknown. There are other ways to be happy. I read that in the manual. I'm trying them out. My Case Manager says this is healthy.

Eight months into my stay, I am chosen. My Case Manager is proud of me.

"That's a respectable amount of time," she insists.

I blush at the compliment.

"The knitting helped," she notes, taking quiet credit for suggesting it.

I nod. However it happened, I'm just glad to have a home.

My new husband's name is Charlie and he lives in Tucson and the first thing he bought with the dowry was a new flat-screen TV. But the second thing he bought was a watch for me, with a thin silver cuff and a small diamond in place of the twelve.

My Placement Team takes me to a diner on the outskirts of town, where Charlie waits in front of a plate of pancakes. He has girlish hands but otherwise he is fine. The Team introduces us and, after some papers are signed, leaves. Charlie greets me with a light hug. He is wearing my husband's cologne. I'm sure it is a coincidence.

I am his second wife. His first wife is in a shelter on a road that leads to the interstate outside Tucson. He tells me not to worry. He didn't cause their broken marriage. She did. I nod, and wish I had a piece of paper so I can take notes.

He asks me how I feel about kids, something he certainly has already read in my file. I answer that I've always wanted them. "We'd been planning," I say. There is an awkward silence. I have broken a rule already. I apologize. He's embarrassed but says it's fine. He adds, "It's natural, right?" and smiles. He seems concerned that I not think badly of him, and I appreciate that. I clear my throat and say again, "I'd like kids." He looks glad to hear it. He calls the waitress over and says, "Get my new wife anything she wants." There's something in his eagerness I think I can find charming.

I am not ready for this. But I've heard that someday I'll barely remember that I ever knew my first husband. I'll picture him standing a long way down a crowded beach. Everyone will be pleased to be on the beach. I'll see something about him that will catch my eye but it won't be his wave, or his smile, or the particular curl of his hair. It will be platonic, something I wouldn't associate with him. It will be the pattern on his bathing shorts; bright, wild, red floral or, maybe, plaid. I'll think something like "What a nice color for bathing shorts. How bright they look against the beige sand." And then the image will disappear and I'll never think of him again. I'm not looking forward to this day. But I won't turn my back on it. As the manual often states, it's my future. And it's the only one I get.

JULIA ELLIOTT

Bride

FROM *Conjunctions*

WILDA WHIPS HERSELF with a clump of blackberry brambles. She can feel cold from the stone floor pulsing up into her cowl, chastising her animal body. She smiles. Each morning she thinks of a new penance. Yesterday, she slipped off her woolen stockings and stood outside in the freezing air. The morning before that, she rolled naked in dried thistle. Subsisting on watery soup and stale bread, she has almost subdued her body. Each month when the moon swells, her woman's bleeding is a dribble of burgundy so scant she does not need a rag.

Women are by nature carnal, the Abbot said last night after administering the sacred blood and flesh. *A woman's body has a door, an opening that the Devil may slip through, unless she fiercely barricade against such entry.*

Wilda's body is a bundle of polluted flesh. Her body is a stinking goat. She lashes her shoulders and back. She scourges her arms, her legs, her shrunken breasts, and jutting rib cage. She thrashes the small mound of her belly. She gives her feet a good working over, flagellating her toes and soles. She reaches back to torture the two poor sinews of her buttocks. And then she repeats the process, doubling the force. She chastises the filthy maggot of her carnality until she feels fire crackling up her backbone. Her head explodes with light. Her soul rejoices like a bird flitting from a dark hut, out into summer air.

Sister Elgaruth is always in the scriptorium before Wilda, just after Prime Service, making her rounds among the lecterns, checking the manuscripts for errors, her hawk nose hovering an inch above each parchment. Wilda sits down at her desk just as the sun rises over the dark wood. She sharpens her quill. She opens her ink pot and takes a deep sniff—pomegranate juice and wine tempered with sulfur—a rich red ink that reminds her of Christ's blood, the same stuff that stains her fingertips. This is always the happiest time of day—ink perfume in her nostrils, windows blazing with light, her body weightless from the morning's scourge. But then the other nuns come bumbling in, filling the hall with grunts and coughs, fermented breath, smells of winter bodies bundled in dirty wool. Wilda sighs and turns back to *Beastes of God's Worlde,* the manuscript she has been copying for a year, over and over, encountering the creatures of God's Menagerie in different moods and seasons, finding them boring on some days and thrilling on others.

Today she is halfway through the entry on bees, the smallest of God's birds, created on the fifth day. She imagines the creatures spewing from the void, the air hazy and buzzing. In these fallen times, bees hatch from the bodies of oxen and the rotted flesh of dead cows. They begin as worms, squirming in putrid meat, and "transform into bees." Wilda wonders why the manuscript provides no satisfactory information on the nature of this transformation, while going on for paragraphs about the lessons we may learn from creatures that hatch from corpses to become ethereal flying nectar eaters and industrious builders of hives.

How do they get their wings? Do they sleep in their hives all winter or freeze to death? Do fresh swarms hatch from ox flesh each spring?

Wilda is about to scrawl these questions in the margins when she feels a tug on her sleeve. She turns, regards the blunt, sallow face of Sister Elgaruth, which nips all speculation in the bud.

"Sister," croaks Elgaruth, "you stray from God's task."

Wilda turns back to her copying, shaping letters with her crimped right hand.

At lunch in the dining hall, the Abbess sits in her bejeweled chair, rubies representing Christ's blood gleaming in the dark mahogany. Though the Abbess is stringy and yellow as a dried parsnip, everybody knows she has a sweet tooth, that she dotes on white flour, pheasants roasted in honey, wine from the Canary Islands. Her Holiness wears ermine collars and anoints her withered neck with myrrh. Two prioresses, Sister Ethelburh and Sister Willa, hunch on each side of her, slurping up cabbage soup with pious frowns. They cast cold glances at the table of new girls.

The new girls have no Latin. They bark the English language, lacing familiar words with the darkness of their mother tongue. One of them, Aoife, works in the kitchen with Wilda on Saturdays and Sundays. Aoife works hard, chopping a hundred onions, tears streaming down her cheeks. She sleeps in a cell six doors down from Wilda's. Sometimes, when Wilda roams the night hall to calm her soul after matins, she sees Aoife blustering through, red hair streaming. And Wilda feels the tug of curiosity. She wants to follow the girl into her room, hear her speak the language of wolves and foxes.

Now, as Wilda's tablemates spout platitudes about the heavy snows God keeps dumping upon the convent in March, the new girls erupt into rich laughter. They bray and howl, snigger and snort. Dark vapors hover over them. A turbulence. A hullabaloo. The Abbess slams her goblet down on the table. And the wild girls stifle their mirth. But Wilda can see that Aoife's strange amber eyes are still laughing, even though her mouth is pinched into a frown.

At vespers, the gouty Abbot is drunk again. His enormous head gleams like a broiled ham. He says that the world, drenched in sin, is freezing into a solid block of ice. He says that women are ripe for the Devil's attentions. He says their tainted flesh lures the Devil like a spicy, rancid bait. The Abbot describes the Evil One scrambling through a woman's window in the darkness of night. Knuckles upon pulpit, he mimics the sound of Satan's dung-caked hooves clomping over cobblestones. He asks the nuns to picture the naked beast: face of a handsome man of thirty, swarthy skinned, raven haired, goat horns poking from his brow, the muscular chest of a lusty layman, but below the waist he's all goat.

It has been snowing since November and the nuns are pale, anemic, scrawny. They are afflicted with scurvy, night blindness, nervous spasms, and melancholy. Unlike the monks across the meadow, they don't tend a vineyard at their convent. And when the Abbot describes the powerful thighs of Satan, the stinking flurry of hair and goat flesh, a young nun screams. A small mousy thing who never says a word. She opens her mouth and yowls like a cat. And then she blinks. She stands. She scurries from the chapel.

After the Abbot's sermon, Wilda tosses on her pallet, unable to banish the image from her mind: the vileness of two polluted animal bodies twisting together in a lather of poisonous sweat. She jumps out of bed and snatches her clump of blackberry brambles. She gives her ruttish beast of a body a good thrashing, chastising every square inch of stinking meat from chin to toes. She whips herself until she floats. God's love is an ocean sparkling in the sun, and Wilda's soul is a droplet, a molecule of moisture lifted into the air. When she opens her eyes, she does not see her humble stone cell with its straw pallet and hemp quilt; she sees heavenly skies in pink tumult, angels slithering through clouds. She sees the Virgin held aloft by a throng of naked cherubs, doves nesting in her golden hair.

In her melodious voice, the Virgin speaks of Jesus Christ her Son, his tears of ruby blood. The Virgin says her son will return to Earth in May to walk among flowers and bees.

When the bell rings for matins, Wilda is still up, pacing, her braids unraveling. Somehow, she tidies herself. Somehow, she transports her body to the chapel, where three dozen sleepy-eyed virgins have gathered at two in the freezing morning to revel in Jesus' love.

At breakfast, Wilda drinks her beer but does not touch her bread. Now she is floating through the scriptorium. She has slept a mere thirty minutes the night before. She has a runny catarrh from standing in the freezing wind with her hood down, and she shivers. But her heart burns, a flame in the hallowed nook of her chest.

You are all Christ's brides, said the Abbot this morning. *Do not break the seal that seals you both together.*

"I am the bride of Christ," Wilda whispers as she sits down at her lectern. She opens her ink, sniffs the blood-red brew. She has a burning need to describe the voice of the Virgin, the frenzy of beating angel wings as the heavens opened to let the Sacred Mother descend. She wants to capture the looks on their faces, wrenched and fierce. But there's Sister Elgaruth, wheezing behind her. Wilda turns, regards the sooty kernel of flesh that adorns Sister Elgaruth's left nostril. Elgaruth is one of God's creatures, magnificent, breathing, etched of flesh and bone.

"Sister," says the old woman, "mind the missing word in your last paragraph."

Elgaruth points with her crooked finger, deformed from decades of copying, too crimped to copy text.

"Forgive me. I will be more mindful."

Sister Elgaruth shuffles off. Wilda eyes the shelves where the unbound vellum is stashed, noting the locked drawer that stores the choicest sheets, stripped from the backs of stillborn lambs. She has never touched the silky stuff, which is reserved for the three ancient virgins who have been penning a psalter for an archbishop.

Now, when Sister Elgaruth departs to the lavatory, Wilda tiptoes over to the old woman's lectern. She opens the first drawer, notes a pot of rosemary balm, the twig Elgaruth uses to pick dark wax from her ears. The second drawer contains a psalter, prayer beads, a bundle of dried lavender. In the third drawer, beneath a crusty handkerchief, is a carved wooden box, four keys within it, looped on a hemp ring. Wilda snatches the keys, hurries to the vellum drawer, tries two keys before unlocking the most sacred sheets. By the time Sister Elgaruth returns, Wilda is back at her desk, three stolen sheets stuffed in her cowl pocket. Her heart, a wild bird, beats within her chest.

She turns back to *Beastes of God's Worlde*.

The goats bloode is so hotte with luste it wille dissolve the hardest diamonde.

In the kitchen, Aoife chops the last carrots from the root cellar, brown shriveled witches' fingers. Aoife is pale, freckled, quick with her knife. She sings a strange song and smiles. She turns to Wilda. In the Abbot's pompous voice, she croaks a pious tidbit about the darkness of woman's flesh—a miraculous imitation. For a second the Abbot is right there in the kitchen, ankle-deep in onion skins, standing in the steam of boiling cabbage. Wilda feels an eruption of joy in her gut. She lets out a bray of laughter. Sister Lufe turns from her pot of beans to give them both the stink eye. Wilda smirks at Aoife, takes up a cabbage, and peels off rotted leaves, layer after slimy layer, until she uncovers the fresh, green heart of the vegetable.

*

Wilda kneels on bruised knees. She has no desk, only a crude, short table of gnarled elm. Tucked beneath it are sheets of lamb vellum, her quills, a pot of stolen ink. She faces east. Her window is a small square of hewn stone. Outside, snow has started to fall again, and Wilda, who has no fire, rejoices in the bone-splitting cold. She's mumbling. Shiver after shiver racks her body. And soon she feels nothing. Her candle flame sputters. She smells fresh lilies.

The Virgin steps from the empyrean into the world of flesh and mud.

The glow from her body burns Wilda's eyes.

The words from her mouth are like musical thunder in Wilda's ears.

"My Son will return to choose a bride," says the Virgin, "a pearl without spot."

And then the Virgin is lifted by angel throng, back into the realm of pure fire.

Wilda sits stunned as the snow thickens outside. She prays. She whips herself. And then she takes up her plume. She tries to describe the beauty of the Virgin. At first, her words get stuck, stunned as flies in a spill of honey. But then she begins with a simple sentence, in tiny, meticulous script.

Whenne the virgin descended I smelde apples and oceane winde.

At Prime Service the Abbess keeps coughing—fierce convulsions that shake her whole body. She flees the chapel with her two prioress flunkies, eyes streaming. The Abbot pauses, and then he returns to his theme of Hell as a solid block of ice, the Devil frozen at its core. Satan is a six-headed beast with thirty-six sets of bat wings on his back. The Evil One must perpetually flap these wings to keep the ninth circle of Hell freezing cold.

Wilda frowns, trying to grasp the paradox of Hell as ice, wondering how this same Devil, frozen at the center of Hell, can also slip through her window at night, burning with lust, every pore on his body steaming. But it's morning, and the Abbot is sober. When he returns for vespers, his imagination inflamed with wine, he will speak of carnal commerce between women and Satan. But this morning his theme is ice.

Today is the first day of April, and a crust of snow covers the dead grass.

The chickens aren't laying. The cows give scant milk.

The meat cellar boasts nothing but hard sausage, oxtails, and salted pigs' feet.

The beets are blighted, the cabbages soft with rot.

But Wilda smiles, for she knows that Christ will return this blessed month, descending from Heaven with a great whoosh of balmy air. She has described the glory in her secret book: trees flowering and fruiting simultaneously, lambs frolicking on beds of fresh mint, the ground decked with lilies as Christ walks across the greening Earth to fetch his virgin bride.

On Sunday, in the kitchen, Aoife puts two bits of turnip into her mouth, mimicking the Abbess's crooked teeth. Crossing her eyes, Aoife walks with the Abbess's arrogant shuffle, head held high and sneering. Wilda doubles over, clutches her gut. She staggers and sputters as laughter rocks through her. Her eyes leak. She wheezes and brays. At last, the mirth subsides. Wilda leans against the cutting table, dizzy, relishing the warmth from the fire. A stew, dark with the last of the dried mushrooms, bubbles in the cauldron. Aoife, still sniggering, places her hand on Wilda's arm. Wilda feels a delicious heat burning through her sleeve. Aoife's smile sparkles with mischief, and the young nun smells of sweat and cinnamon.

Wilda's body floats as she looks into Aoife's honey-colored eyes, pupils shrinking, irises etched with green. Aoife murmurs something in her mother tongue. But then she speaks English.

"Man is a rational, moral animal, capable of laughter."

Aoife removes her hand and turns back to her bucket of turnips.

The Abbess is dead by Tuesday. Her body, dressed in a scarlet cowl, rests on a bier in the chapel. The Abbot, fearing plague, sends a small, nervous prior to conduct the service. The chapel echoes with the coughs of sickly nuns. The prior covers his mouth with a ruby rag. He hurries through the absolution, flinging holy water with a brisk flick of his fingers, and departs. Three farmers haul the body away.

That night, a hailstorm batters the stone convent, sending down stones the size of eggs, keeping the nuns awake with constant patter. Sisters whisper that the world has fallen ill, that God will purge the sin with ice. No one arrives from the monastery to conduct the morning service, and nuns pray silently in the candlelit chapel.

Contemplating the body of Christ, Wilda kneels before her little book, waiting for words to come. She sees him, torn from the cross, limp in the Virgin's arms. He is pale, skinny as an adolescent boy. His side wound, parted like a coy mouth, reveals glistening pomegranate flesh. Other than the flowing tresses and silky beard, Christ is hairless, with smooth skin and nipples the color of plums. He has a woman's lips, a woman's soft, yearning eyes. Wilda imagines him waking up in his tomb, cadaverous flesh glowing like a firefly in the cryptic darkness. His groin is covered with loose gauze. His hair hangs halfway down his back, shining like a copper cape when he emerges into the sunlight.

The world is frozen in sinne, Wilda writes, *frozen until the Lammbbe descendes to walk among floweres and bees. He wille strewe his marriage bed with lilies. Hallelujah!*

Fifteen nuns have been taken by the plague, their bodies carted off by farmers. Not even a prior will set foot in the convent, but the nuns shuffle through their routine, sit coughing and praying in the silent chapel, their hearts choked with black bile. They pine for spring. But the heavens keep dumping grain after grain of nasty frost onto the stone fortress. In mid-April, the clouds thicken, and a freak blizzard descends like a great beast from the sky, vanquishing the world with snow.

Prioress Ethelburh orders the nuns to stay in their rooms praying, to leave only for the lavatory. Kitchen workers will still prepare food but the nuns will no longer gather in the refectory for fellowship. Victuals will be taken from door to door to stave off the contagion.

In the kitchen Aoife is bleary-eyed, and Wilda worries that the plague has struck her. But then the poor girl is weeping over her pot of dried peas.

"What is it, Sister?" Wilda moves toward her.

"Nothing," says Aoife, "just the sadness of winter and death."

But then Aoife pulls up her cowl sleeve, shows Wilda her thin arm—pale and finely shaped, mottled with pink blisters.

Wilda jumps back, fearing contagion.

"Only burns," Aoife whispers, "from Prioress Ethelburh's hellish candle."

Wilda allows her knuckles to stray across Aoife's soft cheek.

"I was out walking in the garden," says Aoife, "watching the moon shine on the snow, and she . . ."

Sister Lufe bustles in with a rank wheel of sheep's cheese, and the two girls jump apart. Aoife dumps melted snow into her pot of dried peas (the well is frozen). Wilda hacks at a black cured beef tongue (the last of it). Outside, the sun glares down on the endless white blight of snow. The trees are rimed with frost, the woodpile obscured, the garden paths obliterated.

Wilda kneels on cold stone, stomach grumbling. For supper she had three spoons of watery cabbage soup and a mug of barley beer. The crude brew still sings in her bloodstream as she takes up pen and parchment.

The Lammbbe will come again, she writes, murmuring the word *Lammbbe,* reveling in its deep, buzzing hum. She closes her eyes, pictures Jesus hot and carnified, walking through snow. Frost melts upon contact with his burning flesh. *Walking accrosse the barren earthe,* she writes, *the Lammbbe wille leeve a hotte traile of lillies.* When he steps into the convent orchard, the cherry trees burst into bloom. *Thirty-six virgines stand in white arraye, pearles withoute spotte.* The nuns stand in order of age upon the lawn, ranging from thirteen-year-old Sister Ilsa to sixty-eight-year-old Elgaruth. Jesus pauses before twenty-three-year-old Wilda. He smiles with infinite wisdom. He touches her cheek with his hand, peers into her eyes to look upon her naked soul. Wilda feels the heat from his spirit. At first she can't look at his face. But then she looks up from the grass and sees him: eyes like molten gold, lips parted to show a hint of pearly teeth, a tongue as pink as a peony.

"My bride," he says.

And cherubim scream withe joye, squirminge naked in the frothe of heavene.

The shrieks grow louder—so loud that Wilda looks up from her book. She's back in the convent, hunkered on the cold floor. She gets up, walks down the hallway, turns left by the lavatory. The screaming is coming from the sad room where nuns are punished, but Wilda has never heard a ruckus in the middle of the night. She peeks in, sees Aoife seated, skirts pulled up, hair wild, eyes huge and streaming. Prioress Ethelburh twists the young nun's arms behind her back. Prioress Willa burns Aoife's creamy left thigh with red-hot pincers. This time, Aoife does not scream. She bites her lip. She looks up, sees Wilda standing in the doorway. Their eyes meet. A secret current flows between them. Ethelburh turns toward Wilda, her mouth wrenched with wrath, but then a violent cough rocks through her. She shakes, sputters, drops to the floor. And Aoife leaps from the chair like a wild rabbit. In a flash she is halfway down the hall.

"Surely mockers are with me," says Prioress Willa, casting her clammy fisheye upon Wilda, "and my eye gazes on their provocation."

The next morning, Ethelburh is dead, her body dragged beyond the courtyard by hulking Sister Githa, a poor half-wit fearless of contagion. Twelve bodies lie frozen near the edge of the wood, to be buried when the ground thaws.

Aoife is singing in her mother tongue, the words incomprehensible to Wilda, pure and abstract as birdsong, floating amid the steam of the kitchen. Poor old Lufe is dead. Hedda and Lark have passed. Only Hazel, the girl who carries bowls from door to door, loiters in the larder, bolder now that Lufe is gone, inspecting the dwindling bags of flour.

"Prioress Willa has taken to her bed," whispers Aoife.

"God bless her soul," says Wilda, crossing herself.

Aoife chops the last of the onions. Wilda picks worms from the flour. And the soup smells strange: boiled flesh of a stringy old hen.

"Sister," says Aoife, her mouth dipping close to Wilda's ear, "I have heard that the Abbess kept food in her chamber. Pickled things and sweetmeats. A shame to let it go to waste, with our sisters half starved and weak."

Snow falls outside the kitchen door, which is propped open with a log to let the smoke drift out. The light in the courtyard is a strange dusky pink, even though it is afternoon. Wilda thinks of Jesus, multiplying fishes and loaves. She sees the bread materializing, hot and swollen with yeast. She pictures the fish—teeming, shimmering, and salty in wooden pails.

"Sister," says Wilda, "you speak the truth."

*

The Abbess lived in the turret over the library, and the two nuns tiptoe up winding stairs. The door is locked. Aoife smirks and fishes a key from her pocket. Aoife opens the door and steps into the room first. Wilda stumbles after her, bumps into Aoife's softness, stands breathing in the darkness, smelling mold and rot and stale perfume—myrrh, incense, vanilla. Aoife pushes dusty drapes aside, discovering windowpanes in a diamond pattern, alternating ruby and clear. The nuns marvel at the furnishings: the spindly settee upholstered in brocade, the ebony wardrobe with pheasants carved into its doors, several gilded trunks, and the grandest bed they have ever seen: big as a barge, the coverlet festooned in crimson ruffles, the canopy draped in wine velvet. Wilda wonders how the crooked little Abbess climbed into this enormity each night, and then she spots a ladder of polished wood leaning against the bed.

Aoife opens a trunk, pulls out forbidden things: a lute, a fur-lined cape, a crystal vial of perfume, and a bottle of belladonna. They find a clockwork mouse that creeps when you wind it up (a mechanism that Aoife, oddly, seems to understand). The girls giggle as the mouse moves across the floor. Aoife strokes the ermine cape as though it is a sleeping beast. Wilda leans against the settee, but does not allow herself to sit. The second trunk is chock-full of dainty food: small clay jars of pickled things, dried fruit in linen sacks, hard sausages in cheesecloth, venison jerky, nuts, honey, wine.

Aoife opens a pot of pickled herring, sniffs, eats a mouthful, chews, and then offers the fish to Wilda. They taste fresh, briny, tinged with lemon. Something awakens in Wilda, a tiny sea monster in her stomach, so weak and shriveled that she hardly knew it existed. She feels it stretching strange tentacles, opening its fanged mouth to unleash a wild groan. Wilda is starving. She gnaws at a twisted strand of venison, tasting forests in the salty meat, the deer shot by a nobleman's arrow, strips roasted over open flame. When Aoife opens a pot of strawberry preserves, she moans as sweetness fills the room—a kind of sorcery, the essence of a sun-warmed berry field trapped in a tiny crock. Aoife eats with her fingers, tears in the creases of her eyes. And then she offers the jar to Wilda. Wilda pauses, feels the monster slithering in her gut, dips a finger, and tastes the rich, seedy jelly.

"Hallelujah!" she whispers, smacking her lips. She eats more strawberries. Offers the pot to Aoife. But Aoife has discovered a stash of sugared almonds. Wilda tries them: butter roasted with cinnamon and cloves, a hint of salt, some other spice, unfamiliar, bewitching. The nuns sit down on the soft settee and spread their feast on a carved trunk. They eat smoked fish, dried apricots, pick-led carrots, and red currant jam. Suddenly very thirsty, they have no choice but to uncork a bottle of wine, passing it between them. After shaving off teal mold with a small gilded knife, they consume a chunk of hard cheese. And then they discover, wrapped in lilac gauze, a dozen pink marzipan rabbits.

The monster in Wilda's stomach lets out a bellow. She can pic-ture it, lolling in a hot stew of food, the scales on its swollen belly glistening. She pops a candy into her mouth, closes her eyes, tastes manna, angel food, milk of paradise. The young nuns drink more wine. And now Aoife is up on her feet. She opens the Abbess's wardrobe, rifles through gowns and cloaks. She pulls out a winter frock, thick velvet, the luminous color of moss, sable fur around the neck and cuffs. Wilda looks away as Aoife undresses.

"How do I look?" Aoife asks, still buttoning up the bodice, con-torting like an acrobat as though she has pulled on fine frocks a hundred times before.

Wilda tries to speak, but the words will not come. Her throat feels dry. She takes another swig of wine.

The dress brings out the secret lights in Aoife's eyes, the swan-like curve of her neck.

Wilda feels ugly, small, though she has not seen her reflection in a good, clear mirror in seven years, not since her parents and brother died and her aunt sent her off to the convent.

Aoife chooses a fur cloak from the wardrobe, slips it over Wil-da's shoulders. Wilda feels cold, but then a feeling of delicious warmth overtakes her, and her spine relaxes. Aoife picks up the lute, strums a strange tune, sings a song in her mother tongue that makes Wilda feel like she's dream flying, her stomach buckling as she soars too fast into whirling stars, the air thin and strange and barely breathable.

Imitating the Abbess, Aoife hobbles over to the bed, climbs up the ladder, peeks over the edge at Wilda, who can't stop laughing.

"It's a boat," Aoife says, crawling around like a child. Wilda re-members her brother, galloping around on his stick horse. Memo-ries like these stopped haunting her two years ago, part of the earthly existence she has kept at bay. Now she remembers the two of them rolling in the garden, flowers in their fists, singing bawdy songs they barely understood, laughing so hard she thought her ribs would crack. She remembers the way her parents would scold them with stanched smiles, trying not to laugh themselves.

Wilda climbs up the ladder. She sits beside Aoife on the high bed. The stiff fabric of the coverlet smells of must and myrrh.

"Look!" says Aoife, opening a cabinet built into the bed's headboard. Inside is a crystal decanter encrusted with a ruby cross, a burgundy liquid inside it. Aoife sniffs, takes a sip.

"Wine," she says dreamily, "though it might be some kind of liqueur."

Aoife offers the bottle. Wilda drinks, tasting blackberries and brine and blood, she thinks, though she has never tasted blood, for the Sacrament does not transubstantiate until it passes into the kettle of the stomach, where it is boiled by the liver's heat, the same way alchemists turn base metals into gold. Some kind of matter floats in the liquid. Wilda feels grit between her teeth. The grit dissolves and the world glows, a fresh surge of pink light shining through red windowpanes.

Aoife's hand scurries like a white mouse over the coverlet to stroke Wilda's left wrist. Their fingers intertwine. Wilda marvels at the deliciousness of the warmth streaming between them.

The two sisters sit holding hands, leaning against thick down pillows, sipping the strange concoction at the very top of a stone fortress, snow falling in the eternal twilight outside—upon the monastery and meadows and forests, upon frozen ponds and farms and villages. They discuss beasts in winter, the mysteries of hibernation, the burrows and holes where furry animals and scaly things sleep.

"Do you think their blood freezes?" whispers Aoife, her breath on Wilda's cheek. "Do you think they dream?"

Wilda has the strange feeling that everyone in the world is dead. That she and Aoife are completely alone in an enchanted castle. That they are just on the verge of some miraculous transformation.

Wilda wakes to the clanging of monastery bells. She clutches her throbbing head. She tries to sit up, thinking she's on her cot. But then she smells musty perfumes, odors of pickled fish and honey, and her cheeks burn as the previous night's feast comes back to her in patches. How had it happened so fast?

Her swollen belly throbs with queasiness, the sea monster slithering in a mash of wine and food. She has no choice but to lean over the bedside and heave a foul gruel onto the floor. Bright sunlight shines through the windows. How long has she been asleep? She turns to Aoife, still dozing beside her. Not Aoife—where is Aoife?—but the Abbess's fur cloak, crumpled, patched with bald spots, sprawling like a mangy bear. She remembers a tale from her childhood, about a fair woman who turned into a bear. The she-bear scratched out the eyes of lovesick hunters and devoured them whole. The bear, like Aoife, had eyes the color of honey. She sang with the voice of a nightingale, luring hunters into deep woods.

Wilda climbs down from the bed, hurries back to her cell, and latches her door. She paces around the cramped space, feeling the rankness of the flesh upon her bones, the puffery of her belly, the sea monster roiling within. Her brow and cheeks are hot. She wants to check on Aoife, see how she feels, laugh about the previous night's feast—a whim, a trifle, nothing—but her skin burns with shame. She pictures Aoife singing in her green dress. She imagines fur sprouting from her freckled skin, yellow claws popping from her fingertips.

Wilda vows to stay in her room without eating, without sleeping, whipping herself until the hideous sea monster ceases to squirm in her belly, until she has purged her flesh of excess fluid and heat and is again a bird-boned vessel of divine love—arid, clean, glowing with the Word. She has a clay bottle of water, almost full, the only thing she needs.

Wilda kneels on the floor, naked, whipping herself for the third time, bored with the effect, not feeling much in the way of spinal tingling, her mind as dull as a scummy pond. She sighs. Tries not to think of Aoife, the lightness of her laughter. She contemplates Christ in his agony—hauling the cross, grimacing as iron nails are hammered into his feet and hands, staring stoically at the sun on an endless afternoon, thorns pricking his roasted brow. But the images feel rote like a rosary prayer. So she hangs her whip on a nail and lies down on her bed. She watches her window, waiting for the day to go dark, the light outside milky and tedious. She hasn't eaten for two days, but her belly feels puffed up like a lusty toad. Contemplating the beauty of Christ's rib cage, the exquisite concavity of his starved and hairless stomach, she shivers.

When she hears the giggle of young nuns running down the hallway outside her door, her heart beats faster. And there's Aoife again, knocking softly with her knuckles.

"Sister Wilda," says Aoife, "won't you take some food?"

Wilda says nothing.

"Sister Wilda," says Aoife, "are you well?"

"I am," says Wilda, her voice an ugly croak, her throat full of yellow bile.

Her heart sinks as Aoife slips away.

When Wilda wakes up, some kind of flying creature is flapping around her room. A candle flickers on her writing table, her book still open there.

She spots a flash of wing in a corner. A dove-sized angel hovers beside her door like a trapped bird wanting out. An emissary, Wilda thinks, come to tell her that Christ is near. Wilda unlatches the door, peeks out into the dark hallway, and lets the creature out. The angel floats, wings lashing, and motions for her to follow. The angel darts down the hall, a streak of frantic light. Wilda lopes after it, feeling dizzy, chilled. They pass the lavatory, the empty infirmary. The angel flies out into the courtyard and flits toward the warming house, where smoke puffs from both chimneys. Crunching through snow, Wilda follows the angel into the blazing room.

The angel disappears with a diamond flash of light.

Fires rage in both hearths. And there, basking on a mattress heaped with fine pillows, is Aoife. Dressed in the green gown, drinking something from a silver communion goblet, Aoife smiles. Hazel lolls beside her in sapphire velvet, munching on marzipan, an insolent look on her face.

"Sister." Aoife sits up, eyes glowing like sunlit honey. "Come warm your bones."

Overcome with a fit of coughing, Wilda can't speak. It takes all of her strength to turn away from the delicious warmth, the smells of almond and vanilla, from beautiful Aoife with her wine-stained lips and copper hair. Hacking, Wilda flees, runs through the frozen courtyard, through empty stone passageways where icicles dangle from the eaves, back to her cell, where she collapses, shivering, onto her cot.

When Wilda wakes up, her room is packed with angels, swarms of them, glowing and glowering and thumping against walls. An infestation of angels, they brush against her skin, sometimes burning, sometimes freezing. She hurries to her desk, kneels, and takes up her plume.

A hoste of angells flashing like waspes on a summer afternoone. My fleshe burned, but I felte colde.

One of the creatures whizzes near her and makes a furious face—eyes bugged, scarlet cheeks puffed. Another perches on her naked shoulder, digging claws into her skin. Wilda shudders, shakes the creature off. A high-pitched humming, interspersed with sharp squeaks, fills the room as the throng moves toward the door. She opens the door, follows the cloud of celestial beings down the hallway, past the infirmary, out into the kitchen courtyard.

Wind howls. Granules of ice strike her bare skin as Wilda follows the angels toward the orchard. Her heart pounds, for surely the moment has come: The fruit grove glows with angelic light. Wilda can see skeletal trees sparkling with ice, a million flakes of wind-whipped snow, the darkness of the forest beyond. And there, just at the edge of the woods, the shape of a man on horseback. The angels sweep down the hill toward the woods and wait, buzzing with frustration as Wilda trudges barefooted through knee-deep snow. But her feet are not cold. Her entire body burns with miraculous warmth. And now she can see the man more clearly, dressed in a green velvet riding suit, a few strands of copper hair spilling from his tall hat. His mouth puckers with a pretty smile. His eyes are enormous, radiant, yellow as apricots.

The Big Cat

FROM *The New Yorker*

THE WOMEN IN my wife's family all snored, and when we visited for the holidays every winter I got no sleep. Elida's three sisters and their bombproof husbands loved to gather at her parents' house in Golden Valley, an inner-ring suburb of Minneapolis. The house was less than twenty years old, but the sly tricks of the contractor were evident in every sagging sill, skewed jamb, cracked plaster wall, tilted handrail, and, most significantly, in the general lack of insulation that caused the outer walls to ice up and the inside to resound.

Every night the sounds were different. Helplessly cognizant, I formed mental scenarios while drifting in and out of sleep. One memorable night, I tossed and turned in a metalworking shop. From the far end of the second-floor hallway came the powerful rip of my mother-in-law's rough-cut saw. From below, on the living room's foldout couches, the intermittent thrum of welders' torches—a wild hissing as the sisters' noses sparked and soldered invisible objects. Beside me, Elida's finishing touch: the high-pitched burr of a polisher perfecting a metal surface. Elida was slight, and she dressed in precise, quiet colors. She sat with her hands folded, wore clear nail polish and almost undetectable makeup. You would never have imagined that such a stark little person could produce such sounds.

Ambien, earplugs, two pillows over my head—nothing could shut the noise out. I lay awake stewing, even though I knew I should feel sorry for them. The sisters and their mother had visited sleep clinics, endured surgery, blown their CPAPs off their faces, tried every nose strip and homeopathic remedy that existed. It wasn't that they liked to snore but that they were incurable. I think they took comfort in solidarity, though. Elida admitted that she loved sleeping in that noisy house, and sometimes they snored in unison—which was terrifying.

One subzero vacation morning, my daughter, Valery, ran her finger across the ice-furred downstairs living-room wall and asked, "What is this, Daddy?"

"Snores," I said, blue with tiredness. "All the snores from last night have stuck to the walls."

Later, after her mother and I had divorced, Valery wistfully recalled that moment as the first time she'd realized how alive with sound the night was—and that all the noise emanated from the women in the family. Later still, she asked her mother at what age she'd begun to snore, and asked me if that was the reason we'd split up. Valery was worried for her own future. I assured her that snoring had had nothing to do with the divorce, which was amicable but also unavoidably painful. I laughed and hugged Valery. I even told her that I had adored her mother's snores. I had never adored them, but I had adored Elida, almost to the point of madness, from the first time we met.

We found each other in Hollywood, as Minnesotan expatriates always do, common sense driving them together—though to leave the Land of Ten Thousand Lakes for a thirsty city built on a desert may speak of some interior flaw. For Elida, it was the compulsive lure of film editing. In my case, the shame of acting. Although I auditioned endlessly and always had work, my parts generally lasted between six and twelve seconds. I rarely had a line. But I had Elida, her intense green stare, her Nordic pallor, even after years of sunlight, her slender, gliding walk, and the dark swerve of her severe haircut. She was mine.

When Valery turned twelve, I was cast in a supporting role in a movie that got a lot of attention. It could have been my fabled break. But Elida suddenly panicked over how unhappy Valery was in high school and decided that the schools in Minneapolis were more nurturing. We moved back. I had to accept the fact that my film career was over. I'd worked steadily and spoken a line or two, given many a meaningful glance, tripped villains, sucker-punched heroes, spilled coffee on or danced around movie stars in revolv-

ing doors. I had appeared in dozens of films, TV episodes, commercials. But Elida hadn't been doing well, and both of us got
better, more reliable jobs back home.

Elida loved the minuscule: the hundreds of tiny decisions that
together produce a great flow of scenes. She applied this love of
detail to her new vocation, planning corporate events. I also loved
the small, when it consisted of learning to say lines a dozen different ways, with different tonal qualities, inflections, and gestures. In
my new job, as a fund-raiser for a vibrant local theater company, I
perfected the gestures and tones that I hoped would coax dona-
tions to my organization.

For my birthday that year, perhaps to console me for the life
I'd given up, Elida somehow managed to clip and splice together
a half-hour movie of my bit parts, which she set to eerily repetitive
music. Shortly after she gave me that gift, which she titled "Man of
a Thousand Glimpses," we parted. I moved out of our downtown
condominium, near nurturing DeLaSalle High School.

For the first couple of months after leaving Elida, I bolted out of
work at exactly 4 p.m. I drove to my tiny apartment impatiently,
hungrily, addicted not to a new relationship but to sleep itself.
Deep rest was a drug. Waking from relaxed oblivion, I vibrated
with an almost tear-inducing pleasure. Why shoot up, I wondered,
when just by depriving the body of uninterrupted sleep for twenty
years you can have ecstasy with no side effects? Except, it might be
said, for Laurene.

It took no time at all before I was sleeping the entire night beside a woman whom I feared I had married too quickly because
she slept like a drunk kitten.

From the beginning, I had to consciously keep myself from
referring to Laurene in casual conversation as "my current wife."
Though it was taken as a joke, I knew better: it was a slip. Laurene
Schotts was the daughter of the owner of an immensely successful
Midwestern sporting-goods chain with outlets in the ex-est of the
exurbs throughout the tristate area. She was also a lover of the theater arts. At the annual gala dinner for my theater company, which
Elida organized pro bono the year we parted, Laurene spoke between the salad and the entrée. Her flattering words of thanks to
our supporters, which screened a plea for still greater largesse, impressed me with their genuine, awkward grace.

Laurene reveled in that sort of gala, where people bid on donated items—the use of time-shares in warm countries, fur coats, ski packages, signed books, hand-painted scarves. Scarves draped our chairs, and we took superb vacations. Laurene was blond, social, generous, and loved to barbecue. Elida was dark, wayward, introverted, frugal, and usually a vegetarian. Laurene could drink a whole bottle of cold Pinot Gris between 5 and 6 p.m. Elida might sip one murderous, snore-inducing glass of Côtes du Rhône between eleven and midnight.

After the divorce, Elida and I met once a month to discuss Valery. We had agreed to do this early on, even when it hurt to see each other. Every time, after we had wincingly established where Valery's college tuition would come from, or whether she needed a new therapist, after Elida had confided the latest news of Valery's boyfriend, who we both hoped would turn out to be simply "experience," we would conclude the hour with a cheerful goodbye, perhaps saying "That wasn't so bad!" or even "Good to see you!" We laughed in relief. We hugged, patted each other on the back, sometimes drank a cup of tea before the drive home. We never kissed, not even on the cheek. Our divorce had been agreeable and final. Our postdivorce meetings were lingering, tedious, and self-congratulatory.

Once Laurene and I were married, however, the meetings with Elida became more difficult. The boyfriend had turned into a problem—we suspected an addiction. We also began, without any warning, to fight. It would start with some obscure thing and progress to even more obscure things. By the end of our meetings, Elida and I were worn out. Then, after one particularly difficult session, still upset as we were saying goodbye, Elida, instead of hugging me, stuck out her hand. I took her hand and held on to it until she met my eyes. Her glare pulled me to her, and I shocked us both by kissing her studious, pale lips. We jumped apart, as though scorched, and turned away. We didn't speak of it.

Our next meeting was set up by e-mail, and I found myself walking eagerly toward Nick's, a restaurant off Loring Park, which was quiet and decorous by day, with leather booths and gauzy curtains that let in glowing white rafts of winter light.

Elida was sitting at the third booth in, and raised a hand as I entered, then put a tissue to her eyes. She had been crying, a rare event. It usually meant, frighteningly, that she'd had some breakthrough realization about me that she'd repressed for years. Warily, I asked her what was wrong. She told me that Valery had started snoring. Her boyfriend had left her, thank goodness, but now Valery was refusing to believe that her mother's snoring hadn't precipitated our divorce.

"Of course it didn't!"

"Maybe not. We had other issues."

"Who doesn't? Twenty good years. One bad year. A thousand little issues came home to roost."

"I thought, you know, because of those good years we might still get back together," Elida said. "Until Laurene. She doesn't snore, right?"

I admitted as much.

"Ah." Elida turned to look out the window, and her dark glinting hair swung sorrowfully alongside her cheek. "The first time we spent the night together."

"St. George Street."

"I warned you I snored. I'd already been to the specialists and had surgery, which only made it worse. It's almost a relief to sleep alone now. At least I'm not blasting a man out of bed."

"I never minded."

I thought of the couch in Los Feliz that had wrecked my back. The walk-in closet with a floor pallet in our Minneapolis condominium. I'd adjourned to these lonely sleeping venues on most nights. I did mind, but her fixed gaze shook my heart.

"Last month you kissed me."

"I did."

We grew perplexed, ate in silence, each secretly examining the other's face from time to time. I was very conscious of the drama of the situation. Any former actor would have been. Elida sussed that out.

"You're trying on expressions," she said, laughing.

It was true. Various expressions crossed my face, but none felt right. The elements wouldn't meld. My eyes would express affection while my mouth was tense. Surprise would lift an eyebrow while my upper lip worked cynically. Embarrassment smote me. At least that was real. I put my face in my hands and tried to breathe, but my hands covering my mouth made me hyperventilate. When

I looked up, Elida was signing the credit-card slip. She folded her napkin.

"Don't get up," she said. "From now on, let's do a phone call. Or e-mail."

"I really hate e-mail," I said, "for personal stuff. Please sit down. We can solve this."

She sat down. Irrationally elated, I ordered a bottle of wine.

"This is a bad idea," Elida said.

"Why? We can talk. How are the ripsaw and the welders?" Elida knew my nicknames for her mother and sisters.

"Ha!" She clinked my glass. "What was I again?"

"The polisher!"

"I don't really mind that," she said. "It's in my line of work, really. I miss you. Maybe we should have an affair where we see each other only by day and never sleep together, you know, at night."

She was speaking whimsically, but we proceeded to do exactly that. We were extremely happy for ten months. To be sure, I felt bad about lying to Laurene, but she noticed nothing. She made few demands, seemed happy enough with my company, and continued to barbecue, even in December. Meanwhile, Valery had left for college, and Elida and I were meeting in our old condominium, overlooking the poisoned brown waters of the Mississippi.

Then one afternoon we were dressed, sipping tea, looking out at the river, when Valery dropped her suitcase inside the door. She was astonished to see us sitting there. She gaped silently for a moment, then clumped down the hall in her big snow boots.

Elida gave me an oddly insolent look. You can live with a person, have an affair with a person, and still suddenly see an unfamiliar flash, like the belly of a fish in the shallows, there and gone. She had known exactly when our daughter would arrive home.

Valery screamed when she saw the untucked covers on our bed, the scattered pillows. She clumped back into the living room.

"How long has this been going on?"

We told her. She began to sob.

"All this time? How selfish! Mean! I could have had you both together. Instead, I've been trying to get used to you apart. I was facing the facts and then . . ."

She pressed her mittened hands to her temples as if to keep her head from flying apart. We all started crying and, for a while, felt miserable. Then Elida snorted, and we burst into hysterical laughter.

It was decided that I would come clean and leave Laurene Schotts. Elida and I would remarry. Although it was strange, the idea gave me an enormous sense of rightness. Things were falling into balance. My elation continued all the way back to Laurene's and my house on Interlachen Boulevard, in Hopkins, facing the golf course. A beautiful stone house, with creamy painted walls, a wet bar in the basement, and a vast screening room for movie-viewing parties. Sitting in my car and looking up the flagstone walk, I thought of the pallet on the floor of the condominium's walk-in closet. I would regret leaving this lavish, comfortable house, bought with Laurene Schotts's money. I would regret leaving Laurene too, the silent comfort of her presence every night.

Laurene pitched a majolica vase, then a framed photograph of us in Peru. She threw a few other breakable objects at the wall and, at last, hefted a crystal unicorn she'd had since the age of ten.

"You'll regret throwing that," I said. "Please don't. I'm so sorry!"

"Dad was right!"

Tears rolled down her face onto her collar, wetting her throat.

I was stricken. I couldn't stop apologizing. Never before had I seen her truly upset or sad.

"Dad was right," she said again. "He said you were after the money. He didn't trust you—a former bit-part actor. He begged me to make you sign a pre-nup, but I said, 'No, you're so wrong! He's the one!'"

Because I had little money, and because money hadn't figured into my first marriage, except for the problem of not having it, I was until that moment unaware that this had even been discussed. I put it out of my mind and didn't think about it until a month later. I had moved out of Laurene's house into a studio apartment. I continued to see Elida only during the day. I wasn't quite ready for the walk-in closet.

"Are you crazy?" Elida said, putting down her teacup one afternoon, after I'd told her the proposed terms of my divorce. "That family is worth more than a hundred million! You could get a settlement. They'd never even miss it."

I waved her off, but every time I thought about how handy, how fantastic it would be to have money, I wavered. With my nonprofit

salary, I could barely afford to soundproof Valery's old bedroom.
I told myself that I'd keep my pride and sleep on the closet floor.
I'd walk away without a cent. But I didn't, of course.

We bought the condominium next door and removed two walls.
This gave us an easy path into a large room, where I set up a huge
screen. Before it, we arranged several couches of immense size
and comfort. I slept there in grateful quiet. I didn't take Laurene
for that much, comparatively speaking, and the Schotts family was
relieved. Still, they hated me enough to threaten for a while to get
me fired.

One night, Elida surprised me by playing the montage of clips
she'd made for my birthday years earlier. It was worse, somehow,
seeing it on that giant screen bought with Laurene's money. There
I was, my trivial works captured for the ages. I hadn't noticed,
when I first viewed the movie, that Elida had made of those fleeting cameos and set pieces a sort of narrative.

"Man of a Thousand Glimpses" started out with crowd scenes,
me here, me there, the nice-looking, unobtrusive bystander reading a newspaper, glancing up at the sound of a gunshot, the man
crossing a street, exiting a bakery, jumping into his car, uncoiling
a hose to water his lawn. Next, a better man appeared, somewhat
older, more heroic: I ran toward a river with a child in my arms;
I was a soldier dragging his buddy to safety; I lowered a dog in a
basket from a burning building, addressed people through a bull-
horn, rushed into waves, and dived toward despairing arms. After
that, I became a good father, inflated bicycle tires, opened refrigerator doors, lay back smiling in my late-night-shopper's easy chair,
had my waist measured, drove several carloads of screaming kids
to sports matches. Small wonder I then got a pounding headache,
clutched my jaw, my leg, my heart, wincing in agony. Next there
came a turning point, which had been much applauded at the
first viewing: I smoked a cigarette in a cheap motel, a beautiful
woman silhouetted in the shower behind me. Afterward, ruined,
I poured myself drink after drink, ordered a third martini, fell off
a barstool, crawled under a table and licked a woman's ankle. I
sank even lower—stuck a gun in a teller's face, took cash from the
drawer of a fast-food register. I palmed an apple from a pile, stole
a moped, a diamond bracelet, a newspaper. These crimes kept me
tossing in bed. I stared at ceilings, my eyes luminous, hollow with

glare, haunted by ghosts, by women, by hallucinations. Sleepless, I got clumsy. I was hit by a car, crushed by a falling girder, devoured by a live volcano, axed, mauled, infected with bubonic plague. I was identified several times, in liverish-green morgue light, by stricken, dignified women. It was shocking the way I just kept on dying, physically, then mentally. A wreck of a man, I leaped from a bridge, a window. I parked on train tracks and drank deeply from a flask. I smiled at the swiftly approaching lights and laughed soundlessly.

The End.

Elida left. I played the movie over and over. How dark was my narrative! Why had Elida killed me off, instead of letting me rescue dogs at the end? This downward trajectory gave me a moral chill. I decided that I had not only wasted my life but had acted ignobly in taking money from Laurene. Although Elida and I had made Valery happy, and I'd thought I was contented with Elida, I knew now, as I'd known before, the nature of her true feelings for me.

I destroyed the movie. It would be years before anyone noticed that my long-ago birthday gift had disappeared and I was once again dispersed into the confetti of B movies, failed TV sitcoms, and clumsy commercials. No one would ever have the cruel patience to assemble my life glimpse by glimpse again.

When the holidays came around, I insisted that we stay at the house in Golden Valley. Why not? I had already counted a million holes in a million ceiling tiles.

The first night at Elida's parents' house, we all had a mirthful, loving dinner, then did the dishes together. Elida's relatives had easily absorbed me back into the family, where my role, though peripheral, was also vital, because I was Valery's father.

After we turned in and Elida fell asleep beside me, I lay on my back waiting. It usually took her an hour or so to really get going, but her sisters and her mother had already begun. Valery and a girl cousin had sneaked a bottle of wine into their sleeping bags and were now drifting off next door.

The real snoring hit with abrupt ferocity. The orderly, mechanical regularity of the metalworking shop had been abandoned. Now it was more like a pack of wolves snarling over a kill. I closed my eyes. On my mental screen I saw lions driving the wolves—or hyenas, maybe—into the veld. On a hill overlooking the bloody feast, a baboon whooped. For many hours, I elaborated on the vivid images that accompanied the soundtrack: a lioness worrying the leg off a carcass, two others fending off a male, raking his ribs with teeth and claws, while their cubs mock-fought nearby. At last, I dropped off.

In the deepest part of the night, I woke. Although Elida's snarls had calmed to the loud, gurgling purr of a big cat digesting prey meat, I came to in a sick sweat, shaking. Perhaps my imagined scenario had triggered some terror from my evolutionary past. I had dreamed that I was the hunted animal, thrown to earth, being eaten alive. The tearing of my flesh, the snap of jaws wrestling at my bones, the blissful lapping as my throat opened—all this seemed absolutely real to me. It took some time for me to understand that Elida's body had not been satiated on mine, that she wasn't purring because she'd swallowed my heart.

BEN FOWLKES

You'll Apologize If You Have To

FROM *Crazyhorse*

WALLACE WENT ALL the way to Florida to fight a Brazilian middleweight he'd never heard of for ten thousand dollars. That's what it had come to.

The Brazilian's name was Thiago something, but everyone called him Cavalo. From what Wallace had gathered, it had something to do with a movie or a TV show that only Brazilian people knew about. No one cared enough to explain it any more than that and anyway Wallace wasn't overly interested. Everything he needed to know about the guy's game he could tell just from looking at him. He had shoulders that looked welded on, a neck that existed mostly in theory. The kind of guy who'd be hell on wheels in a street fight.

"If you take him down, flatten him out, and feed him some elbows," Coach Vee said, "my guess is he'll start thinking of all the other places he'd rather be."

Wallace said he got the message.

"Good," Coach Vee said. "Because I don't feel like repeating it all night."

Right off Cavalo clipped the top of Wallace's head with a glancing left hook. It felt like someone had thrown a phone book at his head and just missed. A follow-up right set off flashbulbs behind his eyes. Enough of this, Wallace decided.

The last thing he remembered was backing Cavalo up against the cage and seeing the Brazilian set his feet. There, Wallace thought. He dropped for the double-leg. The next instant he was looking into Coach Vee's face. It seemed to hover all alone in a

field of light. He was saying something to Wallace, but the sounds
didn't quite match up with the movement of his lips.

"I said just stay down, relax for a second," Coach Vee said.

Wallace asked him what he meant by *stay* down. They were both
standing up.

Coach Vee winced at him.

"Oh," Wallace said, lifting his head up to look around.
"Fuck me."

One ear felt like it was plugged up with wax. The other rang
with a high metallic whine. Somewhere off where he couldn't see,
Cavalo and his coaches were singing in Portuguese. It took him a
second to understand that the field of light around Coach Vee's
face was coming from the ceiling.

"Head kick," Coach Vee told him later, back at the hotel.
"Caught you right as you were changing levels."

There were two narrow beds in the hotel room. Wallace sat on
one and Coach Vee sat on the other. They were both drinking
Miller High Life tallboys. A movie with Denzel Washington was on
the TV.

"Caught you flush too."

Wallace thanked him for clarifying that part.

The left side of his head felt like it had been dug out with a
spoon. He pressed the beer can to his temple but it was nowhere
near cold enough to do anything. On the TV Denzel was yelling at
some guys in a submarine.

"Timed it really well, is the thing," Coach Vee said. "Right as you
were coming in. Bang."

"What are you, his publicist now?" Wallace said. He took a big
gulp of his beer. It tasted of aluminum. It was shit.

"Hey," Coach Vee said. "You asked how it happened."

Had he? Wallace didn't remember. He tried to trace the conversation back to its beginning but couldn't. Then he tried to remember where they'd gotten the beers and he couldn't do that
either. It was like trying to reel yourself in on a rope only to get
halfway there and realize it'd been cut. He knew this happened
to some guys after a knockout, but it had never happened to him.
He'd never been knocked all the way out before. Not like that.
Not *out*-out. Now that he had, he couldn't recommend the experience.

*

They flew back to San Diego the next day. Five hours vacuum-packed into coach seats. Wallace pretended to sleep so he didn't have to watch the stewardesses willing themselves not to stare at the giant bruise on the side of his head. Coach's wife picked them up at the airport and gave Wallace a ride down to his place in Imperial Beach. She asked once how Florida was and when no one said anything neither did she. They drove most of the way like that.

Wallace spent the next three days alone in his condo, sitting in the dark and feeling sorry for himself. He let his cell phone ring until it died and then made a point of not plugging it in. He watched whatever was on TV. He made a couple of attempts at getting drunk, but it wouldn't take. He iced his head until the swelling started going down, leaving behind a darkening triangle of tissue along his temple. It looked like he'd had an accident while ironing.

After three days he'd had enough. He had to do something, get outside, take a walk. Look, he told himself while standing at the sliding glass door to his deck. It's a beautiful fucking day.

He put on his shoes and rolled a joint to keep him company. He didn't want to risk it on the beach, where there might be people, so instead he headed off into the estuary that started in back of the condos and ran all the way down to Mexico like one long green finger pointing the way out. There was a dirt path that dead-ended in about a dozen places, depending on the water level, before eventually snaking its way to the big houses with ocean views on the other side. People didn't go back in the estuary often. The people in the condos looked out on it every day and the people in the big houses on the other side probably never did. They hadn't paid all that money to be close to a saltwater swamp. They paid to look out at the beach. That was fine with Wallace. He lit his joint as he walked.

He'd seen a heron back there once. That had been something. It was back when he first bought the condo, his first year in the Big Show, the same year his daughter was born. He fought three times in Vegas that year. He made a half-million dollars just in purses and bonuses alone. It seemed like only the beginning of the wonderful things that were going to happen for him. Then one day he goes walking in the estuary and rounds a corner right into this enormous bird. He stopped cold, no more than ten feet away. The heron just stood there on long, ridiculous legs, then lifted its wings, big as car doors, and took off. Wallace could hear it chopping at the air as it disappeared toward Mexico.

He thought about the heron as he smoked and walked and let the sun fall on the bruised part of his face. It felt all right. The joint didn't hurt either. He took a long pull on it and when he looked up he saw a man in a big green jacket, too heavy for the weather, coming up the path toward him. Wallace let the hand with the joint fall casually to his side and tried to tilt his head so that his bruise wouldn't be so noticeable. When the man got close, Wallace nodded and moved to pass on one side. The man stepped in front of him and stopped.

"So you're the one who's been smoking weed back here," the man in the green jacket said. He said it with a smile on his face, but it didn't look to Wallace like a smile that was meant to convey any form of happiness.

Wallace still had the joint in his hand. He looked at it stupidly, like it might somehow vanish, then he looked back at the man. The man had thick, dark hair and the cool kind of glasses, the kind people who didn't need glasses might wear. He stared at Wallace like he really expected an answer. Wallace agreed that he was, in fact, smoking weed back here.

"But I wouldn't say I've *been* doing it," he said.

"No?" the man said. "What would you say, then?"

"I'd say I've smoked back here once or twice," Wallace said.

"Once or twice?" the man said. "That's an interesting answer, isn't it?"

Wallace said nothing.

"Are you saying this is the second time, right here?" the man said. "Or are you saying this is the once? Because it seems like you'd remember if it was your first time."

Wallace didn't care for his tone. The man couldn't have been much older than he was. Mid-thirties, maybe. Definitely not past forty. He wasn't a cop. He seemed too hip, or too something. There was no question of whether Wallace could take him, but the last thing he needed was to get into something physical. This didn't seem like the kind of dude you got into a scrap with. This seemed like the kind of dude you assaulted.

Wallace licked his fingertips and pinched the joint out before slipping it in the back pocket of his jeans.

"There," he said to the man. "We good?"

The man looked at him.

"I live right over there," the man said, pointing at a big yellow house on the other side of the estuary. "So I smell it when someone smokes weed back here. My kids smell it. There's no way *not* to smell it. You get what I'm saying?"

"You're saying that you smell it," Wallace said.

"Can you not understand how this would be a problem?" the man said.

Wallace said he understood that the man lived in the yellow house over there and that his kids smelled it when people smoked weed. He said he understood all this perfectly.

"Where do you live?" the man said. "Those apartments?"

"They're condos," Wallace said.

"How about if I came over there and blazed up in front of your kids? How would you like that?"

Wallace chuckled to himself. It was the only way to keep from slapping the man's cool glasses off his face. He'd been having such a nice day too. His first in a while. His high was slipping away and he could hear his own pulse in his ears. *Now, now, now,* went his heartbeat. It'd take him hours to calm back down. It'd fuck up his whole afternoon. He could see it, rolling out in front of him like an old rug.

"Let's agree that you made your point and I learned my lesson," Wallace said. "And then let's get the hell out of each other's way before one of us does something we'll both regret."

The man stood there. He looked at Wallace and then nodded as if a question had just been answered.

"So this is what you do, huh?" the man said, still nodding. "A weekday morning, and this is what you do. Just walk around smoking weed in public. It must be nice."

"It's better than nice," Wallace said.

"Oh, I bet it is," the man said again.

Wallace liked his tone even less now.

"What happened to your face?" the man said.

"Work," Wallace said.

"Sure," the man said, and laughed a mean, bitter laugh. "I'll bet that's why you're out here smoking weed in the middle of the day. Because you're so busy with work, right?"

That did it. Wallace clapped his hand on the man's shoulder, grabbing a handful of his green jacket. The man didn't move except to turn his head and look at Wallace's hand, his eyes going wide like a giant insect had just landed on him. Wallace grabbed the man's opposite sleeve with his other hand.

"Here's what's happening now," Wallace said.

He used a simple foot sweep to sit the man down just off to the side of the trail. It was like he was watching himself do it. The man landed hard and sunk down to his elbows in mud. His face was all confusion and panic, just perfect. Wallace could tell that it hadn't even occurred to him that this had been a possible outcome.

"Oh what the Christ," the man said. Silty mud washed up over his lap. He tried to sit up and only sank further. "Christ!" he said again.

Yeah, Wallace thought, that's going to be trouble. But there it was. He turned on his heels and started back the way he'd come. Behind him he could hear the sucking sound of the man pulling himself out of the mud. The man swore in stupid, broken-off threats at his back. Wallace decided he was going to let the man say whatever he wanted to say. That was a choice he was making.

Wallace took the joint out of his pocket as he walked out and lit it up again. He slowed down so the man could see as he tilted his head back and exhaled the smoke in one luxurious stream. He was four days out from a knockout loss and I-don't-give-a-fuck had settled in.

He spent the next hour standing around in his condo, trying to figure out what to do next. He plugged in his phone and it lit up with all the stuff he'd been avoiding. A voicemail from Coach Vee, asking Wallace to let him know he hadn't died in his sleep. A voicemail from his ex-girlfriend Kim, telling him he'd missed his day to pick up his daughter. A couple texts from some reporter who wanted to talk about the fight. He put the phone in his pocket and decided not to think about it anymore.

He went and looked out the sliding glass door to see if there was any commotion in the estuary. He saw the same dull green mass he looked at every day. If this guy is the type to let something like this go, he told himself, you'll spend the next couple days stressing for nothing. If he's some other type, he's probably already on the phone to the cops, his lawyer, whoever.

Not like it would be hard to find Wallace. Show up to the condos where he'd idiotically admitted to living and ask around for the guy with the cauliflower ear and the giant bruise on the side of his head. It'd take them all of five minutes to zero in on him, and then what? Was that assault? Probably. Everything was these days. Maybe it wasn't the kind of thing you went to jail for, but it would be expensive and dumb and an utter pain in the ass. Plus you did it to yourself for no good reason. And just wait until one of those blogs gets ahold of it. Pro fighter gets knocked out cold in the cage, then comes home and bullies some local yuppie. What a career move.

He got sick of hanging around and waiting so he went up to Coronado to see his daughter. The drive took ten minutes and ended in a different world. Coronado was somewhere people lived on purpose. Old people walked the sidewalks like they were keeping an eye on things. Even the dogs had nice haircuts.

Kim lived with their daughter, Molly, in a big house paid for by Kim's husband, a lawyer in a downtown firm. He was too old for Kim but he was loving and fair and kind to Wallace's daughter in a way that made Wallace feel like every decision he'd ever made with his own life had been wrong. They had the Pacific Ocean and 150 feet of sand for a front lawn. They couldn't complain.

Kim was on the patio when he pulled up. She had the detached nozzle for a garden hose in one hand and an unopened juice box in the other. Her eyes followed Molly as she stalked through the hedges, a plastic Tupperware container outstretched in her hands. It was not quite noon and the marine layer had just finished burning off. Wallace had to squint through the brightness to read their expressions.

"What happened to your face?" Kim asked him.

He smiled at her and then kneeled down to Molly's level. She held the Tupperware in front of her eyes as if she were trying to hide behind it.

"Hello, Mol," he said.

She looked at him through the Tupperware. She didn't say anything.

"We're hunting for lizards," Kim explained. "We could kill an entire morning this way. We have, more than once."

"I see," Wallace said. "Can I play?"

Molly stared straight through him and didn't answer. This was one of her new things, not talking to him. He felt like it was probably meant to get him to do all the talking, or maybe to punish him. He looked at her big eyes and felt exposed. They stood there that way until Kim touched Molly lightly on the top of the head. Molly took it as a signal that she was free to resume the lizard hunt. Wallace watched her go and all he felt was relief.

"We waited for you all day on Sunday," Kim said.

"About that," Wallace said.

"I'm guessing there's a story here that also explains the state of your face," she said.

Wallace told her he had a fight in Florida. He left it at that.

Kim had been around enough fighters to know that if he'd won, he'd have mentioned it already. That was a rule you could count on. Some guy went out to Vegas for a fight and if he won he'd be back in the gym on Monday, not even training, just giving everyone a chance to ask him about it, hear the story of his triumph. If he lost, you wouldn't see him for a week. When you did see him, he wouldn't mention the fight. If you asked him how it went, he'd say it went shitty and leave it at that.

"We've got to figure something out here," Kim said. "You can't just stand her up like that and then show up when you feel like it."

"I know," Wallace said.

"You think she doesn't really notice but she does," Kim said.

"I know," Wallace said again.

"This age, you never know what will end up sticking with them for the rest of their lives," Kim said. "I mean, come on, look at me and my dad."

By all means, Wallace told her. Let's go ahead and make this about that now.

Kim looked at him like she was trying to decide whether it was worth summoning the energy to get angry. Over by the hedges Molly clamped the Tupperware down over some invisible prisoner, then looked back to see if she was being watched.

I made this possible for you, Wallace thought. It's because of me that you can marry a rich lawyer and stay home all day in a big house. You lived with a fighter once and had his baby and followed him into all sorts of bad decisions, so now no one can say you were always boring and domestic.

But that was a shitty way of making himself feel better. Because even if you're right, he told himself, so what?

"You could take her for a little while today," Kim said. "Make up for the weekend you missed, maybe even let her stay the night at your place. She likes that."

Wallace pictured his condo, pictured flinging open the door for Molly, her crinkling her nose at the cloistered stink of three days' worth of grown man wallowing. Or better yet, what if the cops came by? A nice man in a crisp blue uniform knocking on his door to talk about the morning Wallace had spent smoking weed in public and throwing people in the mud. That'd make a great story for Mol to tell in therapy some day. The kind of story that starts, "The last time I saw my dad . . ."

"Why don't you just say you don't want to do it?" Kim said when she saw his face. "At least then I can pretend to respect your honesty."

"It's not the best time," he said.

"It never is," Kim said.

"Fuck it," Wallace said.

He told her about the thing in the estuary. He told it just how it happened, exaggerating his own patience and the other man's obnoxiousness only slightly. When he got to the part about foot-sweeping the man into the mud, Kim looked away from him and shook her head twice in a tight, mean pivot. Wallace said it wasn't that big a deal. It's not like he hit him. It's not like the man was actually physically hurt.

"Right," Kim said. "It's so unimportant you're afraid you're going to get arrested when you go home."

It didn't sound to Wallace like a question, so he didn't answer.

"And you were stoned too? Walking around with a joint like some teenager? Then you drove here, presumably still stoned? And to see your daughter? I mean, what the hell."

"I didn't have a chance to get stoned," Wallace said. "It might have been a lot better for that guy if I did."

"That's why you drove up here rather than just calling, isn't it?" Kim said. "Because you think you might be in trouble and you'd rather not be there for it."

There wasn't anything good he could say.

"God, do you know how boring this kind of thing is now?" she said. "Do you know how stupid?"

Wallace said he did. He was surprised at how much he meant it.

Molly came running around the corner, holding the Tupperware over her head and keeping it very still as she ran. When she got to where they were standing, she extended it up to show them. It was filled with tiny pebbles, and in the center was a snail with a partially crushed shell that oozed air bubbles. Molly's grin beamed out at them. When she saw Wallace looking at her she stopped grinning, then motioned for her mother to lean down so she could whisper to her. Kim did it. Molly watched him as she spoke into her mother's ear.

"Yeah, no," Kim answered her. "That's not going to happen."

Molly made a face like she might cry, then turned and raced off with the Tupperware over her head again. Something felt like it was draining out of him as he watched her.

"She wants the snail to sleep in her bed with her," Kim said once she'd gone. "She doesn't want me to tell you about it."

"And yet here we are," Wallace said.

It was quiet then and Wallace could hear the sound of the ocean drifting across the street at them. The water even *sounded* cleaner up here. He couldn't understand it. Kim asked him what he was going to do now. Wallace said he'd probably take the rest of the week off, then get back in the gym on Monday and start thinking about the next one.

"That wasn't at all what I meant," Kim said. "But I guess you answered my question anyway."

That's how you know these visits are over, Wallace told himself. When you've both reminded each other why you don't do this more often.

He was two blocks from home when he spotted the cop car out front.

Fuck, fuck, fuck, fuck, he thought.

There was just one of them, pulled up to the curb with nobody in it, near as he could tell. He drove right on past and tried to look like he wasn't looking. There was no sign of any actual cop. No sign of a commotion in the courtyard. Just the car.

Haven't there been cop cars parked out front every now and then? he asked himself. Wasn't that something that happened sometimes? Maybe it had nothing at all to do with him.

He kept driving. The afternoon was heating up. Ahead of him

the freeway shimmered. He drove past it, on into Chula Vista. He didn't even know he was driving to the gym until he pulled into the parking lot.

Coach Vee was leaning up against the back wall of the gym, watching two lazy heavyweights pretend to spar. Wallace went over and leaned next to him without a word. The heavyweights moved like two men miming a fight in the shallow end of a pool. The act of keeping their hands up seemed to exhaust them both.

"Somebody please hit someone," Coach Vee said to the heavyweights. "Pretty fucking please."

One of the heavyweights pumped a few jabs, then stepped back and took a deep breath.

"You two are literally killing me," Coach Vee said. "It's a goddamn travesty what you're doing to me right now."

The heavyweights both hooked at the same time. Neither of them hit anything.

Coach looked at Wallace and shook his head. "For my sins," he said.

The round timer dinged. Coach Vee threw his head back and thanked Christ in heaven. Wallace followed him over the wrestling mats and into his cramped little office without being asked. The heavyweights both leaned over at the waist with their gloved hands on their knees.

"So you're alive," Coach Vee said, and plopped down in his cheap leather office chair. He had his laptop open on his desk. The word *Commitment* bounced around the empty black screen, running into the edges and then spinning back out toward the center. Coach Vee's office always made Wallace feel a little claustrophobic. All four walls were plastered with fight photos and magazine covers. The faces pressed in on you. You got more than two people in there at once and everybody had to flatten against the wall just to let someone out.

"I was this close to sending out the search party," Coach said.

Wallace told him he'd listened to his voicemails but didn't feel like they demanded immediate action.

"Even the one where I said 'Call me back' like three or four times at the end?" Coach Vee said.

Wallace grinned. He could be sixty years old and Coach Vee would still have the ability to make him feel like he was Dennis the Menace, running around with a slingshot in his back pocket.

"I'm just saying," Coach said. "Guy suffers a concussion and then falls off the map, least he could do is call his coach and let him know he's not facedown in the bathtub waiting for the neighbors to notice the stink."

"Well. At least you're not being overly dramatic or anything," Wallace said.

"Sure," Coach Vee said. "No big deal. Just a knockout, right? It happens."

Wallace knew what was coming next.

"Of course," Coach Vee said, and leaned back in his chair, letting his eyes drift up the wall past the framed photos of Coach with past champs, Coach in his own glory days, all the way up to the one of Wallace getting the sweat knocked off his head by a straight right from Vladimir Zinoviev.

"It didn't used to," Coach said.

The photo was close to a decade old by now, torn out of a magazine and shoved into a Wal-Mart frame. Zinoviev was a hard-ass ex-Soviet special-forces guy who broke Wallace's orbital in the first minute of the first round out in Atlantic City. Within seconds the swelling nixed his vision in that eye. His depth perception was shit after that. By the start of the second round he felt like he had a water balloon growing out of his face. Coach Vee had told him to make it a ground fight, take it where he could feel rather than see, and he did. He choked Zinoviev out with a rear naked in the third, then spent the next week in New Jersey because they wouldn't let him get on an airplane with his eye like that.

All he had to do now was think about that punch and a glowing warmth would spread out across his face, beginning right on that very spot. It was like his body had its own memory of these things that he couldn't quite access. After that fight Coach Vee told a reporter that it wouldn't have mattered if Zinoviev had hit Wallace with a shovel, he was too stubborn to get knocked out. Wallace understood right away that it was the highest compliment Coach Vee was capable of giving. It was still the only picture on Coach's little Wall of Fame where his fighter wasn't demolishing the other guy or grinning after a victory. The only photo where Coach's guy seems to be the one getting his ass handed to him.

"I should have called you back," Wallace said. "You're right about that."

"I know I am," Coach Vee said. "But you were too busy feeling sorry for yourself. Like you're the first fighter who ever got knocked out in a fight he never should have taken."

Wallace laughed to himself. How many times had he heard Coach telling guys to step up and fight? How many times had he heard that spiel about how you didn't make any money sitting on your couch? But that was before a fight. It wasn't until after that things became so very crystal clear to everyone else.

"Be straight with me, how many more of these are we going to do?" Coach asked him.

Wallace shook his head.

"Bet you've wondered the same thing though, right?" Coach said. "I know you have. Tell me something: when you walked into the gym today, how'd it smell?"

"Like dreams and sunshine," Wallace said. "As always."

"It smelled awful, didn't it?" Coach Vee said. "It made you sick, right? Like you wanted to run out of here and get a shower?"

Wallace didn't say anything. The truth is, that's exactly how it felt, like the stench of old, mildewed leather was sticking to his skin. That smell of stale sweat, other people's feet. That same fight gym smell, but worse. Coach leaned forward and stretched his long arms out on the desk between them. He smiled that sad, conspiratorial smile of his.

"When the smell of the gym makes you sick," Coach said very slowly, emphasizing each syllable, "it's time to quit. I think Marciano said that. I don't know, maybe not Marciano. But whoever said it was right. When you start to hate that smell, it's time. And when it's time, brother." Coach held up his hands and let them drop. Wallace opened his mouth to say something, then didn't. Start talking now, he thought, and you might not be able to stop.

All he needed was a little while to collect himself. He needed a day or two with no Coach Vee, no Kim and no Molly, no asshole neighbor. He needed a second to breathe. He needed some time to figure some things out, and he knew he wasn't going to get it.

Coach Vee leaned back in his chair again and looked up at the photo of Wallace and Zinoviev.

"Wonder what ever happened to that guy," Coach Vee said.

In the photo Zinoviev wore a blank expression and a flat-top that was severe and well out of fashion even then. The halo of sweat around Wallace's head glimmered in the arena lights. There was that warm glow on his cheek again.

"I heard he's a small-time gangster in Brooklyn now," Wallace said, his voice thick and all in his throat.

"Seriously?" Coach Vee said.

"That's what I heard," Wallace said. He said the rumor was that Zinoviev had gone back to work as hired muscle for the same guys he used to serve under in the Soviet army. Or maybe he'd never really stopped working for them, even when he was fighting. Anyway, that was his life now, or so people said.

"Isn't that something," Coach Vee said. "Guy changes continents and still ends up with the same friends."

On his way out Wallace passed the two heavyweights sitting on the floor with their backs leaning against the wall, slowly unspooling their hand wraps as the sweat puddled up around them. Wallace nodded at them and one of them asked how his fight in Florida went.

"Shitty," Wallace said.

They'd given him a watch once, the Big Show had. He hadn't thought about it in years, but now, driving around by himself, he remembered it.

It was a nice one too. Cartier, with diamonds in more places than Wallace had thought possible. He'd never asked for it. No one explained what it was for.

This was back when he was first fighting in the Big Show, after he'd won three straight and people were starting to talk about a title shot. Then, out of nowhere, they had this watch delivered to him. Like, *here.* It wasn't his birthday, wasn't Christmas. His last fight had been two months earlier. The box the thing came in seemed nicer than any luggage Wallace had ever owned. He was scared to take it out. He didn't even wear watches.

He asked his manager to find out who he could thank for it, and maybe see if he could sniff out a reason for it. His manager called back later that day to say it was all taken care of. It didn't seem right, but fine. His manager told him he'd have to get used to stuff like this, that when you're a winner people give you things. They want to. You don't owe them anything for it.

Wallace believed this at the time. That's how dumb he'd been.

Probably about a year later he saw where a lightweight who'd just been cut from the Big Show was trying to sell the exact same watch on eBay. He told the story about how the promoters had given it to him for being their top lightweight prospect, how it was one of a kind, custom-made especially for him. The bidding got up there, then it got ridiculous. In the end the bids were all bullshit, just mean, smart kids fucking with him on the Internet. He never got a dime for it.

Wallace still had his, still in the box in the back of his sock drawer. He couldn't say why. He had the vague feeling that he might need it someday. Maybe he just wanted to know it was there, this watch, a piece of secret evidence. It proved that he'd done something, at least. He hadn't made it all up.

The big yellow house had a huge wooden door and a front yard made of volcanic rocks. Wallace stood on the sidewalk looking at it, trying to imagine what kind of world existed inside. He'd just had enough, was what it was. There was no breeze coming off the ocean and the heat had flattened the afternoon out, leaving it limp and heavy. Whatever was going to happen, Wallace wanted to get it over with.

You'll apologize if you have to, he told himself. Then he said it out loud, just so he'd believe it.

Wallace went up and rang the doorbell. Behind it a little dog barked, clipping its nails across a tile floor as it got closer. A woman told it to hush and it did. Wallace realized he hadn't even considered what he was going to say if someone other than the man in the green jacket answered. He really should have thought about that.

An old woman in a floral print robe pulled the door open just enough to see him. She held the little dog back with her foot. She had thin, bleached hair and the rough, thick skin of a person who'd been willfully abused by the sun for decades. Her eyes were hidden somewhere deep inside her face where Wallace couldn't quite see. She stood there as if waiting for a sales pitch of some kind. Wallace realized he didn't know the man's name, didn't know how to ask for him.

"Is there a man who lives here?" he asked.

"What's happened?" the woman snapped.

Wallace didn't know how to answer that.

"What's he done?" the woman said.

Wallace told her that it wasn't exactly like that. He needed to talk to him, he said.

"We had a misunderstanding earlier," Wallace said. "It was my fault. I wanted to apologize."

The old woman looked down at her dog, as if checking to make sure he'd heard the same thing she had.

"Is this a trick?" she said.

Wallace told her no, it wasn't a trick. She looked at him for what felt like a long time, then she looked down at the little dog.

"We're going to trust this man and let him in to talk to us," she said to the dog. "We're going to trust him and hope he is worthy of that."

Please, Wallace thought. Don't you be crazy. I'm not sure I can handle it right now.

The woman led him into the living room. As he followed her across the tile floors he realized how small she was. Her floral robe trailed on the floor behind her. She stopped in the living room and turned to Wallace like she'd forgotten what they'd come in there for. She suggested that they sit out on the back patio and talk. It was nice out there, she explained. There was shade, and when the wind shifted the right way they could smell the ocean.

"It's delightful," she said and closed her eyes. "Just delightful."

That's when Wallace realized she was drunk. He figured it was better than crazy, but only by a little. The woman told him she was having some pineapple juice and asked him if he'd like a glass.

"I don't want to trouble you," Wallace said.

"It's no trouble," she said. "I like vodka in mine. How do you take yours?"

Wallace said that would be fine. He watched her pull a giant bottle out of the freezer and then pour the thick, syrupy vodka into their glasses. Wallace could smell the booze before he even brought it close to his mouth. He followed her to a glass table on the back patio. The shade from the awning enveloped them.

"I'll tell you right now, it's not often that people come here to talk about my husband and think that they should be the ones apologizing," the woman said when they sat down.

Wallace felt himself flinch at the word *husband*. She had to be at least thirty years older than the man he'd gotten into it with. He wondered whether he'd gotten the wrong place, whether he wasn't caught up in the middle of some big misunderstanding.

"I know," the woman said. "You think I don't recognize that look?"

"I didn't mean anything," Wallace said.

"I can spot that look from across the street," the woman said. "But I don't care. I know it's strange to most people. But most people are strange to me. He was a friend of my son's when they were in high school. Did he tell you that?"

Wallace explained that they hadn't had much of a conversation.

"They weren't best friends," the woman said. "Almost acquaintances, really. Though it doesn't really matter anymore, does it?"

Wallace agreed that it didn't. The woman looked at him over the top of her pineapple drink. Wallace told her about the estuary. The woman listened patiently and gulped her drink as he told her about the joint, the run-in with her husband, the foot sweep into the marsh, all of it. When he heard how it sounded he felt the need to tell her more, if only to explain himself a little, to make it all make sense. If people just knew what you were dragging around with you, he thought, they might cut you some slack. But who had time for that? Who could be troubled?

"He really told you he had children over here?" the woman said when Wallace was done. "You're sure about that?"

Wallace nodded into his glass. The woman pinched her bottom lip.

"That's new," she said. "That's troubling."

Wallace sipped his drink and felt the acid from the pineapple and liquor burning together in his throat.

"The thing about my husband," the woman was saying, "is that idleness gets the better of him. He's not a bad man, but he doesn't have much to do. Sometimes that leads to trouble."

"He doesn't work?" Wallace said, and then wished he hadn't.

"Oh no," she said. "Not for years. I have money, you see, and anyway he's not cut out for most jobs. He's very sensitive. He's not a bad man. But he is very, very sensitive. Does that make sense to you?"

Wallace said it did, and the woman smiled in an appreciative sort of way.

"And you," she said. "Do you work?"

Wallace said that he did, sort of.

"I'm a fighter," he offered.

"As in professionally?" the woman said.

Wallace nodded and tried to put his face as deep into his drink as it would go. It smelled sweet and sticky and boozy, a vague scent of suntan oil.

"That's what happened to your face, then," the woman said, almost to herself. She asked him what it was like, that line of work.

Wallace had to think about it for a second. "It's awful," he said, and then stopped.

That wasn't what he meant. What he meant was that it was the best thing he'd ever done with his life, the only thing he could do well, and what was awful was how it made everything else seem boring and fake. But there wasn't any way to explain that, so he didn't try. Instead he told her not to listen to him, that he was just coming off a bad fight.

"Oh dear," she said. "And what's *that* like?"

He told her it was like breaking up. "You tell yourself, never again. But then, what else is there?"

"I understand completely," the woman said. Wallace decided to believe her. That was a choice he was making.

When her face changed, he followed her gaze back toward the house and saw the man standing on the other side of the screen door, peering out at them. How long had he been there? He had the green jacket slung over one arm. Wallace could see where the dried mud was caked on, just beginning to flake off at the edges. He could see how he must look to the man, drinking pineapple and vodkas with his wife in the afternoon, telling each other about their lives.

The man opened the screen door slowly, two fingers pushing it down the track. The wind shifted. Wallace smelled the ocean. The woman was right. It was delightful.

ARNA BONTEMPS HEMENWAY

The Fugue

FROM *Alaska Quarterly Review*

WILD TURKEY WAKES up. It's the last day of June, and an early summer thunderhead has marched across the peripheral Kansas plain (the lights of town giving out to the solid pitch of farmland) while Wild Turkey slept. He knew it was coming, the lightning spidering forth behind and then above him last night as he walked, the air promising the rain that is now, as Wild Turkey blinks in the thin blue morning, making the rural highway overpass above his head drone, a toneless room of sound below.

Wild Turkey lifts himself out from the body-shaped concrete depression that nestles just under the eaves of the little overpass—that word too big for the little nexus; really it's just one lonely county road overlapping another. He knew to sleep here last night because of the rain and because he saw the overpass was old enough to have this body-shaped concavity, a "tornado bed" they used to call it, and now he reaches up into the dark of the girder's angle and feels around until he finds the ancient survival box for those erstwhile endangered motorists: a flashlight that doesn't work, a rusted weather radio, and—yes—a bottle of water, thick with dust, but Wild Turkey is thirsty and doesn't care. He stands and stretches on the sloped concrete bank, against the theater of the rain. He was right about the long night-walk out along the country road being good for coming down, the darkness being good for discouraging one of his fits, but wrong about being able to make it to the school before morning.

He makes it to the school now, in the rain, sopping wet. The school is, as it ever was, more or less in the middle of a cornfield, and the thick leaves and stalks cough in the rain as Wild Turkey comes once again upon the old buildings. He rounds the tiny campus in the storm as if he is still in junior high, still traipsing from class to class in the cloying polo and khaki uniform. Now, as then, he does not fail to think of the strangeness of time when he sees the buildings—themselves somehow eternal feeling, always but only half in ruin. Even in use (back then, as an ad hoc private Episcopalian school, and now, apparently repurposed as a child-care center) the moldering white portables and darkly aging main brick building sit in situ, oblivious.

Standing on the concrete path along the portables and trying to look into the darkened window of an abandoned room, Wild Turkey has one of his little gyres in time—a brief one, only sending his mind back to those moments when he just an hour ago woke under the little bridge—and he realizes he woke thinking of Mrs. Budnitz, his second-grade teacher, specifically of the rank, slightly fetid scent that would occasionally waft subtly from somewhere inside her gingham dress on a tendril of air in the last weeks of school before summer. Though the scent or smell itself wasn't subtle at all but sharp, rich, pungent, even vaguely sweet, like the smell of human shit anywhere outside a bathroom. Nor was it really a smell so much as an *emanation,* or at least that's how it'd seemed to Wild Turkey, sitting on the carpet in the middle of the room, transfixed by this sensate experience delivered to him on the wavering bough of the window fan's breeze.

They did not have air conditioning installed in their classroom yet and the heat and consequent sweat, secreted beneath Mrs. Budnitz's plain, sturdy dresses and folds of fat and thigh, probably amplified the smell. It was only noticeable every ninth or tenth breath and so not really something Wild Turkey ever felt he could really speak or complain about. But it was distinctly sexual, or carnal in its fleshy, mildly lurid bodilyness—in its intimate note of vaginal musk, though of course this particular understanding would come only later, the experience at the time being importantly a momentary one. The scent refused to linger, and so existed for Wild Turkey mostly in the wince of shame at his own interest, in the same way he sometimes at that age lingered for just a few seconds too long in the school's bathroom over the shit-stained toilet paper in his hand before flushing it, feeling a rush of something he didn't understand. It was oddly comforting, in the end.

And why this smell now, or rather, then, upon waking—why does it chase him? Maybe this school harkens his mind back to that other classroom, Wild Turkey thinks. Though really it's the feeling of it as he drifted on the carpet in Mrs. Budnitz's classroom during "naptime," the confluence of those two sensations—drifting helplessly into a tired, sweaty sleep; drifting helplessly into that intriguing, somewhat disgusting scent. It was a kind of surrender, a voiding of the mind; a reversion to some pre-infantile state of abandon. He's been finding the declensions of that experience in his life ever since, often as he falls asleep, or which he wakes into: the stagnant air of soiled women's bed linen and spilt chamber pot in the small house in Ramadi; the attenuated scent of the bare bed after he and Merry Darwani had anal sex for the first time; the closeness of the rain-soured, coppery metal of the small bridge's girding. Wild Turkey is used to his life proceeding this way: this or that detail of his day stepping down out of some first world of previous, essential experience. These sensate allusions are always only whiffs or pale imitations of the original, in the same way that the rainy, pallid light now breaking from the clouds as the morning regains its heat is cousin to the small fist of bright fire over the limbs of the girl in the courtyard in Ramadi, or the rhythmic flash of the tactical grenade's phosphorous strobe, and all three are mere shavings of the pure white lightning of one of Wild Turkey's fits.

He turns away from the window. There is nothing to see here. It was stupid to come. He begins the long walk back.

Wild Turkey wakes up. He's eight years old, on his back in the middle of the wheat field that has sprung up by chance in the sprawling park behind his parents' subdivision. He does not know why he's on his back, does not remember how he got there. Strangely, however, he does remember what happened just before he woke up, which is that he had his first fit (though he doesn't know to call it that yet, knows only the image lingering spectacularly in his retinas, in the theater of his mind). He'd been running through the field, feeling the itchy stalks resist his stomping feet, and then he'd been standing in the field, caught up by something in the air, by a small flash in the sky, and then he was looking and looking and seeing only the beauty of the high afternoon sun on the blurry tips of the wheat as it rose and fell on the invisible currents of wind. Like on a sea floor, he thought, just before the brightening in the sky, before it turned in a flash into an overwhelming field of white lightning, so much and so close that he remembers nothing else.

Later, he will not tell the marine recruiters or doctors about the fits but will have one anyway on the first night of initiation, before he even gets to boot camp proper. He will be among the guys at the long tables in the gym of the local armory building: the recruits being kept awake all night, forced to keep their hands flat out in front of them, hovering four inches above the tabletop. They are not allowed to move, or to move their hands, or to let their hands touch the tabletop. Then, the lightning.

"Why did you let me stay?" he will ask later, toward the end of actual boot camp, and the instructors will explain (allowing their voices to dilate a little with respect) how he'd looked, sitting there seizing, his hands the only part of him held perfectly still, four inches above the table. Though Wild Turkey will suspect the truthfulness of this, seeing as how he woke up in the wetness of the ditch outside the armory building, his white T-shirt stained with blood from the tips of the chain-link fence he hopped (he guesses) to escape, the faces of the instructors pale moons in their huddle above him. Eventually he will get medicine for his fits, but the medicine will make him spacy, drowsy—the medicine itself in effect simulating the aftereffects of the fits—and so Wild Turkey will be unable to parse his waking. It will never be clear to him whether he is waking from a lacunal fit, the medicine, or a memory, as if all three are essentially the same thing.

Wild Turkey wakes up, but Jeannie has already left the bed. Wild Turkey can see her, if he hangs off the side of the mattress, down the narrow hallway: the bathroom door ajar, the bathroom light golden and warm in the cool, cesious fall morning. They're at his place, the duplex right on top of the train tracks, across the street from the college. Jeannie is doing her hair, naked, still overheated from the shower. She stands in front of the mirror quietly, getting ready for class or work, he can't remember which she has today. He's been home from his deployment for two weeks now and he still can't get ahold of time. In the afternoons he gets in the shower, wastes no minutes, gets out to find it's two hours later.

Last night Wild Turkey took Jeannie out to the old school buildings, overgrown as they are, stilled in the interregnum between their days as the school he and Jeannie went to together and its current incarnation as some daycare's repurposed space. This was something they did in high school too, back when Jeannie still had her green Mustang convertible; late October nights they'd drive out there with sleeping bags and put the top down and park in the middle of the erstwhile baseball field, already half reclaimed by brush, and look at the stars. The buildings were abandoned even back then, or between abandonments; Wild Turkey and Jeannie having decamped for the public high school, the original private school having finally amassed enough non-scholarship families to fund a new building (itself a repurposed old country club) inside city limits.

Later still last night, when they'd gotten too cold and come back to his duplex, Wild Turkey had lain naked with Jeannie on his mattress, which was on the floor, and curled his body around her in-turning fetal position and called out, "Jeannie in a bottle!" which was one of their old jokes, and she'd laughed, sounding half-annoyed at her own easy nostalgic amusement, but then Wild Turkey had repeated it and repeated it, "Jeannie in a bottle! Jeannie in a bottle! Jeannie in a bottle! Jeannie in a bottle! Jeannie in a bottle! Jeannie in a bottle! Jeannie in a bottle! Jeannie in a bottle! Jeannie in a bottle! Jeannie in a bottle! Jeannie in a bottle! Jeannie in a bottle! Jeannie in a bottle! Jeannie in a bottle! Jeannie in a bottle! Jeannie in a bottle! Jeannie in a bottle! Jeannie in a bottle! Jeannie in a bottle!" over and over, with just enough slight vocal modulation and wavering emphasis as to keep it from seeming like a glitch, repeating and repeating, which he did helplessly, "Jeannie in a bottle! Jeannie in a bottle! Jeannie in a bottle! Jeannie in a bottle! Jeannie in a bottle! Jeannie in a bottle! Jeannie in a bottle! Jeannie in a bottle! Jeannie in a bottle! Jeannie in a bottle! Jeannie in a bottle! Jeannie in a bottle! Jeannie in a bottle! Jeannie in a bottle! Jeannie in a bottle! Jeannie in a bottle! Jeannie in a bottle! Jeannie in a bottle! Jeannie in a bottle!" on and on until the sound became extenuated, then lost all tone, then resolved briefly into song before crumbling into over-articulation, each alien phoneme distinct and meaningless. Eventually he'd stopped. Jeannie lay there very quiet, very still, stiffened as she had been from somewhere around the twentieth or twenty-fifth repetition. Then, in the silence after Wild Turkey's voice had ceased, when it was clear he had really stopped, when he finally released her, she very carefully unfolded herself up from the bed and walked silently to the bathroom. Though Wild Turkey knows at some point she must've returned to bed (did she? or did she sleep on the couch?), her presence now in the bathroom seems contiguous to her presence there last night, which makes it hard for Wild Turkey to tell how much time has passed, if any has passed at all.

She finishes doing her hair and makeup and gets dressed in silence. She does not avoid looking at Wild Turkey; she holds his eyes as she pulls on her jeans one leg at a time before turning and letting herself out, her expression level, empty of anger, empty of assessment. When she gets back, if she comes back to the duplex instead of her own apartment, Wild Turkey will be there or he won't, she's already used to that.

Wild Turkey wakes up, the voices of the other men in the unit insistent. They're all in the dining area of the forward operating base, talking to the doctors from the casualty attachment, which is something the other guys on the team get a kick out of, Wild Turkey's never known why. It's Pizza Hut night, which is why the team is all out here in the base's main area, the only real chance for the team and the doctors both to see each other, before the former, their day just beginning now that it's nightfall, slouch back into the restricted-access staging area and ready themselves for their next operation.

Someone is telling the story of how Wild Turkey got his name. Wild Turkey can't see who it is speaking, but it doesn't really matter as the story is now collective, accessed by anyone on the team, each small contortion of detail sponsored by the men's own willingness.

It was back in Carolina, before the team was strictly assembled, when they were all still loosely gathered at the base, waiting to be repurposed. It was the day before Thanksgiving and the commander in charge of the base had a vaguely sadistic obsession with getting the men prepared for the Suck, high concern over the lack of regulatory discipline et cetera, and so had ordered for the men no Thanksgiving meal, and had replaced that order with several shipments of turkey and mashed potato and cranberry sauce MREs, which were dried out, reconstituted, et cetera et cetera, and so Wild Turkey (though he wasn't called that yet) had gone prowling during one of the exercises in the golden leaves of the fall woods, and gotten God's Grace to go with him.

God's Grace was Bob Grace, a gentle-faced, soft-spoken man from Tennessee, eventually included on the team mostly for his perfect marksmanship. He was religious, though very passive about it, and ended up being God's Grace because he often said "God's grace," in a kind of summarizing way, when he saw something that made him feel like speaking. Later, Wild Turkey would see God's Grace get shot through the neck while their vehicle was stalled in traffic at an intersection in Tikrit. This day, though, God's Grace stood calmly at the tree line as Wild Turkey crawled forward slowly over the rural highway, which they weren't supposed to cross.

"So Wild Turkey's out there, doing this dumbass crab-crawl across the highway because just on the other side what has he seen but three fat old birds, turkeys, wild turkeys, rooting around there in the ditch on the other side of the road and this is a no discharge drill and Wild Turkey's got long underwear on beneath his gear and hasn't brought his knife, so he's going to God knows what—wring their necks, or whatever, but only if he can get close enough to grab one of them. Anyway, good old Wild Turkey hears a sound and must be real hungry or maybe just a pussy because he spooks and takes off sprinting at the birds, who of course just completely lose their fucking shit. We're watching this all on the helmet cam back at the comms camp, laughing our fucking asses off."

"So what happens?" one of doctors, a bald little man with glasses, asks.

"They fucking scatter, is what happens, because Wild Turkey's a fucking idiot. You can't chase down a turkey. And so we're all on the line in his earpiece, giving him all this shit about it and what happens just at that exact moment but a semi comes tearing around the corner of this bumfuck nowhere little road and almost kills Wild Turkey, who dives out of the way, only to find, when he gets up, that the fucking semi has taken three of the birds' heads clean off."

There'd been blood all over the highway. Wild Turkey had lain there in the ditch, shaking. In the concussive silence after the semi's blasting passage, Wild Turkey heard God's Grace shift in the leaves behind him. He'd retrieved the headless birds, was holding them out to Wild Turkey with one hand.

"God's grace," God's Grace had said.

Mostly they call Wild Turkey "Wild Turkey," the full name. Sometimes one or two of the black guys call him Jive Ass Turkey, with an unknown level of aggressive irony. Once, after the courtyard in Ramadi, Wild Turkey heard one of the newer guys ask someone in the bunks about him, heard whoever it was readjust his head on the stiff cot before answering, "That's Wild, man, that's just Wild," in that ambiguous way that seemed to mean both the adjective and the proper noun. Ever since Bob Grace got killed, when they mention Bob at all they just smile and call him Gracie, like he was one of their lovers from back in the world who accidentally found himself there with them in the desert.

Wild Turkey has always been mesmerized by their language, the team's utilitarian military patois always morphing what they said just enough to approximate some slightly more surreal world, a language somehow better suited to the world they are actually confronted with. Oftentimes the unthinking word or slight lingual shift ends up being eerily or confusingly apt, in the way that Wild Turkey's friend the TOW missile gunner whom they call Tow Head really does resemble a "towheaded boy" (the phrase surfacing in Wild Turkey's mind from some old novel read in a high school English class), or in the way that Wild Turkey will end up buying fifths of Wild Turkey to take the edge off his highs back at home. The Shit, meaning the desert, the war, Iraq, becomes The Suck becomes The Fuck becomes The Fug becomes The Fugue, finally meaning just everything.

Wild Turkey wakes up. He's sitting in the rear corner of his brother's large backyard patio, the snow having fallen so gently and quietly while he slept that he is now covered with its soft, undisturbed angles. Wild Turkey wakes to the sound of his brother carefully closing the patio door behind him so as not to wake Wild Turkey's sister-in-law; wakes to the click of the motion-sensor light, which his brother has forgotten to turn off, tripping on. His brother approaches the wrought-iron patio table that Wild Turkey sits at, and sets down the familiar foil-wrapped plate. It is very late, and very cold, but the snow has quieted everything.

Wild Turkey's brother is an associate minister or junior minister, Wild Turkey can't remember the exact title, at one of the local churches. Few people in the town know they're brothers. They grew up together only until the age of thirteen, when their mother died and they went to the group home and Wild Turkey couldn't bear to go along to the better group home, the one that required adoption by the church or some family in the church. There'd been something so disgusting to Wild Turkey about the idea that they (the potentially adopted boys) should see their adoption and transport as "God's grace," which is what the man who came to talk to the two brothers said they should think of it as. He just couldn't bring himself to do it and so his brother got out of the state home and he didn't. They got along, though, after that, understood each other in some basic way; the brutality of that state group home (at least for those two months when they'd been fresh meat) a kind of dark night of the soul for both of them, forcing each to make this own manner of unfeeling calculation as to down which road salvation, et cetera, he guesses.

Now Wild Turkey's brother sits down heavily in the snowy chair across from Wild Turkey. He sighs, rests the side of his face in his hand. He's tired, equanimously perplexed by Wild Turkey, by his continued presence here these occasional nights.

The first time Wild Turkey came to his brother's house it was for the same reason as this time: he needed to eat. This is one thing Wild Turkey knows his brother's wife hates about him: she sees him as needlessly homeless, and as what she calls in her unselfconsciously cute little way a "drughead." Both of these assessments are more or less fair, insofar as Wild Turkey does technically have a home back at the duplex (he was officially evicted when he stopped paying rent, but then the building was foreclosed upon and Wild Turkey has just kept living there, the color of the notices on his front door changing every few weeks but nobody really bothering him about it) and yet he sleeps under bridges sometimes, or on the street, or in the fields, or spends all night walking around, high or low on the pills he ingests. Paradoxically, Wild Turkey's sister-in-law doesn't count the duplex as a home, mostly, Wild Turkey guesses, due to the fact that three of the walls now have huge gaping holes, covered only by minimally effective plastic tarp, from which the landlord removed the windows to sell before the bank could take them. Though, in his own defense, it's also true that Wild Turkey doesn't have any money: he gave almost all of it to Jeannie, minus some he gave to Merry Darwani for her broken jaw and some he gave to Tow Head for his new gun.

Wild Turkey doesn't want the money. He brought back from Iraq enough pills to stay in Dexedrine for as long as he wants, and so doesn't really need any money. Sometimes he eats with Jeannie. Sometimes he eats at the shelter. Sometimes he doesn't eat.

Wild Turkey's brother watches him unwrap the plate of leftovers and begin to eat. Neither says anything.

The first time he came to his brother's to eat, Wild Turkey stood in the dining room afterward and listened to his brother help his wife with the dishes in the kitchen. The house was quiet and oddly peaceful in the nighttime lull. Wild Turkey knew his brother and sister-in-law wanted children but had none. His brother's wife had been silent all through dinner. Wild Turkey's brother had talked about his ministry.

Standing there that first time, Wild Turkey heard his brother in the kitchen apologize, his wife sigh.

"It's like with a dog," she said. "If you feed him, he'll just keep coming back."

The look on his brother's face, when Wild Turkey had then risen and peered into the dim kitchen through the half-open door, was exquisitely pained: torn, it seemed to Wild Turkey, between his love for this woman and his real feeling of charity, of grace. His face, upon his return to the dining room (had Wild Turkey stayed around to see it, he's sure), full of resignation at this discrepancy between the practical and theoretical theologies of love, or charity, or whatever.

Now his brother is very still, watching him eat. He does this each time. Wild Turkey doesn't know if the irony of the arrangement—of him now being actually fed like a stray dog: secretly, guiltily, on the back porch, with the implied hope that he *will* keep coming back—is lost on his brother's wife, who tacitly allows it. He doesn't blame her. Wild Turkey knows she was friends with a man in a Bible study group in her old hometown who'd gone on an outreach mission early on in the supposedly safer Kurdish north and been kidnapped and was now missing, presumably beheaded. He knows she has, at some level of consciousness, transferred her anger and grief onto Wild Turkey himself, whom she is convinced committed his own atrocities, in Iraq.

"I am the least of you," Wild Turkey's brother says now, in a kind of bored wonderment, and Wild Turkey isn't sure if he's quoting scripture or paraphrasing scripture or if he has hit, in his unintentional summary of several of Jesus' sentiments, an ambiguous middle-ground in which he can just say something and mean it, or want very much to mean it. Neither speaks. The motion-sensor light trips back off, and they are thrown again into darkness.

Wild Turkey wakes up in the desert. He's in a slight body-shaped depression at the base of a mud wall, over the edge of which sits the fake village. This is a training exercise, the last preparation for the grab team before they go over to the Shit. They are in Arizona. Wild Turkey lies still, listening to the grumbling of the other guys on the team, and watches the mud ruins (fake? real?) seep with the grays and blue of the thin winter sunset.

Sometime before zero dark, Wild Turkey stands paused in his position in the team's tactical column, lined up against the exterior wall of one of the village houses. Inside he can hear the muted noise of a radio. In a minute, at the first man's signal (two consecutive toneless blips of static on the radio earpiece) the men will go into their suite of motion, so practiced and efficient and many-parted as to seem almost balletic. Wild Turkey, who is the DIA officer attached to the team (which really just means he is responsible for the confirmed identification of team extraction targets), breathes in the quiet, in the dark. He closes his eyes and thinks through what is about to happen, the steps so familiar, mechanical, though less in the way of machines than of soul-hollowing boredom. This is why these men were chosen for the grab team, Wild Turkey has often reflected in these moments: because they will do this with perfect disinterest, not keyed up, not even eager in the way of the adrenalized army kids.

But what Wild Turkey thinks of now in the eternal moments before the twin blips throw the night into action is where he is standing, is the fake village, meant to be a simulation but really more of a simulacrum, a psychological agent at play in the men's imaginations. It's all an effort, really, at making their imagination of what they will soon face in Iraq "more real," if such a thing makes sense, Wild Turkey thinks. As if anything could be more or less real than anything else, as if all reality isn't contained in every instance of it, this desert being very apropos of all this in that it really is indistinguishable from the Iraqi desert (though Wild Turkey will only confirm this later) and so contains that other reality, or is contiguous to that other reality. The real desert and the village and the specific house that this one is meant to represent is actually just a double, a repetition. He's had a lot of time to think about it.

Wild Turkey has often been overcome by this sense during their operations in the fake village—this feeling that the real Iraqi village/desert/target house is actually very close by, maybe over the next ridge, and that it is or will be the exact twin of this village. The feeling has spread until Wild Turkey hears two sounds in every one fake mortar explosion or real explosion of blank assault rifle rounds: the exercise's sound and, somewhere behind it, the real one. In a way, this should serve the military's purpose in making the fake village seem more "real" but has instead only emphasized the surrealism of the entire exercise. He wonders when they are actually there, if it will seem finally real. This is what he thinks about, in all the time they have to hurry up and wait, and think.

This is all made worse by the tasks they've been assigned so far in their time in the fake village here in the desert in Arizona. It's a full exercise, meaning as close an acting-out of real operating procedure as they can possibly undertake without actually being in the Shit. The unit was dropped off kilometers from the village. They approached by night. For a week they've been calmly doing reconnaissance on the fake village, on its real inhabitants. Wild Turkey has watched through special optics fat middle-aged men take their tea, slurping it from saucers, has logged the arrival and departure from the water source (a nearby well) of women in flowing fabrics that are given form by the wind. He's listened on his headset to conversations within the crumbling walls of the low houses, his half-learned Arabic lagging behind, keying into family names, locations, et cetera. It's all very authentic.

It's these people that get to him, as Wild Turkey now shifts uncomfortably against the wall, waiting for the signal. The crushing irony of their physical existence here: they are real Iraqi villagers paid to play Iraqi villagers in America; immigrants from Iraq given asylum and money to come to this other desert and this other village and play themselves. They are given whole complicated psychological profiles to enact, Wild Turkey knows; they each have a role and a set of actions or conversations to complete at predetermined points. They each will behave differently when threatened. They are paid for the performance of reality, for the performance of their identities rather than for their identities themselves. It is all very thorough.

Two nights ago, Wild Turkey watched two of the younger subjects, masked by red kaffiyehs, drag one of the "local politicians" out into the square and videotape themselves staging an execution. The grab team received this video on their digital comms link the next morning, though it wasn't the same video as the one taken below, in the fake village, Wild Turkey could tell. He doesn't know if he was supposed to notice this or not, and has decided now it was a real video of a real execution, something scrounged from a dark corner of the Internet.

The whole thing has worked by approximation, which Wild Turkey will especially think later, after Ramadi. Later, actual reality (Wild Turkey crouched in the tactical column outside the actual house in actual Ramadi) will seem also like an approximation of experience somehow, the distance between what happens (as Wild Turkey hears the two blips and rises into action, then later, as the tactical phosphorous strobe breaks the night and the vision of the house's interior into its discrete pulses of scene) and the "real" experience (even then, something slightly Else or Other, as if there is yet another house, the real target, just over the next rise in Ramadi) making his own feelings seem like an exercise too.

Now, however, on this night, with this crowning exercise, something real will occur, Wild Turkey thinks. Someone really will get identified, then grabbed, then extracted. Wild Turkey has spent the entire week identifying the target, going over the tactical plan. He wonders if when the team does penetrate the building, when they've cleared the rooms and assembled the members of the family (a wife, a young teenage daughter, a middle-aged man, and the "cousin" they are housing, who is really the courier for a local "militant faction"), if they'll show real fear, if, taken by surprise by the timing if not the nature of the event, they will revert to their natural human reaction, to terror. Though it occurs to Wild Turkey now (as the tactical column remains paused) that the family members must've had their dreams exploded into violent light and sound many times before as unit after unit was trained here, and Wild Turkey wonders if it must be frustrating to them (especially the teenage girl) that they still feel scared when it happens, that it's still actually terrifying, when they should sort of know it's coming. And it will occur to Wild Turkey later, when he remembers this night's exercise, that this thought was probably the seed of that later momentary feeling, when he will be standing in the rear bedroom in Ramadi, looking down at the partially collapsed head of the teenage girl: that flush of stupid anger at her for not somehow knowing what would happen.

In his ear, Wild Turkey hears the two blasts of static.

Wild Turkey wakes up. Tow Head is driving, drumming his fingers on the wheel, staring straight ahead and humming something that is not the song playing tinnily on the radio as the ancient pickup jounces around on the country road. It is January and so cold the air is almost completely thinned out, knife-edged in Wild Turkey's nostrils and mouth. Tow Head picked him up from the crumbling duplex very early this morning, before first light, and Wild Turkey is coming down, the brutal sobriety of the air helping out.

Tow Head is excited to go shooting at the unofficial range they are now bouncing and fishtailing toward. He's excited about his new gun, the reissued, remade World War II rifle that, in its combination of antique design and modern mechanics, is a sort of simulation of itself, giving Tow Head both of the experiences he seems to want: the struggle of a marksman in Normandy in 1944 and the smooth riflery of all the advances made since.

Tow Head is Wild Turkey's friend, and he isn't doing too well, Wild Turkey thinks, though he's never really been doing too well. He has a big, robust head and brow, but very small shoulders and a wilting torso that makes his whole appearance vaguely downcast and disconcerting to Wild Turkey, like his body has failed the promise of his martial features. This gives Tow Head a puzzled, frustrated mien. He's a good guy, really, always says just what he means, which is why Wild Turkey has agreed to go shooting in the freezing cold even though it's the last thing he really wants to do.

Beside him, Tow Head bops and twitches in his seat. He's like this here in the States, Wild Turkey knows, always a little nervous, never quite holding still or maintaining visual focus on any one thing. He talks very fast (he's talking now, Wild Turkey realizes) and pauses only occasionally to acknowledge the conversant, though not in a way that requires any response. He always has a lot of conversational energy, and jumps from one subject to another according to his inscrutably associative thought. In Iraq he wasn't like this, at least not while Wild Turkey knew him there. When they first met, and Tow Head realized they were both from Kansas, from even adjacent tiny towns, he looked as happy as a small boy.

It's this look that Wild Turkey has kept in mind, when he was giving away all his military pay and set aside the amount for this rifle, which Tow Head, in their previous conversations, always circled back to the subject of.

Wild Turkey hadn't heard from Tow Head for some time when he saw the flyer at the library for the Wounded Hero Arts Share event. This was two weeks ago. The reading was held in one of the public library's anonymous meeting rooms, plastic chairs set up in solemn rows facing a podium. Tow Head was the featured reader. Wild Turkey went by himself and sat far to one side, where there was a chance Tow Head might not see him, beside a covered piano.

Wild Turkey didn't know that Tow Head liked to write, and spent the time while several middle-aged women went through the introductions wondering if this was actually supposed to be some kind of effort at therapy, or if this was a preexisting interest of Tow Head's, or, if it wasn't, if Tow Head could possibly parse his own answer to that question now. Finally Tow Head got up and took the podium and began to read in a deep, affectless voice.

It was a story, sort of, though really it was just a long description of a man making a wooden guitar amplifier from scratch in his garage, which eventually disintegrated into a sort of list of instructions, but in the third person. As Tow Head's voice settled further into its low timbre and the instructions became repetitive, the sum effect became markedly sinister, almost sexual in its fixated self-surety, until the description of the main character's coating and re-coating and recoating again of lacquer on the amplifier's wooden exterior seemed distinctly violent. Before he began, Tow Head had mentioned that the story was about a veteran home from Iraq. Or maybe Wild Turkey only thought he'd said this when really he hadn't.

This was more or less a true story, Wild Turkey knew; Tow Head had told him about fabricating from scratch a wooden electric guitar amplifier in his garage in Kansas, or attempting to fabricate one—now in the library, as in the original recitation, Tow Head reached the point where he fucks up the interior wiring—though Tow Head had begun the reading (this Wild Turkey does remember) by stating the story was fiction. In his uncomfortable plastic chair Wild Turkey wondered at this strange disavowal of the experience, wondered if it really was fiction or if he'd just said it was, or if, ultimately, Tow Head even knew anymore. This experience of the wooden amplifier had presumably happened at least three times, Wild Turkey realized: once in actuality, once in Tow Head's recitation of the story to Wild Turkey in Baghdad, and once in the re-creation of this, his fiction writing—like a matryoshka doll of experience, understandably involuted, confused.

In fact, sitting in that little meeting room in the public library, Wild Turkey was having a very similar experience of confusion due to the particular arrangement of chairs. These same chairs, in this very same formation, were used in the fake/real base near the fake village in Arizona, in the fake (real?) chapel area for the fake/simulated funeral service that they were all required to attend during the exercise. Presumably this was held in order to prepare the men for attending the same thing in reality, in the Shit. They'd been very thorough, Wild Turkey remembered, with a chaplain and soldiers speaking and eulogies that managed to work in vague references to the details of the casualty.

But Wild Turkey had later found, after Googling the name on the fake funeral program, that the service was in fact held for a real soldier, for a real person who'd been killed in Iraq (IED), which made the fake funeral not so much a simulation of a memorial service (as the officers insisted) but a reenactment of it, a doubling, technically a recurrence. It was unclear if the ranking organizers (let alone the chaplain and the volunteer eulogizers) of the fake/real base near the fake village even knew that it was a real person they were memorializing: the fact that the biographical information on the fake funeral program didn't match what Wild Turkey could find about the real soldier killed in action suggested that they didn't know. This also brought up the possibility of sheer coincidence, of the chance that the master designers of the fake Iraq experience had chosen by accident the name of a victim of the real Iraq experience in order to simulate the loss of a real person. The whole thing was very similar, Wild Turkey felt, to the real video of the execution they'd received on their comms link that was supposedly of the fake execution he'd watched through the night optics the night before.

In the library Tow Head finished up, getting to the point that functioned as the end of the story, where the main character finally completes the wooden electric guitar amplifier only to realize that he does not, in fact, own an electric guitar, or even know how to play. In the applause afterward, Tow Head had caught sight of Wild Turkey and waved, compelling Wild Turkey to stay for the reception afterward, where Tow Head hatched the shooting-range plan.

Now they're parked at the edge of the wide field that serves as the range, and Wild Turkey is leaning against the side of the truck, watching Tow Head carefully reload the rifle, bobbing his head to the pulsing techno music coming from the huge boom box he's set up by his feet on the little shooting platform. This is really a skeet range, and Tow Head has insisted that Wild Turkey sling the clay pigeons out into the white plane of the snowed-over field and washed-out winter sky. They have only one of the cheap plastic hand-throwers, so for an hour now Wild Turkey has made the strange side-armed motion, skipping the bright orange clay disks out onto the currents of air. Tow Head is an excellent shot. He's hit each one, the disks wobbling or splitting cleanly in half, their flight turned to mere gravity. He seems to be enjoying himself.

The landscape does in fact resemble Normandy in winter, which is fitting for the rifle, though since Wild Turkey has never actually seen Normandy in winter he supposes it really just resembles what he thinks it would look like. He wants it to look like Normandy in the snow for Tow Head, though, even if it did, Tow Head wouldn't know it.

Tow Head is ready again and Wild Turkey flicks away his cigarette and steps forward. "Ready," Tow Head says, then, "Pull!" and Wild Turkey whips his arm, sending the clay disk high into the air. Tow Head fires, missing, but at the sound of the rifle's report a raft of geese rise into the air from some hidden tufts in the field, their winged shapes very dark against the air. Wild Turkey realizes Tow Head is screaming before he realizes that Tow Head is firing, though the two actions are concurrent. But Tow Head is screaming and Tow Head is firing, and firing, and firing, until Wild Turkey hears the small metallic clink of the ammunition cartridge going empty and there are no more birds in the air. Then Tow Head is running out into the field, slipping, falling down, getting up, still running, still yelling, though now laughing too, the techno music throbbing very loudly and finally Tow Head reaches the area of bloodied snow where he has expertly dropped what must be at least ten birds and Wild Turkey can see him lifting the rifle, holding it at either end above his head like he's wading a river, and

Tow Head is dancing and laughing wildly, the sound rising and rising in joy, and Wild Turkey, watching, loves him, loves him, loves him.

This is six months before Tow Head, who has this day refrained from his usual running obsession with the possibility that he suffered an undiagnosed TBI at some forgotten point during his deployment, will use the replica rifle to shoot himself through his cheekbone, perhaps purposefully making his theory impossible to ever disprove or confirm.

Wild Turkey jars awake. He's in his position, last in the tactical column, crouched against a low mud wall in a residential compound in Ramadi. The target, Wild Turkey knows (the drone's heat imaging burned into the inside of his eyelids), is sleeping in the small house just ahead. The team pads forward quietly in its line. They pause, waiting for the radio signal.

Inside the house, Wild Turkey mentally recites, there will be two civilians (a middle-aged male and a female, presumably his wife) and the target, whom they've previously claimed is a cousin but who is actually a low-level messenger between militias. All are asleep. The operational information has been confirmed, according to the radio clearance an hour earlier, presumably by more drone imaging.

In his ear, Wild Turkey hears the two blasts of static.

There is the sound of the steel ram battering the door open, the loud flash of the tactical stun grenade, the shadowy flow of the bodies in front of Wild Turkey funneling into the house, the shouted commands for the occupants to lie flat on the ground. From all corners of the house, from its four separate rooms, Wild Turkey hears the voices of the team confirming that the rooms are clear. "One female in northwest bedroom," Wild Turkey hears someone tell him either over the radio or the night air. "Holding."

There are several things that are wrong, Wild Turkey thinks, as he stares at the lone male lying facedown in front of him on the carpets of the main room. One is that this male is clearly not either of the males (not the target, and not the middle-aged man) from the assignment profile. Wild Turkey will have to go through the standard procedures to confirm this, but he can see, even in the dark, that the man in front of him is very, very old. The extraction clock in Wild Turkey's head is ticking, ticking. The rest of the

team stands, idly tensed, adjusting their equipment. Wild Turkey
tells them he needs to go see about the female.

In the back bedroom, Specialist Freidel is standing inside the
doorway, watching a teenage girl, who is naked, cower in the far
corner.

"What the fuck?" Wild Turkey says.

Freidel shrugs. The girl in her crouch seems almost feral, eyes
flashing. Wild Turkey, in his real-time catalog of the operation,
struggles to age her, distracted by the combination of her child's
face, her dirty thighs, and half-hidden adolescent breasts.

"Did two men leave this house tonight?" Wild Turkey asks in
half-hearted Arabic. "Where is your mother? Where is your father?
Was there a houseguest tonight? Did he leave?"

The girl doesn't answer, but winces sharply at Wild Turkey's
voice, showing her teeth.

"Bring her into the main room," Wild Turkey says, frustrated.
Freidel steps forward and grabs the naked girl by the upper arm.
He begins to drag her but then she stands up, still resisting.

"I think they gave us the wrong fucking house," Wild Turkey
says (to whom?), and Freidel turns, or starts to turn, starts to say to
Wild Turkey, "What?" when the naked girl rears back, sending one
hand with its nails arcing over, digging into Freidel's neck.

"Goddamn it," Freidel says, or starts to say, as he turns and
brings his weapon's thick stock up and around possibly more
swiftly than he means to, and there is a single sound, something
like a crack, and the naked girl is on the floor at both Freidel's and
Wild Turkey's feet. Her head is unmade: the upper left quadrant
of her skull collapsed, blood very dark on the floor, a jagged-edged
concavity with a fleck of white bone just visible in Wild Turkey's
flashlight here and there, the wound tangling with her hair.

"Fuck!" Friedel says.

"Fuck," Wild Turkey says.

Wild Turkey helps drag the girl's body out into the dirt-floored
courtyard, thinking maybe he can radio for a medical addition to
the extraction, once he gets clear just what the fuck is going on,
but Wild Turkey can see—the girl's complete limpness, eyes lolling
with the dragging motion between whites and wide, black, fixed
pupils; the lack of any rising or falling of the small breasts, now
bared where she lies on her back in the pitch of the night and the
dirt—that she is gone.

"What do we do with this?" Freidel says, voice taut with desperation, and Wild Turkey can feel the stares of the rest of the team, gathered near the doorway out to the courtyard.

Wild Turkey is not afraid. He can write the report exactly as it really happened, he knows, and it will more than likely simply be forgotten, lost, after a brief bureaucratic murmur, to the labyrinth of operational After Action Reports. They'd be more interested in how the team was given the wrong house, the wrong info from the drone, more interested in the failure to extract the messenger man than anything else. Even if the report caught the eye of some officer worried about exposure, all that would happen would probably be that Wild Turkey would be rotated back home, though he didn't want to go back home. Wild Turkey knows all this, looking down at the naked girl with the ruined head, knows that he can report it or not report it, but he can't leave the body as it is. Not to be found, and photographed. Not to be seen. This is when he says it, when he raises his eyes to Freidel's and the others.

"Burn it," he says.

"Burn it," he says.

"Burn it," he says.

He helps them prepare the body. He gets the jug of kerosene from the house's tiny kitchen. He has Freidel get the bed sheets from the room they found her in. The sheets are stained with the blood that has spread on the floor. Freidel deposits them next to the body, which Wild Turkey is pouring the kerosene over. Wild Turkey straightens up. He's holding the tactical phosphorous strobe grenade in his hand.

And does Wild Turkey smell, cut by the fumes of the kerosene, that rank, fetid waft from the girl's bed sheets? Does he feel himself falling for just a second into that complex of faintly vaginal, excretory musk—does it seem familiar to him? And the girl's naked body, shining with the wetness of the kerosene there on the ground before him—what is it that strikes him as so oddly sexual about it? Is it what he saw Freidel doing as Wild Turkey entered the room? Did he see Freidel wrestling with the girl—in what, an effort to restrain her? Did he hear him laughing?

Wild Turkey has the team clear the courtyard and prepare for egress to the extraction point. He will experience this night twice, have two simultaneous nights: the one that now occurs and the one that occurs on paper. He will be honest in his report, but in his honesty he will be no more able to separate what actually happened, for the most part, from the false implantation of memory, of narrative memory, which was coeval with the experience itself. And so the truth of the night will forever feel to Wild Turkey somewhere in between the fragmentation of experience and what he remembers: he will have both seen and not seen what he saw, what he smelled. All of this with one lone exception: the moment when the phosphorous strobe, nestled underneath the naked girl's back and buried beneath the shroud of the soiled bed clothes, ignites, and shatters the night into pulses of pure white light, and the absence of it.

And already, as Wild Turkey watches (though the strobe cannot be watched, though "watching" the strobe would render him temporarily blind, as is the tactical strobe's function), the team, and Wild Turkey along with it, is leaving, clearing the buildings in the neighboring compound just in case, only to discover empty room after empty room of desks, of broken chalkboards (the mistaken compound a school, apparently). Already they are clear of Ramadi's outskirts and jogging into the field where the helicopter will briefly land and collect them; already they are back at the operations base, going to sleep; already Wild Turkey is waking in midfuck with Jeannie; waking in the invigorated air of Merry's room after a punch; already he is waking to the town's lights buzzing with the edge of his pills. He wakes outside the courthouse with Jeannie even though his heart's not really in it; he wakes on his second tour in Iraq, on a pile of rubble in Fallujah, the roar of heavy metal being pumped at the insurgents a toneless room of sound all around him, as he closes his eyes again and falls back into the city air's approximation of Mrs. Budnitz's rankness; he wakes on the adolescent night he loses his virginity to a sweet-faced girl named Helen, who, out of fear of it hurting too much, gets him off manually and only then, as Wild Turkey drifts on the edge of sleep, mounts him unexpectedly; he wakes in the overgrown baseball field outside the country school, remembering the spring afternoon he woke in the outfield years ago in the middle of a game, the air heavy and perfect with the rumor of rain; in the desert, in the lightning, in his crumbling duplex, in the field, in the many rooms of night, Wild Turkey wakes up, he wakes up, he wakes up.

DENIS JOHNSON

The Largesse of the Sea Maiden

FROM *The New Yorker*

Silences

AFTER DINNER, NOBODY went home right away. I think we'd enjoyed the meal so much we hoped Elaine would serve us the whole thing all over again. These were people we've gotten to know a little from Elaine's volunteer work—nobody from my work, nobody from the ad agency. We sat around in the living room describing the loudest sounds we'd ever heard. One said it was his wife's voice when she told him she didn't love him anymore and wanted a divorce. Another recalled the pounding of his heart when he suffered a coronary. Tia Jones had become a grandmother at the age of thirty-seven and hoped never again to hear anything so loud as her granddaughter crying in her sixteen-year-old daughter's arms. Her husband, Ralph, said it hurt his ears whenever his brother opened his mouth in public, because his brother had Tourette's syndrome and erupted with remarks like "I masturbate! Your penis smells good!" in front of perfect strangers on a bus or during a movie, or even in church.

Young Chris Case reversed the direction and introduced the topic of silences. He said the most silent thing he'd ever heard was the land mine taking off his right leg outside Kabul, Afghanistan.

As for other silences, nobody contributed. In fact, there came a silence now. Some of us hadn't realized that Chris had lost a leg. He limped, but only slightly. I hadn't even known he'd fought in Afghanistan. "A land mine?" I said.

"Yes, sir. A land mine."

"Can we see it?" Deirdre said.

"No, ma'am," Chris said. "I don't carry land mines around on my person."

"No! I mean your leg."

"It was blown off."

"I mean the part that's still there!"

"I'll show you," he said, "if you kiss it."

Shocked laughter. We started talking about the most ridiculous things we'd ever kissed. Nothing of interest. We'd all kissed only people, and only in the usual places. "All right, then," Chris told Deirdre. "Here's your chance for the conversation's most unique entry."

"No, I don't want to kiss your leg!"

Although none of us showed it, I think we all felt a little irritated with Deirdre. We all wanted to see.

Morton Sands was there too, that night, and for the most part he'd managed to keep quiet. Now he said, "Jesus Christ, Deirdre."

"Oh, well. OK," she said.

Chris pulled up his right pant leg, bunching the cuff about halfway up his thigh, and detached his prosthesis, a device of chromium bars and plastic belts strapped to his knee, which was intact and swiveled upward horribly to present the puckered end of his leg. Deirdre got down on her bare knees before him, and he hitched forward in his seat—the couch; Ralph Jones was sitting beside him—to move the scarred stump within two inches of Deirdre's face. Now she started to cry. Now we were all embarrassed, a little ashamed.

For nearly a minute, we waited.

Then Ralph Jones said, "Chris, I remember when I saw you fight two guys at once outside the Aces Tavern. No kidding," Jones told the rest of us. "He went outside with these two guys and beat the crap out of both of them."

"I guess I could've given them a break," Chris said. "They were both pretty drunk."

"Chris, you sure kicked some ass that night."

In the pocket of my shirt I had a wonderful Cuban cigar. I wanted to step outside with it. The dinner had been one of our best, and I wanted to top off the experience with a satisfying smoke. But you want to see how this sort of thing turns out. How often will you witness a woman kissing an amputation? Jones, however, had ruined everything by talking. He'd broken the spell. Chris worked the prosthesis back into place and tightened the straps and rearranged his pant leg. Deirdre stood up and wiped her eyes and smoothed her skirt and took her seat, and that was that. The outcome of all this was that Chris and Deirdre, about six months later, down at the courthouse, in the presence of very nearly the same group of friends, were married by a magistrate. Yes, they're husband and wife. You and I know what goes on.

Accomplices

Another silence comes to mind. A couple of years ago, Elaine and I had dinner at the home of Miller Thomas, formerly the head of my agency in Manhattan. Right—he and his wife, Francesca, ended up out here too, but considerably later than Elaine and I—once my boss, now a San Diego retiree. We finished two bottles of wine with dinner, maybe three bottles. After dinner, we had brandy. Before dinner, we had cocktails. We didn't know one another particularly well, and maybe we used the liquor to rush past that fact. After the brandy, I started drinking Scotch, and Miller drank bourbon, and although the weather was warm enough that the central air conditioner was running, he pronounced it a cold night and lit a fire in his fireplace. It took only a squirt of fluid and the pop of a match to get an armload of sticks crackling and blazing, and then he laid on a couple of large chunks that he said were good, seasoned oak. "The capitalist at his forge," Francesca said.

At one point we were standing in the light of the flames, I and Miller Thomas, seeing how many books each man could balance on his out-flung arms, Elaine and Francesca loading them onto our hands in a test of equilibrium that both of us failed repeatedly. It became a test of strength. I don't know who won. We called for more and more books, and our women piled them on until most of Miller's library lay around us on the floor. He had a small Marsden Hartley canvas mounted above the mantel, a crazy, mostly blue landscape done in oil, and I said that perhaps that wasn't the place for a painting like this one, so near the smoke and heat, such an expensive painting. And the painting was masterful too, from what I could see of it by dim lamps and firelight, amid books scattered all over the floor . . . Miller took offense. He said he'd paid for this masterpiece, he owned it, he could put it where it suited him. He moved very near the flames and took down the painting and turned to us, holding it before him, and declared that he could even, if he wanted, throw it in the fire and leave it there. "Is it art? Sure. But listen," he said, "art doesn't own it. My name ain't Art." He held the canvas flat like a tray, landscape up, and tempted the flames with it, thrusting it in and out. . . . And the strange thing is that I'd heard a nearly identical story about Miller Thomas and his beloved Hartley landscape some years before, about an evening very similar to this one, the drinks and wine and brandy and more drinks, the rowdy conversation, the scattering of books, and finally, Miller thrusting this painting toward the flames and calling it his own property and threatening to burn it. On that previous night, his guests had talked him down from the heights, and he'd hung the painting back in its place, but on our night—why?—none of us found a way to object as he added his property to the fuel and turned his back and walked away. A black spot appeared on the canvas and spread out in a sort of smoking puddle that gave rise to tiny flames. Miller sat in a chair across the living room, by the flickering window, and observed from that distance with a drink in his hand. Not a word, not a move, from any of us. The wooden frame popped marvelously in the silence while the great painting cooked away, first black and twisted, soon gray and fluttering, and then the fire had it all.

Adman

This morning I was assailed by such sadness at the velocity of life—the distance I've traveled from my own youth, the persistence of the old regrets, the new regrets, the ability of failure to freshen itself in novel forms—that I almost crashed the car. Getting out at the place where I do the job I don't feel I'm very good at, I grabbed my briefcase too roughly and dumped half of its contents in my lap and half on the parking lot, and while gathering it all up I left my keys on the seat and locked the car manually—an old man's habit—and trapped them in the Rav. In the office, I asked Shylene to call a locksmith and then to get me an appointment with my back man.

In the upper right quadrant of my back I have a nerve that once in a while gets pinched. The T4 nerve. These nerves aren't frail little ink lines; they're cords, in fact, as thick as your pinkie finger. This one gets caught between tense muscles, and for days, even weeks, there's not much to be done but take aspirin and get massages and visit the chiropractor. Down my right arm I feel a tingling, a numbness, sometimes a dull, sort of muffled torment, or else a shapeless, confusing pain.

It's a signal: it happens when I'm anxious about something.

To my surprise, Shylene knew all about this something. Apparently, she finds time to be Googling her bosses, and she'd learned of an award I was about to receive in, of all places, New York—for an animated television commercial. The award goes to my old New York team, but I was the only one of us attending the ceremony, possibly the only one interested, so many years down the line. This little gesture of acknowledgment put the finishing touches on a depressing picture. The people on my team had gone on to other teams, fancier agencies, higher accomplishments. All I'd done in better than two decades was tread forward until I reached the limit of certain assumptions, and stepped off. Meanwhile, Shylene was oohing, gushing, like a proud nurse who expects you to marvel at all the horrible procedures the hospital has in store for you. I said to her, "Thanks, thanks."

When I entered the reception area, and throughout this transaction, Shylene was wearing a flashy sequinned carnival mask. I didn't ask why.

Our office environment is part of the New Wave. The whole agency works under one gigantic big top, like a circus—not crowded, quite congenial, all of it surrounding a spacious break-time area, with pinball machines and a basketball hoop, and every Friday during the summer months we have a happy hour with free beer from a keg.

In New York, I made commercials. In San Diego, I write and design glossy brochures, mostly for a group of Western resorts where golf is played and horses take you along bridle paths. Don't get me wrong—California's full of beautiful spots; it's a pleasure to bring them to the attention of people who might enjoy them. Just, please, not with a badly pinched nerve.

When I can't stand it, I take the day off and visit the big art museum in Balboa Park. Today, after the locksmith got me back into my car, I drove to the museum and sat in on part of a lecture in one of its side rooms, a woman outsider artist raving, "Art is man and man is art!" I listened for five minutes, and what little of it she managed to make comprehensible didn't even merit being called shallow. Just the same, her paintings were slyly designed, intricately patterned, and coherent. I wandered from wall to wall, taking some of it in, not much. But looking at art for an hour or so always changes the way I see things afterward—this day, for instance, a group of mentally handicapped adults on a tour of the place, with their twisted, hovering hands and cocked heads, moving among the works like cheap cinema zombies, but good zombies, zombies with minds and souls and things to keep them interested. And outside, where they normally have a lot of large metal sculptures—the grounds were being dug up and reconstructed—a dragline shovel nosing the rubble monstrously, and a woman and a child watching, motionless, the little boy standing on a bench with his smile and sideways eyes and his mother beside him, holding his hand, both so still, like a photograph of American ruin.

Next, I had a session with a chiropractor dressed up as an elf.

It seemed the entire staff at the medical complex near my house were costumed for Halloween, and while I waited out front in the car for my appointment, the earliest one I could get that day, I saw a Swiss milkmaid coming back from lunch, then a witch with a green face, then a sunburst-orange superhero. Then I had the session with the chiropractor in his tights and drooping cap.

As for me? My usual guise. The masquerade continues.

Farewell

Elaine got a wall phone for the kitchen, a sleek blue one that wears its receiver like a hat, with a caller-ID readout on its face just below the keypad. While I eyeballed this instrument, having just come in from my visit with the chiropractor, a brisk, modest tone began, and the tiny screen showed ten digits I didn't recognize. My inclination was to scorn it, like any other unknown. But this was the first call, the inaugural message.

As soon as I touched the receiver I wondered if I'd regret this, if I was holding a mistake in my hand, if I was pulling this mistake to my head and saying "Hello" to it.

The caller was my first wife, Virginia, or Ginny, as I always called her. We were married long ago, in our early twenties, and put a stop to it after three crazy years. Since then, we hadn't spoken, we'd had no reason to, but now we had one. Ginny was dying.

Her voice came faintly. She told me the doctors had closed the book on her, she'd ordered her affairs, the good people from hospice were in attendance.

Before she ended this earthly transit, as she called it, Ginny wanted to shed any kind of bitterness against certain people, certain men, especially me. She said how much she'd been hurt, and how badly she wanted to forgive me, but she didn't know whether she could or not—she hoped she could—and I assured her, from the abyss of a broken heart, that I hoped so too, that I hated my infidelities and my lies about the money, and the way I'd kept my boredom secret, and my secrets in general, and Ginny and I talked, after forty years of silence, about the many other ways I'd stolen her right to the truth.

In the middle of this, I began wondering, most uncomfortably, in fact with a dizzy, sweating anxiety, if I'd made a mistake—if this wasn't my first wife, Ginny, no, but rather my second wife, Jennifer, often called Jenny. Because of the weakness of her voice and my own humming shock at the news, also the situation around her as she tried to speak to me on this very important occasion—folks coming and going, and the sounds of a respirator, I supposed—now, fifteen minutes into this call, I couldn't remember if she'd actually said her name when I picked up the phone and I suddenly didn't know which set of crimes I was regretting, wasn't sure if this dying farewell clobbering me to my knees in true repentance beside the kitchen table was Virginia's or Jennifer's.

"This is hard," I said. "Can I put the phone down a minute?" I heard her say OK.

The house felt empty. "Elaine?" I called. Nothing. I wiped my face with a dishrag and took off my blazer and hung it on a chair and called out Elaine's name one more time and then picked up the receiver again. There was nobody there.

Somewhere inside it, the phone had preserved the caller's number, of course, Ginny's number or Jenny's, but I didn't look for it.

We'd had our talk, and Ginny or Jenny, whichever, had recognized herself in my frank apologies, and she'd been satisfied—because, after all, both sets of crimes had been the same.

I was tired. What a day. I called Elaine on her cell phone. We agreed she might as well stay at the Budget Inn on the East Side. She volunteered out there, teaching adults to read, and once in a while she got caught late and stayed over. Good. I could lock all three locks on the door and call it a day. I didn't mention the previous call. I turned in early.

I dreamed of a wild landscape—elephants, dinosaurs, bat caves, strange natives, and so on.

I woke, couldn't go back to sleep, put on a long terry-cloth robe over my PJs and slipped into my loafers and went walking. People in bathrobes stroll around here at all hours, but not often, I think, without a pet on a leash. Ours is a good neighborhood—a Catholic church and a Mormon one, and a posh townhouse development with much open green space, and on our side of the street, some pretty nice smaller homes.

I wonder if you're like me, if you collect and squirrel away in your soul certain odd moments when the Mystery winks at you, when you walk in your bathrobe and tasseled loafers, for instance, well out of your neighborhood and among a lot of closed shops, and you approach your very faint reflection in a window with words above it. The sign said SKY AND CELERY. Closer, it read SKI AND CYCLERY.

I headed home.

Widow

I was having lunch one day with my friend Tom Ellis, a journalist—just catching up. He said that he was writing a two-act drama based on interviews he'd taped while gathering material for an article on the death penalty, two interviews in particular.

First, he'd spent an afternoon with a death-row inmate in Virginia, the murderer William Donald Mason, a name not at all famous here in California, and I don't know why I remember it. Mason was scheduled to die the next day, twelve years after killing a guard he'd taken hostage during a bank robbery.

Other than his last meal, of steak, green beans, and a baked potato, which would be served to him the following noon, Mason knew of no future outcomes to worry about and seemed relaxed and content. Ellis quizzed him about his life before his arrest, his routine there at the prison, his views on the death penalty—Mason was against it—and his opinion as to an afterlife—Mason was for it.

The prisoner talked with admiration about his wife, whom he'd met and married some years after landing on death row. She was the cousin of a fellow inmate. She waited tables in a sports bar—great tips. She liked reading, and she'd introduced her murderer husband to the works of Charles Dickens and Mark Twain and Ernest Hemingway. She was studying for a realtor's license.

Mason had already said goodbye to his wife. The couple had agreed to get it all out of the way a full week ahead of the execution, to spend several happy hours together and part company well out of the shadow of Mason's last day.

Ellis said that he'd felt a fierce, unexpected kinship with this man so close to the end because, as Mason himself pointed out, this was the last time he'd be introduced to a stranger, except for the people who would arrange him on the gurney the next day and set him up for his injection. Tom Ellis was the last new person he'd meet, in other words, who wasn't about to kill him. And, in fact, everything proceeded according to the schedule and, about eighteen hours after Ellis talked with him, William Mason was dead.

A week later, Ellis interviewed the new widow, Mrs. Mason, and learned that much of what she'd told her husband was false.

Ellis located her in Norfolk, working not in any kind of sports bar but instead in a basement sex emporium near the waterfront, in a one-on-one peepshow. In order to talk to her, Ellis had to pay twenty dollars and descend a narrow stairway, lit with purple bulbs, and sit in a chair before a curtained window. He was shocked when the curtain vanished upward to reveal the woman already completely nude, sitting on a stool in a padded booth. Then it was her turn to be shocked, when Ellis introduced himself as a man who'd shared an hour or two of her husband's last full day on earth. Together they spoke of the prisoner's wishes and dreams, his happiest memories and his childhood grief, the kinds of things a man shares only with his wife. Her face, though severe, was pretty, and she displayed her parts to Tom unselfconsciously, yet without the protection of anonymity. She wept, she laughed, she shouted, she whispered all of this into a telephone handset that she held to her head, while her free hand gestured in the air or touched the glass between them.

As for having told so many lies to the man she'd married—that was one of the things she laughed about. She seemed to assume that anybody else would have done the same. In addition to her bogus employment and her imaginary studies in real estate, she'd endowed herself with a religious soul and joined a nonexistent church. Thanks to all her fabrications, William Donald Mason had died a proud and happy husband.

And just as he'd been surprised by his sudden intimacy with the condemned killer, my friend felt very close to the widow, because they were talking to each other about life and death while she displayed her nakedness before him, sitting on the stool with her red spike-heeled pumps planted wide apart on the floor. I asked him if they'd ended up making love, and he said no, but he'd wanted to, he certainly had, and he was convinced that the naked widow had felt the same, though you weren't allowed to touch the girls in those places, and this dialogue, in fact both of them—the death-row interview and the interview with the naked widow—had taken place through glass partitions made to withstand any kind of passionate assault.

At the time, the idea of telling her what he wanted had seemed terrible. Now he regretted his shyness. In the play, as he described it for me, the second act would end differently.

Before long, we wandered into a discussion of the difference between repentance and regret. You repent the things you've done, and regret the chances you let get away. Then, as sometimes happens in a San Diego café—more often than you'd think—we were interrupted by a beautiful young woman selling roses.

Orphan

The lunch with Tom Ellis took place a couple of years ago. I don't suppose he ever wrote the play; it was just a notion he was telling me about. It came to mind today because this afternoon I attended the memorial service of an artist friend of mine, a painter named Tony Fido, who once told me about a similar experience.

Tony found a cell phone on the ground near his home in National City, just south of here. He told me about this the last time I saw him, a couple of months before he disappeared, or went out of communication. First he went out of communication, then he was deceased. But when he told me this story there was no hint of any of that.

Tony noticed the cell phone lying under an oleander bush as he walked around his neighborhood. He picked it up and continued his stroll, and before long felt it vibrating in his pocket. When he answered, he found himself talking to the wife of the owner—the owner's widow, actually, who explained that she'd been calling the number every thirty minutes or so since her husband's death, not twenty-four hours before.

Her husband had been killed the previous afternoon in an accident at the intersection where Tony had found the cell phone. An old woman in a Cadillac had run him down. At the moment of impact, the device had been torn from his hand.

The police said that they hadn't noticed any phone around the scene. It hadn't been among the belongings she'd collected at the morgue. "I knew he lost it right there," she told Tony, "because he was talking to me at the very second when it happened."

Tony offered to get in his car and deliver the phone to her personally, and she gave him her address in Lemon Grove, nine miles distant. When he got there he discovered that the woman was only twenty-two and quite attractive, and that she and her husband had been going through a divorce.

At this point in the telling, I think I knew where his story was headed.

"She came after me. I told her, 'You're either from Heaven or from Hell.' It turned out she was from Hell."

Whenever he talked, Tony kept his hands moving—grabbing and rearranging small things on the tabletop—while his head rocked from side to side and back and forth. Sometimes he referred to a "force of rhythm" in his paintings. He often spoke of "motion" in the work.

I didn't know much about Tony's background. He was in his late forties but seemed younger. I met him at the Balboa Park museum, where he appeared at my shoulder while I looked at an Edward Hopper painting of a Cape Cod gas station. He offered his critique, which was lengthy, meticulous, and scathing—and which was focused on technique, only on technique—and spoke of his contempt for all painters, and finished by saying, "I wish Picasso was alive. I'd challenge him—he could do one of mine and I could do one of his."

"You're a painter yourself."

"A better painter than this guy," he said of Edward Hopper.

"Well, whose work would you say is any good?"

"The only painter I admire is God. He's my biggest influence."

We began having coffee together two or three times a month, always, I have to admit, at Tony's initiation. Usually I drove to his lively, disheveled Hispanic neighborhood to see him, there in National City. I like primitive art, and I like folktales, so I enjoyed visiting his rambling old home, where he lived surrounded by his paintings, like an orphan king in a cluttered castle.

The house had been in his family since 1939. For a while, it was a boarding house—a dozen bedrooms, each with its own sink. "Damn place has a jinx or whammy: First, Spiro—Spiro watched it till he died. Mom watched it till she died. My sister watched it till she died. Now I'll be here till I die," he said, hosting me shirtless, his hairy torso dabbed all over with paint. Talking so fast I could rarely follow, he did seem deranged. But blessed, decidedly so, with a self-deprecating and self-orienting humor that the genuinely mad seem to have misplaced. What to make of somebody like that? "Richards in the *Washington Post*," he once said, "compared me to Melville." I have no idea who Richards was. Or who Spiro was.

Tony never tired of his voluble explanations, his self-exege-sis—the works almost coded, as if to fool or distract the unworthy. They weren't the child drawings of your usual schizophrenic outsider artist, but efforts a little more skillful, on the order of tattoo art, oil on canvases around four by six feet in size, crowded with images but highly organized, all on biblical themes, mostly dire and apocalyptic, and all with the titles printed neatly right on them. One of his works, for instance—three panels depicting the end of the world and the advent of Heaven—was called "Mystery Babylon Mother of Harlots Revelation 17:1-7."

This period when I was seeing a bit of Tony Fido coincided with an era in the world of my unconscious, an era when I was troubled by the dreams I had at night. They were long and epic, detailed and violent and colorful. They were exhausting. I couldn't account for them. The only medication I took was something to bring down my blood pressure, and it wasn't new. I made sure I didn't take food just before going to bed. I avoided sleeping on my back, steered clear of disturbing novels and TV shows. For a month, maybe six weeks, I dreaded sleep. Once, I dreamed of Tony—I defended him against an angry mob, keeping the seething throng at bay with a butcher knife. Often I woke up short of breath, shaking, my heartbeat rattling my ribs, and I cured my nerves with a solitary walk, no matter the hour. And once—maybe the night I dreamed about Tony, I don't remember—I went walking and had the kind of moment or visitation I treasure, when the flow of life twists and untwists, all in a blink—think of a taut ribbon flashing: I heard a young man's voice in the parking lot of the Mormon church in the dark night telling someone, "I didn't bark. That wasn't me. I didn't bark."

I never found out how things turned out between Tony and the freshly widowed twenty-two-year-old. I'm pretty sure it went no further, and there was no second encounter, certainly no ongoing affair—because he more than once complained, "I can't find a woman, none. I'm under some kind of a damn spell." He believed in spells and whammies and such, in angels and mermaids, omens, sorcery, wind-borne voices, in messages and patterns. All through his house were scattered twigs and feathers possessing a mysterious significance, rocks that had spoken to him, stumps of driftwood whose faces he recognized. And, in any direction, his canvases, like windows opening onto lightning and smoke, ranks of crimson demons and flying angels, gravestones on fire, and scrolls, chalices, torches, swords.

Last week, a woman named Rebecca Stamos, somebody I'd never heard of, called me to say that our mutual friend Tony Fido was no more. He'd killed himself. As she put it, "He took his life."

For two seconds, the phrase meant nothing to me. "Took it," I said . . . Then, "Oh, my goodness."

"Yes, I'm afraid he committed suicide."

"I don't want to know how. Don't tell me how." Honestly, I can't imagine why I said that.

Memorial

A week ago Friday—nine days ago—the eccentric religious painter Tony Fido stopped his car on Interstate 8, about sixty miles east of

San Diego, on a bridge above a deep, deep ravine, and climbed over the railing and stepped into the air. He mailed a letter beforehand to Rebecca Stamos, not to explain himself but only to say goodbye and pass along the phone numbers of some friends.

Sunday I attended Tony's memorial service, for which Rebecca Stamos had reserved the band room of the middle school where she teaches. We sat in a circle, with cups and saucers on our laps, in a tiny grove of music stands, and volunteered, one by one, our memories of Tony Fido. There were only five of us: our hostess, Rebecca, plain and stout, in a sleeveless blouse and a skirt that reached down to her white tennis shoes; myself in the raiment of my order, the blue blazer, khaki chinos, tasseled loafers; two middle-aged women of the sort to own a couple of small obnoxious dogs—they called Tony "Anthony"; a chubby young man in a green jumpsuit—some kind of mechanic—sweating. Tony's neighbors? Family? None.

Only the pair of ladies who'd arrived together actually knew each other. None of the rest of us had ever met before. These were friendships, or acquaintances, that Tony had kept one by one. He'd met us all in the same way—he'd materialized beside us at an art museum, an outdoor market, a doctor's waiting room, and he'd begun to talk. I was the only one of us even aware he devoted all his time to painting canvases. The others thought he owned some kind of business—plumbing or exterminating or looking after private swimming pools. One believed he came from Greece; others assumed Mexico, but I'm sure his family was Armenian, long established in San Diego County. Rather than memorializing him, we found ourselves asking, "Who the hell was this guy?"

Rebecca had this much about him: while he was still in his teens, Tony's mother had killed herself. "He mentioned it more than once," Rebecca said. "It was always on his mind." To the rest of us this came as new information.

Of course, it troubled us to learn that his mother had taken her own life too. Had she jumped? Tony hadn't told, and Rebecca hadn't asked.

With little to offer about Tony in the way of biography, I shared some remarks of his that had stuck in my thoughts. "I couldn't get into ritzy art schools," he told me once. "Best thing that ever happened to me. It's dangerous to be taught art." And he said, "On my twenty-sixth birthday, I quit signing my work. Anybody who can paint like that, have at it, and take the credit." He got a kick out of showing me a passage in his hefty black Bible—first book of Samuel, chapter 6?—where the idolatry of the Philistines earns them a plague of hemorrhoids. "Don't tell me God doesn't have a sense of humor."

And another of his insights, one he shared with me several times: "We live in a catastrophic universe—not a universe of gradualism."

That one had always gone right past me. Now it sounded ominous, prophetic. Had I missed a message? A warning?

The man in the green jumpsuit, the garage mechanic, reported that Tony had plunged from our nation's highest concrete-beam bridge down into Pine Valley Creek, a flight of 440 feet. The span, completed in 1974 and named the Nello Irwin Greer Memorial Bridge, was the first in the United States to be built using, according to the mechanic, "the cast-in-place segmental balanced cantilever method." I wrote it down on a memo pad. I can't recall the mechanic's name. His breast-tag said "Ted," but he introduced himself as someone else.

Anne and her friend, whose name also slipped past me—the pair of women—cornered me afterward. They seemed to think I should be the one to take final possession of a three-ring binder full of recipes that Tony had loaned them—the collected recipes of Tony's mother. I determined I would give it to Elaine. She's a wonderful cook, but not as a regular thing, because nobody likes to cook for two. Too much work and too many leftovers. I told them she'd be glad to get the book.

The binder was too big for any of my pockets. I thought of asking for a bag, but I failed to ask. I didn't know what to do with it but carry it home in my hands and deliver it to my wife.

Elaine was sitting at the kitchen table, before her a cup of black coffee and half a sandwich on a plate.

I set the notebook on the table next to her snack. She stared at it. "Oh," she said. "From your painter." She sat me down beside her and we went through the notebook page by page, side by side.

Elaine: she's petite, lithe, quite smart; short gray hair, no makeup. A good companion. At any moment—the very next second—she could be dead.

I want to depict this book carefully, so imagine holding it in your hands, a three-ring binder of bright-red plastic weighing about the same as a full dinner plate, and now setting it in front of you on the table. When you open it, you find a pink title page, "Recipes. Caesarina Fido," covering a two-inch thickness of white college-ruled three-hole paper, the first inch or so the usual—casseroles and pies and salad dressings, every aspect of breakfast, lunch, and supper, all written in blue ballpoint. Halfway through, Tony's mother introduces ink of other colors, mostly green, red, and purple, but also pink, and a yellow that's hard to make out; and, as these colors come along, her penmanship enters a kind of havoc, the letters swell and shrink, several pages big and loopy, leaning to the right, and then, for the next many pages, leaning to the left, then back the other way; and here, where these wars and changes begin, and for better than a hundred pages, all the way to the end, the recipes are only for cocktails. Every kind of cocktail.

Earlier that afternoon, as Anne handed the binder over to me at Tony's memorial, she made a curious remark. "Anthony spoke very highly of you. He said you were his best friend." I thought it was a joke, but Anne meant this seriously.

Tony's best friend? I was confused. I'm still confused. I hardly knew him.

Casanova

When I returned to New York City to pick up my prize at the American Advertisers Awards, I'm not sure I expected to enjoy myself. But on the second day, killing time before the ceremony, walking north through midtown in my dark ceremonial suit and trench coat, skirting the Park, strolling south again, feeling the pulse and listening to the traffic noise rising among high buildings, I had a homecoming. The day was sunny, fine for walking, brisk, and getting brisker—and in fact, as I cut a diagonal through a little plaza somewhere above Fortieth Street, the last autumn leaves were swept up from the pavement and thrown around my head, and a sudden misty quality in the atmosphere above seemed to solidify into a ceiling both dark and luminous, and the passersby hunched into their collars, and two minutes later, the gusts settled into a wind, not hard but steady and cold, and my hands dove into my coat pockets. A bit of rain speckled the pavement. Random snowflakes spiraled in the air. All around me, people seemed to be evacuating the scene, while across the square a vendor shouted that he was closing his cart and you could have his wares for practically nothing, and for no reason I could have named I bought two of his rat dogs with everything and a cup of doubtful coffee and then learned the reason—they were wonderful. I nearly ate the napkin. New York!

Once, I lived here. Went to Columbia University, studying history first, then broadcast journalism. Worked for a couple of pointless years at the *Post*, and then for thirteen tough but prosperous years at Castle and Forbes on Fifty-fourth, just off Madison Avenue. And then took my insomnia, my afternoon headaches, my doubts, and my antacid tablets to San Diego and lost them in the Pacific Ocean. New York and I didn't quite fit. I knew it the whole time. Some of my Columbia classmates came from faraway places like Iowa and Nevada, as I had come a shorter way from New Hampshire, and after graduation they'd been absorbed into Manhattan and had lived there ever since. I didn't last. I always say, "It was never my town."

Today it was all mine. Today I was its proprietor. With my overcoat wide open and the wind in my hair, I walked around and for an hour or so presided over the bits of litter in the air—so much less than thirty years ago!—and the citizens bent against the weather, and the light inside the restaurants, and the people at small tables looking at one another's faces and talking. The white flakes began to stick. By the time I entered Trump Tower, I'd had a long, hard, wet walk. I repaired myself in the restroom and found the right floor. At the ceremony, my table was near the front—round, clothed in burgundy, and surrounded by eight of us, the other seven much younger than I, a lively bunch, fun and full of wisecracks. And they seemed impressed to be sitting with me, and made sure I sat where I could see. All that was the good part.

Halfway through dessert, the nerve in my back began to act up, and by the time I heard my name and started toward the podium my right shoulder blade felt as if it were pressed against a hissing old New York steam-heat radiator. At the head of the vast room, I held the medallion in my hand—that's what it was, rather than a trophy; an inscribed medallion three inches in diameter, good for a paperweight—and thanked a list of names I'd memorized, omitted any other remarks, and got back to my table just as another pain seized me, this one in the region of my bowels, and now I repented my curbside lunch, my delicious New York hot dogs, especially the second one, and, without sitting down or even making an excuse, I let this bout of indigestion carry me out of the room and down the halls to the men's lavatory, where I hardly had time to fumble the medallion into my lapel pocket and get my jacket on the hook.

I'd sat down with my intestines in flames, first my body bearing this insult, and then my soul insulted too, when someone came in and chose the stall next to mine. Our public toilets are just that—too public; the walls don't reach the floor. This other man and I could see each other's feet. Or, at any rate, our black shoes, and the cuffs of our dark trousers.

After a minute, his hand laid on the floor between us, there at the border between his space and mine, a square of toilet paper with an obscene proposition written on it, in words large and plain enough that I could read them whether I wanted to or not. In pain, I laughed. Not out loud.

I heard a small sigh from the next stall.

By hunching down into my own embrace and staring hard at my feet, I tried to make myself go away. I didn't acknowledge his overture, and he didn't leave. He must have taken it that I had him under consideration. As long as I stayed, he had reason to hope. And I couldn't leave yet. My bowels churned and smoldered. Renegade signals from my spinal nerve hammered my shoulder and the full length of my right arm, down to the marrow.

The awards ceremony seemed to have ended. The men's room came to life—the door whooshing open, the run of voices coming in. Throats and faucets and footfalls. The spin of the paper-towel dispenser.

Somewhere in here, a hand descended to the note on the floor, fingers touched it, raised it away. Soon after that the man, the toilet Casanova, was no longer beside me.

I stayed as I was, for how long I couldn't say. There were echoes. Silence. The urinals flushing themselves.

I raised myself upright, pulled my clothing together, made my way to the sinks.

One other man remained in the place. He stood at the sink beside mine as our faucets ran. I washed my hands. He washed his hands.

He was tall, with a distinctive head—wispy colorless hair like a baby's, and a skeletal face with thick red lips. I'd have known him anywhere.

"Carl Zane!"

He smiled in a small way. "Wrong. I'm Marshall Zane. I'm Carl's son."

"Sure, of course—he would have aged too!" This encounter had me going in circles. I'd finished washing my hands, and now I started washing them again. I forgot to introduce myself. "You look just like your dad," I said. "Only twenty-five years ago. Are you here for the awards night?"

He nodded. "I'm with the Sextant Group."

"You followed in his footsteps."

"I did. I even worked for Castle and Forbes for a couple of years."

"How do you like that? And how's Carl doing? Is he here tonight?"

"He passed away three years ago. Went to sleep one night and never woke up."

"Oh. Oh, no." I had a moment—I have them sometimes—when the surroundings seemed bereft of any facts, and not even the smallest physical gesture felt possible. After the moment had passed, I said, "I'm sorry to hear that. He was a nice guy."

"At least it was painless," the son of Carl Zane said. "And, as far as anyone knows, he went to bed happy that night."

We were talking to each other's reflection in the broad mirror. I made sure I didn't look elsewhere—at his trousers, his shoes. But, for this occasion, we men, every one of us, had dressed in dark trousers and black shoes.

"Well . . . enjoy your evening," the young man said.

I thanked him and said good night, and as he tossed a wadded paper towel at the receptacle and disappeared out the door, I'm afraid I added, "Tell your father I said hello."

Mermaid

As I trudged up Fifth Avenue after this miserable interlude, I carried my shoulder like a bushel bag of burning kindling and could hardly stay upright the three blocks to my hotel. It was really snowing now, and it was Saturday night, the sidewalk was crowded, people came at me, forcing themselves against the weather, their shoulders hunched, their coats pinched shut, flakes battering their faces, and though the faces were dark I felt I saw into their eyes.

I came awake in the unfamiliar room I didn't know how much later, and if this makes sense, it wasn't the pain in my shoulder that woke me but its departure. The episode had passed. I lay bathed in relief.

Beyond my window, a thick layer of snow covered the ledge. I became aware of a hush of anticipation, a tremendous surrounding absence. I got out of bed, dressed in my clothes, and went out to look at the city.

It was, I think, around 1 a.m. Snow six inches deep had fallen. Park Avenue looked smooth and soft—not one vehicle had disturbed its surface. The city was almost completely stopped, its very few sounds muffled yet perfectly distinct from one another: a rumbling snowplow somewhere, a car's horn, a man on another street shouting several faint syllables. I tried counting up the years since I'd seen snow. Eleven or twelve—Denver, and it had been exactly the same, exactly like this. One lone taxi glided up Park Avenue through the virgin white, and I hailed it and asked the driver to find any restaurant open for business. I looked out the back window at the brilliant silences falling from the street lamps, and at our fresh black tracks disappearing into the infinite—the only proof of Park Avenue; I'm not sure how the cabbie kept to the road. He took me to a small diner off Union Square, where I had a wonderful breakfast among a handful of miscellaneous wanderers like myself, New Yorkers with their large, historic faces, every one of whom, delivered here without an explanation, seemed invaluable. I paid and left and set out walking back toward midtown. I'd bought a pair of weatherproof dress shoes just before leaving San Diego, and I was glad. I looked for places where I was the first to walk and kicked at the powdery snow. A piano playing a Latin tune drew me through a doorway into an atmosphere of sadness: a dim tavern, a stale smell, the piano's weary melody, and a single customer, an ample, attractive woman with abundant blond hair. She wore an evening gown. A light shawl covered her shoulders. She seemed poised and self-possessed, though it was possible, also, that she was weeping.

I let the door close behind me. The bartender, a small old black man, raised his eyebrows, and I said, "Scotch rocks, Red Label."

Talking, I felt discourteous. The piano played in the gloom of the farthest corner. I recognized the melody as a Mexican traditional called "Maria Elena." I couldn't see the musician at all. In front of the piano a big tenor saxophone rested upright on a stand. With no one around to play it, it seemed like just another of the personalities here: the invisible pianist, the disenchanted old bartender, the big glamorous blonde, the shipwrecked, solitary saxophone. And the man who'd walked here through the snow . . . And as soon as the name of the song popped into my head I thought I heard a voice say, "Her name is Maria Elena." The scene had a moon-lit, black-and-white quality. Ten feet away, at her table, the blond woman waited, her shoulders back, her face raised. She lifted one hand and beckoned me with her fingers. She was weeping. The lines of her tears sparkled on her cheeks. "I am a prisoner here," she said. I took the chair across from her and watched her cry. I sat upright, one hand on the table's surface and the other around my drink. I felt the ecstasy of a dancer, but I kept still.

Whit

My name would mean nothing to you, but there's a very good chance you're familiar with my work. Among the many TV ads I wrote and directed, you'll remember one in particular.

In this animated thirty-second spot, you see a brown bear chasing a gray rabbit. They come one after the other over a hill toward the view—the rabbit is cornered, he's crying, the bear comes to him—the rabbit reaches into his waistcoat pocket and pulls out a dollar bill and gives it to the bear. The bear looks at this gift, sits down, stares into space. The music stops, there's no sound, nothing is said, and right there, the little narrative ends, on a note of complete uncertainty. It's an advertisement for a banking chain. It sounds ridiculous, I know, but that's only if you haven't seen it. If you've seen it, the way it was rendered, then you know that it was a very unusual advertisement. Because it referred, really, to nothing at all, and yet it was actually very moving.

Advertisements don't try to get you to fork over your dough by tugging irrelevantly at your heartstrings, not as a rule. But this one broke the rules, and it worked. It brought the bank many new customers. And it excited a lot of commentary and won several awards—every award I ever won, in fact, I won for that ad. It ran in both halves of the twenty-second Super Bowl, and people still remember it.

You don't get awards personally. They go to the team. To the agency. But your name attaches to the project as a matter of workplace lore—"Whit did that one." (And that would be me, Bill Whitman.) "Yes, the one with the rabbit and the bear was Whit's."

Credit goes first of all to the banking firm who let this strange message go out to potential customers, who sought to start a relationship with a gesture so cryptic. It was better than cryptic—mysterious, untranslatable. I think it pointed to orderly financial exchange as the basis of harmony. Money tames the beast. Money is peace. Money is civilization. The end of the story is money.

I won't mention the name of the bank. If you don't remember the name, then it wasn't such a good ad after all.

If you watched any prime-time television in the 1980s, you've almost certainly seen several other ads I wrote or directed or both. I crawled out of my twenties leaving behind a couple of short, unhappy marriages, and then I found Elaine. Twenty-five years last June, and two daughters. Have I loved my wife? We've gotten along. We've never felt like congratulating ourselves.

I'm just shy of sixty-three. Elaine's fifty-two but seems older. Not in her looks but in her attitude of complacency. She lacks fire. Seems interested mainly in our two girls. She keeps in close contact with them. They're both grown. They're harmless citizens. They aren't beautiful or clever.

Before the girls started grade school, we left New York and headed west in stages, a year in Denver (too much winter), another in Phoenix (too hot), and finally San Diego. San Diego. What a wonderful city. It's a bit more crowded each year, but still. Completely wonderful. Never regretted coming here, not for an instant. And financially it all worked out. If we'd stayed in New York I'd have made a lot more money, but we'd have needed a lot more too.

Last night Elaine and I lay in bed watching TV, and I asked her what she remembered. Not much. Less than I. We have a very small TV that sits on a dresser across the room. Keeping it going provides an excuse for lying awake in bed.

I note that I've lived longer in the past now than I can expect to live in the future. I have more to remember than I have to look forward to. Memory fades, not much of the past stays, and I wouldn't mind forgetting a lot more of it.

Once in a while, I lie there as the television runs, and I read something wild and ancient from one of several collections of folktales I own. Apples that summon sea maidens, eggs that fulfill any wish, and pears that make people grow long noses that fall off again. Then sometimes I get up and don my robe and go out into our quiet neighborhood looking for a magic thread, a magic sword, a magic horse.

M & L

FROM *West Branch*

M

IT WAS THAT moment in the reception when women leave their high heels on the porch and men take off their jackets and drape them over chairs. The bride and groom and immediate family members went off with the photographer to take advantage of the late afternoon light. The sun disappeared behind a hill, and what remained in the air was a honeyed glow that forgave the tense smiles and dark circles under their eyes. Miriam and Gloria both wore long yellow bridesmaid dresses, gathering their hems above their knees as they waded through the unmowed grass. Although it hadn't rained, the field behind the house was damp enough to soak through a good pair of leather boots. Miriam waited as Liam rolled up his pants and discarded his socks and shoes by a patch of woods. Then the three of them ducked through a tight web of branches to the neighboring field, owned by a couple who'd struck rich in the music business and now tended to a menagerie of exotic pets.

The camel, explained Miriam, was a real sweetheart. A dromedary rescued from a petting zoo in Pigeon Forge that had gone out of business. At the sight of an apple, she'd growl happily and gently take it from your hand with her long cleft lips. Earlier Gloria had raided the appetizer trays and stuffed a handful of carrot sticks into Liam's jacket pocket, along with his wallet and keys. They all squeezed by a rusted metal gate without splashing their cocktails or ruining their clothes, but were stopped a few feet later by an electric fence, the metal wire so thin that it was nearly invisible.

Unfortunately the camel was nowhere in sight. More than likely she was getting fed in the black tobacco barn that stood at the opposite end of the field.

Liam reached into his jacket pocket for a carrot stick. Miriam had never seen him in a suit before and now that he wore one, she no longer found it impossible to believe he was an attorney. He was six foot four, broad shouldered, and handsome in that peculiar way tall redheads are, like he had too many bones in his face.

"How can we tell if it's on?" Gloria waved her hand over the fence like it was a burner on a hot stove.

Miriam balanced her glass on top of the fence post. She bent over, plucked a blade of grass, and held it out to Liam. They had dated for three years in high school after what had been, at least for Liam, an agonizing crush that could be traced back to the fifth grade. It had begun on the day she was captain for recess basketball. He was the shortest kid back then and always chosen last, shifting from one foot to the other and smiling good-naturedly to show it didn't bother him. She'd admired him because of this, and pitied him a little. So she'd tapped him first. Afterward he seemed to be everywhere, trembling as he passed her a box of markers, staring at her with undisguised longing across the rows of cafeteria tables. It was all tremendously flattering. It was all tremendously irritating. She would ignore him for weeks and then, for reasons she couldn't explain, return a look of equal longing, pass notes to him in the shape of origami cranes, share answers to the math homework, which he always forgot. By seventh grade she had the second-biggest boobs of any girl in the middle school. Grown men honked their horns and whistled as she walked home from the bus stop. Miriam had convinced Liam to steal the answers to a test, hand over his spending money on a field trip to an art museum, buy cigarettes from the vending machine at the pizzeria.

She held out the blade of grass to him. He shook his head no. "Just make sure your hands aren't wet," he said.

Miriam took a deep breath. When she touched the grass to the metal wire, the fine hairs on her arm rose. A low, steady pulse tickled up her neck. It almost hurt. She remembered they had done this in Mrs. Walter's science class, walking past the edge of the schoolyard through the new subdivision, over the creek to the farm with Jersey cattle. One recently escaped, causing a highway accident that left a cow-sized bloodstain on the asphalt for days. The farmer had since installed an electric fence as a precaution. They'd formed a chain that was six children long before the current tapered out. Miriam had held hands with Liam. Did Liam remember how she made a big show of wiping her palm on her jeans so the other kids wouldn't tease her? Miriam was tempted to grab Liam's hand but was stopped by all the possible interpretations of this gesture.

She reached for Gloria's instead. Gloria squealed. Liam rolled his eyes and shook his head.

"Not everyone grew up in the country," Gloria said, reaching for him. The current traveled along the blade and circulated through their bodies. Above the distant chatter of the reception and the hum of cicadas, a bass note thudded inside Miriam's head like a second heartbeat. How pleasant it was to feel invaded by this other heart! The end of the day was beautiful. A bluish softness coated the trees and the grass, and a few fireflies blinked over the field. Had she held Liam's hand she would have squeezed it just now.

They almost forgot the camel. "Leave something for when she gets back," said Miriam. And Liam tossed the carrot sticks far over the fence, where they landed near a water barrel. As they walked to the house, Gloria unfastened her bun and a breeze rippled through her long dark hair. She looked like a pretty maiden in an old painting. Miriam realized that she must look like this too—pretty, old-timey—and became aware of Liam's gaze on the back of her neck. The lights of the house appeared through the trees. The guests had congregated on the patio and were talking loudly while the band tuned up indoors. At the corner of the balcony a man stood alone, loosening his tie. He leaned on his elbows and took a sip from his drink. Miriam stopped. The muscles in her chest contracted over her heart as though she'd plunged into freezing water.

It looked just like Caleb. Same angle of the jaw, same curly brown hair—even the same broken nose. She shook herself. By now she was used to these missightings, these minor hallucinations. The man had turned around and she could see that it was clearly not Caleb. His neck was longer. His smile looked easy. He straightened and walked into the house.

"You all right there?" Liam asked. Few other people would have noticed.

"It's nothing." She looked down into her glass and shrugged. "Seems I've run out of liquor."

Miriam ordered one gin and tonic, one rum and Coke, and watched Liam sign the guestbook in the entryway. You could see his beer belly with his jacket unbuttoned. A few months ago his girlfriend had broken up with him—the same girl he'd left Miriam for, their freshman year of college. She was nothing less than delighted to hear this news. She noted that Liam had clearly not been working out, nor had he lost the apologetic stoop of a tall man who was uncomfortable with his height. He put the pen between his teeth. He had not changed much. All in all he reminded her of a skittish orange cat.

She set his drink on the table and glimpsed the message he had taken so long in writing. *To Beth and John, a beautiful couple. Wishing a long life to you both, full of happiness and love!*

The kindness of these words filled her with shame.

When she looked at him her eyes came up only to the top buttons of his shirt.

"How many for you this year?" he asked, nodding to the surroundings. White and yellow paper lanterns draped the porch and swayed in the wind. Beth, the bride, had fought her mother to put these up. A pack of young nieces and nephews roamed between the tables of appetizers, their lips dyed red from multiple Shirley Temples. Aunts and distant cousins, stepfamily, coworkers, and the friends of grandparents shook hands vigorously and gave half kisses on cheeks. A small wedding with a big reception—the whole effect was like being invited to eat at a nice restaurant with someone else's family.

"Four," she said, squeezing a lime into her gin and tonic. "Not as bad as it could be. You?"

Liam's eyes darted to Miriam's right arm.

"It's gone," she told him, touching her bicep where a patch of skin was discolored. "Took a whole paycheck to get it removed." As soon as Liam had turned eighteen they had driven to a tattoo parlor in downtown Nashville. After years of drawing possible designs in the margins of their notebooks, they'd finally settled on something they hoped they would still like at age thirty—their first initials in medieval-manuscript letters. Miriam had volunteered to go first. Fifteen minutes into the appointment, Liam had gone for some fresh air. He had not returned. When it was over, Miriam had wandered outside and found Liam sitting on the curb three blocks away with his head between his knees.

"I can't do it." He shook his head.

Miriam felt sick. Four hundred dollars. The tattoo burned underneath layers of gauze.

"I just can't do it," he repeated. "I'm sorry, Mir."

She threw up by a lamppost.

Liam had walked to the Pizza Hut and bought her a Sprite. He was afraid he'd regret the tattoo. There was no way they were getting married right after high school like their parents. She'd sat down on the curb, lit a cigarette, and offered it to him. His concerns were legitimate, she'd told him. But even if it didn't work out, at the very least they would want something to remember the other by. Whatever happened, they would always remain friends.

"Have you thought about getting yours removed?" Miriam asked.

"I've thought about it." He rolled the ice around his glass with the little plastic sword. "When people ask I just tell them that the M stands for 'Mom.'" He smiled and looked at her sadly. "They think it's sweet."

"It's different for women." Miriam's ears grew hot. "You never see guys wearing sleeveless tops."

"So you're saying that if you'd gotten it on your ass you wouldn't have it removed?"

Miriam opened her mouth and then closed it.

"It's all right." He laughed and slapped her shoulder.

Miriam struggled to think of something meaningful to say. Tell him, maybe, that she was glad that they had been such good friends, or how on his birthday she thought about calling but never did. She was relieved to see Gloria walk up to them, her face flushed and exasperated. Miriam was requested upstairs. More than likely it was trouble with the bustle. Ten hooks! She followed Gloria up the long winding staircase.

In the dressing room, half-eaten finger sandwiches and overturned plastic cups were strewn across a card table. The bridesmaids' gift bags were lined up neatly by the bathroom door next to a pile of jeans and sneakers. Beth sat at the edge of an antique chair, the tulle of her dress blooming around her so that she looked like a stamen in the center of a giant flower. Gloria shut the door behind Miriam, and Beth glanced at her nervously. Miriam told herself there must be a serious problem with the bouquet toss or speaker system, but looked at Beth's face and knew that it was none of these. She leaned her back into the door.

"Did you see him? Did you see Caleb?" Beth asked.

"I thought I did, out on the patio," Miriam said. "Then I thought I made a mistake." Miriam meant to sound calm but her voice came out falsetto.

"We were hoping to get you up here before you saw him." Beth stood up to embrace her, but Miriam's arms felt too heavy and cold to return the hug. Caleb was being seen out to his car, Beth assured her. Someone would have to explain to John's cousin Mary-Beth why her plus-one had disappeared, but that wasn't so hard. Mary-Beth always had the worst taste in men.

They all sat down on the couch and said nothing. Miriam knew that Beth had already procured some emergency Xanax from her mother. A box of tissues waited on the coffee table. Beth and Gloria sat very straight, poised for her to do something dramatic. They were ready to console, restrain, or calm her. For instance, Miriam might take a lamp and throw it into the mirror, or lock herself in the bathroom for the rest of the night, or march to the bar and eat a jar of maraschino cherries. Any of these actions would have been understandable and acceptable. Miriam waited for a strong feeling to overcome her, but nothing did, or at least nothing she could communicate. A shiver of pleasure ran up her spine. Perhaps he had seen her. Perhaps he saw how well she looked. She sank into the couch, disappointed that he was leaving.

Even though they lived in the same town, Miriam had run across Caleb only a handful of times since the eighth grade. The last time was two years ago. She was visiting home over Christmas break from graduate school, driving her mother's truck to drop some old clothes at Goodwill. Caleb had jogged across the intersection in a polar fleece and a hunter's orange wool hat, his breath leaving puffs of steam in the air. He had looked better than well. He'd looked happy, with a thin, Buddha-like smile across his face. A thick layer of ice had covered the road and it was dark and gray outside. Had a car come and hit him, she would have liked to be the one to call an ambulance. She would ride in the back with him to the hospital. He would wear an oxygen mask and for a moment he would not know who she was but in his daze would mistake her for an angel. Then all at once he'd go wide-eyed with recognition. He would be unable to speak. She would take her glove off to squeeze his hand to let him know she had forgiven him, to demonstrate she no longer wished him dead.

Miriam told no one about these sightings. She treated these few moments with the same guilt and exhilaration others reserved for secret love affairs. Beth threaded her dress around her fingers; Gloria chewed on her lower lip. Everyone looked so pretty and fine today, even when their faces were tight with worry.

"You sure you're all right?" asked Beth. Miriam felt a dry lump form in her throat. In the never-ending list of awful things that happen to people each second, Miriam's awful thing was so small that she could render it insignificant. But whenever she thought it had disappeared completely, it would come back as clear and uncomfortable as a hot light on her face.

She had been only thirteen. She woke up in her underwear in the woods behind the First Baptist Church, covered in mosquito bites. He later admitted in the courtroom that he thought he had killed her by accident. In a panic he covered her body with a few branches and an old tire before running away.

He was three years older than her, the shortstop at the high school and the brother of a friend from the softball team. He brought them Gatorade and oranges and ran a special practice on how to steal bases. When he invited Miriam to drink in the basement with his high school friends, her heart somersaulted.

She spent what felt like hours looking for her clothes. For some reason her sneakers were still on. She had to pee terribly but nothing came out. Finally she covered her chest with her arms and limped across the parking lot to the side door of the church, where a gray-haired woman bolted from her car and threw a blanket across her. Miriam looked down and saw that the blanket had dog hair all over it, that it'd been used as a seat cover and not been washed in a very long time. "Let's call your parents," said the woman. It dawned on Miriam that she had stayed out long past her curfew. She would be grounded forever. Her heartbeat quickened. There was no way her mom would let her go to Myrtle Beach in the summer or play softball ever again. At the thought of her punishment she passed out in the woman's arms.

Miriam assured her friends that everything was all right. People
downstairs would be wondering where the new bride was. Beth
cried and mascara ran down her cheeks. Miriam retraced eyeliner
on Beth's lower lids and dusted blush on her cheekbones. Gloria
poured them all a glass of champagne and toasted Caleb's death
from a flesh-eating disease, or at least testicular cancer. Miriam
forced herself to laugh. The champagne bubbled in her throat
and a longing pooled up inside her. If only he had stayed he would
see how nice she looked tonight. She would walk across the room
and he would fidget nervously, not knowing what she wanted.
Then she would smile and ask how he was doing. She would look
him in the eyes and look at nothing else.

"I'll be right down," said Miriam.

"Want us to wait for you?"

"I could use a moment, if you don't mind."

Beth and Gloria nodded. Miriam went to the bathroom and
locked the door. She wanted to wash her face but that would require putting on her makeup all over again and she would never
make it down in time for the toast. She took a hand towel and ran
it under hot water, wrung it out, and put it over her chest until her
heart slowed down. Someone had forgotten to turn off the curling
iron. She opened and closed its trap. Once it might have calmed
her to press the hot metal to the nape of her neck and hold it until
it burned a flat red mark—but now she was too old to do such a
ridiculous adolescent thing.

Because she had been a minor her name had been kept out of
the newspaper. Everyone in town had known anyway. The gray-
haired lady at the First Baptist Church liked to talk. The drama
teacher had given Miriam a leading role in the high school musical, even though she was only a freshman and her audition was
terrible. Other teachers at school had been extra patient with her,
the way they were with the kids with autism. No one had asked her
to the homecoming dance. Boys had quit talking to her. Except for
Liam. Liam had still shot glances of undisguised longing across the
sea of cafeteria tables, like nothing had ever happened. Because of
him she had begun to remember what she used to feel like.

Miriam quietly walked back down the stairs. She could hear
Beth's dad making a speech, thanking all the loved ones who had

traveled so far to be here on this special occasion. That's what she'd tell Liam tonight. She'd tell him thank you.

L

The camel had the most beautiful long eyelashes. She blinked at Liam and chewed on something in the back of her mouth. After Miriam had gone upstairs, he realized he'd lost his keys and returned to the field to look for them. There was enough light left to maybe spot something metallic shining in the grass, but there was nothing unusual except the dark, humpbacked shape of the camel, who greeted him at the fence. The camel gave a low growl and carefully extended her neck without even grazing the wire. It didn't seem like she wanted to escape. He patted her on her muzzle and saw a large bald patch around her left ear. He rubbed it with his thumb and remembered she'd been rescued from a petting zoo. He hoped a person hadn't hurt her while she was there, but if so the camel seemed to have forgotten all about it.

"Did you eat my keys?" he asked the camel. Her lips felt the cuff of his jacket. "I'm sorry but I didn't bring anything with me." Disappointed, she turned and headed back to the barn.

Liam went back inside the house and retraced his footsteps. He searched on the floor near the long polished wooden bar, the billiards room in the basement with the red leather couch, the parlor with the out-of-print books lining the shelves, the organ whose keys made no sound but a hollow tapping. The house was regularly rented out for banquets, conferences, weddings, memorial services, and family reunions. In the daytime, seniors from the retirement home took piano lessons and played cards in the mint-colored breakfast room. The manager behind the front desk was an attractive older woman with a large silver clip fastening her hair. No keys had been found. She suggested he look in his car while he was at it.

"Please, please, please," he muttered as he jogged to the gravel parking lot. He had locked his sister's keys in the car last Thanksgiving and never heard the end of it. The parking lot had filled up and for a second he couldn't remember where he'd parked Julia's ancient Honda. He wandered the rows of cars when he saw Beth's dad, Mr. Johnston, step into the bright light of the side entrance and follow a man out. Mr. Johnston's large farmer's hands rested on the man's shoulders, but not in a friendly way. They stopped at a truck, where the man turned around and said a few quiet words, keeping his gaze low. When he opened the driver's door the light from inside shone on his face.

If the universe had any fairness in it, Caleb would have been missing a few teeth. He would have aged prematurely, or grown bloated and red-faced from drinking, or haggard and thin from drug use. Had he been a decent man he would have, at the very least, bags under his eyes from not getting a good night's sleep in the past fifteen years. But he looked well-rested, handsome even.

Caleb started his truck and slowly drove down the gravel road. Mr. Johnston stuffed his hands in his pockets and waited till the taillights disappeared before turning back toward the house. Liam discovered his feet would not move. A rush of blood returned to his hands when he unclenched his fists. Miriam had once brought him to the library at the high school and opened the old yearbook with Caleb's picture from his junior year, before he was sent off to juvie. "He doesn't look crazy, does he?" whispered Miriam. Her eyes settled on the page with a kind of unnerving softness. She swallowed and placed the yearbook back onto the shelf. As they walked to math class Liam told her that he'd kill Caleb when he got out. Miriam didn't respond. Or maybe he wouldn't kill him, Liam said. Maybe he'd just break his arms, or beat his face so no woman would look at him.

Miriam had grabbed Liam by the sleeve and pulled him into the stairwell. "That's not why I showed you," she told him. Then what was the point?

"I don't know." Miriam shook her head. She'd dyed her hair red for the school play and the color made her hazel eyes appear bright green. She put a finger in the center of his chest. "If you touch him," she said, "I'll never speak to you again."

He saw from her face that she'd gone to a place deep inside herself, and he knew she would never allow him to go there. That was all right, Liam had decided. He didn't need to understand her secrets to love her completely.

Around eleven o'clock, Miriam dragged Liam from his spot in the corner and onto the dance floor. Up close he noticed the absence of freckles across the bridge of her nose. She always used to get freckles at this point in the summer and tried to cover them up with powder. Her round face had grown sharper, especially when she smiled. Liam felt awkward dancing. "I can hear you counting inside your head," she teased him.

He wondered what Miriam would look like had she simply been a pretty woman at a friend's wedding. Her long blond hair was pulled into a bun with loose pieces around her face. Like all the bridesmaids, she wore a fragrant white flower behind her ear. Nothing in Miriam's movements or behavior indicated that she had seen Caleb, and yet Liam felt certain that she had seen him and was now refusing to let this incident ruin a good party.

They danced four songs in a row when she suddenly leaned into Liam, turning her face so that her temple met the inside curve of his neck.

The feeling it gave him was this: Miriam had been dead for years. She now had returned for one night to dance with him in a large house with all these people who couldn't see her ghost.

He felt an emotional pain so sharp that he staggered into an elderly couple dancing nearby. Miriam apologized and rolled her eyes at Liam. She led them into the next dance, a slow Latin song that brought a little cheer from half the dance floor. It appeared that the entirety of Tennessee had been taking ballroom-dance class since he moved out to California. The best dancers, he noticed, were the grandparents who didn't know the steps but brought with them a generational knowledge of the cha-cha and the Texas swing so that their pear-shaped bodies, their flat and wide rears, their bony shoulders, were all infused with such lightness and grace that the song didn't feel at all foreign. Miriam's right thigh gently pressed the inside of his right leg and they rocked back and forth. The half erection caused by this movement was little more than an erratic wandering of the blood, the result of breaking up with Crystal three months ago. Miriam must have felt the hardening between his legs but instead of moving back she drew him nearer. He realized she must be drunk. When he didn't push her away he realized that he was drunk too.

"What's this type of song called?" he asked over the music.

She said a word in Spanish that he forgot almost immediately, but the word sounded like it could mean both *hello* and *goodbye*, *so long* and *please come here*. When the song came to an end Miriam walked away without saying a word or looking at him, exiting through the tall doors that led out to the back porch. A fiddle swelled into a country tune that everyone knew the chorus to. He excused himself across the dance floor. Outside the paper lanterns dimly lit the porch where a few smokers had congregated, and Miriam waited at the top of the steps for him until he saw her. She disappeared into the dark backyard.

Liam walked down the steps and waited for his eyes to adjust to the darkness. The moon was bright and high, and the sky was full of different shades of gray and dark blue clouds. It felt like it might rain. It felt like it would be a terrible idea to have sex with her in the long insect-ridden grass. He would find her, lead her back inside, and order them both a club soda. He would make sure she found a sober ride home, and the next morning, he'd invite her out to breakfast to let her know there was nothing to be embarrassed about. The grass was wet and cold and Miriam had discarded her shoes, one after the other. He picked these up and held them in his left hand by their straps. He could recall what she had been like before this kind of loneliness. And then everything that had happened to her happened to her, and afterward it was like she carried a bomb inside that couldn't explode. Maybe it wasn't such a terrible idea. Maybe it could make them happy. He found a mark on Miriam's shimmering pale dress and followed it through the trees.

Jack, July

FROM *The New Yorker*

THE SUN WAS a wolf. The fanged light had been trailing him for hours, tricky with clouds. As it emerged again from sheepskin, Jack looked down at the pavement, cursed. He'd been walking around since ten, temperature even then close to ninety. The shadow stubs of the telephone poles and his own midget silhouette now suggested noon. He had no hat, and he'd left his sunglasses somewhere, either at Jamie's or at The Wheel, or they might have slipped off his head. They did that sometimes, when he leaned down to tie his shoes or empty them of pebbles.

Pebbles?

Was that a word? He stopped to consider it, decided in the negative, and then marched on, flicking his thumb ceaselessly against his index like a Zippo. His nerves were shot, but unable to shut down. No off button now. He'd be zooming for hours, the crackle in his head exaggerated by the racket of birds rucked up in towers of palm, tossing the dry fronds. What were they doing? Ransacking sounds. Looking for nuts or dates, probably. Or bird sex. Possibly bird sex. Maybe he should walk to Rhonda's, ask her to settle him. Or unsettle him. Maybe he wanted more. *Share* was what she should do, if she had any. He always shared with her. Not always, but it could be argued.

Rhonda was a crusher, though, a big girl, always climbing on top. Her heft was no joke, and Jack was a reed. Still, he loved her. Ha! That was the tweak coming on. He'd never admit to such a thing when he was flat. Now his immortal brain understood. He wanted to marry Rhonda, haul her up the steps of her double-wide, pump out about fifty kids. In the fly-eye of his mind he saw them, curled up like caterpillars on Rhonda's bed.

Jack picked up the pace. The effect of his late-morning tokes was far from finished. Though he'd pulled nothing but dregs (the last of his stash), it was coming on strong, sparking his heart in unexpected ways.

So much gratitude. Jack made a fist and banged twice on his chest, thinking of Flaco, a school friend, now dead, who'd first turned him on to this stuff—a precious substance whose unadvertised charm was love. It was infuriating that no one ever mentioned this. The posters, the billboards, the PSAs—all they talked about were skin lesions and rotten teeth. Kids, sadly, were not getting well-rounded information. If Jack hadn't lost his phone, he'd point it at his face right now and make a documentary.

Traffic, a lot of it. On Speedway now, a strip-mall jungle, which, according to his mother, used to be lined with palm trees and old adobes, tamale peddlers and mom-and-pop shops. Not that Jack's mother was nostalgic. She loved her Marts—the Dollar and the Quik and the Wal. "Cheaper too," she said. She liked to buy in bulk, always had extra. Maybe he should go to her place, instead of Rhonda's, grab some granola bars, a few bottles of water for his pack. Sit on the old yellow couch under the swamp cooler, chew the fat. He hadn't seen her in weeks.

Weeks?

Again, the word proved thin, suspect. "Mama," he said, testing another—an utterance that stopped him in his tracks and caused his torso to jackknife forward. Laughed to spitting. He could picture her face, if he ever tried to call her that. She preferred Bertie. Only sixteen years his senior, she often reminded him. Bertie of the scorched hair, in her sparkle tops and toggle pants. "What's it short for?" he once asked of her name. She'd told him that his grandfather was a humongous piece of shit, that's what it was short for.

Of course, Jack had never met the famous piece of shit, had only heard stories. Supposedly he and Grandma Shit still lived in Tucson, might be anywhere, two of Jack's neighbors. He might have passed them on the street, or lent them an egg or a cup of sugar.

Jack tittered into his fist. What eggs? What sugar? There was

fuck-all in the fridge. In fact, depending on his location, there
might not even be a fridge.

Buses roared past, their burning flanks throwing cannonballs of
heat at the sidewalk. Jack turned away, moved toward himself, a
murkier version trapped in the black glass façade of a large building. Twenty-two—he looked that plus ten. Of course, a witch's mirror was no way to judge. The dark glass was spooked, not to be
trusted. Hadn't Jamie said, only yesterday, in the lamplit corner
of the guest bedroom, that Jack looked all of sixteen? "Beautiful,"
Jamie had whispered, touching Jack's cheek.

   Beautiful. Like something stitched on a pillow, sentimental crap
from some other era. The lamplit whisperings had made Jack rest-
less, the dissolved crystal blowing him sideways like a blizzard.

   To hell with Jamie! Last week, after partying all night, Jack had
woken up to find Jamie lying beside him, the man's hand crawling
like a snail across the crotch furrows of Jack's jeans. Half dead, in
deep crash, Jack hadn't even been sure they *were* his jeans—the
legs inside them looked too skinny, like a kid's. He'd watched the
snail-hand for a good five minutes, feeling nothing—and then,
with a gush, he'd felt too much. When he leaped from the bed,
Jamie screeched, "Oh my gosh! Oh my gosh!"—apologizing pro-
fusely, claiming he'd flailed in his sleep.

   "Why are you in my bed *at all?*" Jack had asked, storming into the
bathroom with shame-bitten fury. He'd got into the shower, only
to find a bar of soap as thin and sharp as a razor blade—scraped
himself clean as best he could, until he smelled breakfast coming on hot from the kitchen. It had turned out to be silver-dollar
pancakes with whipped cream and chocolate chips. Jack's favorite.
Could the man stoop any lower?

   Jamie just didn't add up. A bearded Mexican with a voice like
a balloon losing air. Wore pleated slacks, but without a belt you
could sometimes glimpse thongs. Didn't smoke, but blew invisible
puffs for emphasis. And the name—Jamie—it sat uncomfortably
on the fence, neutered, a child's name, wrong for anyone over
thirty, which Jamie clearly was. Plus he was fat, which made his
body indecisive, intricately layered with loose slabs of flesh—pot-
belly and motherflaps. "Stay with me, why don't you?" he'd said,
for no discernible reason, at the Chevron restroom sink, where
Jack had been rinsing his clotted pipe.

That had been a week ago, maybe two. They'd been strangers in that restroom, the obese man appearing out of the gloom of a shit stall. His words, *stay with me,* had seemed, to the boy, vaguely futuristic, a beam of light from a spaceship.

Jack should have known better.

The sun drilled the boy's head, looking for something. He closed his eyes and let the bit work its way to his belly, where the good stuff lived, where the miracle often happened: the black smoke reverting to pure white crystal. A snowflake, an angel. He smiled at himself in the dark glass. It was so easy to forgive those who betrayed you, effortless—like thinking of winter in the middle of July. It cost you nothing. Reflexively Jack scratched deep inside empty pockets, then licked his fingers. The bitch of it was this: forgiveness dissolved instantly on your tongue, there was no time to spit it out.

He'd have to remember to speak on this, when he made his documentary.

"Welcome to Presto's!"

The blond girl stood just inside the black door, her face gaily frozen, as if cut from the pages of a yearbook. Jack comprehended none of her words.

"Welcome," he replied, attempting a flawless imitation of her birdlike language. Jack was good with foreigners. Most of his school buds had been Chalupas.

The girl tilted her head; the smile wavered, but only briefly. Her mouth re-expanded with elastic lunacy.

"Ship or print?"

Jack was taken aback. Though it was true he needed to use the bathroom, he was disturbed by the girl's lack of delicacy in regard to bodily functions.

"Number one," he admitted quietly.

"Ship?" she persisted.

Jack felt dizzy. The girl's teeth were very large and very white. Jack could only assume they were fake. Keeping his own dental wreckage tucked under blistered lips, he lifted his hands in a gesture of spiritual peace. "I'm just going to make a quick run to the restroom."

"I'm sorry, they're only for customers."

"George Washington," Jack blurted, still fascinated by the girl's massive teeth.

"What's that?"

"Cherry tree," he continued associatively.

"Oh, like for the Fourth?" asked Blondie.

"Yes," Jack replied kindly, even though he knew she was confusing presidents. Fourth of July would be Jefferson or Adams. Jack had always been sweet on History. In school, when he was miniature, he'd got nothing but A's. Again he sensed the expansiveness of his brain, a maze of rooms, many of which he'd never been in. It didn't matter that he hadn't finished high school, there was an Ivy League inside his head, libraries crammed with books. He just needed to pull them from between the folds of gray matter and read them. Close his eyes and get cracking. See, this was the other thing people never told you about meth. It was educational.

The girl informed him that there were no holiday specials, if that's what he was asking about.

Jack nodded and smiled, tapping his head in pretense of understanding her logic. As he moved quickly toward the bathroom, the girl skittered off in another direction, also quickly.

Perhaps she had to print too. Or take a ship.

Jack giggled and opened a door leading to a storage closet.

"Can I help you?"

"Yes," Jack said to the man inside the closet. "I understand what you're saying."

"What am I saying?" asked the man.

"Perfectly clear," said Jack. He held up his peace-hands, walked back through the room of humming and spitting machines, and exited the building—behind which he quickly peed, before resuming his trek down Speedway.

As soon as he knocked at the trailer door, he was aware of the emptiness in his hands. He should have brought flowers. Or a burrito. He knocked again. Sweat dripped from under his arms, making him feel strangely cold.

"I have flowers," he said to the door.

"Go away," said the door.

"I'm not talking to a door," said Jack. "I don't take orders from doors."

"You can't be here. Why are you here?" The voice was exhausted, cakey. Jack could picture the pipe.

"Baby," he said. "Come on. Why are you being stingy?"

"I'll call the police, I swear to God."

Jack was silent, but stood his ground. He scratched at the door like a cat. After a while, someone said, "Please." The word sounded funny, like a flute. Jack tried saying it again. Even worse. It almost sounded as if he were going to cry.

When the door opened, it did so only a few inches—most of Rhonda's mouth obscured by a chain.

"You cannot be here, Jack."

Jack, who was clearly there, only smiled.

"I'm OK," he assured her.

"You look like shit," said Rhonda.

"Sunburn," theorized Jack. "It's like a hundred and twenty out here." He could barely see the girl—or he could see her, just not recognize her. She seemed different, her hair and her clothes fussed up, neat. He smelled no smoke, only perfume. "What's going on?" he asked, flicking his thumb.

Rhonda made an irritated snort, half laugh, half fart. It seemed to come from her mouth.

Jack, confident he was at the peak of his charm, refused to be put off. "Can you just open the door, so that we can talk like humans, without the frickin' mustache?"

"The what?"

"The . . ." Jack gestured swoopily toward the door. "The frickin' . . ."

"Chain?" suggested Rhonda.

"All I want is, like, *hello*, OK? Like hello, whatever, a glass of water."

The girl grimaced dramatically, egging on Jack's own sense of tragedy.

"I am literally dying, Rhonda."

Jack pressed his face into the door crack, letting the cool air caress his skin. His eyes, blinded from sunlight, barely took in the fact that the girl was gone. After a moment, he heard water running in the sink, the clink of a glass being pulled from a cupboard. He closed his eyes, felt a stirring between his legs. Rhonda had always been so kind.

"I don't need ice," he called out.

"Good. Here you go."

At first Jack wasn't sure what it was. The water thrown in his face was cold. It dripped down his neck and into his shirt, slow trails across his belly. It lingered, drifted lower, like a kind of kiss. Jack licked his lips: the tap water salty, mixed with his sweat. Something was humming too—the bones under his cheeks, near his eyes, vibrating like a tuning fork or an organ at the back of a church.

"Don't cry," he said to Rhonda, who said she wasn't.

"Why would I be crying after a fucking year?"

Jack said, "What year?"—to which Rhonda replied, "I thought you were dead."

She wasn't making a whole lot of sense. Jack asked if she was going fast.

"Are you insane?" said Rhonda. "Those were the worst two months of my life."

"Why don't I come in and we'll take a nap?" suggested Jack.

"Listen to me," the girl said. "You have to lose this address—do you hear me?"

Jack ran a hand over his wet face.

"Please," begged Rhonda. "You have to go. Eric will be home soon."

Jack wondered if she meant *Jack*, since the names were so similar. "Do you mean *me?*" he asked in earnest. He tried to find the girl's eyes—and when he did he saw that she wasn't a girl at all. She was old, practically as old as Bertie. What was more astonishing, though, was the look on her face. There was no love in it whatsoever.

"I don't know you," said Jack.

"Good," said Rhonda, shutting the door.

He stood on some gravel, and felt terrible. Even the little plank of shadow beside the cement wall held no appeal. Was he to lie there, he'd only get the jits.

Walking was what he needed, and to hell with the sun.

That's what people in his position did. They walked, they moved, they got things done. Sitting was no good. Talking was fine, if you had someone. Sex was primal. Jack's body knew the rules. There were any number of ways to keep one's brain from exploding.

People going fast rearranged the furniture, or crawled around looking for carpet crumbs. Anything that used your hands, which, compelled by the imaginative fervor of your mind, became tools in a breathless campaign to change the shape of the world. It was art, essentially. Jack wondered why more people going fast didn't do crafts. He suddenly wished for construction paper and Elmer's glue; glitter, cotton, clay. Once, when he was little, he'd made a kick-ass giraffe from a walnut and some toilet-paper tubes. The legs, ingeniously, had been chopsticks.

Bertie used to leave them for hours, on the days she attended her meetings. She'd always made sure there were coloring books and Play-Doh, carrot sticks and DVDs. Little notes saying *Love* and *Be back soon.* Jack and his sister had in no way been deprived.

His sister? *Fuck.* His sister. She came back to him like sheet lightning. He hadn't seen Lisa since she'd gone away. He clapped his hands, to banish the thought. It was almost funny how, at certain elevations, it was so easy to pretend you didn't know things you could never forget. Jack dug for his phone, to see if he had Lisa's number.

But, being that there was no phone, he pulled up only lint—which he quickly dismissed, into the air, with a puff. He watched it float for a moment, fluttering with indecision, before it drifted down, in a slow sashay, and landed on his shoe.

"Fine," said Jack. "Fine!" He picked up the gray fluff and stuffed it back in his pocket.

Walked around the block to see if he could trick it. He'd done it before. Pull one over on time. Circle back and confuse it. Like one of those Aborigines. They were big walkers too. Ugly fuckers, but the cool thing was they could walk a thousand miles, no problem—and they weren't trying to get to China or some shit like that. What they wanted was to get back to their ancestors—way the fuck past Grandma and Grandpa, all the way back to the lizards and the snakes.

Jack, of course, would have been satisfied with a smaller victory—finding his way back five, six years, to Bertie's crumbling adobe. *Star Trek* and pizza with Lisa. Hell, he'd be fine with getting back to just last year, to the old Rhonda, the Rhonda of the bra-welted back and the cream-cheese thighs, the sad girl he'd met at The Wheel, and whom he'd made happy with snowflakes and black clouds.

Had it really been a year? Jack felt nervous now, flicked his thumb even faster, sensed his shadow growing longer, trailing him like gum stuck to his shoe. Soon, he knew, the freak would come, the soul-suck, if he didn't get one of two things: more crystal or a sound sleep—both of which would require money, because sleep, at this point, wouldn't be free. It would cost a bottle of grain or a six-pack or a pill. Sometimes he wondered why a person couldn't just hit himself over the head with a rock.

He climbed on top of the gas meter and opened the window, as he'd done a million times before. A small, high window, facing the alley. Lisa's window, which Bertie never locked.

A tight fit, even for a skinny drink like Jack. Halfway through, he found himself stuck, but with a series of wriggling bitch-in-heat motions he managed to make it through, headfirst, onto the dusty shrine of his sister's neatly made bed. The friction of passing through the small opening, though, had pulled down his pants, as well as given him an erection. When he stood to hoist his jeans, a young woman in yoga tights entered the room, dropped a pear, and screamed.

Jack, thinking the pear was some sort of grenade, covered his head, leaving his erection exposed.

The woman moved quickly to the bureau and grabbed a bead-encrusted candlestick that Lisa had made in sixth grade. Jack, watching the drama through smoke-scented fingers, calmed, seeing the familiar prop. Plus, the grenade, bearing teeth marks, was obviously a ruse.

"I'm not here to hurt you," said Jack—a comment that, judging by the woman's anguished face, failed to impart the cordiality he wished to convey. The woman squealed and fled the room.

"I just want to see Bertie," Jack called out, pulling up his pants. "I'm her son. I'm Jack."

The idea of having to explain his existence exhausted him. When he walked into the living room, the woman was still clutching the candlestick—a lathe-turned beauty, to which Lisa had glued hundreds of tiny red beads. Jack had lent her the epoxy himself, a leftover tube from one of his build-it-yourself dinosaur sets.

"You can put that down," said Jack.

"Look," said the woman, "Beatrice isn't here. She won't be back for a while."

"Who?"

"You're looking for your mother?"

Jack felt a peculiar flutter in his gut.

"I'm meeting her in a—in a bit," stammered the woman. "I'll just—I'll let her know you were here."

"What did you call her?" asked Jack.

The woman took a step back. "Nothing. What?"

"Her name," Jack stated as calmly as possible, "is Bertie."

"Well, that's not how I know her," said the woman in yoga tights, who, even with the upraised candlestick, seemed to smile, a quick flash of arrogance.

"I can see your vulva," said Jack.

The woman covered her crotch with the candlestick. "My God, do you even know what you're saying?"

"It's inappropriate is all I'm saying," replied Jack, strolling over to the yellow couch. He sat at the far right, where the air of the swamp cooler always hit you square in the face. As kids, he and Lisa used to fight over this spot. "Fifteen minutes each," Bertie used to say, making them share the luxury equally. "Otherwise I'll shut the damn thing off." Frickin' Solomon, that was his mother all right. A part-time Christian with a gutter mouth.

Beatrice? For fucking real? How could Jack not have known this—or, more important, why had this information been kept from him? "I don't think you know what you're talking about," he said to the woman.

But she wasn't listening. She was on the telephone, giving an address Jack recognized. He made a blah-blah-blah gesture with his hand, as the woman prattled into the phone.

Why did no one wish to have a legitimate exchange with him? He was a good person, a personable person, a person with a heart the size of a fucking bullfrog. Couldn't the woman in yoga tights understand that there was no need to involve the police?

"I live here," said Jack.

The woman said, "Thank you," and hung up the phone. "I've called the—"

"I know," interrupted Jack. He crossed his legs, willing himself to stay calm. Anyway, it would take them at least ten minutes to get here. This wasn't a zip code anyone rushed to, especially the cops.

"Do you want to get arrested?" the woman asked. "I mean, do you *want* to be like this?"

"Like what?" asked Jack.

"Do you realize how much pain you've caused Beatrice?"

"Who are you, exactly?" Jack had the thought to have Yoga Tights arrested when the police arrived. "How do you even know my mother?"

"We're *room*mates," the woman articulated with unnecessary aggression.

Jack had a vision of pillow fights, s'mores, back rubs.

"Disgusting," he said.

"What's disgusting?"

Jack didn't reply—glass houses and all. He might as well be talking about himself and Jamie. He stood, annoyed, and walked over to the mirrored cabinet in the corner of the room. It seemed distinctly smaller than it had when he was little, like a toy version of the real thing. He kneeled before it, turned the silver latch, opened the doors. He stared inside, uncomprehendingly (*What the fuck?*), pushed around envelopes and stamps, a pile of old phone bills. He shoved his hands to the far back. Not even a bottle of Tio Pepe or crème de menthe.

"We don't keep any in the house," the woman said.

Jack scowled. He knew Bertie better than that.

"In case you care to know, your mother is doing really well."

Wonderful! thought Jack. Applause!

He stood, dusted himself off regally, as if he might dismiss the in-creeping panic. "I just need to get a few bottles of water."

In the kitchen, in the pantry, he pulled the cord, turned on the light. Well stocked, as usual. For Judgment Day, Bertie had always been prepared. With food, if not with mercy. "I can't be held responsible," Bertie liked to say. In a more generous mood, everything was God's plan, God's doing. Jack took six bottles of water and ten granola bars, stuffed them into his pack.

"Help yourself, why don't you?" the woman said.

Unbelievable. Un-fucking-believable. Jack turned to her. She was standing in the doorway, still holding the candlestick.

"Do you even know who that belongs to? Do you even know who made that?"

But the woman had no interest in discussing the relics of Jack's childhood. "Just take what you want and go," she said. "Beatrice would probably be pissed anyway, if I got you arrested. I don't know why she should be, though. You've been a very toxic influence on her." She shook her head, puffing air bullishly from her nose. "Everyone at Fellowship thinks so too, but your mother is, like, deluded."

The woman moved the candlestick from one hand to the other. Jack looked at her hard, just to make sure she wasn't Lisa. No one really knew what Lisa looked like these days.

You could always tell by the eyes, though—and when Jack looked at those he knew that Yoga Tights was not his sister.

"You're not even a very good replacement," he said.

"Replacement for what?" she asked.

But Jack did not deign to answer. He zipped his pack and, without even bothering to take the loose change visible on the counter, scurried out the back door.

He cut through neighbors' yards to avoid running into the cops. He leaped over stones, over crevices, over brown lawns and tiny quicksilver lizards. His speed exhilarated him and then made him feel distinctly ill. When he finally heard the sirens, he was three blocks away, in an alley frilly with trash. He lurched to a stop, sending up clouds of dust. A dry wind blew grit into his eye.

Fuck. He needed an improvement in his itinerary, like immediately. But he had no leverage. Not even two bucks for the bus. He should have taken the coins from Bertie's kitchen. Probably no more than a dollar, but a dollar was enough to get started. Four quarters in a newspaper lockbox and you could steal the lot, sell them from some busy intersection. Old-school, but it worked—even if, sometimes, it took five hours to make five bucks.

"What's that?" Jack said to his stomach, which was mumbling something vague but insistent. He fed it a granola bar, and immediately vomited. Drank some water. Vomited again.

Dirt, weeds, a huge prickly pear like a coral reef. Jack covered his burning head with his T-shirt, exposing his belly. Why hadn't the Founding Fathers planted more shade trees out here? Probably because the bastards had never made it this far west. The only people who'd ventured this far, back then, were derelicts and thieves. Uprooted types, not prone to plant things.

Jack was leaning philosophically against a fence for several minutes before he spotted the dog, sleeping on the other side. Not a pit, just some big floppy collie. Still, it reminded him of Lisa.

How could an animal sleep in this heat with all that fur? Jack kneeled in the alley, winding his fingers through the chain-link. *"Psst."* Rattled the fence. "Hey! Buster!"

The dog opened one eye, too stunned to get up. Shook a leg epileptically.

"You're just gonna lie there?" Piles of dried shit everywhere, like a miniature wigwam village. Again Jack rattled the fence.

"What are you doing? Why are you bothering him?" A little man with a lopsided beard, like a paintbrush that had dried crooked, appeared at a window.

"I'm not bothering him," said Jack. "I thought he was someone else."

"He's a dog," said the man. "He ain't got nothing to do with you."

Jack, riled, was ready to argue the point, but then let it go. He could see that the man was old, and so was the dog. Besides, his mouth was dry, and as he tried to get up his legs buckled.

The man snapped his fingers in Jack's direction. "No funny business!"

Jack nodded and backed away. "I'm going."

He walked about ten feet before he stopped, opened his backpack, and pulled out another granola bar—which he quickly unwrapped and tossed over the fence. "Get up for that, I bet."

The dog didn't hesitate. "I thought so," said Jack.

Instantly, though, the old man shot from the back door and pulled the food from the dog's mouth.

"It's not poison!" shouted Jack. "It's granola!"

A firecracker went off in the distance, and Jack turned. Next time, he thought, I'll do *that*—stick a firecracker in the damn granola.

For years, he'd hated every dog and experienced a paralyzing weakness in their presence. Now, despite the occasional flash of cruel intention, Jack's anger had mostly turned into something else. A dog, any dog, was like the relentless sunshine: mind-alteringly sad. Jack sat on the curb, touched his hand to blazing macadam.

Sometimes it could be burned out of you—the pain.

But no, the past was here, before him now like a mirage, wavering with tiny figures, holograms he recognized.

Resistance is futile, the Borg say.

Because not only had he run into a dog; he'd run out of his stash as well—and running out of crystal was like running out of time, sinking back into the mud that was your life. No dusting of white snow to prettify the view. With a mad, flea-scratching intensity, Jack scraped out the stem of his pookie, but what fell from it was worthless: a few flakes of irredeemable tar. The holograms grew to full size and came closer.

"*Grrr,*" said Jack, hoping he didn't sound like an animal.

Jack had been with his sister that day—a summer morning, playing Frisbee in a field. The Frisbee had gone over a fence.

The dog was black, not huge, the size of a twenty-gallon ice chest.

After the attack, Jack wondered if they'd really killed it. The police had used the words *put to sleep,* but Jack had worried that the owners might have somehow woken the animal up and were hiding it inside their house. Lisa's fears, no doubt, had been far worse—but Jack had known better than to ask her.

Anyway, Lisa couldn't really talk after it happened. She had a lot of problems with her jaw. With everything, really. Her right hand was so nerve-damaged that she had to use her left, which she never got very good at. She shook a lot, refused to eat, mostly drank smoothies. Her pinkie was missing.

Her face, though, was the worst. Even after two surgeries, it looked like something badly made, lumpy—as if a child had made it out of clay. It was less a face than the idea of one, preliminary, a sketch—but careless, with terrible proportions and slightly skewed; primitive—a face that might be touching in art, but in life was hideous.

"Look at that!" Bertie had shouted at the lawyer, showing him pictures of what Lisa had looked like before. "*Beautiful.* And this is what they're saying she's worth?"

The settlement had not been much. "An outrage," Bertie said to anyone who would listen. She tried to get another lawyer to take on the case. Jack would sit with his mother in cluttered offices, staring at the floor, telling the suits what he'd seen. "Happens every seven seconds," one lawyer said with disturbing enthusiasm, as if discussing the odds of winning the lottery. "Plus, you know how people in Tucson love their Rotts and their pits." Unfortunately, he explained, a jackpot settlement was usually tied to an attack catching the right wave of publicity. "Your moment has probably passed," he said with a wince, a shrug.

"That baby," Bertie would complain, referring to what she considered Lisa's competition.

The same summer, a two-year-old had been mauled near Sabino Canyon. There'd been a fund-raising campaign. "Foothills," Bertie had scoffed, after seeing the child's parents on television, their big house on a ridge. "As if they need help! We should start our own campaign," she'd muttered, after a sip, to Jack.

"We could make posters," he'd suggested sheepishly.

"Posters, TV commercials, the whole shebang." His mother pulled more deeply from her Captain Morgan mug, the ice clinking like money inside a piggy bank.

"Wanna make them pop, though," she said of the posters. "Need to get us some big-ass pieces of paper."

It would have been easy. Jack was artistic (everyone said so), and Bertie had balls. But, in the end, they'd never done a thing; never called a TV station or decorated a coffee can with ribbons and a picture of Lisa's face. Never took the case back to court—even though it was clear, after the initial surgeries, that Lisa would require more. The procedures couldn't be rushed, though. The doctor had recommended that Lisa wait before going back under the knife: "Too much trauma already. Let's see how the current work heals."

What little remained of the settlement money was kept in a separate account, like a vacation fund or a Christmas club, some perverse dowry. Money for the future, earmarked for surgery.

Jack had helped, at some point, hadn't he? Standing at the edge of the alley, he scratched his leg—a vague recollection that he'd given Lisa some of his own skin. It had been more compatible than Bertie's.

In the fall, Lisa had refused to go back to school for her junior year. She mostly stayed inside, in her bedroom. There was a lot of pain medication—which was apparently, Jack learned, something to be shared. "I'm in pain too," Bertie had cried, defensively, when he caught her one night with the bottle. "Anyway," she chided, changing the subject, "your sister can't live in a fog for the rest of her life. She needs to get a job."

Jack didn't understand why a person in Lisa's position couldn't be allowed to stay inside, in a dark bedroom, for the rest of her life. Bertie had a thing, though, about self-improvement and positive thinking, which often made her children shrink from her as if she were a terrorist.

Amazingly, Lisa had found a job fairly quickly, full-time at a tele-marketing firm. "You see," Bertie had chirped. "Up and at 'em," practically shoving Lisa out the door, her hair strategically feath-ered over her cheeks. "Minimum wage," Lisa said, and Bertie re-plied that there was no shame in that. All day, Lisa had sat in a cubicle, talked on the phone in her new funny voice. But maybe, thought Jack, the people his sister called just assumed she had a toothache, or an accent.

No one on the phone would have known that his sister was a high school dropout in Tucson—or that she'd been mutilated. That was a word no one had used—not the doctors or Lisa's friends or even the truth-obsessed women from Bertie's so-called church. No one ever said *maimed, destroyed, ruined.*

Bitten, people preferred to say, modestly, as if Lisa's misfortune had been the work of an ant, or a fly.

Jack rubbed his eye, swatted his cheek. As he headed downtown in long, loping strides, his body was dangerously taut, a telephone wire stretched between time zones. He needed to bring his think-ing back to 2000-whatever-the-fuck-it-was—*this* day, *this* street. "Ex-cuse me," he said to a woman with a briefcase and praying-mantis sunglasses—but before he could explain his purpose, she darted away and leaped into a black sedan. The woman obviously had issues; even from inside the vehicle, she was waving her hands at him in extreme sign language: *no tengo no tengo no tengo.*

After an hour and a half, he'd managed to assemble two dol-lars (a few quarters from a laundromat, a few obtained by outright begging). When he climbed onto the bus and dropped the coins in the chute, they made a sound like a slot machine promising a payout.

"What are you waiting for?" asked the driver.

"Nothing," mumbled Jack, taking a seat at the back.

He'd been looking forward to the air conditioning, but now it made him shake—the cold air, like pins on his face. Sometimes he'd met Lisa after her shift, to accompany her home. She hadn't liked to take the bus alone. She'd wanted Jack to ride with her in the mornings as well—but how could he? He was fifteen; he had school.

Anyway, the afternoons were enough. The walk to the back of the bus had always seemed to take a lifetime. People stared, kids laughed. Lisa never said anything, but sometimes she took Jack's hand, which embarrassed him: what if people thought she was his girlfriend? Sometimes he could hear her breathing; sometimes, a sound in her throat like twigs snapping.

That same year, Jack met Flaco. The first time they went fast together, in Flaco's enamel-black bedroom, it was like, *oh yes*—total understanding, total big picture, all the nagging little details washed away. Soon Jack stopped meeting Lisa after work. He let her take the bus alone, with nothing but her feathered hair to protect her; her head drooping like a dead flower; a white glove on her right hand like Michael Jackson, the pinkie stuffed with cotton.

It was OK, though. Because the funny thing was, he'd been able to love her more, and with less effort, from a distance. He felt that by going fast he was actually helping Lisa, he was helping all of them. He was building a white city out of crystal, inside his heart. When it was finished, there'd be room for everyone. For the first time in his life Jack had understood Bertie's nonsense about positive thinking, about taking responsibility for your own life. After Jack met Flaco, there were nights he didn't come home at all. Sometimes their flights lasted for days. Bertie might have complained, but she too was spending more and more time at her meetings. It was no surprise when Lisa said she was going away.

"Away? Where could you possibly go?" cried Bertie.

Lisa said she'd heard there was a good doctor in Phoenix; she'd start there.

"For how long?" Bertie had asked—and when Lisa didn't answer—"And I suppose you plan on taking the money with you?"

"It *is* mine," said Lisa.

No one could argue with that.

Jack pulled the cord, made his way to the rear exit of the bus. The door opened with a life-support hiss.

Whiplash of light coming off a skyscraper. Jack held up his hand to block the sun's reflection, a roundish blur of ghostly ectoplasm that hovered somewhere around the twentieth floor—which the boy's street sense interpreted, correctly, as roughly five o'clock.

Please be over soon, he thought, knowing full well that the day would linger for hours yet. Even after sunset, the heat would be terrible—the sidewalks, the streets, the buildings, radiating back the fire they'd absorbed all day. There'd be no relief until well after midnight.

Jack walked south, toward the barrio, toward the sound of fire-crackers, the whistle of bottle rockets. Later, at dark, the neon pompoms would come—the big holiday displays at the foothills resorts, and the city-sponsored show on Sentinel Peak, which half the time had to be stopped due to the scrub catching on fire. From the valley, you could watch the flames flowing down the mountain like lava. People looked forward to that as much as to the fire-works.

Jack walked with no particular purpose and was surprised when he found himself standing before Flaco's house. There was the white storybook fence around the neatly swept yard; the saint with her garland of artificial flowers, standing on a lake of tinfoil. At the Virgin's feet, a weird mix of things: playing cards and plastic beads, and what looked like pieces of old bread. Jack had always loved this diorama, which lived inside a little cage like a chicken coop. To protect it from the rain, Flaco's mother had explained.

He wondered if she'd still recognize him, maybe give him some *carne seca* wrapped in a tortilla as thin as tissue paper. In so many ways, his life had started in this house. A thousand hopes and dreams. Jack wondered if they were still in there, inside Flaco's spray-painted bedroom. Wondered too if there might be any crys-tal left in one of the old hiding spots.

Five years was a long time, though. Someone would already have smoked it or flushed it down the drain. And besides, Jack didn't have the stamina to crawl through another window. He was done with windows and doors. He half considered climbing inside the chicken coop with the saint.

The sadness bloomed in his belly. It always started there—a radioactive flower, chaotic, spinning out in weird fractals until it found its way to his arms and legs, his quivering lips. Then the telltale buzz of electricity in his hair.

See, this was the reason it was better to go fast with another per-son—so that when you crashed, you weren't alone. The high too was better when shared. Sometimes he and Flaco, as a team, could increase the effect of the drugs, pinballing around the bedroom, generating so much heat they could barely stand the feel of their clothing. Often they'd ripped off their shirts, lain next to each other on the bed, watched in amazement as their words turned into flames, rose into the air like rockets.

Flaco—and this was something Jack wished to mention in his documentary—Flaco had not died from crystal. It had been something else, something stupid, a car.

Walking away from the imprisoned saint, Jack passed old women putting lawn chairs along the street, claiming spots. *Brujas* in flowered smocks and slappy flip-flops, some with brooms, territorial. Later they'd sit there with glasses of watermelon juice and watch the fireworks, the burning mountain.

Farther south now, past Birrieria Guadalajara, where he and Flaco used to eat everything, even tongue.

Lengua.

Words no longer seemed chimeric to Jack, no longer seemed approximations for something else. They were earthbound now, which was what happened when you were sober. Jack clenched his fists—untrimmed nails digging into his flesh. All he wanted was to find a safe place before the blooms made a mess of the sky.

He stopped at the railroad tracks. Stopped right between the iron rails, kicked aside some trash, and sat. In his dark jeans, his dirt-brown shirt, they might not even see him. *"Ow,"* he said, because of the stones as he lay down.

While the sun cooked him, he became aware of how dirty he was. He could smell himself, even a slight tang of shit. Disgusting. His breath stank—and his stomach was bubbling, an ungodly flatulence from a diet of protein bars and black smoke. It was understandable why others would despise him. Most people lived their entire lives straight and had no ability whatsoever to see through surfaces—unlike Jack, who'd been schooled in crystal and who understood how easy it was to forgive.

Who knew if Lisa forgave him? He hoped she didn't. He was the one who'd thrown the Frisbee over the fence, a total spaz, missing Lisa by a mile. She'd pulled a face and told him to go get it. "You're closer," he'd shouted back. "You get it."

Jack turned his head, to see if he could spot the train. Flicker of distant traffic: metal and glass. Lost saguaros, catatonic, above which birds drifted in slow circles, like pieces of ash. To the east, the mountains, shrouded in dust, were all but invisible. The train would come eventually, the crazy quilt of boxcars, the fractious whistle.

Oh, but it was so boring waiting for death! Jack had come to the tracks before. When the signal light began to flash, he jumped up. He wasn't an idiot.

Besides, he couldn't help himself; his sadness was like a river, carrying him home.

"You don't like your life, make up another one." Something Bertie used to say. Her children had, in the end, listened to her.

Jack kept running, and when he got to Jamie's he didn't knock; he walked right in, sat at the table.

It wasn't long before Jamie came into the kitchen in his phony orange kimono ("*Mijo! Mijo!*"), flapping his arms, flushing, like something out of a Mexican soap opera.

And though Jack didn't laugh, he remembered the part of himself that had—and not so long ago. Still, he flinched when the man tried to touch his face.

In the silence that followed, Jamie began to smile.

"What?" said Jack—and Jamie said, "I'm just looking at you."

"Why?"

"Do I need a reason?"

Jack shrugged, evasive. "I'm sort of hungry."

"Well," Jamie said grandly, "you're dealing with an expert on that subject. The only question is: animal, vegetable, or *mineral?*" This last word sugarcoated, singsong.

Jack looked up, hopefully.

"Yes, *mijo.*" Jamie patted the pocket of his kimono. "I do I do I do."

"I do," repeated Jack, feeling his heart leap straight into the man's fat little hand.

Sh'khol

FROM *Zoetrope: All-Story*

IT WAS THEIR first Christmas in Galway together, mother and son. The cottage was hidden alongside the Atlantic, blue-windowed, slate-roofed, tucked near a grove of sycamore trees. The branches were bent inland by the wind. White spindrift blew up from the sea, landing softly on the tall hedges in the back garden.

During the day Rebecca could hear the rhythmic approach and fall of the waves against the shore. At night the sounds seemed to double.

Even in the wet chill of the December evenings, she slept with her window open, listening to the roll of the water sweeping up from the low cliffs, rasping over the run of stone walls, toward the house, where it seemed to pause, hover a moment, then break.

On Christmas morning she left his present on the fireplace, by the small tree. Boxed and wrapped and tied with red ribbons. Tomas tore the package open, and it fell in a bundle at his feet. He had no idea what it was at first: he held it by the legs, then the waist, turned it upside down, clutched it dark against his chest.

She reached behind the tree and removed a second package: neoprene boots and a hood. Tomas stripped his shoes and shirt: he was thin, strong, pale. When he tore off his trousers, she glanced away.

The wetsuit was liquid around him: she had bought it two sizes too big so he could grow into it. He spread his arms wide and whirled around the room: she hadn't seen him so happy in months.

She gestured to him that they would go down to the water in a few hours.

Thirteen years old and there was already a whole history written in him. She had adopted him from Vladivostok at the age of six. On her visit to the orphanage, she had seen him crouched beneath a swing set. His hair was blond, his eyes a pellucid blue. Sores on his neck. Long, thin scars on his lower back. His gums soft and bloody. He had been born deaf, but when she called out his name he had turned quickly toward her: a sign, she was sure of it.

Shards of his story would always be a mystery to her: the early years, an ancestry she knew nothing about, a rumor that he'd been born near a rubbish dump. The possible inheritances: mercury, radiation sickness, beatings.

She was aware of what she was getting herself into, but she had been with Alan then. They stayed in a shabby hotel overlooking the Bay of Amur. Days of bribes and panic. Anxious phone calls late in the night. Long hours in the waiting room. A diagnosis of fetal alcohol syndrome gave them pause. Still, they left after six weeks, swinging Tomas between them. On the Aeroflot flight, the boy kept his head on her shoulder. At customs in Dublin, her fingers trembled over the paperwork. The stamp came down when Alan signed. She grabbed Tomas's hand and ran him, laughing, through arrivals: it was her forty-first birthday.

The days were good then: a three-bedroom house in Stepaside, a series of counselors, therapists, speech experts, and even her parents to help them out.

Now, seven years on, she was divorced, living out west, her parents were gone, and her task had doubled. Her savings were stretched. The bills slipped one after the other through the letterbox. There were rumors that the special school in Galway might close. Still, she wasn't given to bitterness or loud complaint. She made a living translating from Hebrew to English—wedding vows, business contracts, cultural pamphlets. There was a literary novel or two from a left-wing publisher in Tel Aviv: the pay was derisory, but she liked stepping into that otherness, and the books were a stay against indifference.

Forty-eight years old and there was still a beauty about her, an olive to her skin, a sloe to her eyes, an aquiline sweep to her nose. Her hair was dark, her body thin and supple. In the small

village she fit in well, even if she stood at a sharp angle to the
striking blondness of her son. She relished the Gaeltacht, the shifting weather, the hard light, the wind off the Atlantic. Bundled up
against the chill, they walked along the pier, amongst the lobster
pots and coiled ropes and disintegrating fishing boats. The rain
slapped the windows of the shuttered shops. No tourists in winter.
In the supermarket the local women often watched them: more
than once Rebecca was asked if she was the *bean cabhrach*, a word
she liked—the help, the nanny, the midwife.

There was a raw wedge of thrill in her love for him. The presence of the unknown. The journey out of childhood. The step into
a future self.

Some days Tomas took her hand, leaned on her shoulder as
they drove through the village, beyond the abandoned school-
house, past the whitewashed bungalows toward home. She wanted
to clasp herself over him, shroud him, absorb whatever came his
way. Most of all she wanted to discover what sort of man might
emerge from underneath that very pale skin.

Tomas wore the wetsuit all Christmas morning. He lay on the floor,
playing video games, his fingers fluid on the console. Over the rim
of her reading glasses, Rebecca watched the gray stripe along the
sleeve move. It was, she knew, a game she shouldn't allow—tanks,
ditches, killings, tracer bullets—but it was a small sacrifice for an
hour of quiet.

No rage this Christmas, no battles, no tears.

At noon she gestured for him to get ready: the light would fade
early. She had two wetsuits of her own in the bedroom cupboard,
but she left them hanging, pulled on running shoes, an anorak, a
warm scarf. At the door Tomas threw his duffle coat loose around
the neoprene.

—Just a quick dip, she said in Irish.

There was no way of knowing how much of any language Tomas
could understand. His signing was rudimentary, but she could tell
a thing or two from the carry of his body, the shape of his shoulders, the hold of his mouth. Mostly she divined from his eyes. He
was handsome in a roguish way: the eyes themselves were narrow,
yes, but agile. He had no other physical symptoms of fetal alcohol,
no high brow, no thin lip, no flat philtrum.

They stepped out into a shaft of light so clear and bright it seemed made of bone. Just by the low stone wall, a cloud curtained across and the light dropped gray again. A few stray raindrops stung their faces.

This was what she loved about the west of Ireland: the weather made from cinema. A squall could blow in at any time and moments later the gray would be hunted open with blue.

One of the walls down by the bottom field had been reinforced with metal pipes. It was the worst sort of masonry, against all local tradition, but the wind moved across the mouths of the hollow tubes and pierced the air with a series of accidental whistles.

Tomas ran his hand over the pipes, one by one, adjusting the song of the wall. She was sure his fingers could gauge the vibrations in the metal. Small moments like these, they crept up, joyously sliced her open.

Halfway toward the water, he broke into a Charlie Chaplin walk—feet pointed out, an imaginary walking stick twirling as he bent forward into the gale. He made a whooping sound as he topped a rise and caught sight of the sea. She called at him to wait: it was habit now, even if his back was turned. He remained at the edge of the cliff, walking in place, rotating his wrist. Almost a perfect imitation. Where had he seen Chaplin? Some video game maybe? Some television show? There were times she thought that, despite the doctors, he might still someday crack open the impossible longings she held for him.

At the precipice, above the granite seastack, they paused. The waves hurried to shore. Long scribbles of white. She tapped him on the small of his back where the wetsuit bunched. The neoprene hood framed his face. His blond hair peeked out.

—Stay where it's shallow now. Promise me.

She scooted behind him on her hunkers. The grass was cold on her fingertips. Her feet slid forward in the mud, dropped from the small ledge into the coarse scree below. The rocks were slick with seaweed. A small crab scuttled in a dark pool.

Tomas was already knee-deep in the cove.

—Don't go any farther now, she called.

She had been a swimmer when she was a child, had competed for Dublin and Leinster both. Rows of medals in her childhood bedroom. A championship trophy from Brussels. The rumor of a

scholarship to an American university: a rotator cuff injury had cut
her short.

She had taught Tomas to swim during the warmth of the summer. He knew the rules. No diving. End to end in the cove. Never
get close to the base of the seastack.

Twice he looked as if he were about to round the edge of the
dark rock into the deeper water: once when he saw a windsurfer,
yet again when a yellow kayak went swiftly by.

She waved her arms: Just no more, love, OK?

He returned to her, fanned the low water with his fingers,
splashed it high around her, both arms in a Chaplin motion.

—Stop it, please, said Rebecca softly. You're soaking me.

He splashed her again, turned away, dove under for ten seconds, fourteen, fifteen, eighteen, came up ten yards away, spluttering for air.

—Come on, now. Please. Come in.

Tomas swam toward the seastack, the dark of his feet disappearing into the water. She watched his wetsuit ripple under the surface. A long, sleek shadow.

A flock of seabirds serried over the low waves in a taunt. Her
body stiffened. She edged forward again, waited.

I have, she thought, made a terrible mistake.

She threw off her coat and dove in. The cold stunned the length
of her, slipped immediately along her skin.

The second she climbed from the water, she realized she had left
her phone in the pocket of her jeans. She unclipped the battery,
shook the water out.

Tomas lay on the sand, looking up. His blue eyes. His red face.
His swollen lips. It had been easy enough to pull him from the
cove. He hadn't struggled. She'd swum up behind him, placed her
hands gently behind his shoulders, interlocked his fingers, pulled
him ashore. He lay there, smiling.

She whipped her wet hair sideways, turned toward the cliff. A
surge of relief moved along her spine when she glanced back: he
was following her.

The cottage felt so suddenly isolated: the small, blue windows,
the bright half-door. He stood in a puddle in the middle of the
floor, his lips trembling.

Rebecca put the phone in a bag of rice to soak the moisture, shook the bag. No backup phone. No landline. Christmas Day. Alan, she thought. He hadn't even called. He could have tried earlier. The thought of him in Dublin now, with his new family, their tidy house, their decorations, their dramas. A simple call, it would have been so easy.

—Your father never even phoned, she said as she crossed the room.

She wondered if the words were properly understood, and if they were, did they cut to the core: *your father, d'athair, abba?* What rattled inside? How much could he possibly catch? The experts in Galway said that his comprehension was minimal, but they could never be sure; no one could guess his inner depth.

Rebecca tugged the wetsuit zip and gently peeled back the neoprene. His skin was taut and dimpled. He lay his head on her shoulder. A sound came from him, a soft whimper.

She felt herself loosening, drew him close, the cold of his cheek against her clavicle.

—You just frightened me, love, that's all.

When darkness fell, they sat down to dinner—turkey, potatoes, a plum pudding bought from a small store in Galway. As a child in Dublin, she had grown up with the ancient rituals. She was the first in her family to marry outside the faith, but her parents understood: there were so few Jews left in Ireland, anyway. At times she thought she should rebuild the holiday routines, but little remained except the faint memory of walking the Rathgar Road at sundown, counting the menorahs in the windows. Year by year, the number dwindled.

Halfway through the meal they put on the party hats, pulled apart the paper crackers, unfolded the jokes that came within. A glass of port for her. A fizzy orange drink for him. A box of Quality Street. They lay on the couch together, his cheek on her shoulder, a silence around them.

She cracked the spine on an old blue hardcover. Nadia Mandelstam.

Tomas clicked the remote and picked up the game stick. His fingers flitted over the buttons: the mastery of a pianist. She wondered if the parents had been gifted beyond the drunkenness, if one day they had looked out of high conservatory windows, or painted daring new canvases, or plied themselves in some poetic realm, against all the odds—sentimental, she knew, but worth risking anyway, hope against hope, a faint glimmer in the knit of neurons.

Christmas evening slipped away, gradations of dark outside the window.

At bedtime she read to him in Gaelic from a cycle of ancient Irish mythology. The myths were a sort of music. His eyes fluttered. She waited. His turmoil. His anger. Night rages, the doctors called them.

She smoothed his hair, but Tomas jerked his shoulder and his arm shot out. His elbow caught the side of her chin. She felt for blood. A thin smear of it appeared along her fingers. She touched her teeth with her tongue. They were intact. Nothing too bad. Perhaps a bruise tomorrow. Something else to explain in the village store. *Timpiste beag*. A small accident, don't worry. *Ná bac leis.*

She leaned over him and fixed her arms in a triangle so that he couldn't bash his head off the wall.

Her breath moved the fringe of his hair. His skin was splotchy with small, dark acne. The onset of an early adolescence. What might happen in the years to come, when the will of his body surpassed the strength of her own? How would she hold him down? What discipline would she need, what restraint?

She moved closer to him, and his head dipped and touched the soft of her breast. Within a moment he was thrashing in the sheets again. His eyes opened. He ground his teeth. The look on his face: sometimes she thought the fear edged toward hatred.

She reached underneath the bed for a red hatbox. Inside lay a spongy black leather helmet. She lifted it out. *Kilmacud Crokes Are Magic!* was scrawled in silver marker along the side. Alan had worn it during his hurling days. If Tomas woke and began bashing again, it would protect him.

She lifted his head and slipped it on, tucked back his hair and fastened the latch beneath his chin. Gently, she pried open his mouth and set a piece of fitted foam between his teeth so they wouldn't crack.

Once he had bitten her finger while asleep, and she had given herself two stitches—an old trick she had learned from her mother. There was still a scar on her left forefinger: a small red scythe.

She fell asleep beside him in the single bed, woke momentarily unsure of where she was: the red digits on the alarm shining.

The phone, Rebecca thought. She must check the phone.

She went to the fridge for a bottle of white wine, stoked her bedroom fire, put Richter on the stereo, settled the pillows, pulled a blanket to her chest, opened the bottle, and poured. The wine sounded against the glass, a kindling to sleep.

In the morning Tomas was gone.

She rose sleepily at first, gathered the blanket tight around her neck. A reef of light broke through the bare sycamores. She turned the pillow to the cool side. She was surprised by the time. Nine o'clock. The wine still lay on her breath, the empty green bottle on the bedside table: she felt vaguely adulterous. She listened for movement. No video games, no television. A hard breeze moved through the cottage, an open window perhaps. She rose with the blanket around her. The cold floor stung her bare feet. She keyed the phone alive. It flickered an instant, beeped, fell dead again.

The living room was empty. She pushed open the door of his room, saw the hanging tongue of bed sheet and the helmet on the floor. She dropped the blanket from around her shoulders, checked under the bed, flung open the cupboard.

In the living room, the hook where the wetsuit had hung was empty.

The top half of the front door was still latched. The bottom half swung panicky in the wind. She ducked under, wearing only her nightgown. The grass outside was brittle with frost. The cold seeped between her toes. His name was thrown back to her from among the treetops.

The sleeves of grass slapped hard against her shinbones. The wind played its tune over the pipes. She spied a quick movement at the edge of the cliff—a hunched figure darting down and away, bounding along the cliff. It appeared again, seconds later, as if out of the sea. A ram, the horns curled and sharp. It sped away along the fields, through a gap in the stone wall.

Rebecca glanced down to the cove. No shoes on the rocks. No duffle coat. Nothing. Perhaps he had not come here at all. Good God, the wetsuit. She should never have bought it. Two sizes too big, just to save money.

She ran along the cliff, peered around the seastack. The wind blew fierce. The sea lay silver and black, an ancient, speckled mirror. Who was out there? There must be a coast guard boat. Or an early morning kayaker. A fishing craft of some sort. The wind soughed off the Atlantic. Alan's voice in her head. *You bought him what? A wetsuit? Why, for crying out loud?* How far might he swim? There were nets out there. He might get tangled.

—Tom-as! Tom-as!

Perhaps he might hear her. A ringing in his ears, maybe, a vibration of water to waken his eardrum. She scanned the waves. Snap to. Pull yourself together for fucksake.

She could almost see herself from above as she turned back for the cottage: her nightdress, her bare feet, her hair uncoiled, the wet wind driving against her. No phone, no fucking phone. She would have to get the car. Drive to town. The Gardaí. Where was the station, anyway? Why didn't she know? What neighbors were home? You bought him what? What sort of mother? How much wine did you drink? Fetal alcohol.

The wind bent the grass blades. She stumbled forward over the low wall, into the garden, a sharp pain ripping through her ankle. At the back of the cottage the trees curtsied. The branches speckled the wall with shadows. The half-door swung on its hinges. She ducked under, into his bedroom again. *Kilmacud Crokes Are Magic!* Still the phone did not work.

At the kitchen counter she keyed the computer alive. The screen flared: Tomas at six in Glendalough, blond hair, red shorts, shirtsleeves flapping as he sauntered through the grass toward the lake. She opened Skype, dialed the only number she knew by heart. Alan answered on the sixth ring. Jesus. What had she done? Was she out of her fucking mind? He would call the police, the coast guard too, but it would take him three or four hours to drive from Dublin. Phone me when you find him. Hurry. Just find him. He hung up into a sudden, fierce silence.

Rebecca put her head to the table. When she closed Skype, the background picture of Tomas appeared once more.

She ran to her bedroom, struggled into her old wetsuit. It chafed her body, tugged across her chest, scraped hard against her neck.

A menace of clouds hung outside. She scanned the horizon. The distant islands, humped and cetacean. The sweep of headland. Gray water, gray sky. Most likely he'd swum north. The currents were easier that way. They'd gone that direction in summer. Always close to shore. Reading the way the water flowed. Where it frothed against rocks, curved back on itself.

A small fishing boat trolled the far edge of the bay. Rebecca waved her hands—ridiculous, she knew—then scrambled down along the cliff face, her feet slipping in the moist track.

Halfway to the beach she stopped: Tomas's tennis shoes lay there, neatly pointed toward the sea. How had she missed them earlier? She would remember this always, she knew: she turned the shoes around, as if at any moment he might step into them and return, plod up to the warm cottage.

No footprints in the sand: it was too coarse. No jacket, either. Had he left his duffle behind? Hypothermia. It could come on within minutes. She had bought the wetsuit so big. He was more likely to be exposed. Where would he stop? How long was he gone now? She had woken so late. Wine. She had drunk so much wine.

She pulled a swimming cap hard over her hair and yanked the zip tight on her wetsuit. The teeth of it were stiff.

Rebecca waded in, dove. The cold pierced her. Her arms rose, rose, rose again. She stopped, glanced back, forced herself onward. Her shoulder ached.

She saw his face at every stroke: the dark hood, the blond hair, the blue eyes.

Out past the seastack, she moved along the coast, the sound of the waves in her ears, another deafness, the blood receding from her fingers, her toes, her mind.

A novella had arrived from the publisher in Tel Aviv eight months before, a beautifully written story by an Arab Israeli from Nazareth: an important piece of work, she thought.

She had begun immediately to translate it, the story of a middle-aged couple who had lost their two children. She had come upon the phrase *sh'khol.* She cast around for a word to translate it, but there was no proper match. There were words, of course, for *widow, widower,* and *orphan,* but none, no noun, no adjective, for a parent who had lost a child. None in Irish, either. She looked in Russian, in French, in German, in other languages too, but could find analogues only in Sanskrit, *vilomah,* and in Arabic, *thakla,* a mother, *mathkool*, a father. Still none in English. It had bothered her for days. She wanted to be true to the text, to identify the invisible, *torn open, ripped apart, stolen*. In the end she had settled upon the formal *bereaved*, not precise enough hardly, she thought, no mystery in it, no music, hardly a proper translation at all, bereaved.

It was almost noon when she was yanked in by the neck of her wetsuit. A coast guard boat. Four men aboard. She fell to the deck, face to the slats, gasping. They carried her down to the cabin. Leaned over her. A mask. Tubes. Their faces: blurry, unfocused. Their voices. Oxygen. A hand on her brow. A finger on her wrist. The weight of water still upon her. Her teeth chattered. She tried to stand.

—Let me back, she shouted.

The cold burned inside her. Her shoulder felt as if it had been ripped from its socket.

—Sit still now, you'll be all right. Just don't move.

They wrapped her in silver foil blankets, massaged her fingers and toes, slapped her twice across the cheek, gently, as if to wake her.

—Mrs. Barrington. Can you hear me?

In the blue of the skipper's eyes she thought she saw Tomas. She touched his face, but the beard bristled against her hand.

The skipper spoke to her in English first, then Irish, a sharpness to his tone. Was she sure Tomas had gone swimming? Was there any other place he might be? Had he ever done this before? What was he wearing? Did he have a phone? Did he have any friends along the coast?

She tried to stand once more, but the skipper held her back.

The wind buffeted the cabin windows, whitened the tops of the waves. A few gulls darted acrobatically above the water. Rebecca glanced at the maritime maps on the wall, enormous charts of line and color. A furnace of grief rose up in her. She peered out past the stern, the widening wake. The radio crackled: a dozen different voices.

She was making the sounds, she knew, of an animal.

The boat slowed suddenly, pulled into a slipway. A fine shiver of spray stung her face. She did not recognize the area. A lamplight was still shining in the blue daytime: a faint glow, a prospect of dark. Onlookers huddled by their cars, pointing in her direction. Beams of red and blue slashed the treetops. Rebecca felt a hand at her shoulder. The skipper escorted her along the pier. One of her blankets slipped away. She was immediately aware of her wetsuit: the tightness, the darkness, the cold. A series of whispers. She was struck by the immense stillness, the silence, not a breath of wind. *Sh'khol.*

She turned, broke free, ran.

When they pulled her from the water a second time, she saw a man hurrying toward her, carrying his cell phone, pointing it at her, watching the screen as he filmed her rising from the low, gray waves: she would, she knew, be on the news in just a few hours.

—Tomas, she whispered. Tomas.

A sedative dulled her. A policewoman sat in a corner of the room, silent, watching, a teacup and saucer in her hands. Through the large plate-glass window Rebecca could see figures wandering about, casting backward glances. One of them appeared to be scribbling in a notebook.

The Gardaí had set up in the living room. Every few moments another phone rang. Cars turned in the narrow laneway outside the cottage, their tires crunching on the gravel.

Somebody was smoking outside. She could smell a rag of it moving through the house. She rose to shut the bedroom window.

Something has ended, she thought. Something has finished. She could not locate the source of the feeling.

She paused a moment and strode across the floor toward the door. The policewoman uncrossed her legs but did not rise from the wicker chair. Rebecca strode out. The living room fell quiet, except for the static of a police radio. A wine bottle on the table. A discarded party hat. The scraps of their Christmas dinner heaped in the sink, swollen with dishwater.

—I want to join the search parties.

—It's best for you to stay here.

—He can't hear the whistles, he's deaf.

—Best stay in the cottage, Mrs. Barrington.

She felt as if she had chewed a piece of aluminum, the pain in her head suddenly cold.

—Marcus. My name is Marcus. Rebecca Marcus.

She pushed open the door of Tomas's room. Two plainclothes police were sifting through his cupboard drawers. On his bed was a small plastic bag marked with a series of numbers: strands of hair inside. Thin and blond. The detectives turned to her.

—I'd like to get his pajamas, she said.

—I'm sorry, miss. We can't let you take anything.

—His jammies, that's all I want.

—A question. If you don't mind.

As the detective approached, she could smell the remnants of cinnamon on him, some essence of Christmas. He struck the question sharply, like a match against her.

—How did you get that bruise?

Her hand flew to her face. She felt as if some jagged shape had been drawn up out of her, ripping the roof of her mouth.

Outside, the early dark had taken possession of everything.

—No idea, she said.

A woman alone with a boy. In a western cottage. Empty wine bottles strewn about. She looked over her shoulder: the other guards were watching from the living room. She heard the rattle of pills from the bathroom. An inventory of her medicine. Another was searching her bookshelves. *The Iron Mountains. Factory Farming. Kaddish. House Beautiful. The Remains of the Day.* So, she was under suspicion. She felt suddenly marooned. Rebecca drew herself to full height and walked back toward the living room.

—Ask that person outside to please stop smoking, she said.

He came down the laneway, beeping the car horn, lowered the window, beckoned the guard over: *I'm the child's father.*

Alan had lost the jowls of his occasional drinking. The thinness made him severe. She tried to look for the old self that might remain, but he was clean-shaven, and there was something so deeply mannered about him, a tweed jacket, a thin tie pushed up against his neck, a crease in his slacks. He looked as if he had dressed himself in the third person.

He buried his face in Tomas's duffle by the door, then sank theatrically to his knees, but was careful to wipe the muck when he rose and followed her to her bedroom.

The policewoman in the corner stood up, gave a nervous smile.

Rebecca caught a glance at herself in the full-length mirror: swollen, disheveled.

—I'd like to be alone with my wife, Alan said.

Rebecca lifted her head. *Wife:* it was like a word that might remain on a page, though the page itself was plunged into darkness.

Alan repositioned the wicker chair and let out a long sigh. It was plain to see that he was seeking the brief adulation of grief. He needed the loss to attach itself to him. Why hadn't she woken? he asked her. Was the door to her bedroom open or closed? Had she slept through her alarm? Had Tomas eaten any breakfast? How far could he swim? Why didn't you get him a wetsuit that fit? Why didn't you hide it away? Did you give him his limits? You know he needs his limits.

She thought about that ancient life in the Dublin hills, the shiny kitchen, the white machinery, the German cars in the pebbled driveway, the clipped bushes, the alarm system, the security cameras, the *limits,* yes, and how far the word might possibly stretch before it rebounded.

—Did he have gloves on?

—Oh stop, please, Alan.

—I need to know.

The red lights of the clock shone. It had been twelve hours. She lay on the bed.

—No, he had no gloves, Alan.

She could not shake the Israeli story from her head. An Arab couple had lost their two children to two illnesses over the course of five years: one to pneumonia, the other to a rare blood disorder. It was a simple story—small, intimate, no grand intent. The father worked as a crane driver in the docklands of Haifa, the mother as a secretary in a corrugated-paper firm. Their ordinary lives had been turned inside out. After the children died, the father filled a shipping container with their possessions and every day moved it, using the giant crane and the skyhooks, to a new site in the yard, carefully positioning it alongside the sea: shiny, yellow, locked.

—He feels invincible, doesn't he?

—Oh Jesus, Alan.

The search parties were spread out along the cliffs, their hopeless whistles in the air, her son's name blown back by the wind. Rebecca pushed open the rear sliding doors to the balcony. The sky was shot through with red. A stray sycamore branch touched her hair. She reached up. A crushing pain split her shoulder blade: her rotator cuff.

Cigarette smoke lingered in the air. She rounded the back of the cottage. A woman. Plainclothes. The whistles still came in short, sharp bursts.

A loss had lodged itself inside her. Rebecca gestured for the cigarette, drew long and hard on the filter. It tasted foul, heavy. She had not smoked in many years.

—He's deaf, you know, she said, blowing the smoke sideways.

A tenderness shone in the detective's eyes. Rebecca turned back into the house, pulled on her coat, walked out the front door and down toward the cliffs.

A helicopter broke the dark horizon, hovered for a moment right above the cottage, its spotlight shining on the stone walls, until it banked sharply and continued up the coast.

They went in groups of three, linking arms. The land was pot-holed, hillocked, stony. Every now and then she could hear a gasp from a neighboring group when a foot rolled across a rock, or a lost lobster pot, or a bag of rubbish.

The stone walls were cold to the touch. The wind ripped under a sheet of discarded plastic. Tiny tufts of dyed sheep wool shone on the barbed wire: patterns of red and blue.

Along the coast small groups zigzagged the distant beaches in the last of the light. Dozens of boats plied the waves. The bells on the ancient boats tinkled. A hooker went by with its white sails un-furled. A fleet of kayaks glided close to the shore, returning home.

The moon rose red: its beauty appeared raw and offensive to her. She turned inland. The detectives walked alongside. Rebecca felt suspended between them. Cones of pale torch beam swept through the gathering darkness.

At an abandoned home, roofless, hemmed in by an immense rhododendron bush, a call came over the radio that a wetsuit had been found, over. The male detective held a finger in the air, as if figuring the direction of the wind. No, not a wetsuit, said the voice, high alert, no, there was something moving, high alert, stand by, stand by, there was something alive, a ripple in the water, high alert, high alert, yes, it was a body, a body, they had found some-thing, over, a body, over.

The detective turned away from her, moved into the overgrown doorway, shielded the radio, stood perfectly still in the starlight until the call clarified itself: it was a movement in the water, discard, they had seen a seal, discard the last report, only a seal, repeat, discard, over.

Rebecca knew well the legend of the selkie. She thought of Tomas zippering his way out into the water, sleek, dark, hidden.

The female detective whispered into the radio: For fucksake, be careful, we've got the mother here.

The word lay on her tongue now: *mother, máthair, em.* They went forward again, through the unbent grass, into the tunnels of their torches.

Alan's clothing was folded on the wicker chair. His knees were curled to his chest. A shallow wheeze came from the white of his throat. A note lay on her pillow: *They wouldn't let me sleep in Tomas's room, wake me when you're home.* And then a scribbled, *Please.*

They had called off the search until morning, but she could hear the fishing boats along the coast, still blasting their horns.

Rebecca took off her shoes, set them by the bedroom fire. Only a few small embers remained, a weak red glow. The cuffs of her jeans were wet and heavy from the muck. She did not remove them.

She went to the bed and lay on top of the covers, pulled up a horsehair blanket, turned away from Alan. Gazing out the window, she waited for a bar of light to rise and part the dark. A torchlight bore past in a pale shroud. Perhaps there was news. At the cliff he had twirled the imaginary cane. Where had he learned that Chaplin shuffle? The sheer surprise of it. The unknowability. Unspooling himself along the cliff.

From the living room came the intermittent static of the radios. Almost eighteen hours now.

Rebecca pushed her face deeper into the pillow. Alan stirred underneath the sheets. His arm came across her shoulder. She lay quite still. Was he sleeping or awake? How could he sleep? His arm tightened around her. His hand moved to her hair, his fingers at her neck, his thumb at the edge of her clavicle.

That was not sleep. That was not sleep at all.

She gently pushed his arm away.

Another torch bobbed past the window. Rebecca rose from

the bed. A gold-backed hairbrush lay on the dressing table. Long strands of her dark hair were tangled up inside it. She brushed only one side of her hair. The damp hem of her jeans chilled her toes and she walked toward the wicker chair, covered herself in a blanket, looked out into the early dark.

When dawn broke, she saw the door open slightly, the female detective peeping in around the frame, something warm in the flicker that went between them. Alan stirred, pale in the bed, and moaned something like an excuse. His pinkish face. His thinning hair. He looked brittle to her, likely to dissolve.

In the kitchen the kettle was already whistling. A row of teacups were set along the counter. The detective stepped forward and touched her arm. Rebecca's eyes leaped to catch hers, a brief merged moment.

—I hope you don't mind. We took the liberty. There's no news yet.

The presence of the word *yet* jolted her. There would, one day, be news. Its arrival was inevitable.

—We took one of Tomas's shirts from the wash basket.

—Why? said Rebecca.

—For the dogs, the detective said.

Rebecca wanted suddenly to hold the shirt, inhale its odor. She reached for the kettle, tried to pour through the shake in her hands. So there would be dogs out on the headland later. Searching for her son. She glanced at her reflection in the window, saw only him. His face was double-framed now, triple-framed. He was everywhere. Out on the headland, running, the dogs following, a ram, a hawk, a heron above. She felt a lightness swell in her. A curve in the air. A dive. She gripped the hem of the counter. The slow, sleek slip of the sea. A darkening underwater. The shroud of cold. The coroner, the funeral home, the wreaths, the plot, the burial. She felt herself falter. The burst to the surface. A selkie, spluttering for air. She was guided into a chair at the table. She tried to lean forward to pour the tea. Voices vibrated around her. Her hands shook. Every outcome was unwhisperable. She had a sudden thought that there was no sugar in the house. They needed sugar for their tea. She would go to the store with Tomas later. The news agent's. Yes, that is where she would go. Inland along the bend of narrow road. Beyond the white bungalow. Crossing at the one traffic light. Walk with him past the butcher shop, past the sign for tours to the islands, past the turf accountant, past the shuttered hotel, the silver-kegged alleyway, into the news agent's on Main Street. The clink of the anchor-shaped bell. The black-and-white linoleum floor. Along the aisle. The sharp smell of paraffin. Past the paper rack set up on lobster pots, the small blue and orange ropes hanging down, old relics of the sea. She would walk beyond the news of his disappearance. Bread, biscuits, soup. To the shelf where the yellow packets of sugar lay. We cannot do without sugar, Tomas, second shelf down, trust me, there, good lad, get it, please, go on, reach in.

She wasn't sure if she had said this aloud or not, but when she looked up again the female detective had brought one of Tomas's shirts, held it out, her eyes moist. The buttons were cold to the touch: Rebecca pressed them to her cheek.

From the laneway came the sound of scraping branches. Van doors being opened and closed. She heard a high yelp, and then the scrabble of paws upon gravel.

She spent the second morning out in the fields. Columns of sunlight filtered down over the sea. A light wind rippled the grass at the cliff edge. She wore Tomas's shirt under her own, tight and warm.

So many searchers along the beaches. Teachers. Farmers. Schoolchildren holding hands. The boats trawling the waters had trebled.

At lunchtime, dazed with fatigue, Rebecca was brought home. A new quiet had insinuated itself into the cottage. The policemen came and went as if they had learned from long practice. They seemed to ghost into one another: almost as if they could slip into one another's faces. She knew them, somehow, by the way they drank their tea. Food had arrived, with notes from neighbors. Fruit bowls. Lasagna. Tea bags and biscuits. A basket of balloons, of all things: a scribbled prayer to Saint Christopher in a child's hand.

Alan sat next to her on the couch. He put his hand across hers. He would, he said, do the media interviews. She would not have to worry about it.

She heard the thud of distant waves. The labored drone of a TV truck filtered down from the laneway.

A Sunday newspaper called, offering money for a photograph.

Alan walked to a corner of the cottage, cupped his phone, whispered into the receiver. She thought she heard him weeping.

Pages from the Israeli novel were strewn across her desk. Scribbles in the margins. Beside the pages, Mandelstam's memoir lay open, a quarter of the way through. Russia, she thought. She would have to tell them in Vladivostok, let them know what had happened, fill out the paperwork. The orphanage. The broken steps. The high windows. The ocher walls. The one great painting in the hallway: the Bay of Amur, summertime, a yacht on its water, water, always water. She would find the mother and father, explain that their son had disappeared swimming on the western seaboard of Ireland. A small apartment in the center of the city, a low coffee table, a full ashtray, the mother wan and withdrawn, the father portly and thuggish. My fault. I gave him a wetsuit. All my fault. Forgive me.

She wanted the day to peel itself backward, regain its early brightness, its possibility, its pour into teacups, but she was not surprised to see the dark come down. It was almost two days now.

Alan sat in the corner, curled around his phone. She almost felt a sadness for him, the whispered *sweetheart,* the urgent pleading and explanations with his own young children.

That night, lying next to him, Rebecca allowed his arm across her waist. The simple comfort of it. She heard him murmur her name again, but she did not turn.

At daylight she totaled up the hours: forty-eight.

Rebecca rose and walked out into the morning, the dew wet against her plimsolls. The television truck hummed farther up the laneway, out of sight. She stepped across the cattle grid. The steel bars pushed hard into the soles of her feet. A muddy path led up the hill. The grass in the middle was green and untrodden. Moss lay slick on the stone wall.

A piece of torn plastic was tangled in the high hedges. She reached in and pulled it out, shoved it deep into her pocket: she had no idea why.

Water dripped from the branches of nearby trees. A few birds marked out their morning territory. She had only ever driven this part of the laneway before. It was, she knew, part of an old famine road.

Rebecca stood awhile: the hum from the TV truck up the road seemed to cancel out the rhythm of the sea.

She leaned into the hard slope of the road, opened the bar of the red gate, stepped over the mud. The bolt slid back perfectly into its groove. She walked the center grass up and around the second corner to where the TV truck idled against the hedges. Inside, silhouetted against a pair of sheer curtains, three figures were playing cards. The curtains moved but the figures remained static. Across the front seat a man lay slumped, sleeping.

A small group of teenagers huddled near the back of the truck, sharing a cigarette, their breath shaping clouds of white in the cold. They nudged each other as she approached.

She stopped, then, startled by the sight. Alone, casual, adrift. He sauntered in behind the group, unnoticed. A brown hunting jacket hung from his shoulders. A hooded sweatshirt underneath. His trousers were rolled up and folded over. The laces of his boots were open and the tongues wagged sideways. Steam rolled off him, as if he had been walking a long time.

His mouth was slightly open. His lip was wet with mucus. Mud and leaves in the fringes of his hair. Under his right arm he carried a dark bag. The bag fell from his arm, and he caught hold of it as he moved forward. A long, gray stripe. The wetsuit. He was carrying the wetsuit.

He had not yet seen her. His body seemed to drag his shadow behind him: slow, reluctant, but sharp. *Sh'khol.* She knew the word now. *Shadowed.*

The door of the TV truck opened behind her. Her name was called. Mrs. Barrington. She did not turn. She felt as if she were skidding in a car.

She was aware of a bustle behind her, two, three, four people piling out of the truck. The impossible utterance of his name. Tomas. Is that you? Turn this way, Tomas. A yell came from the teenagers. Look over here. They had their phones out. Tomas! Tomas! Turn this way, Tomas.

Rebecca saw a furred microphone pass before her eyes. It dipped down in front of her, and she pushed it away. A cameraman jostled her. Another shout erupted. She moved forward. Her feet slipped in the mud.

Tomas turned. She took him in her arms with a surge of joy.

She held his face. The paleness, the whites of his eyes. His was a gaze that belonged to someone else: a boy of another experience.

He passed the wetsuit to her. It was cold to the touch and dry.

The news had gone ahead of them. The cheers went up as they rounded the corner toward the garden. Alan ran along the laneway in his pajamas, stopped abruptly when he saw the television cameras, grabbed for the gap in the cotton trousers.

Rebecca shouldered Tomas through the gauntlet, her arm encircling him tightly, guiding him to the front door.

In the cottage, a swathe of light dusted the floor. The female detective stood in the center of the room. Her name badge glinted. Detective Harnon. It struck Rebecca that she could name things again: people, words, ideas. A warmth spread through the small of her back.

A smell of turf smoke came off Tomas's clothing. It was, she later realized, one of the few clues she would ever get.

The cottage filled up behind her. She saw a photographer at the large plate-glass window. All around her, phones were ringing. The kettle whistled on the stove. A fear had tightened Tomas. She needed to get him alone. The photographer shoved his camera up against the windowpane. She spun Tomas away as the flash erupted.

Morning light stamped itself in small rectangles on the bedroom floor. Rebecca closed the window blinds. The helmet was lying on the bed. His pajamas were neatly folded and placed on a chair. She ignored the knocking at the door. He was shivering now. She held his face. Kissed him.

The door opened tentatively.

—Leave us be, please. Leave us be.

She touched the side of his cheek, then shucked the brown jacket from his shoulders. A hunting jacket. She checked the pockets. A few grains of thread. A small ball of fur. A wet matchbook. He lifted his arms. She peeled the sweatshirt up over his head. His skin was tight and dimpled.

A piece of leaf fell from his hair to the floor. She turned him around, looked at his back, his neck, his shoulder blades. He was unmarked. No cuts, no scrapes.

She looked down at Tomas's trousers. Denims. Too large by far. A man's denims. Fastened with an old purple belt with a gold clasp. Clothing from another era. Gaudy. Ancient. A bolt of cold ran along her arms.

—No, she said. Please, no.

She reached for him, but he slapped her hand away. The door rattled again behind her. She turned to see Alan's face: the stretched wire of his flesh, the small brown of his eyes.

—We need a detective in here, she said. Now.

In the hospital it was still bright morning and the air was motionless in the low corridors and muddy footprints lay about and the yellow walls pressed in upon them and the pungent odor of antiseptic made her go to the windows and the trees outside stood static and the seagulls cawed up over the rooftops and she stood in the prospect of the unimaginable, the tangle of rumor and evidence and fact, and she waited for the doctors as the minutes idled and the nurses passed by in the corridors and the trolleys rattled and the orderlies pushed their heavy carts and an inexhaustible current of human misery moved in and out of the waiting room every story every nuance every pulse of the city hammering up against the wired windows.

The water poured hard and clear. She tested its warmth against her wrist. Tomas came into the bathroom, dropped his red jumper to the floor, slid out of his khakis, stood in his white shirt, clumsily working the buttons.

She reached to help, but he stepped away, then gestured for her to leave while he climbed into the swimming togs. So, he wanted to wear shorts now while she washed him. Fair enough, she thought.

The house was quiet again. Only the sound of the waves. She keyed her new phone alive. A dozen messages. She would attend to them later.

After a moment she returned to the bathroom with her hands covering her eyes.

—Ta-da! she said.

He stood there, pale and thin in front of her. The swimming shorts were far too tight. Along his slender stomach she could see a gathering of tiny, fine hairs that ran in a line from his belly button. He hopped from foot to foot and cupped his hands over the intimate outline of his body.

He had been untouched. That is what Detective Harnon had

said. He was slightly dehydrated but untouched. No abuse. No cuts. No scars. They had run all manner of tests. Later the detective had asked around the village. Nobody had come forward. There were no other clues.

They wanted him to come in for evaluation the following week. A psychologist, she said. Someone who might piece together everything that had happened, but Rebecca knew there'd never be any answers, no amount of probing could solve it, no photographs, no maps, no walks along the coastline. She would go swimming with him again, soon, down to the water. They would ease themselves into the shallows. She would watch him carefully negotiate the seastack. She would guide him away from the current. Perhaps some small insight might unravel, but she was aware she could never finally understand.

The simple grace of his return was enough. *I live, I breathe, I go, I come back, I am here now.* Nothing else.

Rebecca tested the water again with her fingers. She helped Tomas over the rim of the tub. Goose bumps appeared on his skin. His ribs were sharp and pale. He fell against her. The wet of his toes chilled her bare feet. She threw a towel around his shoulders to warm him, then guided him back toward the water. He finally placed both feet in the bath and let the warmth course up through his body. He cupped his hands in front of his shorts. She put her hand on his shoulder and, with gentle insistence, got him to kneel.

He slid forward into the water.

—There we go, she said in Hebrew. Let me wash that mop.

She perched at the edge of the bath, took hold of his shoulder blades, ran a pumice stone over his back, massaged the shampoo into his hair. His skin was so very transparent. The air in his lungs changed the shape of his back. She applied a little conditioner to his scalp. His hair was thick and long. She would have to get it cut soon.

Tomas grunted and leaned forward, tugged at the front of his shorts. His shoulders tautened against her fingers. She knew, then, what it was. He bent over to try to disguise himself against the fabric of his shorts. Rebecca stood without looking at him, handed him the soap and the sponge.

Impossible to be a child forever. A mother, always.

—You're on your own now, she said.

She moved away from him, closed the door and stood outside in the corridor, listening to his stark breathing and the persistent splash of water, its rhythm sounding out against the faint percussion of the nearby sea.

Thunderstruck

FROM *StoryQuarterly*

I.

WES AND LAURA had not even known Helen was missing when the police brought her home at midnight. Her long bare legs were marbled red with cold, and she had tear tracks on her face, but otherwise she looked like her ordinary placid awkward middle-school self: snarled hair, chapped lips, pink cheeks. She'd lost her pants somewhere, and she held in one fist a seemingly empty plastic garbage bag, brown, the yellow drawstring pulled tight at its neck. Laura thought the policemen should have given her something to cover up. Though what did cops know about clothing: maybe they thought that long black T-shirt was a dress. It had a picture of a pasty overweight man in swashbuckler's clothes captioned, in movie marquee letters, LINDA.

"She's twelve!" Wes told the police, as though they were the ones who'd lured his daughter from her bed. "She's only *twelve*."

"Sorry, Daddy," Helen said.

Laura grabbed her daughter by the wrist and pulled her in before the police could change their minds and arrest her, or them. She took the garbage bag from Helen, uncinched the aperture, and stared in, looking for evidence, missing clothing, wrongdoers.

"Nitrous oxide party," said the taller officer, who looked like all the Irish boys Laura had grown up with. Maybe he was one. "They inhale from those bags. The owner of the house is in custody. Some kid had a bad reaction, she threw them all onto the lawn. The others scattered but your daughter stayed with the boy in distress. So there's that."

"There's that," said Wes.

Helen gave her mother a sweet, sinuous, beneath-the-arm hug. She'd gotten so tall she had to stoop to do it; she was Laura's height now. "Mommy, I love you," she said. She was a theatrical child. She always had been.

"You could have suffocated!" Laura said, throttling the bag.

"I didn't put it over my head," said Helen.

Laura ripped a hole in the bottom of the bag, as though that were still a danger.

This was her flaw as a parent, she thought later: she had never truly gotten rid of a single maternal worry. They were all in the closet, with the minuscule footed pajamas and hand-knit baby hats, and every day Laura took them out, unfolded them, tried to put them to use. Kit was seven, Helen nearly a teenager, and a small, choke-worthy item on the floor still dropped Laura, scrambling, to her knees. She could not bear to see her girls on their bicycles, both the cycling and the cycling *away*. Would they even remember her cell-phone number, if they and their phones were lost separately? Did anyone memorize numbers anymore? The electrical outlets were still dammed with plastic, in case someone got a notion to jab at one with a fork.

She had never worried about breathing intoxicating gas from Hefty bags. Another worry. Put it on the pile. Soon it might seem quaint too.

She blamed her fretting on Helen's first pediatrician, who had told her there was no reason to obsess about Sudden Infant Death Syndrome. "It'll happen or it won't," said Dr. Moody. Laura had found this an unacceptable philosophy. Her worry for the baby had heat and energy: how could it be useless? Nobody had warned her how deeply babies slept, how you couldn't always see them breathing. You watched, and watched, you touched their dozy stomachs to feel their clockwork. Even once the infant Helen started sleeping through the night, Laura checked on her every two hours. Sometimes at 2 a.m. she was so certain that Helen had died she felt an electric shock to the heart, and this (she believed) started Helen's heart too: her worry was the current that kept them both alive. Kit too, when Kit, a surprise, crashed sweetly into their lives.

Maybe that was what happened to Helen. She was supposed to be an only child. She'd been promised. Kit was a flirtatious baby, a funny self-assured toddler. She made people laugh. Poor awkward honking Helen: it would be hard to be Kit's older sister. Growing up, Laura had hated the way her parents had compared her to her brother—Ben was good at math, so there was no point in her trying; Laura was more outgoing, so she had to introduce her brother to friends—but once she had her own children she understood comparison was necessary. It was how you discovered their personalities: the light of one child threw the other child into relief, no different from how she, at thirteen, had known what she looked like only by comparing the length of her legs and the color of her hair to her friends and their legs and their hair.

Helen hit her sister; Helen was shut in her room; afterward all four of them would go to the old-fashioned ice cream parlor with the twisted wire chairs. She and Wes couldn't decide when to punish and when to indulge, when a child was testing the boundaries and needed discipline, and when she was demanding, in the brutish way of children, more love. In this way, their life had been pasted together with marshmallow topping and hot fudge. Shut her in her room. Buy her a banana split. Do both: see where it gets you.

Helen sneaking out at night. Helen doing drugs.

Children were unfathomable. The same thing that could stop them from breathing in the night could stop them from loving you during the day. Could cause them to be brought home by the police without their pants or a good explanation.

That long night Laura and Wes interrogated her. Laura, mostly, while Wes examined the corners of Helen's bedroom and looked grief-struck. Whose house? Laura asked. What had she been doing there? What about Addie, her best friend, Addie of the braces and the clarinet? Was she there? Laura wanted to know everything. No, that wasn't true. She wanted to know nothing, she wanted to be told there was nothing to worry about: she wanted from Helen only consolation. She knew she couldn't yell comfort out of her but she didn't know what else to do. "What were you *thinking?*" she asked Helen, too loudly, as though it was thinking that was dangerous.

Helen shrugged. Then she pulled aside the neck of the T-shirt to examine her own shoulder and shrugged again. Over the bed was a poster that matched her T-shirt: the same guy, light caught in the creases of his leather pants, pale lipstick, dark eyeliner.

"What happened to your nose?" Laura asked.

Helen covered it with her hand. "Someone tried to pierce it."

"Helen! You do not have permission."

Wes said, looking at the poster, "Linda sure is pretty."

"*He's* not Linda," said Helen. "Linda's the *band*."

Laura sat down next to her. Helen's nose was red, nicked, but whoever had wielded the needle had given up. "Beautiful Helen, why would you?" Laura said. Helen bit her lip to avoid smiling straight out. Then she looked up at the poster.

"He must be hot in those pants," Wes said.

"Probably," said Helen. She slid under her bedclothes and touched her nose again. "I'm tired, I think."

"Poor Linda," said Wes. He rubbed his face in what looked like disbelief. "To suffer so for his art."

"We'll go to Paris," Wes told Laura. It was 4 a.m.

"Yes." They were exhausted, unslept. Helen seemed like an intelligence test they were failing, had been failing for years. Better to flee. Paris. "Why?" she said.

"Helen's always wanted to go."

"She has?"

"All those children's books. *Madeline*. Some Richard Scarry mouse, I think. Babar. Kit's old enough to enjoy it now. We'll—we'll get Helen painting lessons. Kit too, if she's interested. Or I'll take them to museums and we'll draw. Eat pastries. Get *out* of here. Your brother's always offering us booty from his frequent flier millions. Let's say *yes*. Let's *go*."

The biggest ice cream sundae in the world. Wes taught printmaking at a community college and had the summer off. Laura worked for a caterer and was paid only by the job. They'd have to do it frugally but they could swing it.

"All right," said Laura. They stayed up till morning, looking at apartments on the Internet. By 7 a.m. Ben had e-mailed back that he was happy to give them the miles; by eight they had booked the flights. They arranged for one of Wes's students to look after the house and the dog for the five weeks they'd be gone. It was astonishing how quickly the trip came together.

The plan was to disrupt their lives, a jolt to Helen's system be-

fore school started again in the fall. The city would be strange
and beautiful, as Helen herself was strange and beautiful. Perhaps
they'd understand her there. Perhaps the problem all this time
was that her soul had been written in French.

They flew overnight from Boston; they hadn't been on a plane
since before Kit was born. Inside the terminal they tried to lead
the family suitcases, old plaid things with insufficient silver wheels
along the keels, prone to tipping. Honeymoon luggage from the
past century: that was how long it had been since they'd traveled.
At Charles de Gaulle, all of the Europeans pulled behind them
like obedient dogs their long-handled perfectly balanced bags.
They murmured into their cell phones. Laura patted her pocket,
felt the switched-off phone that she'd been assured would cost too
much to use here, and felt sorry for it. Her suitcase fell over like a
shot dog. Only Helen seemed to understand how to walk through
the airport, as though it were a sport suited to the pubescent female body, a long-legged stride that made the suitcase heel.

Outside the morning was hot, and French, and blinding, and
Wes was already loading the cases into the trunk of a taxi with the
grim care of a man disposing of corpses. Laura thought: *What a
bad idea this was.* She squeezed into the back of the cab between
the girls, another old caution: proximity sometimes made them
pinch each other. She had to fold her torso like the covers of a
book. Wes got into the passenger seat and unraveled the piece of
paper with the address of the apartment they'd rented over the
Internet.

"*Excusez-moi,*" Wes said to the driver. "*Je parle français très mal.*"
The cab driver nodded impatiently. Yes, very badly, it was the most
self-evident sentence ever spoken: anything Wes might have said
in French would have conveyed the same information. The driver
took the scrap from Wes's hand.

"*L'appartement,*" said Helen, "*se trouve dans le troisième arrondissement, je crois, monsieur. Cent-vingt-deux rue du Temple.*"

At this the driver smiled. "*Ah! Bon! Merci, mademoiselle. Le
troisième, exactement.*"

They were so smashed into the back, Laura couldn't turn to
look at Helen. "You speak French!" she said, astounded.

"I *take* French, Mommy. You know that. I don't *speak* it."

"You're fluent!" said Laura.

The street was crooked, and the taxi driver bumped onto the sidewalk to let them get out. In English he said, "Welcome here." Across the street were a few wholesale jewelry and pocketbook stores, and Laura was stunned by how cheap the merchandise hanging in the window looked, and she wondered whether they'd managed to book an apartment in the only tacky quarter of Paris. The door to their building was propped open. The girls moaned as they walked up the stairs, dragging their bags. "I thought it was on the *fourth* floor," said Helen, and Wes said, "They count floors differently here."

"Like a different alphabet?" said Kit.

The staircase narrowed the farther up they went, as though a trick of perspective. At the top were two doors. One had an old-fashioned business card taped to it. *M. Petit.* That was their contact. Wes knocked, and a small elderly man in an immaculate white shirt and blue tie answered.

"*Bonjour!*" he said. He came out and led them to the other door. He held on to the tie, as though he wanted to make sure they saw it. "*Bienvenue, venez ici. Ici, ici, madame, monsieur, mademoiselles.*"

"*Je parle français très mal,*" said Wes, and there was that look again. M. Petit dropped his tie.

"You do it, Helen," said Laura.

"*Bonjour, monsieur,*" said Helen, and he brought them around the apartment and described everything, pantomiming and saying, "*Comprenez?*" and Helen answered in a nasal, casual, quacking way, "*Ouah. Ouah. Ouah.*"

"What did he say?" Wes asked when M. Petit had gone.

"Something about hot water," she said. "Something about garbage. We need to get calling cards for the phone. He lives next door if we need anything."

"Something about garbage," said Kit. "Real helpful."

The apartment was tiny but high-ceilinged, delightful, seemingly carved from gingerbread: a happy omen for their trip, Laura decided. The girls would sleep in twin beds in one room, Wes and Laura across the hall in a bed that was nearly double but not quite. A three-quarters double bed, like the three-quarters cello that Helen played. The windows looked out on next-door chimney pots. The living room was the size of its oriental rug. The kitchen included a sink, a two-burner hot plate, a waist-high fridge, and a tabletop oven. It was the oldest building any of them had ever stood in.

"Why are the pillows square?" Kit asked.

"They just *are*," said Helen knowingly. She leaned her head out the little window. *Five stories up and no way to shimmy down*, thought Laura. Helen said, "I want to stay here forever."

"We'll see," said Wes. "Come on. Let's go. Let's see Paris."

Jet lag and sunshine turned the city hallucinogenically beautiful. "We'll keep going," said Wes. "Till bedtime. Best way to deal with jet lag." Down the rue des Francs Bourgeois, through the place des Vosges over to the Bastille, along the river, across one bridge, and another: then they stood staring at Notre Dame's back end, all its flying buttresses kicking at Laura's sternum.

"Notre Dame is *here*?" said Helen. An insinuating wind tugged at the bottom of her shirt; she held it down.

"In Paris, yes," said Wes.

"But we just *walked* to it?"

Wes laughed. "We can walk everywhere."

They kept walking, looking for the right café, feeling the heat like optimism on their limbs. Laura swore Helen's French got even better as the day went on: she translated the menu at the café, she asked for directions, she found the right amount of money to pay for mid-afternoon crepes. She negotiated the purchase of two primitive prepaid cell phones, one for Wes and one for Laura. At home the girls had phones, but in Paris they would always be with one of their parents.

What was that odd blooming in Laura's torso? A sense that this was how it happened: you became dependent on your children, and it was all right.

They kept moving in order to stay awake until it was sort of bedtime. At six Laura thought she could feel the sidewalk tilting up like a Murphy bed, and they went to the tiny grocery store behind their building, got bread and meat and wine, and held up the line first when they didn't understand they needed to pack their own groceries, and again when they couldn't open the slippery plastic bags. Once they were out, they felt triumphant anyhow. Wes raised the baguette like a sword.

They turned down their little street. Up ahead of them a heavy-set woman hurried in the middle of the road with a funny hitch, then suddenly turned, worked a shiny black girdle to mid-thigh, and peed in the gutter, an astounding flood that stopped the Langfords.

Helen said, "Awesome."

"That," said Kit, "was impressive."

"City of lights," said Wes.

In their medieval apartment, they ate like medieval people, tearing bread with their teeth, spreading butter with their fingers. They all went to bed at the same time, the girls in their night-gowns—Kit's patterned with roses, Helen's another Linda XXL T-shirt. "Good night, good night," said Laura, standing between their beds. They had never shared a room, her girls. Then she and Wes went across the hall to the other room.

The necessary closeness of the three-quarters bed amplified everything. Her tenderness for Wes, who had been so sure this was the right thing; her worries about how much money this trip would cost; her anxiety at having to use her threadbare high school French. She understood this was the reason she was thirty-six and had never been to Europe. It was a kind of stage fright.

In the morning they discovered that the interior walls were so thin they could hear, just behind the headboard, the noise of M. Petit emptying his bladder as clearly as if he'd been in the same room. It was a long story, the emptying of M. Petit's bladder, with many digressions and false endings.

"We're in Paris," whispered Wes.

"I thought there would be more foie gras and less pee," Laura whispered back.

"Both," said Wes. "There will be plenty of both."

In Paris Helen became a child again. She was skinny, pubescent, not the lean dangerous blade of a near-teen she'd seemed at home, in skin-tight blue jeans and oversized T-shirts. In Paris you could buy children's shoes and children's clothes for a person who was five-two. The sales were on, clothing so cheap they kept buy-ing. Helen chose candy-colored skirts and T-shirts with cartoon characters.

At le boulevard Richard-Lenoir, near the Bastille, Helen bought a vinyl purse with a long strap, in which she kept a few euros, a ChapStick, her name and address, a notebook for writing down her favorite sights. She walked hand in hand with Kit: they were

suddenly friends, as though their fighting had been an allergic reaction to American air. Both girls picked up French as though by
static electricity, and they spoke it to each other, tossing their hair
over their shoulders. *"Ouais,"* they said, in the way that even Laura,
whose brain seemed utterly French-resistant, now recognized as
how Parisians quackingly agreed.

There were so many *pâtisseries* and *boulangeries* and *fromageries*
that they rated the pain au chocolat of one block against the pain
au chocolat of the next. The candy shops were like jewelry stores,
the windows filled with twenty-four-carat bonbons. The caterer
Laura worked for had given her money to smuggle back some
young raw-milk cheeses that were illegal in the United States, and
Laura decided to taste every Reblochon in the city, every Sainte-
Maure de Touraine, so that on the last day she could buy the best
and have them vacuum-packed against the noses of what she liked
to imagine were the U.S. Customs Cheese Beagles.

Paris was exactly what she had expected and nothing like it. The
mullioned passages full of stamp shops and dollhouse-furniture
stores, the expensive wax museum the girls wanted to go back and
back to despite not recognizing most of the counterfeit celebrities,
the hot chocolate emporia and the bare-breasted bus-stop ads.
These were things she had not known were in Paris but felt she
should have. The fast-food joint called Flunch, the Jewish district
with its falafel ("Shall we have f'laffel for flunch," Wes said nearly
every day). She never really got her bearings in the city, no matter how she studied the map. Paris on paper always looked like a
box of peanut brittle that had been dropped onto the ground, the
Seine the unraveled ribbon that had held it together.

"What's your favorite thing in Paris?" Wes asked.

"My family," she answered. That was the truth.

After a while they bought a third pay-as-you-go phone for Helen
and Kit to share, so the girls could go out in the city together after lunch. Then Wes and Laura would go back to the apartment.
She thought every languishing marriage should be prescribed a
three-quarter bed. They didn't even think to worry about M. Petit
on the other side of the wall until later, when news of his careful,
decorous life floated back to them: a ringing phone, a whistling
teakettle, a dainty plastic clatter that could only be a dropped button. This was why it was good to be temporary, and for the neighbors to be French.

"How did you know?" Laura asked Wes.

"What do you mean?" he said.

"Helen. How *good* she'd be here."

"I don't know. I just—I felt it. She is, though, isn't she? Good. Sweet. Back to her old self."

Her old self? Laura thought. Helen had never been like this a day in her life.

Still, it was a miracle: take the clumsy, eager-to-please girl to Paris. Watch her develop *panache*.

Then it was August. It was hot in Paris. Somehow they hadn't realized how hot it would be, and how—Laura thought sometimes—how dirty. The heat conjured up dirt, centuries of cobblestone-caught filth. It was as though Paris had never actually been clean, as though you could smell every drop of blood and piss and shit spilled in the streets since before the days of the revolution. Half the stores and restaurants shut for the month, as the sensible Parisians fled for the coast. French food felt tyrannical. When they chose the wrong place to eat, a café that looked good but where the skin of the *confit de canard* was flabby and soft, the bread damp, it didn't feel like bad luck: it felt as though they'd fallen for a con. As though the place had hidden the better food in the back, for the actually French.

Laura was ready to go home. August was like a page turning. July had felt lucky: August, cursed. From the first day, Laura would think later, no mistake.

The day of Helen's accident—or perhaps the day before; they would never know exactly when the accident happened—she was as lovely and childish as ever. In the makeup section of the Monoprix, she lipsticked a mouth on the edge of her hand, the lower lip on her thumb and the upper on her index finger.

"*Bonjour,*" she said to her mother, through her hand.

"*Bonjour, madame,*" said Laura, who did not like speaking French even under these circumstances. The Monoprix was air-conditioned. They spent a lot of time there.

France had refined the features of Helen's face—Laura had always thought of them as slightly coarse, the thick chap-prone lips, the too-bright eyes—the face, Laura thought now, of a girl who would do anything for a boy, even a boy who didn't care. Her own face, once upon a time. But in Paris Helen had changed. She had lost the eagerness, the oddness, the blunt difficulty of her features. She had become a Parisienne. Laura tucked the label of Helen's shirt in, felt the warmth of her back, and with the force of previously unseen heartache she knew: they would fly back in three days and nothing, nothing would have changed. They would step back into the aftermath of all they hadn't dealt with.

"Are you looking forward to going home?" Laura asked.

Helen pouted. Then she jutted her thumb out, made her bee-stung hand pout too. *"Non,"* she said. *"J'adore Paris.* I'd like to stay here forever."

"Not me," said Kit. "I miss Frogbert."

"Who?" said Helen.

"Our *dog,*" said Kit. "Oh, very funny."

"Forever," Helen said again. "Daddy!" she called across to her father, who was just walking into the store with an antique lampshade. He wanted to stay in France forever too. Laura could imagine him using the lampshade as an excuse: *How can we get this on the plane? We'd better just stay here.*

"Look!" he said. "Hand-painted. Sea serpents."

And they were, a chain of lumpy, dimwitted sea serpents linked mouth to tail around the hem of the shade. It was a grimy, preposterous thing in the gleaming cosmetic aisle of Monoprix.

Helen took it with the flats of her palms. "It's awesome," she said. "Daddy, it's perfect."

Laura did not think she had ever seen that look on Helen's face—not just happiness, but the wish to convey that happiness to someone else, a generosity. That was the expression Laura tried to remember later, to paste down in her head, because soon it was gone forever, replaced with a parody of a smile, a look that was not dreamy but dumbstruck, recognizable, not Cinderella asked to the ball, but a stepsister, years later, finally invited back to the palace, forgiven. Because twelve hours later, Wes and Laura, asleep in their antique bed, heard a familiar, forgotten noise: Wes's American cell phone, ringing in the dresser drawer. Why was it on? Laura answered it.

"Have you a daughter?" said the voice on the other end.

The voice belonged to a nurse from the American Hospital of Paris, who said that a young girl had been brought in with a head injury.

"She have a shirt that say *Linda*," said the nurse. "She fell and striked her head."

Laura went to the girls' room, the phone pressed to her ear. Kit was asleep among the square pillows and the overstuffed duvet. Her hair was sweat damp. Helen's bed was empty. Laura looked to the window, as though it was from there she'd fallen, the pavement below upon which she'd struck her head. But it was locked into place, ajar to let the air in but fixed. If Helen had left the apartment it would have been the ordinary way.

"*Je ne comprends pas,*" Laura said, though the nurse was speaking English.

"She need someone here," said the nurse. "It's bad."

2.

This was why you had two children. This is why you didn't. Wes stood outside their old, old, unfathomably old building. There were no taxis out and he couldn't imagine how to call one. He wondered whether he'd wanted to come to Paris because of the language: the way he'd felt coddled by lack of understanding, delighted to be capable of so little. By now he could get along pretty well but this question, how Paris worked in the middle of the night, seemed beyond his abilities. Who he needed: Helen, to help him make his way to Helen. The Métro didn't run this late, he knew that much. Upstairs Kit slept on, Laura watching over her, which was why he was alone on the street. She was the spare child. The one who wasn't supposed to be here. The one who was all right. In his panic he had not wanted to go away from her: he'd wanted to crawl into Helen's empty bed, not even caring how warm or cold the sheets were, how long she'd been gone, as though that child were already lost and the only thing to do was watch over the girl who was left.

He GPSed directions on his smartphone, the American one. Four and a half miles, in a wealthy suburb called Neuilly-sur-Seine. He would walk: he couldn't think of an alternative. If he saw a taxi he would flag it down but the main thing was movement. Westward, as fast as he could, and then he felt he was in a dull, extravagant, incredible movie. He had a quest, and every person

he passed seemed hugely important: the man carrying the dozing child, who asked for directions Wes couldn't provide (he hid
the phone, he didn't want to stop); the two police carrying riot
shields though Wes could not hear any kind of altercation that
might require them; the old woman in elegant, filthy clothing
who was sweeping out the rhomboid front of a café. All summer
he and his women had walked. "It's the only way to understand
a city," Wes had said more than once, "we are *flâneurs.*" Now he
understood that wandering taught you nothing. Only when you
moved with purpose could you know a place. Toward someone,
away from someone. "Helen," he said aloud, as he walked beneath
the Périphérique's looping traffic. He had not driven a car in over
a month. They looked like wild animals to him. Everything looked
feral, in fact. He wanted a weapon.

It took him more than an hour to get to the upscale western
suburb of the American Hospital. By then the sun was rising. He
stumbled in, shocked by the lights, the people. He didn't want
to talk to anyone but Helen, he just wanted to find her, but he
knew that was impossible so he stopped at the lit-up desk by the
door. The sign above it said INFORMATION. Was that *INforMAtion*
in English, or *informaCEEohn* in French?

"J'arrive," he said, as the waiters did in busy restaurants, though
they meant *I will* and not *I have.* He added, "I walked here."

The man behind the desk had short greasy bangs combed down
in points, like a knife edge. "Patient name?"

Wes hesitated. What sort of shape was she in? What information
had Laura given the hospital? "Helen Langford." He found some
hope inside him: of course Helen was conscious. How else would
they have got Wes's American phone number? She wouldn't have
remembered the French one.

"ICU," said the man with the serrated hair.

But it turned out that Helen had taken her mother's American
phone, had been using it all summer to call first the United States
and then Paris, to text, to take pictures of herself. When the battery drained, she swapped it for Wes's, recharged, swapped them
back. The hospital had found the phone in her pocket, had gone
through the contact list and eventually found him.

The ICU doctor was a tall man with heavy black eyebrows and
silver sideburns. Wes felt dizzied by his perfect English, his uniden-
tifiable accent, the rush of details. Helen had been dropped off at

the front door by some boys. She probably had not been injured in this neighborhood: the boys brought her here, as though *American* were a medical condition that needed to be treated at a specialist hospital. They had done a CAT scan and an MRI. The only injury was to her head. She had fallen upon it. Her blood screened clean for drugs but she'd had a few drinks. "Some sweet wine, maybe, made her clumsy. Hijinks," said the doctor, dropping the initial *h*. *Ijinks*. Not an Anglophone then. "Children. Stupid."

"Is she dead?" he asked the doctor.

"What? No. She's had a tumble, that's true. She struck her head. Right now, we're keeping her unconscious, we put in a tube." The doctor tapped his graying temple. "To relieve the pressure."

What was causing pressure? "Air?" Wes said.

"Air? Ah, no. Fluid. Building up. So the tube—" The doctor made a sucking noise. "So far it's working. Later today, tomorrow, we will know more."

Wes had expected his daughter to be tiny in the bed, but she looked substantial, womanly. Her eyes were closed. The side of her head was obscured by an enormous bandage, with the little slurping tube running from it. No, not slurping. It didn't make a sound. Wes had imagined that, thanks to the doctor.

Her little room was made of glass walls, blindered by old-fashioned wheeled screens. There was nothing to sit on. For half an hour he crouched by the bed and spoke to her, though her eyes were closed. She was slack. Every part of her.

"Helen," he said, "Helen. You can tell us anything. You should, you know." They'd been the kind of parents who'd wanted to know nothing, or the wrong things. It hit him with the force of a conversion: all along they'd believed what they didn't acknowledge didn't exist. Here, proof: the unsayable existed. "Helen," he said to his sleeping daughter. "I will never be mad at you again. We're starting over. Tell me *anything*."

A fresh start. He erased the photos and texts from the phone: he wanted to know everything in the future, not the past. Later he'd regret it, he'd want names, numbers, the indecipherable slang-ridden texts of French teenagers, but as he scrolled down, deleting, affirming each deletion, it felt like a kind of meditative prayer: *I will change. Life will broaden and better.*

Half an hour later he stepped out to the men's room and found

Kit and Laura wandering near the vending machines. Kit had been weeping. *Oh, the darling!* he thought. Then he realized that Laura had been grilling her. She was not a sorrowful little sister. She was a confederate.

"We took a taxi," said Laura miserably.

"Good," said Wes.

"Nobody will tell me anything," said Laura. "The goddamn desk."

"All right," said Wes. "She's—"

"How did she *get* here?" said Laura. "Who dropped her *off?*"

"Nobody knows," said Wes, which was what he'd understood.

"Somebody does!"

"Look," said Wes. Before they went to see Helen, he wanted to explain it to her. What he knew now: they needed to talk about everything. They needed to be interested in their daughters' secrets, not terrified. He sat them down on the molded bolted-together plastic chairs along the walls. He was glad for the rest. "We're lucky. They dropped her off, they did that for us."

"Cowards," said Laura.

Wes sat back and the whole line of chairs shifted. Cowards would have left her where she was. Bravery got her here. He knew what kind of kid he'd been, a scattering boy, who would not have stopped to think till half a mile away. Adrenaline flooded your conscience like an engine you then couldn't start. But Helen hadn't been that kind of kid. She had stayed with the boy in distress, the officers of a month ago had said, and the universe had repaid her.

"I'm sorry," said Kit. "I'm so, so sorry." She was still wearing her rose-patterned nightgown, with a pair of silver sandals. She looked like a mythical sleep-related figure: Narcolepta, Somnefaria. As soon as he thought that, Wes felt the need to sleep fall over his head like a tossed sheet.

"Who are they?" Laura suddenly asked Kit. "You must have met them."

"She'd leave me somewhere and make me promise not to budge."

"French boys?"

"I don't know!" said Kit.

Every night for a week, Helen had sneaked out to see some boys. She had met them on one of the sisters' walks together; the next walk, she sat Kit down on a park bench with a book and told her to stay put. At night, she took either her mother's or her father's American cell phone; Kit slept with their shared phone set to vibrate under her pillow. When Helen wanted to be let back in, she called till the buzzing phone woke up Kit, who sneaked down the stairs to open the front door.

Kit was going to be the wild child. That's what they had said, back when she was a two-year-old batting her eyes at waiters, giggling when strangers paid attention. It was going to be Kit sneaking out of the house in the middle of the night, Helen lying to protect her.

You worked to get your kids to like each other and this was what happened.

They went to the ICU. When Kit saw her sister, she began to cry again. "I don't know anything else," she said, though nobody was asking. "I just—I don't know."

Laura stayed by the door. She put her arm around Kit. She could not look at anyone. Wes thought she was about to pull the wheeled screens around her, as though in this country that was how you attended your damaged child. A mother's rage was too incandescent to blaze unshaded. "How do they even know she fell?" she whispered. "Maybe she was hit with something, maybe—was she raped?"

Wes shook his head uneasily. There was Helen in the bed. They needed to go to her.

"How do you *know*?" said Laura.

"They checked."

"I will kill them," she said. "I will track down those boys. I hate this city. I want to go home." At last she looked at Wes.

"We can't move her yet."

"I know," said Laura, and then, more quietly, "I want to go home *now*."

Well, after all: he'd had the width of three *arrondissements* to walk, getting ready to see Helen. As a child he'd been fascinated by the bends—what scuba divers got when they came to the surface of the ocean too fast to acclimate their lungs to ordinary pressure. You had to be taken from place to place with care. Laura had gone from apartment to taxicab to hospital too quickly. Of course she couldn't breathe.

But it didn't get any easier as the day went on. She looked at Helen, yes, and arranged her hair with the pink rattail comb a nurse had left behind. All the while, she delivered a muttering speech, woven of curses: she cursed their decision to come to Paris; she cursed the midmorning's comically elegant doctor who inflated her cheeks and puffed when asked about Helen's prognosis; she damned to hell the missing boys.

"They *say* boys," said Laura, "but if they didn't see them, how do they know?"

"We need to solve the problems we can, honey," said Wes.

That afternoon Kit and Laura took the Métro back to the city. Kit was seven, after all.

He didn't get back to the apartment until ten. Laura was already in bed but awake. They talked logistics. In two days they were scheduled to fly home. It made more sense for Laura to stay with Helen—she was a freelancer, Wes's classes started in a week—but there was the question of language. The question of Paris.

"I'll stay," Wes said. They were in bed. Beyond, M. Petit's apartment was silent. Kit was asleep in the twin bedroom on the other side of the hall.

Laura nodded. "Shouldn't we all?" Then she answered herself. "Third grade."

"Third grade," said Wes. School started for Kit in a week too. She shouldn't miss it. "We've got the phones. Imagine what this used to be like." They'd talked about that, how appallingly easy technology made it to be an expat these days. "Listen, I'm sure, I'm sure in a week, or two—we can bring her home."

Neither of them could wonder aloud what change in Helen's condition would allow that.

"Where will you stay?" Laura asked.

"Oh, God. I hadn't thought."

He knocked the next morning on M. Petit's door. Two young men answered. One of them was holding some dark artwork in a large frame. The other held an unfurled newspaper and was folding a cup into one of its panes.

"*Bonjour,*" said Wes, and then he couldn't think of what to say.

"English?" said one of the men, a balding redhead.

"Yes. American." Wes pointed at the door behind him.

"Ah!" said the redhead, and Wes could see M. Petit in his expression. In both of their faces, actually. His sons. The redheaded man explained: their father had died suddenly, unexpectedly.

"Oh, no," said Wes. "I am sorry." He felt a tender culpability, as though his own disaster had seeped through the walls and killed the old man. He tried to remember the last time he'd heard M. Petit's morning routine.

"So you see," said the redhead. "We must pack."

"We've had an accident," said Wes. "My family. An emergency. I was wondering if I could extend the lease."

"Ah, no. No. Actually my daughter is moving in, next week, with her husband. Newlyweds."

Wes nodded. He felt a tweak in his chest, disappointment or despair. He needed to stay, as cheaply as possible, and he couldn't imagine where he might start looking for shelter, or how long it would take.

"But," said the son. "Would you like—you could perhaps rent this?" He pointed at the floor of M. Petit's apartment, the same warm burnt orange tiles as next door. Wes peered down the hallway into the murk. "Very sudden, you see."

"Yes," Wes said. "Thank you. *Merci. Merci mille fois.*"

He took the semester off from school. His department head said they'd figure things out so he could still draw a salary—a course reduction, a heavier load in the spring. Better to solve it now for everyone involved than to wonder every day whether Wes might be coming back.

On the day of the flight he and Laura and Kit went to the hospital. Kit said goodbye to her sister tearfully, tenderly, crawled into the bed and stroked Helen's hair and said, "I promise, I promise, I promise." What promise? Wes thought she would tell him when they said goodbye at the airport, though when they got there Kit was awkward, unhappy, her hands bunched under her chin as though, if he tried to draw her close, she would fight him off with her elbows. "Goodbye, Kitty," he said. She nodded.

He thought then that he should find a place to lie down, like Helen. You said goodbye to someone differently if they were supine. But he didn't see any benches, and if he lay on the ground, he'd be pummeled by European feet and suitcases. Security, perhaps. Send ahead his belt and shoes (only in prisons and airports did a stranger tell you to take them off). Put his sad sorry body down. Kit might not fall for it at first. *"Dad,"* she would say, humiliated, because now she had to bear the humiliation for her sister as well. But then, surely, as he disappeared, his head, shoulders, beltless waist, as the agents saw the truth of his kidneys, his empty pockets, she would run to him, grab at his feet—no. Feet first, so that she had enough time to whisper that promise in his ear.

In the end he picked her up. He couldn't remember the last time he'd done that. Her toes knocked against his shins. "We'll talk every day," he said.

"I know," she answered.

Then he kissed Laura. "Call me when you get in."

"It will be too late."

"No," he said. "Not possible."

He watched them go through the checkpoint. Laura kept waving, *go, go,* but he couldn't, not until they disappeared from sight.

He took the train back into the city, to move his suitcase into M. Petit's apartment. The furniture was ancient, fringed, balding. The windows looked onto the courtyard, not the street. It felt like the depressed cousin of the apartment where they'd been so happy. The right place to be, in other words. The bathroom had a slipper tub, deep and short, with a step to sit on. How had M. Petit climbed into it? The bed was in a loft. No octogenarian should have to use a ladder to go to sleep. Everything in the world now looked like something to fall from. He decided he would sleep on the little L-shaped couch, in case M. Petit had died in the bed. He put the sea-serpent lampshade in the middle of the coffee table and fell asleep. He surprised himself by sleeping through the night. He checked the phone: a text from Laura, *Arrived will call in my morning/your afternoon.* He went, for the third day, to the hospital.

The border between consciousness and coma was not as defined as Wes had been taught by television to expect. They'd stopped sedating her. Helen did not come bursting to the surface, as though from a lake. She rose out of unconsciousness by millimeters over the next few days. Her nose woke up. Her forehead. Her cheeks. Her eyes. The pressure in her skull abated; the ventric tube came out.

She had the daft look of a saint. Even her hands were knotted together at her chest, as though in prayer. Her mouth was open. The nurses combed her hair, what was left of it, and then called in the hospital's hairdresser, who cropped it like Jeanne d'Arc's.

In the hospital Wes studied Helen as he had when she was an infant. Around and around her face, the knotted fingers, the angles of her shoulders. She wasn't a baby, of course. She was a girl, thirteen in a month, with breasts, whose body would keep going further into adulthood no matter whether her brain could catch up. The doctors said it was still too early to tell.

He tried to find his daughter in the face, but she'd been so completely revised, and then he tried to comfort himself: Helen was past worry. The worst would not happen to her because it already had. There were no decisions to be made right now. She wouldn't die. She was, for the moment, beyond any psychological complexities. He had to be here. That he could manage.

At the end of every day, he walked back to Paris, all four and a half miles: beneath the Périphérique, through the seventeenth arrondissement, down le boulevard Malherbes, and he spoke to Laura, his ear throbbing against the plastic of the phone. She sounded far away, relieved. He related the latest diagnosis: they were still assessing whether Helen's brain injury was focal or diffuse. Her brain was still swollen in her skull. It might take her years to recover. Laura told him the news of America: the insurance company was being extraordinarily good at working with the hospital; the cell-phone company would not forgive the nearly thousand-dollar bill for Helen's purloined Parisian phone calls and text messages. Sometimes Kit was there, though there were swimming lessons and play dates and flute lessons or just the sound of the slamming door as she went outside.

"We miss you," Laura would say.

"We miss you too," he answered.

"*You* miss us. Helen doesn't miss anything."

"We don't know."

"I feel it."

"OK," he said, because she might have been right.

By the time they'd talked themselves out he was back in the third arrondissement, and then he would zag towards the river. He walked as they had their first jet-lagged day, to exhaust himself before climbing the stairs to M. Petit's apartment, so he could fall asleep without hearing the noises of the granddaughter and her husband in that three-quarter bed on the other side of the wall. Or on the sofa, or any corner of his old home. Sometimes he thought, *That's us still, and I am M. Petit,* and he tried to find the part of the wall that bordered on what had been the girls' bedroom. Maybe he would hear them scheme. Maybe this time he could stop it.

Or maybe he'd just hear the neighbors fucking.

One night on the way home he found a little store that catered to Americans, big boxes of sugary cereal, candy bars, and he wanted to buy them for Helen, whose nasogastric tube had just been taken out, though she was fed only purees. The store carried every strain of American crap. French's mustard, Skippy peanut butter, Stove Top stuffing, even Cheez Whiz. He'd been gone long enough from the U.S. that he felt sentimental about the food, and he'd been in Paris long enough to feel superior to it.

Then he saw the red-topped jar of Marshmallow Fluff.

"Something sweet for you," he said to Helen the next morning. He hunted around for a spoon and found only a tongue depressor. That would do.

Helen closed her eyes as the Fluff went in, as her round mouth irised in around the stick. Wes felt electrified. Before this moment Helen had been a blank, as mysterious to him as she must have been to the emergency room when she'd first arrived: a girl who'd dropped from the sky. Unidentified. Cut off from her history.

Now she opened her eyes, and he could see, for the first time, Helen looking out of them, though (he thought) she couldn't see anything. She was sunk in the bottom of a well. Everything above her was hidden in shadows. He could see her trying to make something out. Her mouth, agape, opened further, with muscle, intent, greed: *more.*

He dug out a larger dollop. Closed eyes, closed mouth, but when the tongue depressor went in Helen began to cough. It was a terrible wet sound.

"Are you all right?" he said. He wondered whether he should put his finger in her mouth, scoop it out, and then he did, and Helen bit down. First just pressure, the peaks of her molars, then pain. He tried to pull out his finger. "Wow. Helen," he said. "Helen, please, Helen, help! Help!" and then her jaw relaxed, and he stood with his wet, indented finger, panting.

The doctor on the floor was Dr. Delarche, the tall woman who'd so infuriated Laura. By the time she peered into Helen's mouth all the Fluff had melted away except a wisp on her upper lip.

"What is this?" she asked Helen. She touched her chin, looking over her face. "*Hein?* This sticky thing."

Wes still held his sore finger. "Fluff."

"Floff?" The doctor turned to him. "What is this floff?"

The lidless jar had fallen to the bed—he pulled it out from under the blanket, and inclined the mouth toward the doctor. "Marshmallow, um, *crème*," he said, pronouncing it the French way. "You put it on bread, with peanut butter."

Dr. Delarche looked incredulous. "No," she said. "This is not good for the body. Even without traumatic brain injury but certainly with. No more floff."

"OK," he said, exhilarated.

His mistake had been to believe that the girl in the bed wanted nothing. But that *was* Helen, and Helen was built of want. She longed, she burned, even if she couldn't move or swallow Marshmallow Fluff. He wished he could find her boys so they could sit on the edge of the bed and read to her; he wished he could take her into the city, let her drink wine.

Well, then. He needed to find what she wanted, and bring it to her.

That evening, after the walk, he found himself on a street that seemed lined with art supplies: a pen shop, a painting shop, a paper store. In the paint shop he bought a pad that you could prop up like an easel, and watercolors in a little metal case with a loop on the back for your thumb, for when you painted *plein air.* It was the sort of thing he'd have bought for the girls in an ordinary time. He hadn't painted himself since graduate school—he'd been a printmaker, and that's what he taught—and it had been even longer since he'd used watercolors. But Helen had. She'd taken lessons at home. Perhaps she could teach him. That's what he would tell her.

"Ah!" said the doctor, when she saw him set up the pad. "Yes. Therapy. Very good. This will help."

They began to paint.

Yes, Helen was there, she was in there. She could not form words. She smiled more widely when people spoke to her but it didn't seem to matter what they said. But with the brush in her hand—Wes just steadying—she painted. At first the paintings were abstracts, fields of yellow and orange and watery pink (she never went near blue) overlaid with circles and squares. She knew, as he did not, how to thin the paint with water to get the color she wanted.

Helen was moved to a private room on another floor. The hospital manicurist ("How very Parisian!" said Laura, when he told her) gave her vamp red toes and fingernails. Wes's favorite nurse, a small man who reminded him of a champion wrestler from his high school, devised a brace from a splint and a crepe bandage to help with the painting, so that Helen could hold her wrist out for longer, though she still needed help from the shoulder.

"She's painting," said Wes on the phone. He'd blurted it out at the end of a conversation, standing in front of the front door of the building: until then he hadn't realized he'd been keeping it a secret.

"What do you mean?" asked Laura.

He explained it to her: the brace, the watercolors.

"What is she painting?"

"Abstracts. I'll take a picture, you can see."

There was a silence.

"What?"

"Nothing. I sighed. You mean she's painting like an elephant paints."

"What do you mean?"

"There's an elephant who paints. Maybe more than one. They stick a brush in its trunk and give it a canvas. The results are better than you'd think. But it's not really painting, is it? It's moving with paint. She doesn't know what she's doing."

"She does," said Wes. "She's getting better."

"By millimeters."

"Yes! Forward."

"What good is forward, if it's by millimeters?" said Laura. "How far can she possibly go?"

"We don't know!"

"I wish she had—" Laura began. "I just don't know what her life is going to be like." Another silence.

Wes knew it wasn't sighing this time. He said, "Listen. I gotta go."

He had not had a drink since the early morning call from the hospital; he'd had the horrible thought he might have woken up and caught Helen sneaking out that night, had he been entirely sober. Now he thought about picking up a bottle of wine to take to M. Petit's. He passed by the gym he'd seen before, which was still open though it was ten at night. A woman sat at street level in a glass box, ready to sign him up. She wore ordinary street clothes, not exercise togs.

"*Bonjour, madame,*" he said. "*Je parle français très mal.*"

"*Ah, no!*" said the woman. "*Très bien.*"

She seemed to be condescending to him, but in a cheerful, nearly American way.

The actual gym was in the basement. By American standards it was small, primitive, but there were free weights—he'd lifted pretty seriously in college—and a couple of treadmills. From then on he came here after his long walk, his phone conversation with Laura, because only exertion blunted the knowledge that Laura wished that Helen had died. He hoped Laura had something to do, to blunt her own knowledge that he knew she felt this way and disagreed.

For some reason one of the personal trainers took a dislike to him and was always bawling him out in French, for bringing a duffle bag onto the gym floor, for letting his knees travel over his toes when he squatted, for getting in the way of the French people who seemed always to be swinging around broom handles as a form of exercise. The trainer's name was Didier, according to the flyers by the front desk; his hair was shaved around the base of his skull, long on top. Like an *oignon*, Wes thought. Didier drank ostentatiously from a big Nalgene bottle filled with a pale yellow liquid, and it pleased Wes to pretend he was consuming his own urine. It was good to hate someone, to have a new relationship of any kind with no medical undertones.

When I've been here a year, he thought one night, as he performed deadlifts in the power rack, *when we find the right place to live, me and Helen—then I'll get a girlfriend.* The thought seemed to have flown into his head like a bird—impossible, out of place, smashing around. It didn't belong there. It couldn't get out.

After three weeks, Helen was not just better, but measurably better: she held her head up, she turned to whoever was speaking, she squeezed hands when people said her name.

And she painted. The abstracts had hardened, angled, until Wes could see what she meant. She was painting Paris. Back in the U.S. they had thought Helen had talent and they'd seized on it, bought her supplies, sent her to classes, not just painting but sculpture, pastel, photography. The problem was content, no better than any suburban American girl's: Floating princesses. Pretty ladies. Ball gowns.

Now she painted stained glass and broken buildings in sunshine, monuments, gardens. He could feel her hand struggling to get things right. She drew faces with strange curves and bent smiles. The first time she signed her name in the corner in fat bright letters, Wes burst into tears.

Staff and visitors took her paintings away, without asking, and Wes had to hide the ones he particularly wanted. He was waiting for the right one to mail to Laura, he told himself, but every day's paintings were better than the last. He wanted to send the best one.

One morning he ran into Dr. Delarche on his way to Helen. *"Monsieur,"* she said, and beckoned him. Wes was alarmed. There was never any news from doctors about Helen. He either had to ask or see for himself. And besides, Dr. Delarche worked in the ICU.

"I must ask you something," she said.

He nodded.

"My husband is a documentarist. I wonder—I told him about Helen and her painting. He wishes to do a little film."

"Oh!" said Wes. "Yes!"

The *documentariste* was a shaggy handsome Algerian named Walid who made Wes like Dr. Delarche better: he had an air of joy and incaution. "You don't mind?" he said. His camera was one of those cheap handheld things, a Flip—Laura's mother had given them one the year before. Wes had better video capabilities on his Nikon, back at the flat. He imagined most of the footage would feature the profile of Walid's wide callused thumb.

He didn't tell Laura about the filming. She would tell him to throw the doctor's husband out of the room. *Do not turn our child into a freak show,* she would have said—

—but Wes knew that was all that Helen had ever really wanted. Not love, and not quotidian attention: since she was a child she liked to scare and alarm her parents and strangers and he did not believe anymore that it was some sort of coded message—a cry for love! She just wants you to talk to her! Helen wanted love but no ordinary sort. She wanted people to gape. Left alone in the U.S., she would not just have had her nose pierced, nor her ears, she would not have got just black forked tattoos across the small of her back: she would have obliterated herself with metal and ink, put plugs in her earlobes, in her lips. People would have stared at her. They would have winced and looked away. She wanted both.

Now she had both.

He was not stupid enough, not optimistic enough, to think that she would have made this bargain herself. She wouldn't have given up the boys in some strange part of Paris, offering her wine, watching her do something stupid before she fell. But if she was in bed in a hospital, she would—not *would*, but *did*—want to be the most interesting girl in the bed who ever was. Filmed and fussed over. Called, by the more dramatic of the nurses, miraculous. Visited by the sick children of the hospital, who were brought by well-meaning religious volunteers.

Helen's room was a place of warmth and brightness. Everyone said so. Walid kept filming, though Wes was never clear to what end.

"Perhaps," said Walid one day, "when we are finished, the boys she was with? They will see this film."

"They could come to visit!" said Wes.

"Eh?" said Walid. He stopped filming and regarded Wes. "Turn themselves in. Repent. That's a terrible thing, to abandon a girl, isn't it? You are American and you want them dead," he explained. "We, of course, do not believe in the death penalty. Anymore: we have had our bumps. But still. Terrible thing."

"She is an inspiration," said Dr. Delarche one day as Wes and Helen painted. "This is not a bad thing." Dr. Delarche leaned against the wall in the lab coat she made look chic: it was the way she tucked her hands in the pockets. Since Wes had agreed to let Walid film, she came to the room nearly every day, though never when Walid himself was around. Maybe she had a crush on him, though that seemed very un-French. He had a crush on her.

"The light in the paintings," she said to him. "Like Monet, *hein?*"

"God, no," said Wes. "I hate Monet. Where you going, Helen? Red? Here's red."

"Renoir," suggested Dr. Delarche.

"Worse. No," said Wes, "I will take your side against the Italians with wine, and coffee, and even ice cream, but painting? They have you beat. The French are too pretty."

"We are pretty," Dr. Delarche agreed. "And cheese also, we are better. Wine, of course. Everyone know that. So then. You are making plans?"

He shook his head pleasantly, not knowing what she meant.

"Soon Helen will go," she said.

"Die?" he said. He stopped his hand and felt the pressure of Helen wanting to move, but he pulled the brush from the brace and set it down. He was sorry he'd said the word in front of her.

"Ah, no!" said Dr. Delarche. She sounded insulted that he'd misunderstood her so badly. The French, in his experience, were often insulted by other people's stupidity. "From here."

"To another hospital."

"Home. To the United States. You will talk to the social workers, see what they know—she is better. Of course. She is much, much better, and now she is strong enough to travel. So, hurrah, isn't it? You will go home to your family."

"Of course," he said.

He left the hospital then; he almost never walked out of the building during the day. Neuilly-sur-Seine looked like a stage set built by someone who had never been to Paris and imagined it was boring: clean nineteenth-century buildings with mansard roofs, little cafés that served coffee in white china cups, nothing notable or seedy. He thought about taking Helen back to M. Petit's apartment and he realized that was the real reason he'd started going to the gym: he lifted weights so that he could lift Helen. Five flights up. Into the slipper bath. Around Paris, even. He'd walked enough of the city to know it was a terrible place for a wheelchair. No Americans with Disabilities Act, no cutouts in curbs. It would be easier on foot.

He would carry her to the Jardin des Plantes. They would paint the animals in the zoo, visit the mosaic tearoom at the mosque. In his head he saw her improve by time lapse: her mouth closed, she sat straighter. He didn't care that their short-term visas would expire in two weeks. He could not picture them in America.

If she could not walk or speak in America, then she would not walk or speak for the rest of her life, and that was something he would not accept.

But when he called Laura on his way home that night, she said she was coming in two days. Kit would stay with friends. Her brother had given her a last-minute ticket. She wanted to see for herself how Helen was doing.

As Wes waited at the airport he worried he wouldn't recognize his wife—he always worried this, when meeting someone—and his heart clattered every time the electric double doors opened to reveal another exhausted traveler. When she came out, of course, he knew her immediately, and he felt the old percolation of his blood of their early dates, when he loved her and didn't know what would happen. *That's her,* he thought. She crossed the tile of the airport and it was no mirage of distance. She fell into him and he loved her. He felt ashamed of every awful thought he'd had about her for the past weeks. They held each other's tiredness awhile.

"You feel different," she said. "Thinner. You look kind of wonderful. How's Didier?"

"I hate him with every fiber of my being. You look more than kind of wonderful."

She shook her head. Then she said, "I don't want to go back there."

"Where?" he said. "Oh. Well, that's where Helen is."

"That's not where Helen is."

"She's better. She's—she'll know you're there." As soon as he'd said it he realized he'd been telling Laura the opposite, to comfort her: Helen didn't really know who was there and who wasn't and therefore it was all right that Laura and Kit were thousands of miles away in America.

"Really?" said Laura.

"Yes."

"How does she show it?"

They headed down to the airport train station. Wes had already bought the tickets back into Paris. At last he said, "She's painting. She's still painting, Laura."

The train stopped in front of them with a refrigerated hiss and they stepped on. "I know."

"What?"

"Kit showed me. On YouTube. I mean, it doesn't show her painting. She's not really, is she. I don't believe it."

He had heard about news traveling on the Internet, but he imagined that was gossip, or affairs, or boss badmouthing: it traveled locally, not from country to country.

"Who's really painting?" said Laura. "The therapist, or someone. One of those religious women. In some of the shots you can see a hand steadying her elbow."

"Helen," said Wes. "I promise. Come on. She'll show you."

At the Gare du Nord, Laura said, "Let's take a cab. Let's go see Helen."

"Don't you want to drop off your suitcase?"

She shook her head. "I wish you'd found another place to stay."

They went to the stand along the side of the station. He hadn't been inside a taxi since their first day in Paris. Mornings, he went to the hospital underground, afternoons he came back by foot. He felt suddenly that every national weakness a people had was evident on its highways.

"Do you have cash?" Laura asked as they pulled up.

"I thought you did."

"I just got here. I have dollars."

He dug through his pockets and found just enough. They stepped outside.

"I hate it here," Laura said, looking at the clean façade of the hospital.

"I know. I hate it too."

"No. You're better than me. You don't hate it. You hate the situation. That's the right response. Me, I want to run out the door and never come back. I would, if I could."

"This way," he said. "They moved her."

At first Wes was struck by how good Helen looked, the pink in her cheeks, the nearly chic haircut, and then he glanced at Laura and then he understood how little, really, their daughter had changed. It had been six weeks. She looked dazed and cheerful. She couldn't speak.

"Hi, honey," said Wes. "Look. Mommy's here."

"Oh, God," said Laura.

"Sshh," said Wes.

But Laura was by the bed. She touched Helen's cheek. "Honey," she said. "Sweetheart. Shit." She looked down the length of Helen and pulled up the sheet: her bent knees with the pillow between, the wasting muscles, the catheter tube. She shook her head, rearranged the sheet. "I know, I know what you think of me, Wes."

"I don't—"

"It's not that it's not her. It's that—whoever this person in the bed is, she's where my Helen should be. That's what I can't get over and it's what I know I have to."

Laura was wearing a dress she had bought in the July sales when they'd first arrived, red, with blue embroidered flowers on the shoulders like epaulets. She had belted it too tight. She had lost weight too.

"Just sit," he said to her. "There are chairs. Here's one. We'll paint. Shall we paint, Helen?"

He wound the brace around her wrist, always a pleasing task, and slid in Helen's favorite long-handled brush, meant for oils, not watercolors. He propped up the pad on the wheeled table that came over the bed, got the water, the colors, dampened the paints. They began.

"You're doing it," said Laura.

"No," he said patiently. "I'm just steadying her hand."

"Then let go," said Laura.

He did, and he believed it would happen: her hand would sail up, like a bird tossed in the air. It would just keep flying. Yes, that was right. If anything, he wanted to tell Laura, he was holding her hand too still, he was interfering. She didn't need him anymore.

But her hand went ticking down to the bottom of the page, and stopped.

Helen's jaw worked, and Laura and Wes watched it. She had not made a noise in weeks. She did not make one now. The short haircut looked alternately gamine and like a punishment. Wes picked her hand back up, placed it, let go. Tick, tick, to the bottom of the page.

"So you see," said Laura.

Wes shook his head. No. She'd needed the help but he was not capable of those paintings.

And if he was, what did that mean? The paintings were what was left of Helen.

"She's not a fraud," said Wes.

"No, I don't think she is," said Laura. "I don't think she's anything. She's not at home, Wes."

"Isn't she?" said Wes.

"No," said Laura. She tapped her head. "I mean here, in her brain, she's not at home. It doesn't matter where her body is. Her body will be at home anywhere. But it matters where *your* body is. We need to take her home and you too."

"It isn't just me who's seen it," said Wes.

"Who doesn't love a miracle girl," said Laura, but with love. "I wanted one too, honestly. I would have loved it, if it had been real."

But, thought Helen—because Helen *was* at home, Helen heard everything—wasn't it more of a miracle this way? Her mother was right. She could not move her hands: that was her father. But she saw the pictures in her head, those fields with the apartment blocks, that golden light—and she couldn't move her hand to get them on the paper. Her father did. There was the miracle everyone spoke about, in English and in French. The visiting nuns said it was God, but it was her father who took her hand and painted the pictures in her head. Every time he got them right: the buildings, the light posts, those translucent floating things across her field of vision when she wasn't exactly looking at anything, what as a child she thought of as her conscience—*floaters,* her father once told her they were called. "I have them too," he'd said. They were worse in the hospital, permanent static. She saw, he painted the inside of her snow-globe skull, all those things whizzing around when she fell—the water tower on top of the building, the boy who'd kissed her, the other boy who'd pushed her, those were their faces in the corner of the page, the bottles of wine she'd drunk—back home she'd had beer and peppermint schnapps and had drunk cough syrup, but not wine. Wine was everything here. Those boys would come visit her. They'd promised they would when they dropped her off. She had to stay put. *Don't let her take me, Daddy.* Her mother hadn't looked her in the eye since she'd come into the room, but when had she, ever, ever, ever, thought Helen. All her life, she'd been too bright a light.

"Careless Helen," said Laura, and then to Wes, "Do you know, I think I've only just forgiven her."

"What for?" asked Wes.

She rubbed her nose absentmindedly. "Funny smell. What is that?"

Not medicine nor illness: the iridescent polish the manicurist had applied to Helen's toes.

In order to wake up every morning, thought Wes, he'd convinced himself of a lot of things that weren't true. He could feel some of his beliefs crumble like old plaster—life in Paris, walking the streets with Helen in his arms, revenge on Didier, even Dr. Delarche's crush. Of course they would go back to the States, where Kit was, they would talk to experts, they would find a facility, they would bring Helen home as soon as they could, where she would be visited by Addie of the braces and the clarinet, and boys from her school. She might never walk again. But her body would persist. It was broken but not failing. She was theirs for the rest of their lives, and then Kit would inherit her. That was what Laura had seen from the first day, and it had crushed her, and she was only just now shifting that weight from her chest.

Helen painted. That was real. He knew his own brain, what it could make up and what it couldn't. He looked at his wife, whom he loved, whom he looked forward to convincing, and felt as though he were diving headfirst into happiness. It was a circus act, a perilous one. Happiness was a narrow tank. You had to make sure you cleared the lip.

THOMAS McGUANE

Motherlode

FROM *The New Yorker*

LOOKING IN THE hotel mirror, David Jenkins adjusted the Stetson he disliked and pulled on a windbreaker with a cattle-vaccine logo. He worked for a syndicate of cattle geneticists in Oklahoma, though he'd never met his employers—he had earned his credentials through an online agricultural portal, much the way that some people became ministers. He was still in his twenties, a very bright young man, but astonishingly uneducated in every other way. He had spent the night in Jordan at the Garfield Hotel, which was an ideal location for meeting his ranch clients in the area. He had woken early enough to be the first customer at the café. On the front step, an old dog slept with a canceled first-class stamp stuck to its butt. By the time David had ordered breakfast, older ranchers occupied several of the tables, waving to him familiarly. Then a man from Utah, whom he'd met at the hotel, appeared in the doorway and stopped, looking around the room. The man, who'd told David that he'd come to Jordan to watch the comets, was small and intense, middle-aged, wearing pants with an elastic waistband and flashy sneakers. Several of the ranchers were staring at him. David had asked the hotel desk clerk, an elderly man, about the comets. The clerk said, "I don't know what he's talking about and I've lived here all my life. He doesn't even have a car." David studied the menu to keep from being noticed, but it was too late. The man was at his table, laughing, his eyes shrinking to points and his gums showing. "Stop worrying! I'll get my own table," he said, drumming his fingers on the back of David's chair. David felt that in some odd way he was being assessed.

The door to the café, which had annoying bells on a string, kept clattering open and shut to admit a broad sample of the community. David enjoyed all the comradely greetings and gentle needling from the ranchers and felt himself to be connected to the scene, if lightly. Only the fellow from Utah, sitting alone, seemed entirely apart. The cook pushed dish after dish across her tall counter while the waitress sped to keep up. She had a lot to do, but it lent her a star quality among the diners, who teased her with mock personal questions or air-pinched as her bottom went past.

David made notes about this and that on a pad he took from his shirt pocket, until the waitress, a yellow pencil stuck in her chignon, arrived with his bacon and eggs. He turned a welcoming smile to her, hoping that when he looked back the man would be gone, but he was still at his table, giving David an odd military salute and then holding his nose. David didn't understand these gestures and was disquieted by the implication that he knew the man. He ate quickly, then went to the counter to pay. The waitress came out of the kitchen, wiping her hands on a dishcloth, looked the cash register up and down, and said, "Everything OK, Dave?"

"Yes, very good, thanks."

"Put it away in an awful hurry. Out to Larsen's?"

"No, I was there yesterday. Bred heifers. They held everything back."

"They're big on next year. I wonder if it'll do them any good."

"They're still here, ain't they? I'm headed for Jorgensen's. Big day."

Two of the ranchers had finished eating and, Stetsons on the back of their heads, chairs tilted, they picked their teeth with the corners of their menus. As David put his wallet in his pocket and headed for the door, he realized he was being followed. He didn't turn until he was halfway across the parking lot. When he did, the gun was in his stomach and his new friend was smiling at him. "Name's Ray. Where's your outfit?"

Ray had a long, narrow face and tightly marcelled dirty-blond hair that fell low on his forehead.

"Are you robbing me?"

"I need a ride."

Ray got in the front seat of David's car, tucked the gun in his pants, and pulled his shirt over the top of it, a blue terry-cloth shirt with a large breast pocket that contained a pocket liner and a number of ballpoint pens. The flap of the pocket liner said "Powell Savings, Modesto, CA."

"Nice car. What're all the files in back for?"

"Breeding records—cattle-breeding records."

"Mind?" He picked up David's cell phone and, without waiting for an answer, tapped in a number. In a moment, his voice changed to an intimate murmur. "I'm there, or almost there—" Covering the mouthpiece, he pointed to the intersection. "Take that one right there." David turned east. "I got it wrote down someplace, East 200, North 13, but give it to me again, my angel. Or I can call you as we get closer. OK, a friend's giving me a lift." He covered the mouthpiece. "Your name?"

"David."

"David from?"

"Reed Point."

"Yeah, great guy I knew back in Reed Place."

"Reed Point."

"I mean, Reed Point. Left the Beamer for an oil change, and Dave said he was headed this way. Wouldn't even let me split the gas. So, OK, just leaving Jordan. How much longer, Morsel? Two hours! Are you fucking kidding? OK, OK, two hours. I'm just anxious to see you, baby, not being short with you at all."

Lifting his eyes to the empty miles of sagebrush, Ray snapped the cell phone shut and said, sighing, "Two fucking hours." If it weren't for the gun in his pants, he could have been any other aging lovebird. He turned the radio on briefly. *Swap Shop* was on the air: "Broken refrigerator suitable for a smoker." Babies bawling in the background. He turned it off. David was trying to guess who Ray might really be—that is, if he was a fugitive from the law, someone he could bring to justice, in exchange for fame or some kind of reward, something good for business. He had tried everything he could to enhance his cattle-insemination business, even refrigerator magnets with his face on them that said "Don't go bust shipping dries."

He asked, "Ray, do you feel like telling me what this is all about?"

"Sure, Dave. It's all about you doing as you're told."

"I see. And I'm taking you somewhere, am I?"

"Uh-huh, and staying as needed. Jesus Christ, if this isn't the ugliest country I ever seen."

"How did you pick me?"

"I picked your car. You were a throw-in. I hadn't took you along you'd've reported your car stolen. This way you still got it. It's a win-win. The lucky thing for you is you're my partner now. And you wanna pick up the tempo here? You're driving like my grandma."

"This isn't a great road. Deer jump out on it all the time. My cousin had one come through the windshield on him."

"Fuckin' pin it or I'll drive it like I did steal it."

David sped up slightly. This seemed to placate Ray and he slumped by the window and stared at the landscape going by. They passed an old pickup truck, traveling in the opposite direction, a dead animal in the back with one upright leg trailing an American flag.

After they'd driven for nearly two hours, mostly in silence, a light tail-dragger aircraft with red-and-white-banded wings flew just overhead and landed on the road in front of them. The pilot climbed out and shuffled toward the car. David rolled down his window, and a lean, weathered face under a sweat-stained cowboy hat looked in. "You missed your turn," the man said. "Mile back, turn north on the two-track." Ray seemed to be trying to send a greeting that showed all his teeth but he was ignored by the pilot. "Nice little Piper J-3 Cub," Ray said.

The pilot strode back to the plane, taxied down the road, got airborne, and banked sharply over a five-strand barbed wire, startling seven cows and their calves, which ran off into the sage, scattering meadowlarks and clouds of pollen. David turned the car around.

Ray said, "Old fellow back at the hotel said there's supposed to be dinosaurs around here." He gazed at the pale light of a gas well on a far ridge.

"That's what they say."

"What d'you suppose one of them is worth? Like a whole Tyrannosaurus rex?"

David just looked at Ray. Here was the turn, a two-track that was barely manageable in an ordinary sedan and David couldn't imagine how it was negotiated in winter or spring, when the notorious local gumbo turned to mud. He'd delivered a Charolais bull near here one fall, and it was bad enough then. Plus, the bull had torn up his trailer and he'd lost money on the deal.

"So, Dave, we're about to arrive and I should tell you what the gun is for. I'm here to meet a girl, but I don't know how it's gonna turn out. I may need to bail and you're my lift. The story is, my car is in for repair. You stay until we see how this goes and carry me out of here, if necessary. My friend here says you're onboard."

"I guess I understand, but what does this all depend on?"

"It depends on whether I like the girl or not, whether we're compatible and want to start a family business. I have a lot I'd like to pass on to the next generation."

The next bend revealed the house, a two-story ranch building with little of its paint left. Ray gazed at the Piper Cub, which was now parked in a field by the house, and at the Montana state flag popping on the iron flagpole. *"Oro y plata,"* he said, chuckling. "Perfect. Now, Davey, I need you to bone up on the situation here. This is the Weldon Case cattle ranch, and it runs from here right up to the Bakken oil field, forty miles away, which is where all the *oro y plata* is at the moment. I'm guessing that was Weldon in the airplane. I met Weldon's daughter, Morsel, through a dating service. Well, we haven't actually met in real time, but we're about to. Morsel thinks she loves me, and we're just gonna have to see about that. All you have to know is that Morsel thinks I'm an Audi dealer from Simi Valley, California. She's going on one photograph of me standing in front of an Audi flagship that did not belong to me. You decide you want to help, and you may see more walkin'-around money than you're used to. If you don't, well, you've seen how I put my wishes into effect." He patted the bulge under his shirt. "I just whistle a happy tune and start shooting."

David pulled up under the gaze of Weldon Case, who had emerged from the plane. When he rolled down the window to greet the old man again, Case just stared, then turned to call out to the house. "It's the cowboy way," Ray muttered through an insincere smile. "Or else he's retarded. Dave, ask him if he remembers falling out of his high chair."

As they got out of the car, Morsel appeared on the front step and inquired, in a penetrating contralto, "Which one is it?" Ray raised his hands and tilted his head to one side, as though modestly questioning himself. David noted that the gun was inadequately concealed and turned quickly to shake Weldon Case's hand. It was like seizing a plank.

"You're looking at him," Ray called out to Morsel.

"Oh, Christ," she yelled. "Is this what I get?" It was hard to say whether this was a positive response or not. Morsel was a scale model of her father, wind-weathered and, if anything, less feminine. Her view of the situation was quickly clarified as she raced forward to embrace Ray, whose look of suave detachment was briefly interrupted by fear. A tooth was missing, as well as a small piece of her ear. "Oh, Ray!"

Weldon looked at David with a sour expression, then spoke, in a lusterless tone: "Morsel has made some peach cobbler. It was her ma's recipe. Her ma is dead." Ray put on a ghastly look of sympathy, which seemed to fool Morsel, who squeezed his arm and said, "Started in her liver and just took off."

A small trash pile next to the porch featured a couple of played-out Odor-Eaters. David wondered where the walkin'-around money Ray had alluded to was supposed to come from. "Place is kind of a mess," Morsel warned. "We don't collect but we never get rid of."

As they went into the house, Weldon asked David if he enjoyed shooting coyotes. He replied, "I just drive Ray around"—Ray turned to listen—"and whatever Ray wants I guess is what we do . . . whatever he's into." David kept to himself that he enjoyed popping coyotes out his car window with the .25–06 with a Redfield rangefinder scope and a tripod that he'd got from Hill Country Customs. David lived with his mother and had a habit of telling her about the great shots he'd made—like the five-hundred-yarder on Tin Can Hill with only the hood for a rest, no sandbags, no tripod. David's Uncle Maury had told him a long time ago, "It don't shoot flat, throw the fuckin' thing away."

David, who enjoyed brutally fattening food, thought Morsel was a good cook, but Ray ate only the salad, discreetly lifting each leaf until the dressing ran off. Weldon watched Ray and hardly said a word, as Morsel grew more manic, jiggling with laughter and enthusiasm at each lighthearted remark. In fact, it was necessary to lower the temperature of the subjects—to heart attacks, highway wrecks, cancer—in order to get her to stop guffawing. Weldon planted his hands flat on the table, rose partway, and announced that he'd use the tractor to pull the plane around back. David was preoccupied with the mountain of tuna casserole between him and the peach cobbler and hardly heard him. Ray, small and disoriented next to Morsel, shot his eyes around the table, looking for something he could eat.

"Daddy don't say much," Morsel said.

"*I* can't say much," Ray said, "with *him* here. Dave, could you cut us a little slack?"

"Sure, Ray, of course." David got up, still chewing.

"See you in the room," Ray said sharply, twisting his chin toward the door.

Weldon had shown them their room by walking past it and flicking the door open without a word. It contained two iron bedsteads and a dresser, atop which were David's and Ray's belongings, the latter's consisting of a JanSport backpack with the straps cut off. David was better organized, with an actual overnight bag and a Dopp kit. He had left the cattle receipts and breeding documents in the car. He flopped on the bed, hands behind his head, then got up abruptly and went to the door. He looked out and listened for a long moment, eased it closed, and shot to the dresser, where he began rooting through Ray's belongings: rolls of money in rubber bands, generic Viagra from India, California lottery tickets, a passport identifying Raymond Coelho, a woman's aqua-colored wallet, with a debit card in the name of Eleanor Coelho from Food Processors Credit Union of Modesto, Turlock grocery receipts, a bag of trail mix, and the gun. David lifted the gun carefully with the tips of his fingers. He was startled by its lightness. Turning it over in his hand, he was compelled to acknowledge that there was no hole in the barrel. It was a toy. He returned it to the pack, fluffed the sides, and sped to his bed to begin feigning sleep.

It wasn't long before Ray came in, singing "Now Is the Hour" in a flat and aggressive tone that hardly suited the lyrics: "Sunset glow fades in the west, night o'er the valley is creeping! Birds cuddle down in their nest, soon all the world will be sleeping. But not you, Dave. You're awake, I can tell. I hope you enjoyed the song. It's Hugo Winterhalter. Morsel sang it to me. She's very nice, and she needs a man."

"Looks like you got the job."

"Do what? Hey, here's what's going on with me: I'm starving."

"I'm sure you are, Ray. You ate like a bird."

"I had no choice. That kind of food gathers around the chambers of the heart like an octopus. But right behind the house they got a vegetable garden, and my plan for you is to slip out and bring me some vegetables. I've been told to stay out of the garden. Don't touch the tomatoes—they're not ripe."

"What else is there?"

"Greens and root vegetables."

"I'm not going out there."

"Oh, yes, you are."

"What makes you think so?"

Ray went to his pack and got out the gun.

"This makes me think so. This will really stick to your ribs, get it?"

"I'm not picking vegetables for you, or, technically speaking, stealing them for you. Forget it."

"Wow. Is this a mood swing?"

"Call it what you want. Otherwise, it's shoot or shut up."

"OK, but not for the reason you think. I prefer not to wake up the whole house."

"And the body'd be a problem for you, as a houseguest and new fiancé."

"Very well, very well. This time." Ray put the gun back in his pack. "You don't know how close you came."

"Whatever."

David rolled over to sleep, but he couldn't stop his thoughts. He should have spent the day at Jorgensen's with his arm up a cow's ass. He had a living to make and, if it hadn't been for his inappropriate curiosity about Ray and Morsel, he'd already be back in Jordan, looking to grab a room for the night. But the roll of money in Ray's pack and the hints of more to come had made him wonder how anxious he was to get back to work. There was opportunity in the air and he wanted to see how it would all play out.

"Ray, you awake?"

"I can be. What d'you want, asshole?"

"I just have something I want to get off my chest."

"Make it quick. I need my Z's."

"Sure, Ray, try this one on for size: the gun's a toy."

"The gun's a what?"

"A toy."

"You think a gun's a toy?"

"No, Ray, I think *your* gun's a toy. It's a fake. And looks like you are too."

"Where's the fuckin' light switch? I'm not taking this shit."

"Stub your toe jumping off the bed like that."

"Might be time to clip your wings, sonny."

"Ray, I'm here for you. Just take a moment to look at the barrel of your so-called gun, and then let's talk."

Ray found the lamp and paced the squeaking floorboards. "Taking a leak off the porch. Be right back," he said. Through the open bedroom door, David could see him silhouetted in the moonlight, a silver arc splashing onto the dirt, his head thrown back in what David took to be a plausible posture of despair.

By the time Ray walked back in he was already talking: ". . . an appraiser in Modesto, California, where I grew up. I did some community theater there, played Prince Oh So True in a children's production and thought I was going places, then *Twelve Angry Men*—I was one of them, which is where the pistol came from. I was the hangman in *Motherlode*. Got married, had a baby girl, lost my job, got another one, went to Hawaii as a steward on a yacht belonging to a movie star, who was working at a snow-cone stand a year before the yacht, the coke, the babes, and the wine. I had to sign a nondisclosure agreement, but then I got into a fight with the movie star and got kicked off the boat at Diamond Head. They just rowed me to shore in a dinghy and dumped me off. I hiked all the way to the crater and used the restroom to clean up, then took the tour bus into Honolulu. I tried to sell the celebrity drug-use story to a local paper, but it went nowhere because of the confidentiality agreement. Everything I *sign* costs me money. About this time, my wife's uncle's walnut farm was failing. He took a loan out on the real estate, and I sold my car, which was a mint, rust-free '78 Trans Am, handling package, W-72 performance motor, Solar Gold with a Martinique Blue interior. We bought a bunch of FEMA trailers from the Katrina deal and hauled them to California. We lost our asses. The uncle gases himself in his garage, and my wife throws me out. I moved into a hotel for migrant workers and started using the computers at the Stanislaus County Library and sleeping at the McHenry Mansion. One of the tour guides was someone I used to fuck in high school and she slipped me into one of the rooms for naps. I met Morsel online. I told her I was on hard times. She told me she was coining it, selling bootleg Oxycontin in the Bakken oil field, but she was lonely. It was a long shot. Montana. Fresh start. New me. Bus to Billings and hit the road. I made it to Jordan, and I had nothing left. The clerk at that fleabag barely let me have a room. I told him I was there for the comets. I don't know where I come up with that. Breakfast at the café was my last dime and no tip. I had to make a move. So what happens now? You bust me with Morsel? You turn me in? Or you join us?"

"You pretty sure on the business end of this thing?" David asked, with a coldness that surprised him.

"A hundred percent, but Morsel's got issues with other folks already in it. There's some risk, but when isn't there, with stakes like this? Think about it, Dave. If you're at all interested in getting rich, you tell me."

Ray was soon snoring. David was intrigued that all these revelations failed to disturb his sleep. He himself was wide awake, brooding over how colorless his own life was in comparison with Ray's. Ray was a con man and a failure, but what had *he* ever done? Finish high school? High school had been anguish, persecution, and suffering, but even in that he was unexceptional. He'd never had sex with a mansion tour guide. He'd had sex with a fat girl he disliked. Then the National Guard. Fort Harrison in the winter. Cleaning billets. Inventorying ammunition. Unskilled maintenance on UH-60 Blackhawks. Praying for deployment against worldwide towel heads. A commanding officer who told the recruits that the president of the United States was "a pencil-wristed twat." Girlfriend fatter every time he went home. He still lived with his mother. Was still buying his dope from the same guy at the body shop he'd got it from in the eighth grade.

Perhaps it was surprising he'd come up with anything at all, but he had: Bovine Deluxe, LLC, a crash course in artificially inseminating cattle. David took to it like a duck to water: driving around the countryside detecting and synchronizing estrus, handling frozen semen, keeping breeding records—all easily learnable, but David brought art to it, and he had no idea where that art had come from. He was a genius preg-tester. Whether he was straight or stoned, his rate of accuracy, as proven in spring calves, was renowned. Actually, David *preferred* preg-testing stoned. Grass gave him a greater ability to visualize the progress of his arm up the cow's rectum. His excitement began as soon as he donned his coveralls, pulled on his glove, lubed it with OB goo, and stepped up to the cow stuck in the chute. Holding the tail high overhead with his left hand, he got his right hand all the way in, against the cow's attempt to expel it, shoveled out the manure to clear the way past the cervix, and finally, nearly up to his shoulder, grasped the uterus. David could nail a pregnancy at two months, when the calf was smaller than a mouse. He never missed, and no cow that should have been culled turned up without a calf in the spring. He could tell the rancher how far along the cow was by his informal gradations: mouse, rat, Chihuahua, cat, fat cat, raccoon, beagle. Go through the herd, or until his arm was exhausted. Throw the glove away, write up the invoice, strip the coveralls, look for food and a room.

Perfect. Except for the dough.

He'd once dreamed of owning jewels, especially rubies, and that dream was coming back. Maybe glue one on his forehead like a Hindu. It'd go over big on his ranch calls.

Morsel made breakfast for her father, David, and Ray—eggs, biscuits, and gravy. David was thinking about Ray's "last dime" back in Jordan versus the rolls of bills in his pack and watching Weldon watch Ray as breakfast was served. Morsel just leaned against the stove while the men ate. "Anyone want to go to Billings today to see the cage fights?" she asked. David looked up and smiled but no one answered her. Ray was probing around his food with his fork, pushing the gravy away from the biscuits, and Weldon was flinching. Weldon wore his black Stetson with the salt-encrusted sweat stain halfway up the crown. David thought it was downright unappetizing, not the sort of thing a customer for top-drawer bull semen would wear. At last Weldon spoke at top volume, as though calling out to his livestock.

"What'd you say your name was?"

"Ray."

"Well, Ray, why don't you stick that fork all the way in and eat like a man?"

"I'm doing my best, Mr. Case, but I will eat nothing with a central nervous system."

"Daddy, leave Ray alone. You'll have time to get to know each other and find out what Ray enjoys eating."

When Morsel brought Ray some canned pineapple slices, he looked up at her with what David took to be genuine affection.

She turned to David and said, "It's all you can eat around here," but the moment he stuck his fork back in his food she put a hand in his face and said, "That's all you can eat!" and laughed. David noticed her cold blue eyes and thought he was beginning to understand her.

To Weldon, she said, "Daddy, you feel like showing Ray 'n' 'em the trick?" Weldon stopped his rhythmic lip pursing.

"Oh, Morsel," he said coyly.

"C'mon, Daddy. Give you a dollar."

"OK, Mor, put on the music," he said with a sigh of good-humored defeat. Morsel went over to a low cupboard next to the pie safe and pulled out a small plastic record player and a 45-rpm record, which proved to be a scratchy version of "Cool Water," by the Sons of the Pioneers. Weldon swayed to the mournful tune and then seemed to come to life as Morsel placed a peanut in front of him and the lyrics began: "Keep a-movin', Dan,/Don't you listen to him, Dan./He's a devil not a man." Weldon took off his hat and set it upside down beside him, revealing the thinnest comb-over across a snow-white pate. Then he picked up the peanut and, with sinuous movements, balanced it on his nose. It remained there until near the end of the record—"Dan, can you see,/That big green tree,/Where the water's runnin' free"—when the peanut fell to the table and Weldon's chin dropped to stare at it. When the record ended, he replaced his hat, stood without a word, and left the room. For a moment it was quiet, and then came the sound of Weldon's plane cranking up.

"Daddy's pretty hard on himself when he don't make it to the end of the record," Morsel said glumly, as she cleared the dishes. Heading for the living room, she added, "Me and Ray thought you ought to see what dementia looks like. It don't look good and it's expensive."

David had taken care to copy out the information from Ray's passport onto the back of a matchbook cover, which he tore off, rolled into a cylinder, and put inside a bottle of aspirin. And there it stayed until Ray and Morsel headed off to the cage fights. David used his cell phone and 411 Connect to call Ray's home in Modesto and chat with his wife or, as she claimed to be, his widow. It took two calls, a couple of hours apart. The first try, he got her answering machine: "You know the drill: leave it at the beep." On the second try, he got Ray's wife. David identified himself as an account assistant with the Internal Revenue Service and Ray's wife listened only briefly before stating in a firm, clear, and seemingly ungrieving voice that Ray was dead: "That's what I told the last guy and that's what I'm telling you." She said that he had been embezzling from a credit union, left a suicide note, and disappeared.

"I'm doing home health care. Whatever he stole he kept. Killing himself was the one good idea he come up with in the last thirty years. At least it's kept the government from garnisheeing my wages, what little they are. I been through all this with the other guy that called, and we have to wait for his death to be confirmed before I get no benefits. If I know Ray, he's on the bottom of the Tuolumne River, just to fuck with my head. I wish I could have seen him one more time to tell him I gave his water skis and croquet set to Goodwill. If the bank hadn't taken back his airplane, I would have lost my house and been sleeping in my car. Too bad you didn't meet Ray. He was an A-to-Z crumb bum."

"I'm terribly sorry to hear about your husband," David said mechanically.

"I don't think the government is 'terribly sorry' to hear about anything. You reading this off a card?"

"No, this is just a follow-up to make sure your file stays intact until you receive the benefits you're entitled to."

"I already have the big one: picturing Ray in hell with his ass *en fuego*."

"Ah, you speak a bit of Spanish, Mrs. Coelho?"

"Everybody in Modesto 'speaks a bit of Spanish.' Where you been all your life?"

"Washington, D.C.," David said indignantly.

"That explains it," Mrs. Coelho said, and hung up.

Of course he had no car when we met, David thought. No need to leave a paper trail by renting cars or buying tickets on airplanes. He'd got done all he needed to get done on the Modesto library computers, where he and Morsel, two crooks, had found each other and gone into business without ever laying eyes on each other.

Before heading to Billings, Morsel had told David how to get to the Indian smallpox burial ground to look for beads. Otherwise, there was nothing to do around here. He wasn't interested until he discovered the liquor cabinet and by then it was early evening. He found a bottle marked Hoopoe Schnapps, with a picture of a bird on its label, and gave it a try: "Bottoms up." It went straight to his head. After several swigs, he was unable to identify the bird but he was very happy. The label said that the drink contained "mira-belles," and David thought, Hey, I'm totally into mirabelles.

As he headed for the burial ground, David was tottering a bit. Rounding the equipment shed, he nearly ran into Weldon Case, who walked by without speaking or apparently seeing him. Behind the ranch buildings, a cow trail led into the prairie, then wound toward a hillside spring that didn't quite reach the surface, visible only by the greenery above it. Just below that was the place that Morsel had told him about, pockmarked with anthills. The ants, Morsel claimed, carried the beads to the surface, but you had to hunt for them.

David sat down among the mounds and was soon bitten through his pants. He jumped to his feet and swept the ants away, then crouched, peering and picking at the anthills. His thighs soon ached from squatting, but then he found a speck of sky blue in the dirt, a bead. He clasped it tightly in one hand while stirring with the other and flicking away ants. He didn't think about the bod-ies in the ground beneath him. By the time it was too dark to see, his palm was filled with Indian beads and he felt elevated and still drunk.

As he passed the equipment shed, he made out first the silhou-ette of Weldon Case's Stetson and then, very close, the face of Wel-don himself, who gazed at him before speaking in a low voice. "You been in the graves, ain't you?"

"Yes, to look for beads."

"You ought not to have done that, feller."

"Oh? But Morsel said—"

"Look up there at the stars."

"I don't understand."

Weldon reached high over his head. "That's the crow riding the water snake," he said, and turned back into the dark.

David was frightened. He went to the house and got into bed as quickly as he could, anxious for the alcohol to fade. He pulled the blanket up under his chin, despite the warmth of the night, and watched a moth batting against an image of the moon in the win-dow. When he was nearly asleep, he saw Morsel's headlights wheel across the ceiling, then turn off. He listened for the car doors, but it was nearly ten minutes before they opened and closed. He rolled close to the wall and pretended to be asleep, while the front door opened quietly. Once the reverberation of the screen-door spring had died down, there was whispering that came into the bedroom. He felt a shadow cross his face as someone peered down at him. Soon the sound of muffled copulation filled the room, stopped for the time it took to raise a window, then resumed. David listened more and more intently, until Ray said, in a clear voice, "Dave, you want some of this?"

David stuck to his feigned sleep until Morsel laughed, got up, and walked out with her clothes under her arm. "Night, Ray. Sweet dreams."

The door shut and, after a moment, Ray spoke. "What could I do, Dave? She was after my weenie like a chicken after a June bug." Snorts, and, soon after, snoring.

Morsel stood in the doorway of the house, taking in the early sun and smoking a cigarette. She wore an old flannel shirt over what looked like a body stocking that revealed a lazily winking camel toe. Her eyes followed her father as he crossed the yard very slowly. "Look," she said, as David stepped up. "He's wetting his pants. When he ain't wetting his pants, he walks pretty fast. It's just something he enjoys."

Weldon came up and looked at David, trying to remember him. He said, "This ain't much of a place to live. My folks moved us out here. We had a nice little ranch at Coal Bank Landing, on the Missouri, but one day it fell in the river. Morsel, I'm uncomfortable."

"Go inside, Daddy. I'll get you a change of clothes."

Once the door had shut behind him, David said, "Why in the world do you let him fly that airplane?"

"It's all he knows. He flew in the war and dusted crops. He'll probably kill himself in the damn thing."

"What's he do up there?"

"Looks for his cows."

"I didn't know he had cows."

"He don't. They all got sold years ago. But he'll look for them long as he's got fuel."

Morsel turned back to David on her way inside. "I can't make heads or tails of your friend Ray," she said. "He was coming on to me the whole time at the cage fights, then he takes out a picture of his wife and tells me she's the greatest piece of ass he ever had."

"Huh. What'd you say to that?"

"I said, 'Ray, she must've had a snappin' pussy because she's got a face that would stop a clock.' He didn't like that too much. So I punched him in the shoulder and told him he hadn't seen nothing yet. What'd you say your name was?"

"I'm David."

"Well, Dave, Ray says you mean to throw in with us. Is that a fact?"

"I'm sure giving it some thought."

David was being less than candid. He would have slipped away the day before if he hadn't felt opportunity headed his way on silver wings.

"You look like a team player to me. I guess that bitch he's married to will help out on that end. Long as I never have to see her."

David had an unhappy conversation with his mother, but at least it was on the phone, so she couldn't throw stuff.

"The phone is ringing off the hook! Your ranchers are calling constantly, wanting to know when you'll get there."

"Ma, I know, but I got tied up. Tell them not to get their panties in a wad. I'll be there."

"David!" she screeched. "This is not an answering service!"

"Ma, listen to me. Ma, I got tied up. I'm sparing you the details but relax."

"How can I relax with the phone going off every ten seconds?"

"Ma, I'm under pressure. Pull the fucking thing out of the wall."

"Pressure? You've never been under pressure in your life!"

He hung up on her. He couldn't live with her anymore. She needed to take her pacemaker and get a room.

That week, Morsel was able to get a custodial order in Miles City, based on the danger to the community presented by Weldon and his airplane. Ray had so much trouble muscling Weldon into Morsel's sedan for the ride to assisted living that big strong David had to pitch in and help Ray tie him up. Weldon tossed off some frightful curses before collapsing in defeat and crying. But the God he called down on them didn't hold much water anymore, and they made short work of the old fellow. At dinner that night, Morsel was a little blue. The trio's somewhat obscure toasts were to the future. David looked on with a smile; he felt happy and accepted and believed he was going somewhere. His inquiring looks were met by giddy winks from Morsel and Ray. They told him that he was now a "courier," and Ray unwound one of his bundles of cash. He was going to California.

"Drive the speed limit," Ray said. "I'm going to get to know the airplane. Take it down to the oil fields. It's important to know your customers."

"Do you know how to fly it?" This was an insincere question, since David had learned from the so-called widow about Ray's re-possessed plane.

"How's thirteen thousand hours sound to you?"

"I'll keep the home fires burning," Morsel said, without taking the cigarette out of her mouth.

David had a perfectly good idea of what he was going to Califor-nia for, but he didn't ask. He knew the value of preserving his ig-norance. If he could keep his status as a simple courier, he was no guiltier than the United States Postal Service. "Your Honor, I had no idea what was in the trunk, and I am prepared to say that under oath or take a lie-detector test, at your discretion," he rehearsed.

He drove straight through, or nearly so. He stopped briefly in Idaho, Utah, and Nevada to walk among cows. His manner with cattle was so familiar that they didn't run from him but gathered around in benign expectation. David sighed and jumped back in the car. He declined to pursue this feeling of regret.

It was late when he got into Modesto, and he was tired. He checked into a Super 8 and woke up when the hot light of a Cali-fornia morning shone through the window onto his face. He ate in the lobby and checked out. The directions Ray had given him proved exact: within ten minutes, he was pulling around the house into the side drive and backing into the open garage.

A woman came out of the house in a bathrobe and walked past his window without a word. He popped the trunk and sat quietly as she loaded it, then closed it. She stopped at his window, pulling the bathrobe up close around her throat. She wasn't hard to look at, but David could see you wouldn't want to argue with her. "Tell Ray I said be careful. I've heard from two IRS guys already." David said nothing at all.

He was so cautious that the trip back took longer. He stayed overnight at the Garfield again, so as to arrive in daylight, and got up twice during the night to check on the car. In the morning, he skipped eating at the café for fear he might encounter some of his rancher clients. Plus, he knew that Morsel would take care of his empty stomach. He was so close now that he worried about everything, from misreading the gas gauge to flat tires. He even imagined the trunk flying open for no reason. Now he drove past fields of cattle with hardly a glance.

He had imagined a hearty greeting, an enthusiastic homecoming, but the place was silent. A hawk sat on the wire that ran from the house to the bunkhouse, as though it had the place to itself. It flew off reluctantly when David got out of the car. Inside, there were soiled plates on the dining-room table. Light from the television flickered without sound from the living room. David walked in and saw the television first—it was on the shopping network, a close-up of a hand dangling a gold bracelet. Then he saw Morsel on the floor with the channel changer in her hand. She'd been shot.

David felt an icy calm. Ray must have done this. He checked the car keys in his pocket and walked out of the house, stopping on the porch to survey everything in front of him. Then he went around to the equipment shed. Where the airplane had been parked in its two shallow ruts lay Ray, also shot, a pool of blood extending from his mouth like a speech balloon without words. He'd lost a shoe. The plane was gone.

David felt as if he were trapped between the two bodies, with no safe way back to the car. When he got to it, a man was waiting for him. "I must have overslept. How long have you been here?" He was David's age, thin and precise in clean khakis and a Shale Services ball cap. He touched his teeth with his thumbnail as he spoke.

"Oh, just a few minutes."

"Keys."

"Yes, I have them here." David patted his pocket.

"Get the trunk for me, please." David tried to hand him the keys. "No, you."

"Not a problem."

David bent to insert the key but his hand was shaking and at first he missed the slot. The lid rose to reveal the contents of the trunk. David didn't feel a thing.

Madame Lazarus

FROM *The New Yorker*

MANY YEARS AGO, after I retired from the bank, James brought
a small terrier to our apartment in Paris. I told him I did not want
it. I knew he was trying to keep me occupied, and it is a ridiculous
thing, to have a dog. Maybe one day you rise from bed and say, "I
would like to pick up five thousand pieces of shit." Well, then, I
have just the thing for you. And for a man to have a small dog—it
makes you a fool.

"Please," James said. "Let's just see how it goes."

I considered the dog, a blond female no bigger than a cat. She
had long hair like whiskers over her eyes, so she seemed always to
be raising her eyebrows. She sat down, as if she knew that would
help her case. James is English and wanted to call her Cordelia,
not for *Lear* but for an English novel. It was not the name I would
have chosen, but it was not worth the argument. He did a ringmas-
ter act with some toys—a knot of cloth, a ball, a round bed—to
show me how good this would be. I had long associated terriers
with the barking arts, but this one did not bark. She sniffed at the
toys and the bed, waiting for my decision.

The next day James was gone to Brazil or Argentina, leaving
me with the dog. He had an import business and was often away.
I think Cordelia had already guessed that he was not a sure thing,
and she looked at me for our next move.

I took her outside to do her business. She was not allowed to
go in the impasse, where the cars park and the concierge is always
watching, so we went out through the gate to the street. We walked

around Paris. We went to the Bois de Boulogne, and there a hawk circled, eyeing Cordelia like a snack.

"Don't even think of it," I told this hawk.

People spoke to me who would not have before, and they wanted to pet Cordelia, who let them. When we arrived home, Desi was there to make lunch, and she cried out and dropped to her knees to rub the ears of the dog. Desi is from Indonesia, very proper, and she had worked for me for many years, but I had never seen such a display. Cordelia licked her face in greeting, and Desi laughed. Then I sat to read the paper, and Cordelia curled herself into my lap.

At first I believed that the appearance of love from a dog is only a strategy, to win protection. Cordelia chose me because I was the one to feed her and to chase away the hawks and the wolves. But after a time we crossed over a line, Cordelia and I. We went out each day to chase the pigeons and smell the piss of other dogs on the trees, and we came home to read the paper. The look with the eyebrows was sometimes skeptical about my actions, and sometimes a question that I understood. There were no arguments except silent ones—*I do not want to go there on the leash*—and these could be easily solved. Her hair needed to be cut, so I found a woman to do it, who tied pink ribbons over Cordelia's ears. She hated these ribbons. You could see she was ashamed. I told the groomer no more—she is too dignified for this. And, if she feels shame, then why not other emotions? A creature's eyes are on you all the time, or the warm body is next to you. There is an understanding. And I think this becomes something like love.

I am older now than I thought possible. I did not believe I would ever be this ancient person. The doctor says I should have no wine at lunch, for my heart. But if you cannot have a little wine with your lunch, there is no life. If you are as old as I am, you believed a German would shoot you in the head before you were old enough to have sex with another human being. Everything beyond that becomes extra. The things people do to live long—drinking so much water, running up and down to ruin the knees—this is what the doctor should warn about.

James is young, far younger than I. When you are the older man, you can be equal, for a time. He has youth and beauty, but you have money and experience. You know many people, and you can take him to Portofino, to Biarritz, to Capri. It is an old story.

But the years go by, and your doctor is concerned for your heart. Your joints are not so good. You don't want to look in the mirror when you go to take a bath. And the man you love is still strong and young, more or less. He travels a great deal. He is away more often. The dog knew the first time she saw him: he was not the one to rely on.

My ex-wife, Simone, comes for lunch sometimes, and we talk of our sons, who are long grown and have children of their own. One lives in New York and the other in Zurich—they are both in the banking. They know James, of course, but they do not like him. There is no reason they would. They are serious men, and James is not. Their children, my grandchildren, are charmed by him. They consider James an uncle. He is the correct age, and he is willing to play with them in a way adults are not. And Simone accepts him, which is in some ways a remarkable thing.

Simone looks as she always did, although she says this is only because I never saw her, not really. But I do: she is an elegant woman, all angles, gold bracelets on thin, tan wrists. And she understands what it is to be old, which is a comfort. After she leaves, Desi clears away the lunch dishes, and I take Cordelia out for a walk.

There came a point when I realized that James was in Paris only when there was an important party. Every person has one great gift, and James is unequaled at an important party. He is good-looking, of course, with the well-cut brown hair and the trim body and the bespoke suit. He has a brilliant smile, very warm and interested and sincere, and when he talks to people they feel special. He has many other abilities, but this one above all. They want to do business with him because of this attention. He is never looking over the shoulder to see who else is at the party. Who he is talking to, this person gets everything.

But then we go home, and the attention goes off like a light. He does not give me the warm and interested smile. He says a thing or two about the party, in the French he speaks like an Englishman but very well. He looks at his phone, swiping with his thumb. He takes his expensive clothes off carelessly, leaves them on the furniture like a child. He has had money always, and good looks, and was his mother's darling. He says Desi will pick up the clothes, although I tell him this is not her job. He says of course it is, what else is her job? He is careful only with his shoes. He puts them on wooden shoetrees in the closet, then goes into the bathroom and closes the door.

I think of the first boy I loved, two lifetimes ago. He came to my family's house, and I ran inside from playing and saw him standing with his mother. He had a light behind his eyes and a crown of silken curls. He was like someone standing in the sun, even in the dim, cool room. I was still very young, and it was a shock, because it was the first time I knew who I was. He was older than I, and he understood also—I could see that.

Then came the war, and the people fleeing Paris, and the Germans in the city. I was sent to England to live with some cousins, and I did not know what happened to this boy. He stayed behind. When I discovered him again, in a nightclub after the war, he did not like to talk about those years. The beauty that could help him in another time was not so useful during the Occupation. The Germans would be happy to kill him, or to send him to build their bunkers, which would be the same, and I do not know how he escaped. He said he tried to help the Maquis, but the people he knew did not want him. He did not seem strong, or robust. He was not a saboteur. Perhaps he could get information, but they did not trust how he would do it.

He was arrested at the end of the war, when the Germans were in a panic, and they simply left him in prison with no food. When I saw him in the nightclub he had the *tuberculose* from this prison, but he was still extraordinarily handsome. He seemed very pitiful to me, and very desirable.

My older brother had his own flat then, to be independent, but I still lived in the family house. This boy came to visit me when my parents were away. I knew my father would not approve, but it was exciting. I remembered the way the boy had lit up the old carpets, the paintings, the dust floating in the air.

One night, the boy and I were eating dinner at one end of the long table in my family house—he was always hungry—when he began to cough. The sound was wet and terrible, and the coughing did not stop. There was blood on the napkin, and his face was purple around the eyes, and then something went very wrong. There was so much blood, and he was coughing, dying, there on the dining-room floor. I didn't know what to do, how to stop this hemorrhage. I thought, He will open his eyes in a minute, he will smile, he will wipe his mouth and say, "No, no, do not worry. I am fine." But it did not happen. I heard a roaring like the sea in my ears. My hands were shaking.

I telephoned the doctor and my brother, and they came. My brother was furious, concerned only with the scandal of this disreputable nightclub boy dying in our family house. "You should have put him in a bathtub," he said. "For the blood."

I stared at him. When was I to carry him upstairs? There would be blood everywhere if I did this.

The doctor was kinder, more practical. He asked if there would be semen on the body, or inside it. I was shocked by the question, but I said no. It was the truth. He said this would make it easier. He asked me to help carry the boy to his car, and I lifted the shoulders. The doctor took the legs. He weighed so little. The head dropped back—the pale face, the bruised eyes—and I could not look, I was filled with horror. The doctor took him away in his car to the morgue and said I was never to speak of it. *N'en parlons plus jamais.* And, you see, still I find I do not want to say his name.

The housekeeper would arrive in the morning, so my brother helped me clean. I moved very slowly, my arms and legs frozen, while my brother gave me orders. I ran cold water on the napkins and towels in the sink, for the blood. I knew I could never repay what the doctor had done. I also knew that my brother would now have the moral advantage over me for the rest of my life. That is what I thought with my hands in the cold pink water, feeling sorry for myself, when it was the boy I loved who was dead.

Within the year, I met Simone. She was very appropriate, with a good family, the most graceful lines in a dress. She was in every way correct, and I must have proposed, because there was an engagement, a great announcement. I had never seen my father so happy. My mother was not so sure, but we had no way of discussing this at that time. There was the momentum of the approaching wedding—it was like climbing into an enormous car without brakes. The party, all the people watching, the flowers and the caterers. In front of everyone I knew, I put my grandmother's ring on Simone's elegant hand and made promises that I could not keep.

Cordelia sleeps on our bed, in the wide gulf between James and me. But she is old now, like me, and she gets down and pees on the rug. I go for the bottle of Perrier, the towel. Then she pees in the hall. James is still asleep, so I clean the hall floor and leave the bottle there. I put on my clothes quietly, and I take the dog outside.

Cordelia starts to go in the impasse, which she knows is not allowed. The concierge will come out, the neighbors will complain, it will be a whole issue. I speak to Cordelia, I pull on her leash, but she does not want to move. I pull harder. Finally she follows, very slowly. I could pick her up, but she needs to walk, just a little. This is the important thing, not to stop moving.

On the pavement outside the gate, she stands and seems to think about something far away. Her eyes are cloudy. She does not do a shit. She makes a strange sound and falls over. Her feet go up in the air, like a dead dog in a cartoon.

Here I become not so dignified. I fall down on my knees on the pavement and put my hands on Cordelia's chest. I feel no heartbeat, and I try to remember the rules. Two fingers for babies, or you break the ribs. Cordelia is about this size. I put my two fingers on her chest and start to push. I think about the heartbeat—how fast? My own heart is pounding in my ears, too fast, but Cordelia is small. Perhaps the rhythm is right. I press down with each loud pulse in my head.

People walk around me on the street. I can feel them stare. A few speak: they ask can they help, should they call an ambulance. I only feel for the pulse. I think, absurdly, of the boy coughing and dying on my floor, in another time. I could not press on his chest because the blood was coming from his lungs, and everything had broken loose. I did not know what to do.

Now I press and press. My knees ache, and I think there is broken glass on the pavement, cutting into my skin, but it is only sand and grit. Minutes go by, and more minutes. My arms tremble. I count the times I push, and then stop counting. I wonder if I have broken Cordelia's ribs. Someone told me once that this pressing does not work without the *truc machin*—the paddles to the heart. I think if I could open the bony chest I could hold the heart in my hand and squeeze it until it began to beat again.

Maybe someone should call an ambulance. But what would the driver say, arriving to see me with an old dog? Do they have this service for animals? I have no feeling in my hand.

"Il est mort," a helpful person says, standing over me. A young man this time.

"Elle," I say. The dog has her feet in the air. The world can see she is not a male. Do the young know nothing? But when I look at her I think he is right—she is dead.

"Ouais, bien, elle est morte," the young man says. And then he is gone.

I continue to press. I look at my watch, but I do not know what time we came outside.

And then Cordelia coughs. She opens her cloudy eyes. She seems to feel the indignity of her position, and she wriggles until her legs are under her. She coughs again, and shakes her head. She raises her eyebrows, as if to say how ridiculous we are, sitting in the street. What am I thinking, to make her so foolish? I struggle to my feet and pick her up, ignoring the people who stare. I carry her into the impasse. I can feel her heart beating against my arm. We take the tiny elevator—I have no strength for the stairs. In the faded bronze mirror, I have never looked so old.

In the apartment, James is awake, holding the Perrier bottle, in a white cotton dressing gown that Desi has ironed. He rubs his face, runs his fingers in his hair. "I didn't know where you were," he says.

"Outside." My voice is hoarse.

"Another accident?" The green bottle is bright against the white cotton.

"The dog is killing me," I say, and I hand Cordelia into his arms. "She was dead. Now she's not."

"Dead?" he says.

But I have no explaining left in me. My legs will not hold me up. "I'm going to bed." I go into the bedroom, take off my clothes, step around the piss on the rug, and climb beneath the covers. Then I hear a scratching at the door, which opens, and small footsteps. Cordelia climbs the little carpeted steps at the end of the bed, which James bought when she couldn't jump up anymore—there is still tenderness in him—and I feel the small body curl beside me. We sleep.

James calls the vet, and we take the dog together. The vet says Cordelia is mostly blind, and deaf, and demented. But she wags her tail, she eats some food. She puts on a good show, for the vet.

James asks the doctor, in many different ways, if Cordelia's quality of life is not diminished. This is a code, a hint. He wants the vet to say maybe it is time to kill the dog. I find this more upsetting than I should. But the vet is cheerful and will not say the words. He pretends not to understand. He calls the dog Madame Lazarus and says it is a miracle, she has returned from the dead. Cordelia licks my hand as we drive home: a steady, appreciative lick. She knows.

The next morning, James leaves again, for Amsterdam, Dubai, I don't know. Somewhere is a schedule. Desi comes to clean and make lunch, and I tell her what happened. We study the dog together. Cordelia wags her tail at us, she eats. But she cannot turn her head to the right anymore, only to the left. She turns her whole body in a circle when she wants to look right. No one asks how Lazarus felt after he came out of the tomb. Maybe it was not so good. Maybe he fell over and died again as soon as the people were not watching.

Desi goes to work on the spot on the rug, and I think of the morning after the doctor took the boy away, when the housekeeper found that I had washed some napkins and towels. She was French, her gray hair in a tight knot. It was not normal for me to wash anything. She frowned down at the place where the carpet was wet and a little pink, and I told her I had spilled the soup. She looked at me in the steady way of a *maîtresse* in school. And then she went back to her work and said nothing.

Sometimes Cordelia takes her small steps into an empty room and stands there, staring. I follow to see what she sees: the furniture, the pictures on the walls. But can she see them? She is listening, maybe, for James's voice. She stands there a long time, waiting for something that does not come.

I begin to carry her up and down the stairs and out to the street. Sometimes, after pissing on the rug, she cannot do it outside. I know this feeling, so I squeeze her to help, while people pass by. A river comes out. I carry her a bit so she can smell the air, and I think, My God, what comes next?

What comes next is a morning, three months later, when Cordelia does not get out of bed. I carry her to the street, but she cannot stand up. She does not wag her tail. She does not eat. I call James on his mobile in some other country. He sounds busy at first, but then he is listening, paying attention. The tenderness is there. He says, "*Chéri,* maybe it's time."

I wait for Desi to arrive. We speak English together, because she does not speak so much French, after so many years. Enough to shop and to eat. She lives with other Indonesians, it is not necessary. "Come with me to the vet," I say.

Desi's eyes slide away from me, and I see she does not want to go, but then she collects her bag. I carry Cordelia, and we find a taxi. I cannot drive and hold the dog also, and Desi does not drive. The taxi driver talks on his mobile, the radio is low—all in Arabic. Desi sits with her hands folded on her bag. Cordelia is very still in my lap.

I think about seeing that boy the first time, when I was only a child, before everything happened. The crown of hair, the dazzling eyes, the bolt of understanding. *N'en parlons plus jamais.*

At the vet's office, I ask Desi to come to the back with me, but she shakes her head. She will wait.

The vet greets Cordelia, cheerful as before. "Madame Lazarus!" he says. But I do not want more jokes. I put her on the table. The doctor examines her. I press my hands together to stop the shaking. I feel a skip in my heart and think of the wine I will have at lunch.

"Ah, Cordelia," the doctor says, stroking her. *"Tu n'es pas immortelle, après tout."*

Cordelia looks for the source of the touch, with her cloudy eyes.

The doctor says it might be time. He says all the lines James suggested to him before, about the diminishing quality of life. I ask him to wait a moment. I go out to the waiting room, where Desi is sitting with a girl with purple hair and a small diamond in her nose. A big sheepdog lies at the girl's feet. It lifts its heavy head to look at me, to see if I am a threat.

"Desi," I say. "The vet says it's time. Will you come in?"

Desi shakes her head, tears in her eyes. "I can't," she whispers. "I can't see it."

"Don't make her," the purple-haired girl says. She has a German accent. "It's terrible. I was here two months ago, with my old dog, and I cried for a week after."

I look at the German girl, whose business it is not. She is strong, a little heavy in the hips. I am the age of her grandfather. I do not want to talk about her dog, killed in this doctor's office.

I turn back to Desi. "Please come in," I say.

But Desi says no. She has cooked my food, cleaned my house,

picked up after James for so many years I cannot count. Her job is to do as I ask, but she will not do this. "I can't," she says, and she is pleading.

So I go back alone to the room where Cordelia is on the table. Her eyes look at nothing. James was right to bring her home, to give me something to take care of.

"You look terrible," the vet tells me. "Sit down."

The nurse brings me a glass of water and says something comforting.

I think of James, our long life together, his shoetrees in the closet, his clothes on the floor. The dog is the last string to tie him to me, and now—snip. Soon I will start walking into the bedroom, staring at nothing, listening for voices that are not there.

"It's your decision," the vet says.

I nod.

"You can hold her," the nurse says, and she puts Cordelia into my arms. Then she puts a pad on my leg like a diaper, beneath the dog, and I think, This will be bad.

Cordelia sniffs my hand, licks it once, and I am no longer sure about the quality of her life. She can still smell the world, she can still love. But then I remember the morning. Her legs not holding her up. I wish for a wild moment that I had brought Simone with me, my loyal wife, but she has never liked dogs. *Allergique.* The doctor is working—he ties a tourniquet on Cordelia's leg, and then he prepares a needle. I think he will miss, he will jab it in my arm. But he doesn't, he slips it into her thin leg where I can't imagine there is a vein.

Cordelia looks around the room for something. We have to wait some minutes for the tranquilizer to work. I feel her pulse in her throat and think again that this is a mistake. Three months ago, I got on my knees to push blood through this small body, and now I am letting the doctor kill her. She closes her eyes, and I think I will tell him this is wrong, but he is already there with another needle, another injection. Cordelia flinches, she makes a little sigh. Then her head sinks, and her chin is on my hand, her throat soft. The white pad on my leg becomes heavy—she has gone in the wrong place one more time. The doctor takes her from me, and the nurse puts her hand on my shoulder.

Out in the waiting room, the German girl has her arm around Desi, and the two of them are crying. The sheepdog's head is on the girl's knee. Desi looks at me, her eyes wet and swollen, and I wonder, for the first time, if Cordelia will be the last string for Desi, also. She could find a new job and start again. She might find children to care for, to delight her as Cordelia did. It would be more interesting than an old man.

I reach into my pocket for my wallet, but the receptionist shakes her head, makes a little gesture of sympathy. This is something, at least. They do not make you pay.

If we lived in the country, we could wrap Cordelia in a blanket and bury her, but we have nowhere, so we leave her with the vet. My arms feel empty. Outside, we wait for a taxi. I see an old man walking down the street, bent almost in half, even older than I. He would have been a young man during the war, but old enough to fight or to work or to run. I think I need something to carry. My mind is confused. I have just killed my dog. A taxi pulls up to the curb.

I turn to Desi, who is blowing her nose, looking at something in the street. Her black hair has some gray now. I never see her outside, in the sunlight. Her bag, bright yellow, hangs on her arm.

"Don't leave me," I say.

Desi looks up, surprised. Her eyes are red. The taxi is waiting, impatient. I think I will say everything now, I will speak of everything. There is not so much time.

"Please don't leave," I say.

SHOBHA RAO

Kavitha and Mustafa

FROM *Nimrod*

THE TRAIN STOPPED abruptly, at 3:36 p.m., between stations, twenty kilometers from the Indian border, on the Pakistani side. Kavitha looked out the window, in the heat of afternoon, and saw only scrubland, an endless yellow plain of dust and stunted trees, as far as the eye could see. She knew what this meant. One of the men in the berth, the tall one Kavitha had been eyeing, calmly told the women to take off all their jewels and valuables and put them in their shoes. They'll search *everything*, he said with meaning, which made the young woman in the corner blush. Two or three of the women gasped. The old lady started crying. There were eleven people crowded into their berth, including Kavitha and her husband, Vinod. They were all from Islamabad and had been squeezed onto the wooden benches of this train now for seven hours. There was an older couple who seemed to be traveling with their middle-aged son and his wife. The young woman in the corner was traveling with her mother and older brother. And the tall man was with his son, or so Kavitha presumed, though they looked nothing alike. The boy was not more than eight or nine years old but, of all of them, he seemed to remain the calmest, even more so than his father. He serenely took two thin pebbles, a curled length of twine, and a chit of paper, maybe a photograph, from his pockets and put them in his shoe.

They heard a clamor farther down the train, a few baleful screams, then a series of thuds. Every door would be barred, they all knew, but when they were done looting the train, Kavitha hoped they would let it continue on as it was. She had heard stories, though: sometimes they uncoupled the bogies and sent them in different directions. At other times, they forced the men to disembark and allowed the women and children to continue. More than once, she had heard, they boarded with kerosene. Kavitha reached out and took Vinod's hand. It was out of habit, she realized, but it was still a comfort. They had talked of this, now and then, in the course of their ten-year marriage: which one might die first. Kavitha had always insisted that she wanted to go first, that she could not possibly bear the pain of living without Vinod. But that was a lie. She knew very well she would manage just fine without him, maybe even better than she had with him. Their marriage, arranged by their families when she was sixteen and he twenty-two, aside from one or two instances, had been mostly uneventful. Boring, really. He'd seemed handsome enough on the wedding dais but when she took a long look at him, a week or so after the wedding, his forehead was squat, and his eyes were dull. As the months went by, she noticed that the dullness persisted; his eyes flickered for a moment, maybe two, when he was on top of her, but then they died out again. Dull eyes? her friends had exclaimed. Just be happy he doesn't beat you. True, true, Kavitha had agreed, but she secretly wondered if perhaps that is what it would take to bring his gaze to life: violence.

There were four of them. The one who entered the berth first had a distended ear, fanned out like a cabbage leaf, and was clearly the leader. He stepped inside, holding a machete by his side, by the handle, swinging it like a spray of flowers. The others crowded behind him, holding sticks, and one a metal rod. Now there were fifteen in the berth meant for six, the heat growing even more unbearable, and the middle-aged man, the one who was there with his wife and parents, lunged, with a cry, at the metal bars of the train's windows, trying to loosen them. It was pointless. They were welded in place. His wife and mother tried to calm him but he was weeping.

Look, how sweet, the leader said, We have a baby in the berth. The leader smiled serenely, looked at each of them in turn, then put his hand on the shoulder of the man at the barred window and said, Here, let me help you. The man—with a tremulous look, his face stained by tears, his hands and shirtfront stained by the rust from the window—turned and looked at him. Come, come, the leader said, let me show you the way out. He pushed the others aside, and led the man to the door. The man, still shaking, the surprise of being led from the berth hardening into flight, took one quick look at his wife and parents and bolted out of the berth.

Cabbage leaf smiled. You see how easy that was, he said.

They stood in silence.

Would any of *you* like to leave? he asked. A fly buzzed. They waited motionless, as if they had all anticipated the sounds of the scuffle that reached them from the other end of the bogie, followed by a loud thump, a scream, and then a strange and preternatural quiet. The old lady—the mother of the man who'd left the berth—let out a long, piercing wail. Now, now, the leader said, there's no need for that. Then his voice dropped, it grew fangs. Your jewels, he said.

It was a rainy afternoon. Kavitha was at home, preparing the evening meal of roti and dal with spinach and sweet buttermilk. Vinod was the tax collector for the district of Taxila and was home no later than eight every night. She sweetened the buttermilk because Vinod preferred sweet buttermilk to salty, and she didn't have a preference. In fact, in the time since they'd been married, it seemed to her that she'd lost most of her preferences. She had once liked taking evening walks, but he'd always said he was too tired. She had liked weaving jasmine into her hair, but their scent had made him nauseous. When she noticed fallen eyelashes on her cheeks, she'd put them on the back of her palm, close her eyes, and make a wish. Then she'd blow on them. If they flew away, she liked to think the wish would come true. If not, she'd wait patiently for another eyelash. She'd believed this since she was a child. He noticed her once, collecting the eyelash, blowing it away, and asked her what she was doing. He hardly ever asked her about herself, so Kavitha looked at him, astonished, then talked for ten minutes about the eyelashes, and the wishes, and the waits, sometimes lengthy, for the next one.

Vinod's eyes seemed to flicker—or so she thought—and then he frowned.

What is it? she asked.

That's the most ridiculous thing I've ever heard, he said. It's just plain silly.

So what? Kavitha said; I'm not asking you to do it. It was the

first time she had talked back to him, and she felt good for having
done it.

That was when he slapped her. Not hard, but just enough so
that she understood. Understood what, she wondered. She looked,
in the instant after the slap, into his eyes. They were empty. Not
a flicker. Not a sign of anger, or regret, or even satisfaction. She
looked down. She too felt empty.

That was years ago.

On this night, after preparing the evening meal, Kavitha sat at the
window of their flat. Vinod would be home in an hour. The window was big and looked out onto a row of facing flats, and most
clearly into the flat directly opposite. A young couple lived in it,
Kavitha had noticed, and she liked to watch them especially. This
was about the time the young husband was due home, and Kavitha
waited anxiously for his arrival. It was not that they were ever lewd
or inappropriate, or even that they did anything interesting or unusual; it was just that there was such sweetness between them. She
could tell just by their gestures, by how they moved, by how their
bodies seemed to lighten the moment the other walked through
the door. On previous afternoons, she'd noticed that the young
wife wore a plain cotton sari during the day and, just before her
husband was to arrive, she would change into a more colorful fancy
sari. Today when she emerged from the back room, she had on a
yellow sari. Kavitha squinted and thought that it might be chiffon,
with a blue border of some sort. The breeze swept up her pulloo
as she walked from room to room. She looked like a butterfly. She
looked like the petals of a flower. When the husband arrived, he
had clearly brought home snacks to eat with their tea—perhaps
pakora or maybe samosas, Kavitha guessed—because the young
wife dashed to the kitchen and returned with a plate. Then she
went back and, after a few minutes, brought out their teas on a
tray. Kavitha watched them with envy. She nearly cried with it.

Your jewels, he repeated.

The middle-aged wife and the mother of the recently departed
man wept silently. It was odd, but it felt like only now, only after
there was one fewer person in the berth, did a pall descend on the
group. They moved slowly; the shadow of the train lengthened.

The August heat was oppressive. Sweat trickled down their faces, their clothes stuck to their bodies. Flies entered the berth in droves but the passengers were too scared to swat them away, to make any sudden movements. Kavitha licked her lips and tasted salt. Hurry up, the leader said. The three other men were outside the door, standing guard, Kavitha assumed. The leader, though, watched the passengers keenly. Each of the women had left a small piece of jewelry visible, so they wouldn't suspect the ones in their shoes—Kavitha had left her earrings in, the young woman her nose-ring, the middle-aged and the elderly mother a few bracelets. They took them off and placed them in a pile on the wooden bench. Cabbage leaf looked at the pile, shook his head, and laughed. I *know* you have more jewelry than that, he said. When he finished laughing, he said, Would you like me to help you look?

The women glanced from one to the other, then they looked at the men.

Cabbage leaf—whose name was Ahmed; Kavitha had heard one of the men guarding the door call him that—waited patiently. When no one moved, he placed his machete next to the pile, seated himself beside it, and said, I'm going to enjoy this. Then he wrapped his arm around the waist of the young woman standing closest to him, and pulled her onto his lap. Yes, I am, he breathed into her neck, pulling her chunni off her shoulder.

The brother of the young woman lurched forward. His mother caught the very end of his wrist but he slipped out. It didn't seem possible in such a tiny space, with so many people crowded into it, but it felt to Kavitha as if he sailed across the berth, his arms reached out as if to strangle the bandit. But Ahmed was quicker. He swerved to the side, so that the brother landed in a heap against the seat. And in a flash of metal, one of the outside guards, the one with the rod, swung at the brother. All Kavitha heard was the *thwack* of metal against bone. The brother let out a howl, gripping his arm. Blood spurted from the wound. His mother kneeled next to him, using the pulloo of her sari to staunch the blood. It wouldn't stop. It was now covering the floor of the berth, pooling around their shoes.

My shoes, Kavitha thought.

Get him out of here, Ahmed growled, We have enough flies as it is. The guard went into the passageway and yelled for help.

Another one of the guards came in, and he and the one with the metal rod dragged the brother out. He whimpered as he left the berth.

You see what happens to heroes, Ahmed said.

Their berth was the last in the bogie, on the far end, next to the lavatories. Kavitha, seated next to the door and directly across from the little boy, caught a glimpse of the tiny steel sink that was used by the passengers to brush their teeth, and it was against this sink that the brother was propped up. Blood was still pouring out of the gash on his arm and she wondered if he might die. She looked up, and the little boy was watching her. There was, she noticed, intention in his gaze, and she looked away only when Ahmed addressed her.

You, the leader said, pointing to Kavitha, Give me that.

She had forgotten about her mangal sutra. She'd swapped the gold chain of her wedding necklace for turmeric-soaked thread just before the trip, for safety's sake, but the round lockets were made of gold. How could she have forgotten? She slipped it over her head and handed it to him. Vinod seemed to wince. Was it for her or for the gold? Ahmed bounced it in his palm—the wedding necklace she'd not once taken off in ten years—up and down, up and down, as if weighing the gold. It must still hold the warmth of my skin, she thought. And then she felt a thrill, a rush of heat, flooding her body, to think that a man, any man, held in his hand the warmth of her body.

The boy was still looking at her. Kavitha couldn't understand it—his stare—but she felt too faint to return it. She hadn't eaten in over seven hours; they had emptied their water bottle three hours ago. She closed her eyes. There had been a pregnancy in Kavitha and Vinod's marriage, but the child had been stillborn. The stillbirth had been a culmination of many years of trying for children, and the next time Vinod had reached for her, an appropriate number of weeks after the failed pregnancy, she had looked at him evenly, a little sadly, and said, Please. No more. In her memory, that was the second instance of a flicker passing across his eyes. She knew it was unfair—all of it—but she felt gratitude toward Vinod for understanding, for not having touched her since, and in a small way, he had increased, incrementally, her love for him.

When she opened her eyes, Ahmed was by the window. He

was searching the bags of the older couple. The many buckles and belts had been hacked off by the machete, but there were still bundles tucked under the wooden seats, and the couple and their daughter-in-law were making matters worse by their distress, by opening and reopening the same bundles and folding and refolding the same clothes. Most of these clothes were now strewn across the berth. Vinod, who was sitting next to Kavitha, reached over and patted her hand, as if to calm her, but she was already strangely calm. Even with one of the guards standing right next to her, on the other side of the door, close enough to touch, so close that his metal rod was within Kavitha's arm's reach.

When she looked again at the boy, he was looking straight back at her. This time, she slowly came to understand that he was trying to tell her something. But what? Kavitha watched him. And as she did the boy raised his right index finger to his right ear and tapped it. She stared at him. Why was he tapping his ear? Did it hurt? She turned to Vinod but his attention was fixed on Ahmed. When Kavitha spun back, the boy was pointing toward the guard, the one who was standing by the door. What could he mean? She guessed now that he wanted her to listen, but to what? The guard was silent, unmoving. The only other sound was an occasional scream from another bogie, loud enough to travel through the train. There must be other men, in other parts of the train. She had assumed it: these four could not possibly subdue a whole train. But why would he want her to listen to *that*? She strained her ears some more. There were a few night sounds that reached her, an owl, perhaps, or a bulbul, but those were infrequent and could hardly be the reason for the boy's signaling. She knew he wasn't deaf or mute because she'd seen the boy and his father conversing earlier. So what was it?

Then there was a lull. A quiet. For a few seconds, a few precious seconds, there was no screaming, no wailing. Ahmed was busy looking through a bag, and even the old couple and the daughter-in-law were restrained, stoic as they gathered their remaining tattered bags. And that was when she heard it. Footsteps. At first, they meant nothing to her. She looked at the boy, perplexed. He had heard them too, and she knew because he nodded. *They* were what he had wanted her to hear. But why? Kavitha concentrated. Footsteps. She heard them approaching, growing louder. And louder. And then, just as the footsteps passed the guard in front of their door, she arched her neck and saw that it was one of the guards who had come with Ahmed. So he was patrolling the bogie. She had assumed all three guards were standing outside their door, but now it made sense that one of them would have to patrol the passengers in the other berths.

She sat back and looked at the boy. She hardly had a chance to blink when, in the next instant, the other guard passed the one at the door, *going the other way.* She nearly gasped. *Two* of the guards were patrolling. And not only that, since theirs was the last berth in their bogie, one of the guards, at any given time, was probably in the next bogie over. He wasn't even *in* their bogie, let alone anywhere near their berth.

She had thought there were three men outside the door. But there was only one.

Kavitha had no idea what any of this meant, but she knew it meant something. She nearly reached out and hugged the boy. And he seemed to know it because he smiled.

Kavitha sat back. She held her breath. She knew there was not much time. Ahmed had already moved on to searching the bags of the younger sister and her mother. She mapped out the layout of their bogie in her head. There were eight berths, exactly like theirs, behind them. Those berths were being patrolled just as theirs was, except Ahmed had already looted the other eight berths. In front were the two doors, facing each other, that led on and off the train. Past the doors were the lavatory and the sink. And against this sink the brother still slumped. He seemed conscious, but barely. Between the lavatory and the sink area was a narrow passageway that led to the next bogie. She knew all their hope was in front, where the doors were, but that was all she knew.

She thought about the layout, and she despaired. There was no way out, not with a guard standing by the door, and two more approaching or within earshot. It would have to be lightning quick, before the two patrol guards could be alerted, but even then . . .

She looked at Vinod. It was growing dark outside, and all the lights in the train had been extinguished, but she could still see his face, wary of Ahmed's movements, watching him as he unpacked the suitcases of the mother and her daughter. Vinod's body was as it had always been, since the day they'd married, slim, straight-backed, the recent gray at his temples only accentuating his seriousness, his reserve. She wanted, for the first time in the ten years she'd known him, to collapse into his arms. She wanted to weep. She wanted to say, There has to be a way out. How are you holding up? he whispered. Instead of answering she rested her forehead against his upper arm and felt the knobbiness of his shoulder bone, its hardness against the hardness of her forehead; she felt in that moment that the answer must lie in the body, in its unquenchable will to live. Her gaze fell on the little boy's feet; they dangled off the floor of the train and his shoes hung loose around them, a size too big. The end of the piece of twine he'd put in them was visible, near his left ankle. She looked at the piece of twine and then she lifted her head.

The boy still seemed as though he was listening to the footsteps, and when he noticed her gaze, Kavitha pointed at his shoes and gestured for him to pass her their contents. The boy waited for Ahmed to turn away, just as Kavitha had hoped he would, and quickly handed her the two thin, flat pebbles and the piece of twine. There had been a chit of paper, she recalled, but this he kept for himself. Again, nothing was quite clear in her mind, but never had two rocks and a piece of twine seemed to hold so much promise. The contents of her shoes—a necklace, some rings, and a set of matching bracelets—held none.

Kavitha waited. She didn't know what she was waiting for, but she knew she had to wait.

Ahmed, in the meantime, had found the jewelry in the shoes of the young woman. Kavitha became aware of it only when he laughed out loud and said, So *that's* where they are. He turned to face the rest of the berth. Everybody, he said, swinging his machete, his voice rising at their collusion, take them off.

Kavitha slowly undid the buckle of her sandals; all this time, the hem of her sari had covered them. Her necklace fell out first. Ahmed picked it up with his machete. It dangled off the tip like a lizard, like something writhing, and not meant to be touched. He added it to the pile of jewelry on the bench. Just as he turned back toward her, the old man, standing in the corner by the window, clutched at his chest. He let out a long groan and collapsed onto the seat. His daughter-in-law shrieked. His wife was bent over him, pleading, *Kya bhath hey?* What's wrong? Air, someone said, give him air. Ahmed's face bristled. The daughter-in-law rose to take the old man outside, but Ahmed pushed her down. Stay where you are, he seethed. He needs air, she pleaded, he might die. You all might, Ahmed said. He summoned the guard posted at the door. Get the old man some air, he said, and stand where I can see you. The guard stepped into the berth and led the old man to the door. They stood just outside, in the passageway.

Kavitha counted to ten in her head. One of the guards went by. Then the other.

I need to use the lavatory, she said.

The others were busy emptying their shoes. Ahmed took no notice of her.

I said I have to use the lavatory.

Shut up.

It's female trouble, she said.

Vinod gave her a sharp look. Ahmed paused. Leave your shoes here, he said, the pile of jewelry rising behind him like a hill of sand.

The boy looked at Kavitha. She looked back at him.

The brother, the one slumped by the sink, lifted his eyes when she came out of the berth. The bleeding had slowed, it seemed to her, but he was clearly weak. He had gone pale; his clothes and skin were soaked with blood. For a fleeting moment, she thought she might help him, perhaps even by simply lifting him to a sitting position, but she knew there was no room for that. No time. She passed the old man, the guard, both at the window facing the berth, and when she reached the brother, she kneeled swiftly next to his ear, shoved one of the pebbles into his hand (his left; the good one), and whispered, Throw it. Throw it the moment I come out of the lavatory.

She jumped up and ducked inside. Had he heard? Was he even conscious? She listened for the footsteps of the guards. She could no longer hear them, not with the door closed, only when they were just outside the lavatory door would she be able to hear. Breathe, she told herself, taking a breath. Breathe again, she said. And she did this over and over and over again, thinking only of the little boy.

The lavatory had no window. Just a squat toilet, a tap for water, and a handle for grip. The hole was open and showed the gravel on the tracks. She looked through the hole, lined with excrement, and saw the gravel. Every stone the same color, quarried in some distant place, and varying only slightly in shape. The years following the stillbirth had been like that. She had often wondered, during those years, whether she should have named the baby. She decided it was better that she hadn't. Not because she would have felt a greater loss—there was not, she knew, a loss any greater—but because naming the child, a girl they had told her, would have been an act of bravery, and she didn't want to be brave. She wanted all the fears and weakness of a dark, unnamed place. And she wanted to love the child in that way, without hope and without a name.

When both guards had passed and been gone a few seconds, she opened the lavatory door. At the sound of the door, the brother seemed to wake as if from a deep sleep. He looked at the pebble, a little too long, a little too long, Kavitha fretted, then flung it down the corridor. Ahmed yelled, What was that? The guard, the one by the old man, took a few tentative steps past the berth.

This was the moment. This was it.

Kavitha darted past the brother, reached in, and grabbed the little boy's hand. They jumped from the train, through the door near the lavatory, and as soon as they hit the ground, Kavitha handed the little boy one end of the twine, shoved him against the door, and said, Hold it. Tight. She held the other end, on the other side of the door. Ahmed came racing out, they held on until he tripped, and leaped out of the way so they wouldn't break his fall. Then they ran.

It was dark. There were a few stars, not many. The sliver of moon cast hardly any light. They scurried under the bogie, up a few cars, toward the engine, and lay on the couplings, facedown, their arms wrapped tight around them. Neither spoke. Kavitha waited until the guards had run past, checking under the bogies and inside them, then indicated the ladder that led to the roof of the train. They climbed up—the rungs digging into Kavitha's bare feet—and crawled to the middle, if for no other reason than to be at the halfway point in case they had to run in either direction. It was from this vantage point that Kavitha saw a road in the distance, a full kilometer away, at least; a thin, dark ribbon that she assumed was a road. But it was empty, not a car or a lorry or a bullock cart passed.

The night deepened.

She could not have said how much time had gone by when she saw a small light in the distance, almost a puncture in the night sky. It grew—slowly, because it was so far away. There, she whispered, look. The boy raised his head. What do we do, he said. They waited. The light got bigger. Alarmingly fast. She knew there was no way for both of them to reach the road before the light passed them. She studied the ground. Near the train was a small tree. Further along was what looked to be a pile of luggage.

She handed the boy the second pebble.

She saw, after a time, his small, murky shape moving to the tree. Then the luggage. He had told her, before he'd descended the ladder, that he'd aimed pebbles at moving trains lots of times, in his village. I never missed, he boasted. Kavitha didn't point out to him that the moving light was not a train, but something much smaller. She didn't tell him, but it's dark. And she didn't say, we only get to play this game once.

She heard a clink. Didn't she? What else could it be? There was nothing for many, many kilometers surrounding the train. That was of course why Ahmed and his men had picked this spot. And that's what she had thought while traveling on the train: that to journey through such emptiness was to invite it inside.

The light stopped.

The driver of the lorry, a burly Sikh who spoke very little, except to say, I'm going to Attari, no further, ignored Kavitha. But we have to get the police, she said, the authorities, the military, I don't know. That train is under siege, she cried. My husband is on it, his father. People are hurt. The cabin of the lorry was dark. She turned from the driver to the boy. He was staring out of the window. He wasn't my father, the boy said, falling silent again.

Kavitha looked at him, as if for the first time. What's your name? she asked.

Mustafa.

A Muslim. But why was he going to India? They drove on and on, eastward.

You didn't miss, she said to Mustafa. Then she said, Was that luggage?

No.

What was it?

Kerosene, he said.
And she too fell silent.

They reached Attari late the next morning. She'd learned from Mustafa that the man she'd taken to be his father was a Hindu friend of his parents', entrusted to take their son to relatives living in East Pakistan. But where are your parents? she'd asked. He'd looked away, and said nothing. After a moment he'd turned to her and said, My cousins are waiting.

She knew she would take him there. He refused to take another train, and she was not keen on it, either, so they traveled slowly, overland by road. Mostly lorries and bullock carts, a passing car if they were fortunate. She had silver anklets she'd pushed up her calves, so that Ahmed wouldn't see, and she traded these for money. It ran out well before they got to East Pakistan. In the presence of other people, the two were often silent, letting them assume they were mother and son. That seemed easiest.

Sitting for these long stretches of quiet, Kavitha was surprised by how often she thought of Vinod. She knew he was gone, that she was now a widow. The awareness was not startling. Not even frightening. I was widowed long ago, she thought. And she knew that on the train, when she'd laid her head on his shoulder and had felt the roundness and knobbiness of a bone so funny, so irreverent, so unlike him, she had said her goodbye.

They were on a horse cart, nearing East Pakistan. Maybe a day, no more. It was late afternoon. It was a covered, two-wheeled cart and Kavitha lay in its shade, dozing. Mustafa lay beside her. The motion of the cart woke her (or was it a dream?) and she said to Mustafa, What happened to us, it's ours. Yours and mine. Don't speak of it.

And in his half-sleep, perhaps also dreaming, Mustafa heard, You are mine. Don't speak. And so he never did.

JOAN SILBER

About My Aunt

FROM *Tin House*

THIS HAPPENS A lot—people travel and they find places they like so much, they think they've risen to their best selves just by being there. They feel distant from everyone at home who can't begin to understand. If they're young, they take up with beautiful locals of the opposite sex; they settle in; they get used to how everything works; they make homes. But usually not forever.

I had an aunt who was such a person. She went to Istanbul when she was in her twenties. She met a good-looking carpet seller from Cappadocia. She'd been a classics major in college and had many questions to ask him, many observations to offer. He was a gentle and intelligent man who spent his days talking to travelers. He'd come to think he no longer knew what to say to Turkish girls, and he loved my aunt's airy conversation. When her girlfriends went back to Greece, she stayed behind and moved in with him. This was in 1970.

His shop was in Sultanahmet, a well-touristed part of the city, and he lived in Fener, an old and jumbled neighborhood. Kiki, my aunt, liked having people over, and their apartment was always filled with men from her husband's region and expats of various ages. She was happy to cook big semi-Turkish meals and make up the couch for anyone passing through. She helped out in the store, explained carpet motifs to anyone who walked in—those were stars for happiness, scorpion designs to keep real scorpions away. In her letters home, she sounded enormously pleased with herself—she dropped Turkish phrases into her sentences, reported days spent sipping *çay* and *kahve*. She sent home to Brooklyn a carpet she said was Kurdish.

Then Kiki's boyfriend's business took a turn for the worse. There was a flood in the basement of his store and a bill someone never paid and a new shop nearby that was getting all the business. Or something. The store had to close. Her family thought this meant that Kiki was coming home at last. But no. Osman, her guy, had decided to move back to his village to help his father, who raised pumpkins for their seed oil, as well as tomatoes, green squash, and eggplant. Kiki was up for the move; she wanted to see the real Turkey. Istanbul was really so Western now. Cappadocia was very ancient and she couldn't wait to see the volcanic rock. She was getting married! Her family in Brooklyn was surprised about that part. Were they invited to the wedding? Apparently not. In fact, it had probably happened already by the time they got the letter. "Wearing a beaded hat and a glitzy head scarf, the whole shebang," Kiki wrote. "I still can't believe it."

Neither could any of her relatives. But they sent presents, once they had an address. A microwave oven, a Mr. Coffee, an electric blanket for the cold mountains. They were a practical and liberal family; they wanted to be helpful. "I know it's hard for you to imagine," Kiki wrote, "but we do very well without electricity here. Every morning I make a wood fire in the stove. Very good-smelling smoke. I make a little fire in the bottom of the water heater too."

Kiki built fires? No one could imagine her as the pioneer wife. Her brother, Alan (who later became my father), was always hoping to visit. Kiki said not a word about making any visits home. No one nagged her; she'd been a touchy teenager, given to sullen outbursts, and everyone was afraid of that Kiki appearing again.

She stayed for eight years. Her letters said, "My husband thinks I sew as well as his sisters" and "I'm rereading my copy of Ovid in Latin. It's not bad!" and "Winter sooo long this year, I hate it. Osman has already taught me all he knows about the stars." No one could make sense of who she was now. There were no children and no pregnancies that anyone heard about, and the family avoided asking.

Her brother was just about to finally get himself over for a visit when Kiki wrote to say, "Guess what? I'm coming back at last. For good." No, the husband was not coming with her. "My life here has reached its natural conclusion," Kiki wrote. "Osman will be my dear friend forever but we've come to the end of our road."

"So who ran around on who?" the relatives kept asking. "She'll never say, will she?"

Everybody wondered what she would look like when she returned. Would she be sun-dried and weather-beaten, would she wear billowing silk trousers like a belly dancer's, would the newer buildings of New York amaze her? None of the above. She looked like the same old Kiki, thirty-one with very good skin, and she was wearing jeans and a turtleneck, possibly the same ones she'd left home with.

Her luggage was a mess, woven plastic valises baled up with string, very third world, and there were a lot of them. She had brought back nine carpets! What was she thinking? She intended to sell them.

Her brother always remembered that when they ate their first meal together, Kiki held her knife and fork like a European. She laughed at things lightly, as if the absurdity of it all wasn't worth shrieking over. She teased Alan about his eyeglasses ("you look like a genius in them") and his large appetite ("has not changed since you were eight"). She certainly sounded like herself.

Before very long, she moved in with someone named Marcy she'd known at Brooklyn College. Marcy's mother bought the biggest of the rugs, and Kiki used the proceeds to rent a storefront in the East Village where she displayed her carpets and other items she had brought back—a brass tea set and turquoise beads and cotton pants with tucked hems that she herself had once worn.

The store stayed afloat for a while. Her brother wondered if she was dealing drugs—hashish was all over Istanbul in the movie *Midnight Express,* which had come out just before her return. Kiki refused to see such a film, with its lurid scenes of mean Turkish prisons. "Who has *nice* prisons?" she said. "Name one single country in the world. Just one."

When her store began to fail and she had to give it up, Kiki supported herself by cleaning houses. She evidently did this with a good spirit; the family was much more embarrassed about it than she was. "People here don't know *how* to clean their houses," she would say. "It's sort of remarkable, isn't it?"

*

By the time I was a little kid, Kiki had become the assistant director of a small agency that booked housekeepers and nannies. She was the one you got on the phone, the one who didn't take any nonsense from clients or workers either. She was friendly but strict and kept people on point.

As a child I was a teeny bit afraid of her. She could be very withering if I was acting up and getting crazy and knocking over chairs. But when my parents took me to visit, Kiki had special cookies for me (I loved Mallomars) and for a while she had a boyfriend named Hernando who would play airplane with me and go buzzing around the room with me on his back. I loved visiting her.

My father told me later that Hernando had wanted to marry Kiki. "But she wasn't made for marriage," he said. "It's not all roses, you know." He and my mother had a history of having, as they say, their differences.

"Kiki was always like a bird," my father said. "Flying here and there."

What a corny thing to say.

I grew up outside Boston, in a small suburban town, whose leafy safety I spurned once I was old enough for hip disdain. I moved to New York as soon as I finished high school, which I barely did. My parents and I were not on good terms in my early years in the city, but Kiki made a point of keeping in touch. She'd call on the phone and say, "I'm thirsty, let's go have a drink. OK?" At first I was up in Inwood, as far north in Manhattan as you can get, so it was a long subway ride to see her in the East Village, but once I moved to Harlem it wasn't quite so bad. When my son was born, four years ago, Kiki brought me the most useful baby stuff, things a person couldn't even know she needed. Oliver would calm down and sleep when she walked him around. He grew up calling her Aunt Great Kiki.

The two of us lived in a housing project, but one of the nicer ones, in an apartment illegally passed on to me by an ex-boyfriend. It was a decent size, with good light, and I liked my neighbors. That fall the TV started telling us to get prepared for Hurricane Sandy, and Oliver had a great time flicking the flashlight on and off (a really annoying game) and watching me tape giant X's on the window glass. All the kids on our floor were hyped up and excited, running around and shrieking. We kept looking out the win-

dows as the sky turned a sepia tint. When the rains broke and began to come down hard, we could hear the moaning of the winds
and things clattering and banging in the night, awnings and trees
getting the hell beaten out of them. I kept switching to different
channels on the TV so we wouldn't miss any of it. The television
had better coverage than my view out the window. A newscaster
in a suit told us the Con Ed transformer on Fourteenth Street exploded! The lights in the bottom of Manhattan had gone out! I
made efforts to explain electricity to Oliver, as if I knew. Never,
never put your finger in a socket. Oliver wanted to watch a better
program.

At nine-thirty my father called to say, "Your aunt Kiki doesn't
have power, you know. She's probably sitting in the dark." I had
forgotten about her entirely. She was on East Fifth Street, in the
no-electricity zone. I promised I'd check on Kiki in the morning.

"I might have to walk there," I said. "It's like a hundred and
twenty blocks. You're not going to ask about my neighborhood?
It's fine."

"Don't forget about her, OK? Promise me that."

"I just told you," I said.

The next day the weather was shockingly pleasant, mild, with a
white sky. We walked for a half-hour, which Oliver really did not
like, past some downed trees and tossed branches, and then a cab
miraculously stopped and we shared it with an old guy all the way
downtown. No traffic lights working, no stores open—how strange
the streets were. In Kiki's building, I led Oliver up four flights of
dark tenement stairs while he drove me nuts flicking the flashlight
on and off.

When Kiki opened the door onto her pitch-black hallway, she
said, "Reyna! What are you doing here?"

Kiki, of course, was fine. She had plenty of vegetables and
canned food and rice—who needed a fridge?—and she could
light the stove with a match. She had daylight now and candles for
later. She had pots of water she could boil to wash with. She had
filled the tub the night before. How was *I*? "Oliver, isn't this fun?"
she said.

Oh, New Yorkers were making such a big fuss, she thought. She
had a transistor radio so the fussing came through. "I myself am

enjoying the day off from work," she said. She was rereading *The Greek Way* by Edith Hamilton—had I ever read it? I didn't read much, did I?—and she planned to finish it tonight by candlelight.

"Come stay with us," I said. "Wouldn't you like that, Oliver?"

Oliver crowed on cue.

Kiki said she always preferred being in her own home. "Oliver, I bet you would like some of the chocolate ice cream that's turning into a lovely milk shake."

We followed her into the kitchen, with its painted cabinets and old linoleum. When I took off my jacket to settle in, Kiki said, "Oh, no. Did you get a new tattoo?"

"*No.* You always ask that. You're phobic about my arms."

"I'll never get used to them."

I had a dove and a sparrow and a tiger lily and a branch with leaves and some small older ones. They all stood for things. The dove was to settle a fight; the sparrow was the true New York bird; the tiger lily meant boldness; and the branch was an olive tree in honor of Oliver. I used to try to tell Kiki that they were no different from the patterns on rugs. "Are you a floor?" she said. She accused my tattoos of being forms of mutilation as well as forms of deception over my natural skin. According to what? "Well, Islamic teaching, for one thing," she said.

Kiki had never been a practicing Muslim but she liked a lot about Islam. I may have been the only one in the family who knew how into it she'd once been. She used to try to get me to read Averroës, she thought he was great, and Avicenna. Only my aunt would believe that someone like me could just dip into twelfth-century philosophy if I felt like it. She saw no reason why not.

"Oliver, my man," she was saying now, "you don't have to finish if you're full."

"Dad's worried about you," I told Kiki.

"I already called him," she said. It turned out her phone still worked because she had an old landline, nothing digital or bundled.

She'd been outside earlier in the day. Some people on her block had water but she didn't. Oliver was entranced when Kiki showed him how she flushed the toilet by throwing down a potful of water.

"It's magic," I said.

When we left, Kiki called after us, "I'm always glad to see you, you know that." She could have given us more credit for getting all the way there, I thought.

"You might change your mind about staying with us," I called back, before we went out into the dark hall.

I had an extra reason for wanting her to stay. Not to be one of those mothers who was always desperate for babysitting, but I needed a babysitter.

My boyfriend, Boyd, was spending three months at Rikers Island. He was there for selling five ounces of weed (who thinks that should even be a crime?). For all of October I'd gone to see him once a week, and it made a big difference to him. I planned to go that week, once the subways were running and buses were going over the bridge again. But it was hard bringing Oliver, who wasn't his kid and who needed a lot of attention during those toyless visits.

I loved Boyd but I wouldn't have said I loved him more than the others I'd been with. Fortunately no one asked. Not even Boyd. There was no need for people to keep mouthing off about how much they felt, in his view. Some degree of real interest, some persistence in showing up, was enough. Every week I saw him sitting in that visitors' room in his stupid jumpsuit. The sight of him—heavy-faced, wary, waiting to smile slightly—always got to me, and when I hugged him (light hugs were permitted), I'd think, *It's still Boyd, it's Boyd here.*

Oliver could be a nuisance. Sometimes he was very, very whiny after standing in so many different lines, or he was incensed that he couldn't bring in his giant plastic dinosaur. Or he got overstimulated and had to nestle up to Boyd and complain at length about some kid who threw sand in the park. "You having adventures, right?" Boyd said. Meanwhile, I was trying to ask Boyd if he'd had an OK week and why not. I had an hour to give him the joys of my conversation. Dealing with those two at once was not the easiest.

I got a phone call from Aunt Kiki on the second day after the hurricane. "How would you feel about my coming over after work to take a hot shower?" she said. "I can bring a towel, I've got piles of towels."

"Our shower is dying to see you," I said. "And Oliver will lend you his ducky."

"Kiki Kiki Kiki Kiki Kiki!" Oliver yelled when she came through the door. Maybe I'd worked him up too much in advance. We'd gotten the place very clean.

As soon as my aunt emerged from the bathroom, dressed again in her slacks and sweater and with a steamed-pink face under the turban of her towel, I handed her a glass of red wine. "A person without heat or water needs alcohol," I said. We sat down to meatloaf, which I was good at, and mashed potatoes with garlic, which Oliver had learned to eat.

"This is a feast," she said. "Did you know the sultans had feasts that went on for two weeks?"

Oliver was impressed. "This one could go on longer," I said. "You should stay over. Or come back tomorrow. I mean it."

Tomorrow was what I needed—it was the visiting night for inmates with last names from *M* to *Z*.

"Maybe the power will be back on by then," Kiki said. "Maybe maybe."

At Rikers, Boyd and the other inmates had spent the hurricane under lockdown, no wandering off into the torrent. Rikers had its own generator, and the buildings were in the center of the island, too high up to wash away. It was never meant to be a place you might swim from.

"You know I have this boyfriend, Boyd," I said.

Kiki was looking at her plate while I told her, as much as I could in front of Oliver, the situation about the weekly visits. "Oh, shit," she said. She had to finish chewing to say, "OK, sure, OK, I'll come right from work."

When I leaned over to embrace her, she seemed embarrassed. "Oh, please," she said. "No big deal."

What a mystery Kiki was. What could I ever say to her that would throw her for a loop? Best not to push it, of course. And maybe she had a boyfriend of her own that I didn't even know about. She wasn't someone who told you everything. She wasn't showering with him, wherever he was. Maybe he was married. A man that age. Oh, where was I going with this?

When Kiki turned up the next night, she was forty-five minutes later than she'd said she'd be, and I had given up on her several times over. She bustled through the door, saying, "Don't ask me how the subways are running. Go, go. Get out of here, go."

She looked younger, all flushed like that. What a babe she must've once been. Or at least a hippie sweetheart. Oliver clambered all over her. "Will you hurry up and get out of here?" she said to me.

The subway (which had only started running that day) was indeed slow to arrive and very crowded, but the bus near Queens Plaza that went to Rikers was the same as ever. After the first few stops, all the white people except me emptied out. I read *People* magazine while we inched our way to the bridge to the island; love was making a mess of the lives of a number of celebrities. And look at that teenage girl across the aisle in the bus, combing her hair, checking it in a mirror, pulling some strands across her face to make it hang right. *Girl,* I wanted to say, *he fucked up bad enough to get himself where he is, and you're still worried he won't like your hair?*

Of course, I was all moussed and lipsticked myself. I had standards. But you couldn't wear anything too revealing—no rips or see-through fabrics—they had rules. *Visitors must wear undergarments.*

After I stood in a line and put my coat and purse in a locker and showed my ID to the guards and got searched and stood in a line for one of Rikers' own buses and got searched again, I sat in a room to wait for Boyd. It was odd being there without Oliver. The wait went on so long, and it wasn't like you could bring a book. And then I heard Boyd's name read from the list.

Those jumpsuits didn't flatter anyone. But when we hugged, he smelled of soap and Boyd, and I was sorry for myself to have him away so long. "Hey there," he said.

"Didn't mean to get here so late," I said.

Boyd wanted to hear about the hurricane and who got hit the worst. Aunt Kiki became my material: "Oh, she had her candles and her pots of water and her cans of soup and her bags of rice, she couldn't see why everybody was so upset."

"Can't keep 'em down, old people like that," he said. "Good for her. That's the best thing I've heard all week."

I went on about Kiki's gameness. How she'd taught me the right way to climb trees when I was young, when my mother only worried I'd fall on my head.

"I didn't know you were a climber. Have to tell Claude."

His friend Claude, much more of an athlete than Boyd, had recently discovered the climbing wall at some gym. Boyd himself was a couch potato, but a lean and lanky one. People told him he looked like Lebron James, only skinnier. Was he getting puffy now? A little.

"Claude's a monster on that wall. Got Lynnette doing it too." Lynnette was Claude's sister. And Boyd's girlfriend before me. "Girls can do that stuff fine, he says."

"When did he say that?"

"They came by last week. The whole gang."

What gang? Only three visitors allowed. "Lynnette was here?"

"And Maxwell. They came to show support. I appreciated it, you know?"

I'll bet you did, I thought. I was trying not to leap to any conclusions. It wasn't as if she could've crept into the corner with him for a quickie, though you heard rumors of such things. Urban myths.

"Does Claude still have that stringy haircut?"

"He does. Looks like a root vegetable. Man should go to my barber." The Rikers barber had given Boyd an onion look, if you were citing vegetables.

"They're coming again Saturday. You're not coming Saturday, right?"

I never came on Saturdays. I cut him a look.

"Because if you are," he said, "I'll tell them not to come."

You couldn't blame a man who had nothing for wanting everything he could get his hands on. This was pretty much what I thought on the bus ride back to the subway. Oh, I could blame him. I was spending an hour and a half to get there every week and an hour and a half to get back so he could entertain his ex? I was torn between being pissed off and my principles about being a good sport. Why had Boyd told me? The guy could keep his mouth shut when he needed to.

Because he didn't think he needed to. Because I was a good sport. What surprised me even more was how painful this was starting to be. I could imagine Boyd greeting Lynnette, in his offhand,

Mr. Cool Way. "Can I believe my eyes?" Lynnette silky and tough, telling him it had been too long. But what was so great about Boyd that I should twist in torment from what I was seeing too clearly in my head?

I was on the bus during this anguish. I wanted Boyd to comfort me. He had a talent for that. If you were insulted because some asshole at daycare said your kid's shoes were unsuitable, if you splurged on a nice TV and then realized you'd overpaid, if you got fired from your job because you used up sick days and it wasn't your fault, Boyd could make it seem hilarious. He could remind you it was part of the ever-expanding joke of human trouble. Not just you.

When I got back to the apartment, Oliver was actually asleep in his bed—had Kiki drugged him?—and Kiki was in the living room watching the Cooking Channel on TV.

"You watch this crap?" I said.

"How was the visit?"

"Medium. Who's winning on *Chopped*?"

"The wrong guy. But I have a thing for Marcus Samuelsson." He was the judge who had a restaurant right in Harlem, a chef born in Ethiopia, tall and rangy and very good-looking. *So*, I wanted to ask Kiki and I almost did, *is the whole fucking world about men?*

"Oliver spilled a lot of yogurt on the floor but we got it cleaned up," she said.

I wanted a drink, I wanted a joint. What was in the house? I found a very old bottle of Beaujolais in the kitchen and poured glasses for us both.

"When does he get out?" Kiki asked.

"They say January. He's holding up OK."

"He has you."

"You don't have to tell me if you don't want to, but when you got divorced," I said, "was it because one of you had been messing around with someone else?"

"Whooh," Kiki said, "where did that come from?"

"Someone named Lynnette has been visiting Boyd."

Kiki considered this. "Could be nothing."

"So when you left Turkey, why did you leave?"

"It was time."

I admired Kiki's way of deciding what was none of your business, but it made you think there was business there.

It was my bad luck that Con Ed got its act together the very next evening, so electricity flowed in the walls of Kiki's home to give her light and refrigeration and to pump her water and the gurgling steam in her radiators. I called her to say Happy Normal.

"Normal is overrated," she said. "I'll be so busy next week."

"Me too," I said.

Oliver hardly ever had sitters. He was in daycare while I went off to my unglamorous employment as a part-time receptionist at a veterinarian's office (it paid lousy but the dogs were usually nice) and at night I took him with me if I went to see friends or Boyd, when I used to stay with Boyd. Sometimes Boyd had a cousin who watched him.

"Oliver wants to say hi," I told my aunt.

"I *love* you, Great Kiki!" Oliver said.

This didn't move her to volunteer to sit for him another time, and I thought it was better not to ask again so soon.

Oliver wasn't bad at all on the next visit to Rikers. The weather was colder and he got to wear his favorite Spider-Man sweater, which Boyd said was very sharp.

"Your mom's looking good too," Boyd said to Oliver.

"Better than Lynnette?"

I hadn't meant to say any such whiny-bitch thing; it leaped out of me. I was horrified. I wasn't as good as I thought I was, was I?

"Not in your league," Boyd said. "Girl's nowhere near." He said this slowly and soberly. He shook his onion head for emphasis.

The rest of the visit went very well. Boyd suggested that Oliver now had the superpower to spin webs from the ceiling—"You going to float above us all, land right on all the bad guys"—and Oliver was so tickled he had to be stopped from shrieking with glee at top volume.

"Know what I miss?" Boyd said. "Well, that, of course. Don't look at me that way. But also I miss when we used to go ice skating."

We had gone exactly twice, renting skates in Central Park, falling on our asses. I almost crushed Oliver one time I went down. "You telling everyone you're the next big hockey star?" I said.

"I hope there's still ice when I get out," he said.

"There will be," I said. "It's soon. Before you know it."

Kiki had now started to worry about me; she called more often than I was used to. She'd say, "You think Obama's going to get this Congress in line? And how's Boyd doing?"

I let her know we were still an item, which was what she wanted to know. Why in God's name would I ever think of splitting up with Boyd before I could at least get him back home and in bed again? What was the point of all these bus rides if I was going to skip that part?

"You wouldn't want me to desert him at a time like this," I said.

"Be careful," she said.

"He's not much of a criminal," I said. "He was just a bartender selling on the side, not any big-time guy." I didn't have to tell her not to mention this to my father.

"Anybody can be in jail, I know that," Kiki said. "Hikmet was in jail for thirteen years in Turkey."

I thought she meant an old flame of hers but it turned out she meant a famous poet who was dead before she even got there. A famous Communist poet. She'd read all his prison poems.

Boyd wasn't in jail for politics, although some people claimed the war on drugs was a race war, and they had a point. My mom and dad were known to smoke dope every now and then, and was any cop stop-and-frisking them on the streets of Brookline?

"So can I ask you," I said, "were there drugs around when you were in Turkey?" What a blurter I was these days. "Were people selling hash or anything?"

"Not in our circles. I hate that movie, you've seen that movie. But there was smuggling. I mean in antiquities, bits from ancient sites. People went across to the eastern parts, brought stuff back. Or they got it over the border from Iran. Beautiful things, really."

"It's amazing what people get money for."

"If Osman had wanted to do that," she said, "he wouldn't have become a farmer. It was the farming that made me leave, by the way."

I was very pleased that she told me.

"And he left off farming five years later," she said. "Isn't that ironic?"

"It is," I said.

"I still write to Osman. He's a great letter writer."

This was news. Did she have all the letters; how hot were they; did he e-mail too? Of course, I was thinking: *Maybe you two should get back together.* It's a human impulse, isn't it, to want to set the world into couples.

"The wife he has now is much younger," Kiki said.

By December I'd gotten a new tattoo in honor of Boyd's impending release. It was quite beautiful—a birdcage with the door open and a line of tiny birds going toward my wrist. Some people design their body art so it all fits together, but I did mine piecemeal, like my life, and it looked fine.

Kiki noticed it when it was a week old and still swollen. She had just made supper for us (overcooked hamburgers but Oliver liked them) and I was doing the dishes, keeping that arm out of the water. Soaking too soon was bad for it.

"And when Boyd is out of the picture," Kiki said, "you'll be stuck with this ink that won't go away."

"It's my history," I said. "My arm is an album."

"What if Boyd doesn't like it?"

"It's for *me*," I said. "All of these are *mine*."

"Don't be a carpet," she said.

"You don't really know very much about this," I said, "if you don't mind my saying."

Why would I take advice from a woman who slept every night alone in her bed, cuddling up with some copy of Aristotle? What could she possibly tell me that I could use? And she was getting older by the minute, with her squinty eyes and her short hair cut too close to her head.

It was snowing the day Boyd got released from Rikers. I was home with Oliver when Claude went to pick him up. He didn't want me and Oliver seeing him then, with his bag of items, with his humbling paperwork, with the guards leaning over every detail. By the time I got to view Boyd he was in our local coffee shop with Claude, eating a cheeseburger, looking happy and greasy. Oliver went berserk, leaping all over him, smearing his snowy boots all over Boyd's pants. I leaped a little too. "Don't knock me over," Boyd said. "Nah, knock me over. Go ahead."

"Show him no mercy," Claude said.

Already Boyd looked vastly better than he had in jail, and he'd
been out only an hour. "Can't believe it," he said. "Can't believe
I was ever there." He fed french fries to Oliver, who pretended to
be a dog. Boyd had his other hand on my knee. We could do that
now. "Hey, girl," he said. The snow outside the window gave everything a lunar brightness.

The first night he stayed with me, after it took forever to get Oliver
asleep in the other room, I was madly eager when we made our
way to each other at last. How did it go, this dream—did we still
know how to do this? Knew just fine, though there were fumbles
and pauses, little laughing hesitations. I had imagined Boyd would
be hungry and even rough, but no, he was careful; he looped
around and circled back and took some byways before settling on
his goal. He was trying, it seemed to me, to make this first contact
very particular, trying to recognize me. I hadn't expected this from
him, which showed what I knew.

At my job in the vet's office my fellow workers teased me about being sleepy at the desk. They all knew my boyfriend had returned
after a long trip. Any yawn brought on group hilarity. "Look how
she walks, she hobbles," one of the techs said. What a raunchy
office I worked in. All I said was, "Laugh away, you're green with
envy."

I was distracted, full of wayward thoughts—Boyd and I starting
a restaurant together, Boyd and I running off to Thailand, Boyd
and I having another kid, maybe a girl, what would we name her,
Oliver would like this—or would he? I lost focus while I was doing
my tasks at the computer and had to put up with everyone saying
how sleepy I was.

Jail doesn't always change people in good ways, but in Boyd's case
it made him quieter and less apt to throw his weight around. He
had to find a new job (no alcohol). I was proud of him when he
started as a waiter in a diner just north of our neighborhood, a
big challenge to his stylish self. This was definitely a step down for
him, which he bore grudgingly but not bitterly. After work his hair
smelled of frying oil and broiler smoke. His home was not exactly
with me—he was officially living at his cousin's, since he no longer
had his apartment—but he spent a lot of nights at my place. I

liked the cousin (it was Maxwell, who had once babysat for Oliver) but he had a tendency to drag Boyd out to clubs at night. In my younger days I liked to go clubbing same as anyone, but once I had Oliver it pretty much lost its appeal. I had reason to imagine girls in teensy outfits throwing themselves at Boyd in these clubs, but it turned out that wasn't the problem. The problem was that Maxwell had a scheme for increasing Boyd's admittedly paltry income. It had to do with smuggling cigarettes from Virginia to New York, of all idiotic ways to make a profit. Just to cash in on the tax difference. "Are you out of your fucking mind?" I said. "You want to violate probation?"

"Don't shout," Boyd said.

"Crossing state lines. Are you crazy?"

"That's it," Boyd said. "No more talking. You always have opinions. Topic closed. Forget I said a word."

I didn't take well to being shushed. I snapped at him and he got stony and went home early that night. "A man needs peace, is that too much to ask?"

"You think I give a fuck?" I said.

I was with Kiki the next day, having lunch near my office. She was checking up on me these days as much as she could, which included treating me to a falafel plate. I told her about the dog I'd met at my job who knew three languages. It could sit, lie down, and beg in English, Spanish, and ASL. "A pit-bull mix. They're smart."

"You know what I think?" Kiki said. "I think you should go live somewhere where you'd learn another language. Everyone should, really."

"Someday," I said.

"I still have a friend in Istanbul. I bet you and Oliver could go camp out at her place. For a little while. It's a very kid-friendly culture."

"I don't think so. My life is here."

"It doesn't have to be Istanbul, that was my place, it's not everyone's. There are other places. I'd stake you with some cash if you wanted to take off for a while."

I wasn't even tempted.

"It's very good of you," I said.

"You'll be sorry later if you don't do it," she said.

She wanted to get me away from Boyd, which might happen on its own, anyway. I was touched and insulted both at once. And then I was trying to imagine myself in a new city. Taking Oliver to a park in Rome. Having interesting chats with the locals while I sat on a bench. Laughing away in Italian.

My phone interrupted us with the ping that meant I was getting a text. "Sorry," I said to Kiki. "I just need to check." It was Boyd, and I was so excited that I said, "Oh! From Boyd!" out loud. *Sorry, baby* was in the message, and some other things that I certainly wasn't reading to Kiki. But I chuckled in joy, tickled to death—I could feel myself getting flushed. How funny he could be when he wanted. That Boyd.

"Excuse me," I said. "I just have to answer fast."

"Go ahead," Kiki said, not pleasantly.

I had to concentrate to tap the letters. It took a few minutes and I could hear Kiki sigh across from me. I knew how I looked, too girly, too jacked up over crumbs Boyd threw my way. Kiki was not glad about it. She didn't even know Boyd. But I did—I could see him very distinctly in my mind just then, his grumbling sweetness, his spells of cold scorn, his bragging, his ridiculous illusions about what he could do, and the waves of tenderness I had for him, the sudden pangs of adoration. I was perfectly aware (or just then I was, anyway) that some part of my life with Boyd was not entirely real, that if I pushed it too hard a whole other feeling would show itself. I wasn't about to push. I wanted us to go on as we were. A person can know several things at once. I could know all of them while still being moved to delight by him—his kisses on my neck, his way of humming to the most blaring tune, his goofing around with Oliver. And I saw that I was probably going to help him with the cigarette smuggling too. I was going to be in it with him before I even meant to be.

I was going to ride in the car and count the cash; I was going to let him store his illegal cigarettes in my house. All because of what stirred me, all because of what Boyd was to me. All because of beauty.

I had my own life to live. And what did Kiki have? She had her job making deals between the very rich and the very poor. She had her books that she settled inside of in dusty private satisfaction. She had her old and fabled past. I loved my aunt, but she must have known I'd never listen to her.

When I stopped texting Boyd, I looked up, and Kiki was dabbing at her plate of food. "The hummus was good," I said.

"They say Saladin ate hummus," she said. "In the eleven hundreds. You know about him, right? He was a Kurd who fought against the Crusaders."

She knew a lot. She was waiting for me to make some fucking effort to know a fraction as much. Saladin who? In the meantime —anyone looking at our table could've seen this—we were having a long and unavoidable moment, my aunt and I, of each feeling sorry for the other. In our separate ways. How could we not?

North

FROM *One Story*

MY FATHER MADE it as far as Little Iceland. That was the name of the iceberg they found his notebook frozen into, interred like a fossil. At least that was the name written on one of the last pages of his notebook, under a sketch of what might or might not have been the iceberg. There was the question, in those days, of what to name. The impulse was to lay claim to each new fragment of the unknown. Label everything. But icebergs do as they please. They form and break so quickly, it is possible to claim one one day, only to watch it divide itself out of existence the next.

What my mother said: we do what we can to make things stick.

My father was an explorer. Every few years, he packed his things —clothes, boots, notebooks, tins of food—and kissed my mother goodbye. She watched from the steps of their cabin in northern Idaho as he hoisted his bag onto his shoulder and set off down the path to the main road. When he got to the gap in the trees where the path bent back like a hairpin, he stopped and waved, a figure no bigger than her thumb.

He came close to dying enough times she stopped keeping track. Back then, people traveling to the places he did disappeared because of all kinds of things: exhaustion, hypothermia, trichinosis, bears. For a long time, my father was lucky. The things that went missing were largely expendable: food, sled dogs, scientific measuring tools whose cost got chalked up to an expedition's overhead. Still, some things are irreplaceable. By his thirtieth birthday, the only fingers remaining on his left hand were his ring finger, index finger, and thumb.

But my father was a stubborn man. He had an internal compass, he said. It just kept pointing north. Once, at my mother's insistence, he went to see the local doctor in Coolin. The doctor frowned: "Strange," he said, shaking the thermometer. "Let's try that again." But my father laughed and hopped down off the examining table. He'd always known ice ran through his veins, he said. It was only a matter of time before the rest of him froze.

One day my father did what anyone might have predicted. He hoisted his pack onto his back, waved through the gap in the trees, boarded the train that wound through the Selkirk Mountains, got off in Seattle, and was never heard from again. My mother waited years, but the body was never found. For that reason she went on for a long time believing he might come back. When I was younger, and thought love was something the world owed you, I had to hide in my room when I wanted to cry over it, this great unfairness.

The sea captain who found my father's notebook frozen into the side of Little Iceland came all the way to northern Idaho to hand-deliver it to my mother.

We all thought very highly of your husband, he said. The world could use more men like him.

My mother nodded. She said the notebook had clearly been left there intentionally. It was stuffed inside a specimen jar, stoppered, carefully sealed with wax. The pages were in perfect condition, she pointed out, the words only a little smudged here and there.

The sea captain nodded. The balloon could have landed anywhere, he said, sunk anywhere. The water would have carried the party's belongings miles from where they died. With time, their bodies would have been dispersed in this way as well.

Or, my mother said, he could have deliberately thrown it overboard. *A clue,* she called it, as though the whole thing—my father, the balloon, the years of waiting, all of it—was no more than a puzzle waiting to be solved.

Every love story begins with a discovery: amidst the ordinary, the sublime.

*

This is how it begins.

My mother and her sisters were crossing the road in the town of Sumpter, North Dakota, when a buggy stopped in front of her and a man leaped out. He wore a tall hat, wide red suspenders. His boots were covered in mud, his coat filthy and ragged along the hem, but he walked up to my mother as though they'd known each other all their lives.

"Good afternoon." He stood there, smiling at her.

My mother had never seen a smile like his. It was a smile like a magician's, full of hidden wonders.

"Allow me to introduce myself," he said, tipping his hat, and her sisters giggled into their handkerchiefs.

My mother had never set foot outside of Sumpter. Her family was close-knit, clannish, five girls born to a Virginia preacher who'd ended up in a dusty town in the middle of nowhere because the Lord commanded him so. His wife liked to remind anyone who would listen that the Lord hadn't commanded *her* to go anywhere. She would have stayed in Virginia forever, if anyone cared. She would have stayed there till the end of time.

There wasn't much for my mother and her sisters to do in Sumpter. They spent long afternoons sewing on the porch, watching the dusty streets turn copper-colored in the sun.

But my mother was not quite like her sisters. She'd been taken to the town physician frequently as a child, because she did strange things to her body even God couldn't seem to explain. She ripped the nail clean off her thumb once because, she said, she wanted to see her hand plainly. She took a pair of scissors to her braid and chopped the whole thing off, the curls that remained so short her ears showed through like little shells. She slipped out to where the prairie grasses grew high as her shoulders, pulled her dress over her head, and ran through those arid, sweet-smelling fields until her legs buckled under her; she lay there a long time, breathing hard into the hot alluvial soil, letting the bloody taste of it settle across her tongue. She didn't know how to read, but she spent long hours bent over the Bible, moving her lips in a way that might have suggested to anyone who didn't know her that she was praying. She had desires she didn't have words for.

No man will want a wild woman for a wife, her mother told her, not unkindly.

A wild man will, my mother said, and her sisters laughed, because the way she said it made it sound true.

At night, my mother sneaked out to sit on the porch. She needed to breathe, she told her sisters. She couldn't for the life of her understand how anyone slept cooped up like that. She curled herself into the rocking chair, still as a cat. Counted the stars in the sky, memorized the pinprick pattern they punched into the blue. With a little concentration, she found, she could float up among them. Vanish from the porch, the still, too-close air. In the wink of an eye, escape.

This was one of the first things she told my father when he came to call on her the next day.

I should warn you, she said, eyeing him as she used her pinky to coax a sugar tornado up from the bottom of her glass of lemonade. *I have a habit of disappearing.*

But he just tapped his chest and smiled his magician's smile. *Ask me what I do for a living.*

This is how it begins.

My father, Thomas Hamblen, stands on the narrow strip of shoreline. Overhead, the sky burns a brilliant blue. It is late August, and a breeze ripples the surface of the lake. The air at this early evening hour is already cool, but comfortably so. Even a man unaccustomed to the cold could spend the night outdoors without complaint.

My father eases himself down in front of the water, stretching his back against the gravelly sand. He wears a long-sleeved shirt and cotton pants. Slowly, deliberately, he removes his socks.

He has been home for five days. He is afraid he might be losing his mind.

Over the course of the past fifteen years, my father has traveled to the Arctic and back a total of three times. He came within an estimated sixty-odd miles of the North Pole—so close, he tells my mother, he could taste it. He went first as a boy, chosen for his speed and agility. Later, because he retained a boy's hunger for the unknown. He goes where few other men dare. He does so willingly, eagerly. For this reason, he is respected by other explorers. Admired, even. This does not protect him from anything.

For example, loss. He has lost so much by this point it hardly registers when he loses it all over again, his memory stretched over time to a dangerous thinness. What did he lose? A fellow expedition member. A photograph. Ammunition. Mementos—lockets, pocketknives, letters. They slid into the water when an ice floe cracked, or they fell out of his jacket, or he traded them for something necessary, something that in the moment drew the line between life and death. There are nights he lies, sleepless, beside my mother and tries to add it all up: five men, sixteen dogs, five pounds of dried meat plus ten pounds of beans, two notebooks . . . but it is a futile exercise. He gives up and goes back to counting sheep. Easier arithmetic. Or he gets out of the warm bed and goes into the kitchen, where he pours himself whiskey after whiskey, drinking until the numbers disappear.

There are moments on his expeditions, trekking across snow so brilliant its light seems thrown from some alien sun, when my father stops abruptly, drops his head in his hands. He pretends to cough, to sneeze, to wipe at the tiny icicles forming at the corners of his eyes. He has to, to hide what his companions on these long journeys cannot see: he is in love. His face, like a schoolboy's, would give him away.

Now he lies back against the damp stones and watches the setting sun bleed into the blue. Clouds shuttle back and forth, pinking up around their edges until they glow like flesh in candlelight. High above the pine trees, a pair of sharp-shinned hawks turn lazy circles, scouting out mice and voles.

My father shuts his eyes, squeezing until red stars explode against the black.

He blinks, and the sky opens above him like an invitation.

What did the Pole taste like?

Like dirty metal. Like salt. Like this, he tells my mother, and she waits, eyes closed, lips parted for a kiss.

The months between expeditions are never easy. In the absence of imminent disaster, my father finds himself listless, irritable. His appetite vanishes; his body softens like fruit. Days pass and he loses himself in their passing, the predictable sameness of one morning to the next. He loses hours to sleep, or to some strange fugue state between sleeping and waking from which he starts as though from a nightmare, finding himself in the middle of some small task he has no recollection of having begun. He walks outside to fetch water from the creek and wakes with an ax in his hand, his head leaning against the rough, sweet-smelling trunk of a white pine. He opens his battered copy of *Origin of Species* and finds himself on the shore an hour later, left hand aching, as though feeling the loss of those fingers anew. He finds a pencil and sits on a log, copying lines into his notebook until the pain ebbs from his palm. *Great as are the differences between the breeds of the pigeon* . . . he switches the pencil to his right hand, forcing his wrist to curve in a way still unnatural. Over the years, the muscles in those fingers have gained only a little more fluidity, but he keeps at it. *Anticipate the worst,* a fellow explorer once told him—this one of the men now gone, succumbed to something or other in lands unknown. *The only surprise should be finding yourself alive.*

One afternoon a few weeks after he arrives home, my father goes into the kitchen and puts his arms around my mother. He is not a man given to regret, but on this afternoon, the world honeyed by the warm September light, he feels suddenly heavy with it, a sadness that sits on his chest like a stone. He tells my mother he has been a fool to leave her all these years. He says she is what he thinks of every night he is gone. That she is what saves him. When he is with her, he tells her, the cold that has a hold on his body retreats a little. Retracts its claws. He is nothing without her, he tells her. A no one. He is hardly a man at all.

Please, he says.

Forgive me, he says.

For a moment, she stands perfectly still. Through the window, the pine trees are moving their feathered branches in the breeze, the cool, clean smell of them so strong she can feel the rutted surface of their bark beneath her hands, feel the sap lacing itself stickily across her palms.

Then all at once—chattering, her voice too loud—she ducks out from under his arm. *Look!* she says, pushing up her sleeve. Look how strong she's gotten! She makes him feel the sinewy muscles along her shoulder. She has been chopping wood all spring and summer. She put up ten jars of huckleberry jam and ate enough fresh berries she worried her skin might turn blue. There were bears up along the mountainside where the huckleberries grow. She counts off on her fingers: a family of four, two young ones, a mother and three cubs, a solitary giant—male, she thinks. She crept away—so, so quietly—and made it home with her store intact. She caught trout in the stream and dried and smoked it for winter. She made friends with their neighbors in the next cove and has been taking the coach with the wife, Bernice, into town for supplies every few weeks. She stitched a new quilt for their bed. She taught herself how to crochet. She embroidered three separate pillows, one for each chair. She went swimming every afternoon, for hours and hours—See how strong she is? How brown? She thrusts her arm out again. Only two bad storms, and what little damage there was she cleaned up easily. The sun after this long winter a blessing, she says. The sun its own God, she says, making heaven out of—she shakes her head, brushing something off the front of her dress. Heaven, she says. End of story, she says.

He looks at her and sees she is desperately unhappy.

The sun sails from one side of the lake to the other. As it mounts, the air grows heavy with heat. The birds thin out. They retreat into the woods, though the pair of hawks remains, riding air currents carelessly back and forth. When they sight something—a fish sliding under the surface of the lake, a mouse scrabbling through the tangle of huckleberries—they release a thin, high whistle. As the afternoon stretches on, the air cools, and other birds begin to reappear—loons and grebes, the tiny gray-tailed Grunter finch. My father watches the birds coast back and forth, retreating and advancing toward land. By the time the sun begins to slip toward the lake, the bats have joined in, dim shapes flicking back and forth across the water, sailing low to scoop up the bugs congregating just above the surface.

The air is full of flying things.

My father watches. A dull pain uncoils itself along the base of his skull. He has not eaten anything all day, and his brain, despite the pain, feels sharper for it. He slides his notebook from his pocket and starts a few simple sketches—a duck, a finch, a filigree of alder leaves against the sky—before dropping the pencil, his right hand spasming in a way that makes him want to weep. Glancing at the horizon, he catches a ribbon of ice glinting out from behind the distant mountain ridge: it is bluish, glittering, a faint iridescence like a butterfly's wing. When he looks again, it is gone.

The sky is an angry bruise-colored violet by the time my mother makes her way down to the lake's edge. Clouds hang low along the horizon. My father has lain here for hours now, half-shaded by a row of tall cedars. A patch of skin across his left foot stings: sunburn, probably, though most of the feeling in both feet he lost to frostbite years ago, the skin there smooth and white as a cadaver's.

My mother stands over him, smiling. "Resting?"

"Thinking," he says, and she turns away too quickly.

An eagle emerges from a nearby cove, gliding in before flapping its enormous wings—once, twice, spiraling down across the open expanse of lake, sending the house sparrows into a frenzy. The eagle, my father has read, is nearly seven feet across the wingspan, though to see it glide across the cove is to believe it larger still. It is a bird of such grace and power it seems to come from another world. According to the great Darwin, the eagle is the result of centuries of careful genetic winnowing. He is the outcome of a thousand intricate survival games: Does this wingspan help the eagle fly higher or longer? Does this particular curvature of the beak aid or hinder the tearing of flesh? Does the chick with the slightly larger cranial socket hunt more efficiently, or does it die when its head gets stuck in the burrow of some woodland animal it has chased into the underbrush?

The sky is darkening in earnest now, turning indigo and velvety, dense as cream. A cloud drifts out from behind the ridge of trees to his right and my father tries to watch them simultaneously, eagle and cloud, but in the last faint wash of daylight, his eyes refuse to focus. He squints, raises himself on one elbow. Suddenly, the eagle plunges. It drops from the sky like a cannonball, so fast my father barely has time to sit up before the bird is flapping its enormous wings, skidding to an awkward suspension as it scoops one talon into the water and takes off again. Its victory scream is high and loud. Against the rising moon, the outline of a small pike wriggling in the bird's talons is neat and black as a stamp. Up the eagle rises, up, up.

The sky snuffs itself out like a candle.

My father grabs the nearest bit of driftwood and drives it into the pebbles, lights the end on fire. He snatches up his notebook, turns to a fresh page, and draws the eagle coasting, then dropping, then braking against the air—then, as his makeshift lantern sputters and spits, draws the eagle lifting again, the sudden parasol of those wings.

When my mother calls him in for dinner, she has to say his

name three times before he stands. His body is stiff from hours of
inertia. His foot burns. His mouth is so dry his lips have cracked,
the bottom one—when he runs his tongue along it experimen-
tally—weeping a few drops of blood.

But: his mind. His mind vibrates like a plucked string.

My mother sits across the table from him, smoothing the napkin across her knees. She pretends not to notice how quickly he
eats, moving his fork mechanically back and forth until his plate is
clean. When dinner is done, he gets up immediately and goes to
the little desk by the window and sits down. Opens his notebook to
a new page.

Supplies needed for the construction of a balloon, he writes.

When my mother goes to bed, she leaves the candles burning. My
father does not raise his head as she steps past him, putting her
feet down deliberately, rattling the door in its casing. In bed, she
tosses and turns; it is after one by the time she finally blows the
candles out. She lies there in the dark, listening to the scratch of
the pen against paper. She counts the minutes as they pass.

When she wakes, she is still alone. Light leaks in around the
half-closed door; she gets up and crosses the room, pulling a
sweater on over her nightgown to fend off the early morning chill.

My father sits at the desk, scribbling furiously. He does not turn,
and my mother stands there only briefly before slipping out the
back door. Here, in her own home on the edge of a lake so wide
she can't see to the other side, she no longer has to sit outside in
order to breathe. On the nights she finds herself unable to sleep,
she simply leaves. Walks along the trail until she comes to the main
road, then up the hill to where it crests against the sky. When she
reaches the top of the hill, she turns around and looks back at the
cabin, the glint of moonlight off its windows giving it away, like a
telltale heart.

She would like to know how it feels, is all.

The next few months are a slow grind of activity. Each day my father cycles through exhilaration, exhaustion, frustration. Each day
he arrives at the conclusion that he has embarked upon the most
significant journey of his life, one that will write his name beside
Darwin's in the history books. Each day he decides he has finally
gone mad. He sits on the stony beach with a stack of notepaper,

writing letter after letter. He is gathering what he will need to coax his expedition into the realm of possibility: information, interest, hazy promises of involvement, financial and otherwise. Without the necessary funds, the idea will never leave the page. He writes everyone from every expedition he has been a part of since he became a member of this strange club, the club of explorers. He writes John Manley, who once shot and killed the largest polar bear any member of their party had ever seen. *Nanook,* he called it, after the native people's word for the bear. He said he had been waiting his whole life to kill a bear that big.

Dear John, my father writes. *I write to tell you that I have discovered my Nanook. It is attaining the North Pole by way of a balloon.* He writes the head of the science department at the university. He writes the great explorer Adolphus Greely, recently returned from an expedition to Ellesmere Island—the trip for all intents and purposes a disaster, all but six of the twenty-five-man crew dead. *Dear Mr. Greely,* my father writes. *Before I begin my application for your counsel in earnest, may I express to you my utmost admiration for the bravery demonstrated by you and your crew on your most recent Polar Expedition. This is no easy road, he writes. God help all of us who have chosen to journey it.* He writes the celebrated British balloonist Henry Tracey Coxwell, the architect and pilot of such spectacular specimens as *Mars* and *Mammoth: Dear Mr. Coxwell,* my father writes. *It is with great respect for your many accomplishments in the field of aeronautics that I write to you today in search of guidance pertaining to all things balloon.*

He writes Alfred Nobel, whose generosity has made him a coveted contact among adventurers Arctic and other. *Dear Mr. Nobel,* my father writes. *I have not had the pleasure of making your acquaintance, but I understand we hold a similar passion for invention close to our heart. I have a number of ideas pertaining to the recent and unfortunately failed ventures to the North Pole and ways in which I might, with my breadth of experience in the region in question and my extensive knowledge of the conditions related to said region, improve (considerably) upon these failures and, indeed, triumph where others have failed.*

He writes the president of the United States, reasoning that in the off chance some excitable underling may, as he sifts through the mail, find my father's letter and scent the crisp odor of adventure, it will be entirely worth the effort. *Dear Mr. President, I am writing to inform you of a thrilling new development in the field of Arctic exploration, a field in which our brave nation might and indeed by all rights should, I believe, excel. Sir,* he writes, *it is my humble opinion that if given the opportunity I can and shall lead us into the future.* Under his signature he writes "Seasoned Arctic Explorer." At the last minute, he adds: "*and* Inventor."

This is what my father sees when he looks out over the lake: balloon after balloon, rising toward the heavens. A fish flips out of the lake. *Balloon!* In the arc of the fish's body as it leaps out and reenters there is a fluidity that sends him back to his notebook, sketching furiously. That he is entirely unfamiliar with the nuts and bolts of ballooning gives him little pause: he knows the terrain, he knows the cold. He is intimately acquainted with the brutal physics of heat loss and hope. Over the years, he has lined the cabin walls with stacks of books—a vast assortment of weathered encyclopedias, primarily, collected along his journeys and carried back at the expense of more practical acquisitions: canned goods, a sharp knife, warm clothes for my mother, who has darned and re-darned her skirts so many times the mending yarn now blots out the original fabric entirely. No matter. The latest spoils yielded a reasonably well-preserved and fairly recent edition of the *Britannica,* which he flips through with growing impatience.

When he finds what he is looking for, he hesitates only an instant before ripping the page from the spine. The prize? A drawing of the late Frenchman Jean-Pierre Blanchard's balloon—the specifics of its construction antiquated by now but still useful. The drawing itself is quite elegant, a bit of fancy my father had admired in passing and then promptly forgotten—its beauty, he had thought, the indulgence of a fool.

My father bends over his notebook. He begins to sketch.

Here is the envelope, here is the burner, here are the drag ropes, here is the basket. The observation platform in Blanchard's diagram is spare but functional; placed below the burner, it will allow two men to stand watch and take notes on the weather, the clouds, the view as they peer down from their perch. The basket will need to be lined with something warm—sealskin? Something that repels water would be helpful. Rope that can double as ballast. His pen flies over the pages, making a scratching sound as he draws. He turns the page, fills it; turns to another, another.

On her weekly trips to the dry goods store in Coolin, my mother collects stacks of old newspapers and practices her reading at night, one laborious page at a time. My father takes the papers she has already read and draws preliminary sketches across the brittle pages, scrawling through headlines with abandon. *MAN DEAD AT TWENTY* becomes *M N DE D AT TW NTY. STORM APPROACHES COEUR D'ALENE* becomes *T RM AP O CHES C UR D'ALE E.* He uses three entire newspapers in a single afternoon, going through a dozen sketches, two dozen, calculating and recalculating various heights and weights before settling on the proper dimensions for one of the ballast ropes, which he then meticulously copies down into his notebook. My mother watches him take a stack of fresh papers out to the beach and wipes her hands on her apron, takes a loaf of bread from the stove. She puts it in the window to cool, leans forward. Presses her forehead to the glass.

A chipmunk knocks a pinecone down from a nearby tree. My father squints: *balloon!* They will need more ballast than anyone has ever thought necessary. If the balloon is to stay afloat for a matter of days rather than hours, and if it is required of the balloon that it be able to be controlled tightly once they approach the yawning territory of ice and bitter winds, then they will need to harness not only the power of the sun and the air currents but also that of gravity. Sand, my father reads, is the usual thing, but when he draws a sketch of the basket he includes three five-pound sacks of sugar. They can use it in their coffee, pitch what's not needed over the side. He has heard that the Norwegian explorer Fridtjof Nansen, tales of whose recent forays into Greenland have begun to assume the size and heft of myth, takes coffee on every expedition, never mind the vehicle of motion: sled, boat, foot. My father finds the thought of coffee in the air appealing: it is as though, flying, he need not be any less at home than he is on the ground. He sips the coffee my mother has made him and starts a preliminary list:

Coffee, five pounds
Sugar, twelve pounds
Meat, ten pounds
Fowl, ten pounds

When his hand begins to cramp, my father closes his eyes. (His right hand he has abandoned, the work too fine, the degree of control required too high.) The sun burns through his lids, producing a shimmering red glow. *Balloon!* Hot air fills the envelope. The hydrogen hisses like a snake.

If he rounds the bottom of the basket, will it bounce lightly along the ground rather than smash to smithereens? If he can control the drag ropes the way he controls the ropes that guide the sled dogs, keep them from tangling up in one another, what is to stop him from landing the balloon lightly as a feather? Anyone who knows ice knows it must be treated like a beautiful woman: gently, warily, with a firm but respectful hand. He flips the newspaper over and wets the nub of the pencil against his tongue.

A dragonfly lights on his knee, wings quivering as it cleans its front legs.

Balloon!

A letter from Henry Tracey Coxwell arrives. My father takes the envelope down to the lake and opens it there, his heart fluttering girlishly. The letter is brief but cordial. In it Coxwell expresses his enthusiasm for my father's venture and outlines the specific ways in which he would like to be of service: the names of a few potential crew members, a wealthy benefactor acquaintance with a taste for the exotic, a seamstress willing to purchase reams of silk on credit. My father stands a minute, pressing the letter to his lips. It is sunset, and the air has taken on an exquisite shimmer, a wash of blues and violets and pale petal-pinks.

I wish you the very best of luck in your ventures, Coxwell writes. *Godspeed.*

It is only when my father goes to put the letter back in the envelope that he discovers the second sheet tucked into one corner, folded neatly into quarters. He unfolds the quadrants, smoothes it against his arm.

In the dusky quiet, my father lets out a whoop. A single meticulous diagram covers the page: a balloon, perfect as a pearl.

Winter comes and goes. Spring.

My mother sweeps a cluster of fallen elderberry blossoms from the steps. As they whirl up around her broom, she sees they are newspaper, shredded into tiny bits.

The ice melts. The stream that empties into the lake swells and groans, the rushing of its overflow so loud it wakes my mother up at night. She lies there a moment, shivering a little under the thin quilt, then turns onto her side and lifts her nightgown so she can press her bare skin against my father's back. He is burning up all the time now, his body running on some strange, inexhaustible fuel.

She is out clipping the laundry on the line to dry one morning when my father steals all the pillowcases from the linen closet and spends an entire afternoon at the edge of the lake, tossing them into the air, where they billow and collapse like lungs. He pulls the leaves off her favorite alder and sits by the water for days, clumsily sewing them together, blunting her needle until it is unsalvageable. He takes all the silverware from the kitchen drawers; he spends the rest of the week building strange, gleaming cities in the sand. At mealtime they eat with their hands and my mother wonders idly if my father is going insane.

He disappears into the water for hours, swimming toward the horizon until the lake closes behind him. Not so much as a ripple to show where he's gone.

A mallard beats its wings, pitching its feet forward as it slows, flapping hard as it comes down to rest on the shore. Its body is sleek and fat, the feathers glossy. My father rubs his eyes and turns to a fresh page.

Balloon! Balloon! Balloon!

My mother begins spending all her time inside. She stops going into town. Stops wading in the stream, surprising unlucky trout. Stops walking the trails up to where the huckleberries cluster in fat blue-black globes, leaves her needlepoint to languish on the bedside table, the thread slowly unspooling. Instead, she stands in the kitchen, stirring sugar into cup after cup of tea, watching my father through the window. The spoon hitting the cup over and over again makes a sound like a little bell.

One evening, when my father finally emerges from one of his marathon swims, the sun hits him from behind just so; he is golden, glowing. The light is so strong it has the peculiar effect of drawing a second, shimmering man around the first, as though my father has doubled himself, gone into the water and emerged with a twin.

He lifts a hand to his forehead, squinting at something in the trees, and his twin does the same, his hand drawing a streak against the sky like a shooting star.

The spoon falls to the floor with a clatter, my mother's pulse suddenly wild.

That night while my father snores, my mother slips her hands under his nightshirt. She runs her fingers across his ribs, up and down the knobby articulation of his spine. He is so thin these days she might see through him. If she lit a candle and brought it under the sheets, she might see straight in to the mess of organs, that dense, wet tangle. She might see through to his heart, the tireless muscle of his desire.

And her?

In one swift motion, she yanks her nightgown up over her head.

At a certain point he clutches her around the waist and she freezes, her hips lifted a quarter-inch above his. But his hands fall away almost immediately. He groans; once, he murmurs her name. Or maybe it is *sorry*. Maybe it is *glory*. Or *goodbye*. She watches his eyes flutter open, the whites of them in the dark startling. After, she lies back against her pillow and folds her arms across her chest. Warmth rises from her like the mist that comes off the lake in early morning. Or like there is something dangerous running through her, both of them burning up from the same fever.

There are things my father wishes he could explain. Things he would like my mother to understand. The sky there is God, he wants to tell her. The ice is God. The fat, hideous walrus is God.

My mother places a pie in the window to cool, standing a few deliberate inches from the steam that rises from it, smelling of burnt sugar. The nausea has just come on. A little over two weeks ago now, but she'd known when the first day of her bleeding came and went without so much as a vague cramping. She has always been regular as a clock. Her body has never failed her. And now—well, now it has done only what she asked of it. She finds the nausea unpleasant but feels otherwise well enough; she is a little tired, occasionally dizzy. No appetite most of the day, though at times hunger comes upon her so suddenly, with such urgency, she finds herself racing to the kitchen to cram hunks of bread down her throat. It helps both nausea and fatigue to focus on a single point. Standing by the window, she pretends she is on a boat in the middle of a vast ocean, though she has never seen the ocean, never seen a body of water larger than this lake. She has never, truth be told, been anywhere. She grips the edge of the kitchen table, pressing her palms against the wood as her stomach rolls and flips. When she closes her eyes, she sees it: hope the size of a seed.

When my father comes in from chopping wood, cheeks red from exertion, she is standing over the pie, halving it, quartering, slicing it into eight. She does not turn around. All these months, he has never said one word about the balloon. He is like a child, afraid to speak his wish for fear of it never coming true. But of course it is ludicrous to pretend my mother doesn't know. Even before the letters, before he began covering the pages of his notebook with sketches and calculations, filling it with the many blueprints of his dreams—long before any of that, she saw it, the glint in his eye.

She does not know when my father's leaving turned from adventure to abandonment. Nor does she know when the freedom to do with her days what she pleases became its own oppression, but she pins some portion of the change to that afternoon up on the mountainside, picking berries. She had been happy tramping through the underbrush, the sun hitting her full-tilt. Her basket filled to the brim with fruit. She had been looking forward to the jam, to the elbow-deep immersion its making required, those many hours hers to do with as she wished. And then, as she turned halfway down to admire the view, something about the lake, the way it curled around the mountainside, still and unwieldy as a giant's finger—something about that had stopped her in her tracks. She had to lie down right there in the bushes and wait until the roaring in her head subsided. This is what she had meant to tell my father. Not about the bears, but about the loneliness that struck her, sudden as a storm.

She places a slice of pie on his plate.

How many pairs of socks, she says, turning, does he think he'll need this time?

At dinner he eats a little less each night. My mother serves him the same heaping plate, twice as much as covers hers, and he mentally quarters each portion and eats as slowly as he can, ignoring the groans of protest from his gut. They are both eating less and less. Pretending for very different reasons that everything is just as it has always been. She pushes her food around with her fork and drinks plain hot water, cup after cup. She has a headache, she says. She is just tired, she says.

My father stands on the shoreline in his undershirt, watching the moon glaze the frozen lake silver. He flips through his notebook, runs his finger across the pages covered top to bottom with his cramped print, his carefully detailed figures, the lists dutifully numbered and separated according to category. The few letters received in reply he keeps tucked into the back cover, the pages folded and refolded so many times the paper has been worn to unnatural softness, Coxwell's balloon diagram the texture of velvet.

My mother has stopped crying. For this, he is grateful.

A loon calls somewhere not too far from where he stands and he squints into the glowing darkness, searching.

Behind him, the last candle gutters out in the cabin.

Bal-loon, cries the loon. *Bal-loon, bal-loon.*

The weather begins to turn again. The snow melts on the mountainside, sending down water like a biblical flood.

My mother wakes one night to a sensation so strange she nearly cries out: just below her rib cage, under the new softness in her belly, a small wave rolls through her. She lies there in the dark for hours after, pressing her hand against the memory.

The day my father leaves, my mother wakes early. She slips out of bed, pulls his favorite dress over her head. She has made a special trip into town the day before, buying provisions for pancakes: flour, butter, eggs, precious as gold. Even so, it is not until she stands there buttoning her dress in the semi-darkness, her fingers trembling so violently she finally abandons the last few, that she realizes what she will do. What she has been planning to do ever since she felt me in the night, flipping inside her like a little fish.

She stands in the kitchen, whisking salt into the flour. Her heart is everywhere: in her throat, her chest, the heat she feels in her cheeks. She will tell him over breakfast. She will get up from her chair as he wipes the last of the syrup from his plate, take his hand and place his palm flat against her belly, the give where, soon enough, I will push the skin out, taut as a drum.

"John," she will say. "After your father. Dorothy if it is a girl."

What he is leaving behind is no different that what he is leaving for, she will tell him. A truth stranger than any magic: Inside her is the wildest land.

She stands and pours the first of the batter on the griddle, making a neat row of circles. She is humming loudly to cover up the noise of her heart, a tune she used to sing with her sisters—so long ago now she remembers no more than the refrain: *my dear, my sweetheart, my hind.* When my father walks in, she turns away to hide her smile.

"Mary," he says, and when she hears the determination in his voice something that is not me flips over inside her. *"Mary,"* he says urgently. "Listen to me," he says. "I am going to change the world."

And just like that, her smile disappears.

My father has been gone four months the night my mother wakes up to a band of pain like a vise tightening around the swell of her belly. She shifts onto her side and lies still as long as she can stand it. It is dark when she wakes, and as she turns onto one side, then the other, she watches the light begin to seep in around the edges of the curtains. She watches, in particular, one bar the width of her ankle, makes herself guess the length it creeps along the floor. When the pain gets worse, she stands and paces the small living room. It takes ten steps to go from one wall to another. ONE-TWO-THREE-FOUR. She counts out loud. In between contractions, she puts wood into the stove, manages to get a few pots of water boiling. She can't imagine what she will do with the water but she remembers this from her own mother, the pots bubbling on the stove, remembers the births of each of her four younger sisters, the hot, salty smell that filled their small house, the dampness hanging in the air. She remembers the look on her mother's face, after, the blunt incredulousness of it. The broken veins beneath her eyes strange and beautiful, like crushed flowers. She remembers her sisters, each blonder than the last, and she, my mother, dark as an owl. How terrible that love should contain such contradictions. How utterly insane, she thinks, biting down on the pillow, that her body should think it can contain another human being. She ought to have known all along it is madness, this business of belonging. It is lunacy.

As the contractions get stronger, my mother stares out the win-

dow at the water, bright with the last of the moonlight, and counts
off the seconds until they are done. She says the two names to herself, over and over again, like a spell. *John. Dorothy. John. Dorothy.* If
she says them enough times, she reasons, eventually someone will
appear to claim one of them, a stranger she will make her own.

Of course she will know me the instant I come howling into the
world. She will know exactly who I am.

I am born at noon the next day. My mother tells me this is the
first thing she did: she checked the clock. I am still attached to
her when she looks. We are not yet two when she begins to keep
track of me, the seconds I have been alive and then, after she
cuts through the cord herself, cleaving my body from hers with a
kitchen knife, the seconds I have been on my own.

This is what women do, she says.

By which she means she understands that one day I will leave
her too. Lift off the ground, think myself beyond gravity.

Let go.

LAURA LEE SMITH

Unsafe at Any Speed

FROM *New England Review*

THE DAY AFTER his forty-eighth birthday was the same day Theo Bitner's seventy-five-year-old mother friended him on Facebook. It was also the same day his wife told him he needed to see a doctor. Or a therapist. "It's your mood," she said. "It sucks." Counting his mother, Theo now had eight Facebook friends. Sherrill, his wife, had 609. It was just past dawn, in the perfidious part of the day that implied anything was possible when, really, nothing was very likely. He regarded his Facebook profile, the faceless blue bust of a man staring from the margin of the screen where he should, by now, have uploaded a photo of himself. "Theo Bitner is new to Facebook," the caption read. "Suggest a friend for Theo!" Sherrill finished dressing and left the room, and Theo leaned back in his chair. He stared at the ceiling in the corner of the bedroom, where he'd propped his computer, a hulking dinosaur of a tower, on a tiny table made of pressboard. By contrast, Sherrill had a Mac laptop the size of a place mat. She carried it around in a zippered rhinestone bag and took it with her to Starbucks and Crispers.

The estrogen levels at the house, a smallish Tuscan number in an uninspired neighborhood south of St. Augustine, were through the roof, in Theo's opinion. With his daughter Ashley, unemployed and fresh from FSU with a degree in Women's Studies (what the *hell?*), ensconced back in her childhood bedroom, with his mother, Bette, now living in the spare room he'd once fancied his office (the "bonus room," Sherrill called it), and with Sherrill herself generally holding court over the rest of the house, Theo had begun to feel increasingly scuttled, shunted, reduced. There was a conspiracy, he reckoned. He didn't like it.

He turned off the computer and picked up the Craigslist ad he'd printed out. "Corvair!" the ad read. "$5,000. Two models. Call for details." The photo showed a pristine ermine-white Corvair coupe, '66 he was guessing, just sharp as *Jesus* it was, shot against a lush green backdrop of palmettos. He studied the photo and mentally ran down the specs: 95 hp in a rear-engine design, voluptuous Coke-bottle styling, and a seductive glimpse of red upholstery. The car looked like salvation. Beneath the photo was the address for a car auction in Lakeland.

He took a shower and got dressed. He chose a yellow button-down shirt and a pair of dark blue chinos. No tie. Independent sales representatives for dental equipment did not wear ties. He'd learned this. He picked up the Corvair ad and put it in his pocket. In the kitchen, Sherrill and Ashley were eating bagels, and they stopped talking when he entered the room. Sherrill looked at Ashley knowingly and raised her eyebrows.

"Good morning," he said.

"Tell him," Sherrill said.

Ashley sighed.

"Tell him," Sherrill said. "It's the only way he'll learn."

"Tell me what?" Theo said.

Ashley put her bagel down on her plate and turned to regard him. Her eyes were rimmed with a pasty blue sparkly substance, and Theo looked at her, blinking, having lost sight many years ago of the plump, pliant little girl who liked to sit on his foot as he clomped around the house, her arms wrapped tightly around his calf.

"My laundry," Ashley said. She looked at him sadly, enunciated her words clearly, as if he had a hearing impairment. "My laundry is in a *separate* basket. It's not to be *touched*."

"Did I touch it?" he said.

"Yes, you touched it," she said. "You mixed it in with all the other laundry—the towels? The sheets? Your underwear? I mean, gross."

"Well," he said.

"She doesn't want you to touch her laundry," Sherrill said. She gave him a smile that was not really a smile at all. "I don't think that's too much to ask."

"Well, maybe I just won't do any laundry at all," he said. "That way there won't be any confusion."

"Of course," Sherrill said. "He's defensive. Didn't I tell you?" She looked at Ashley, rolled her eyes. "Didn't I tell you he would freak out?"

"I'm not freaking out," he said. He poured a cup of coffee, then stood back and looked at them.

"You're freaking," Sherrill said. "You're always freaking."

Bette entered the kitchen and plodded toward the refrigerator.

"I sent you a friend request," she said.

"I saw that," he said.

"You didn't accept it?"

"I didn't have time."

"Didn't have time? How long does it take to click 'accept'?" She leaned in to pull the butter dish from the refrigerator, and a tiny muffled fart flapped through her dress. "You don't want me in your secret Facebook life, is that it?" She stood up and looked at him. Her face was powdery. Tiny white hairs stood up along her forearms.

"Oof." He shrugged. "I got no secrets," he said.

"What's that supposed to mean?" Sherrill said.

"Look," Ashley said. "All I'm saying is, don't touch my stuff. You can't afford to replace it."

Theo took his coffee out to the back patio, where he squatted on a resin footstool and read the paper. Then he sat still for a few minutes, watching a frog that had gotten caught in the return at the edge of the swimming pool. The frog was pale, exhausted. It flexed its legs and butted its head up against the wall again, again, again, looking for an escape. It had probably been there all night.

"Hooo, buddy," Theo said. "Sucks, don't it?"

He put the coffee down on the pool deck and cupped his hands under the frog to flip it out onto the concrete. The frog crouched, frozen, astonished.

"Go on," Theo said. "You're back in the game." He smiled. "Congratulations, little man."

He found the checkbook in Sherrill's purse, which was hanging on a hook in the laundry room. The washing machine chugged. Two plastic baskets sat on the floor, one marked with a black Sharpie along the rim. DO. NOT. TOUCH., it said. He left the house without another word. He climbed into his minivan, a late model Dodge Caravan, and swatted angrily at the felt headliner dangling across the top of his head.

At the office, Ernie was already waiting for him.

"Bro," Ernie said. "Where you been, bro?" Ernie was fifteen years younger than Theo, though he'd outpaced him long ago in terms of income and ambition. Ernie owned a distributorship for dental equipment, drove a BMW, wore a Rolex. His eyelashes were blacker and longer than any Theo had ever seen on a man. His chest was thick beneath a golfy turtleneck. Theo hated almost everything about him, except for the car.

The fact that Theo worked for Ernie, and not the other way around, was sickening sometimes, when he let himself think about it. He consoled himself with the idea that he was still an "independent" rep, clinging to the concept of autonomy and freedom that the word promised and turning a blind eye to the reality of the relationship, which meant that Theo was free to help line Ernie's pockets with sales without the complications of health benefits or a profit-sharing plan. But the territory—the territory was primo, according to Ernie. The top half of the state, west to Pensacola and south all the way to Tampa. "The sky's the limit on commissions, bro," Ernie said regularly. "Get out there and sell that shit. You whore it, you score it."

This morning Theo settled himself into a metal chair across from Ernie's desk, wishing he'd had more coffee. He flipped through a stack of leads and looked forlornly at his latest commission check.

"Don't get comfy there," Ernie said. "What's on deck today? You got that endodontist in Lakeland? Kelso?"

"Yeah," Theo said. "Kelso. Maybe get him to close on the exam chairs."

"The Premiers?"

"The Basics."

"Shit, Theo," Ernie said. "Upsell that son of a bitch. He needs the Premiers."

"He wants the Basics."

"Upsell him."

Ernie unclipped his cell phone from a belt attachment and peered at the screen. He started texting a message, still talking to Theo. "You gotta get some balls, man. What's the matter with you? Your sales are crap. You gotta upsell this shit. These are *dentists,* man. They're not businessmen. This isn't Steve Jobs. This isn't goddamn Jack Welch."

"I don't even know who Jack Welch is," Theo said.

Ernie stopped texting and stared at him. "And that right there is the problem," he said.

Theo looked away.

"Upsell this shit, man," Ernie said.

"Right," Theo said, but his tone was unconvincing, even to himself. He jiggled his knee, looked at his watch.

"All right, now listen," Ernie said. "Before you go to Lakeland I got this new guy I want you to see. Wainwright. He's got a practice in Palatka." Ernie wrote an address on a piece of paper and slid it across the desk.

"Jesus, Palatka?" Theo said.

"It's on your way," Ernie said. "Sort of. And you need the sales." He raised one eyebrow and looked at Theo pointedly.

Theo pictured the route—Palatka was at least an hour's detour from the beeline he'd been planning to make to Lakeland. And what kind of dentist could be in Palatka, anyway? Theo sighed and picked up the paper from Ernie's desk. "That all?" he said.

"You tell me, bro."

Theo walked out of Ernie's office and looked across the parking lot to where the Caravan sat broiling in the sun. The light was white and fuzzy, and everything was damp with humidity. He did a few quick calculations. It was only nine o'clock. He could make it to Palatka in under an hour, see Wainwright, then be back on the road and make it to Lakeland by early afternoon. If he rushed the second sales call, he could still leave plenty of time to get to the car auction. He slipped his hand into his pocket to make sure the ad was still there.

He pulled into traffic and made for McDonald's, where he ordered a large coffee and a McGriddle to go. He headed south on US-1 and cranked up the van's air conditioning, but the air from the vents was damp and warm. Dead compressor, he thought. Fabulous. He lowered the windows and let the morning's hot air rush in.

This goddamn van. This goddamn Caravan. Why did it have to be a Caravan? Sherrill's castoff relic, bestowed upon Theo against his wishes when she bought herself a Volvo three years ago. A *Cara-*

van. She'd insisted on it ten years ago, when Ashley was a preteen and Sherrill had been driving kids all over town and making eyes at that imbecile PTA president. But now Ashley herself drove a Beetle, and Sherrill had the Volvo, and Theo was stuck driving all over Florida in this fat porker of a van. Putty beige exterior and a gray velour interior. Crap-tastic instrument panel. The whole thing smelled like old socks. Oh, God, the vehicle wrung almost all the joy out of driving. Almost all.

He took a deep breath and willed himself to relax. The traffic was sparse, and the road opened up past Moultrie, so he inched up the speed and felt the wind increase. After a few minutes, he un-buckled his seat belt and steered with his knees while he removed his shirt and draped it over the passenger seat. Stripped down to a T-shirt, he felt liberated, younger somehow. The McGriddle went down easy, and he chased it with the coffee.

His phone buzzed and he looked at it and saw a text from Sher-rill. "You have ckbk?" it said. He dropped the phone into the cup holder and turned on the radio, but it was all static, so he clicked it off and listened to the wind. He followed US-1 south for a stretch, then cut over and pushed through Hastings and Spuds, imagining the aquifer under the blacktop, all these roads cutting through Florida like veins. Like veins in a penis, it occurred to him, and he smiled at the thought of it, the bawdiness, the state of Florida nothing but a big penis hanging down off the bottom of the country, pointing out across the Keys and into the south Atlantic. He laughed out loud. He'd been driving all over the state for years, but he'd never thought of that before today.

In Palatka, Wainwright was a bust. Wouldn't see him. The recep-tionist slid open a frosted glass window and shook her head when he told her his name.

"He's got patients," she said. "He said maybe tomorrow." She looked up at Theo, and his first sensation was one of pity. The girl was not pretty; she had coarse black hair cut in a chunky arrange-ment of bangs that fell heavily across her face. Her lips were over-large, her glasses were smudged with an oily film. She'd clearly been crying recently; her eyes were puffy and her nostrils were raw, damp.

"He told my boss we could meet for ten minutes," Theo said. "I just drove all the way down from St. Auggie."

"He's got patients," she repeated. She sniffed, then offered him a star mint from a bowl on the counter.

"Those good for people's teeth?" he said.

She shrugged. "Try tomorrow," she said. She left the mints on the counter and slid the frosted window closed again, but he could see her shape behind the glass, and he watched her roll her chair across a vinyl mat and start tapping at a keyboard. He took three star mints from the bowl and put them in his pocket. He looked around the waiting room, where only one old man slouched, sleeping, in an uncomfortable-looking chair.

He tapped on the glass again, and the girl rolled across the floor, slid the window open, and looked at him over the top of her glasses. "You sure he won't see me?" he said. "I mean, I totally detoured to come here. I'm trying to get to Lakeland. I could have gotten there a lot faster if I hadn't come here first."

She pursed her lips then and regarded him carefully, holding his gaze a beat longer than he would have expected. The old man in the waiting room gurgled suddenly, waking himself with a small snore, and then nodded off again. Theo glanced at him, but then looked back at the girl, who still regarded him in that odd, unaffected manner.

"Is everything OK?" he asked quietly. She blinked.

"What do you mean?" she said.

He hesitated. "I mean, I know it's none of my business, but you seem upset," he said. His phone buzzed in his pocket, and he ignored it. What was he doing? He had no idea why he was inserting himself into this young woman's drama, whatever it was. He was, generally speaking, not that sort of person. In times of public strife—a husband and wife arguing in a restaurant, a mother spanking her child in a grocery store, a customer bawling out a cashier—he generally looked away. It was just how he was wired.

But now—she blinked again. "I'm fine," she said stiffly. "It's boyfriend stuff." Boyfriend stuff! He could not imagine. She pushed her bangs back off her forehead and he felt an unexpected stirring in his groin. She was young, probably in her late twenties, he guessed, and her body was smooth under her rayon blouse. He could see the small bulge at the top of her bra where her breasts overflowed.

She saw him looking at her, and he caught a flicker in her eyes, a sudden light. She wiped at her nose with a tissue.

"Well, I'm sorry to hear that," he said, and he almost said more, almost said, "Well, his loss!" but he stopped himself, bit his lip. A flicker of a smile crossed her lips.

"Maybe tomorrow," he said finally. "Thank you, anyway." He walked out of Wainwright's office feeling jolted, somehow, more awake. He heard the frosted glass sliding shut behind him as he passed through the front door.

Outside, the heat was ridiculous. He got into the Caravan and took his shirt off again, draping it over the passenger seat. Then he started the van and checked the time—10:35. He calculated his route: county roads for the next hour to backtrack to I-95, then he could head south to Daytona, pick up I-4, and cover the two hours left to Lakeland. Shit! Wainwright! This little detour to Palatka had just cost him most of the morning. He fished his cell phone out of his pocket and called the number on the Craigslist ad. He reached a recorded message saying the car auction closed at five. All right, then. He'd make it, though it would be tight, depending on how long the Lakeland call took. He could blow off the call, he thought, and he paused for a moment, entertaining the notion. Kelso? What would Kelso care? And Ernie would be none the wiser, but the proof would be in the empty commission sheet at the end of the month. He sighed. Fine. Kelso. Upsell to the Premiers. Whatever. But he'd make it quick, still get to the auction before it closed.

As he put the Caravan into reverse, a quick movement caught his eye, and he looked toward Wainwright's office to see the dark-haired receptionist walking toward him, an enormous black purse hanging from the crook of her elbow. He paused. Her heels were too high, and she had to put her weight on the balls of her feet in order to move quickly. She short-stepped up to the Caravan's open passenger window.

"Mr. Bitner," she said. "Can you give me a ride?" Without waiting for an answer she pulled the door open and dropped into the seat beside him.

"Well," he said.

"Please," she said. "Just a little ways. I've got a family emergency."

She was breathing hard, and her chest heaved upward with each breath. Her skirt had caught under her thighs when she sat down, and he felt a flicker of electricity in his veins. She closed the door.

"Please," she said again. She turned and looked straight at him, mouth open slightly, eyes wide. The Caravan's engine hiccuped, then regrouped.

"Okay," he said finally. He pulled his shirt out from behind her and leaned over to lay it on the back seat. "Sure. Where do you need to go?"

"Take a right here," she said. As he pulled out of the parking lot and turned right, she twisted around in her seat and looked out the back window at the receding office building.

"Oh, my God," she said. Then she looked at him again and all traces of her earlier tears were gone, replaced with such elation that he was, once again, astounded.

"What?" he said.

"I just walked out on my job."

"Oh, my," he said. He slowed down.

"Don't stop," she said. "Keep going."

"Was that a good idea?" he said. "I mean, to quit your job just like that?"

She started to laugh, a short giggle at first, then swelling into a guffaw. "I just quit my damn job!" She put her fists out in front of her, dragged them in a rhythmic, sideways square, bounced in her seat. Her skirt rode up higher on her thighs.

He stared at her, then jerked his eyes back to the road.

"All right, there, you're making me a bit nervous," he said. "Are you sure you're OK?"

"Mr. Bitner," she said. "I'm fantastic." He looked over again, and she smiled at him, a huge, dangerous smile. She was not pretty, he thought again, but there was something. Something. He turned away.

"I'm Stacey," she said.

"Where do I turn?" he said.

"Anywhere you want to," she said. "It's totally up to you, Mr. Bitner."

He hesitated, then accelerated slightly, and the wind rushed through the windows, hot and damp.

"It's Theo," he said.

*

He didn't know what to do with her. She was evasive, confusing in her directions, telling him to turn here, not turn there, go straight, go right, go left, just keep going, and he gathered, eventually, that she had no particular destination at all. She clutched her purse on her lap and jittered crazily in her seat, fussing with the radio, rolling the window up, then, realizing the air conditioner didn't work, back down again.

"Look, Stacey," he said finally. "I need to let you out somewhere. I'm trying to get to Lakeland."

"What for?"

"I have a sales call," he said. And then, "And I'm buying a car there." It was the first time he'd said it out loud.

"Really? What kind of car?"

"A Corvair. An antique."

"A Corvette?" she said. "Cool."

"Not a Corvette. A Corvair," he said. "Different."

"Better?"

"Well, no," he admitted. He thought of the checkbook in his pocket. "I only have five thousand dollars. Corvettes are a lot more."

"Too bad," she said.

He pulled into a parking lot at a dry cleaner's.

"Don't stop," she said.

"I gotta stop," he said. "I need to know where to take you."

She looked at him. "Take me to Lakeland with you," she said.

"Stacey."

"No, really, Mr. Bitner. Theo . . . please. Truth is I really need to get to Tampa, but if you get me to Lakeland that's almost there. My mother lives in Tampa. She could come to Lakeland to pick me up."

He hesitated.

"It's only a few hours, right?" she said. "Please, Theo. I'm desperate. I don't have a job. And my boyfriend is an asshole. I don't want to go back. Please? I'll give you some gas money."

"You don't even know me," he said. "How do you know I'm not a rapist? A murderer?"

She laughed. "Oh, I can tell," she said.

"Well, I could be," he said, stubborn.

She clasped her hands under her chin, looked up at him from

under her glasses, pursed her lips. "Please?" she said. "Please, please, please?"

It was too hot to idle at the dry cleaner's. The air was stagnant in the van. A bead of sweat appeared on her upper lip, and he stared at her for a moment, then pulled out of the dry cleaner's and headed south. When the phone buzzed in his pocket and he saw the message was from Ernie, he turned the damn thing off and put it in the glove box.

They made it back to I-95 in record time and merged with the southbound traffic. On the interstate, he took the van up to seventy and felt the sweat cooling on his neck. She raised her voice over the rushing wind and told him about her boyfriend.

"He's a lot older than me," she said. Her hair was blowing crazily around the front seat. "Probably your age."

"Thanks."

"I'm just saying."

"But he's a waste," she said. "I hate him."

"Then why are you with him?"

"That's what I've been asking myself, Theo." She rolled her eyes. She rummaged in her purse, found a hair tie, and pulled her hair into a raffish bun atop her head. Then she swapped out her glasses for an enormous pair of sunglasses, and the result was, surprisingly, quite fetching. "He's a day trader, right? So he spends all day on the computer, looking at the stocks, making decisions. Or so he says. But I look at his Google history. I know what he's doing."

A semi truck passed on the right at an alarming speed, and Theo swerved slightly.

"He's looking at porn. It's disgusting," she said.

"Well, I'm sorry," Theo said. He wasn't sure how else he should respond.

"Why do men look at porn, Theo?" she said. He glanced over, and she was looking at him accusingly over the top of the sunglasses.

"I don't know," he said, feeling guilty. "Not all men do."

"You do," she said. "Don't you?"

He shrugged, defeated.

"I thought so," she said. She sighed. "Well, what about you and this car, then? It's, like, old?" she said.

"1966," he said.

"And it's a Corv-what?"

"Corvair," he said. "It's a beautiful car." He paused, then changed lanes to maneuver around a sluggish Civic. "It got a bad safety rap once, though," he said. Ralph Nader, God bless him. Theo often thought that if it hadn't been for Nader, he'd never be able to afford the Corvair, which had been eviscerated in the media in 1965 after Nader penned a damning account of the car's rear-engine instability and wonky suspension. "Unsafe at any speed," Nader had proclaimed. General Motors protested mightily and launched an aggressive redesign and accompanying PR campaign, but the damage was done, and by 1967 the Corvair was out of production.

"Wow. So you're buying a dangerous car," Stacey said.

"Nah," he replied. "It's fine. They fixed the problem in the later models. It was just those early years that were bad." He shifted position to reach into his pocket and pull out the ad, which he unfolded and handed to Stacey. He caught a glimpse of the photo as he handed her the paper, and his heart caught slightly when he realized that every mile on the road was a mile closer to the little car, its power, its grace, its tenacious, ballsy, bantam presence. Corvair! The name made him want to shout.

"Well," she said. She took her sunglasses off and squinted at the photo, then put the glasses back on and sighed. "Safety's not all it's cracked up to be, anyway," she said. She folded the paper and slid it back into Theo's pocket, letting her fingers linger beneath the fabric for a beat, it seemed.

He stared at her until she pointed back to the road, and then he jerked his eyes back to the front. "You are one hundred percent correct about *that*," he said.

She flipped open the center console and started flipping through CDs, and he was embarrassed by the selection.

"Susan Boyle?" she said. "Oh, Theo, really?"

"It's my wife's," he said.

She raised an eyebrow.

She was a talker, it turned out. She took off her shoes and propped her bare feet up on the Caravan's dashboard and chattered on about all number of topics: Lady Gaga, *Extreme Home Makeover,* even NASCAR when they passed the Speedway in Daytona, and Theo was impressed with her range. "That Dale Junior is something else," she said. "I'd fry chicken for him any night of the week."

"Would you, now," he said. He glanced over at her, tried to imagine what this meant, exactly. But then she caught sight of a WANTED billboard featuring a row of convicts, and she sat up straight.

"Look at them, there," she said. "Bad guys. On the loose." She pointed at the billboard and squinted at it until they went past. "They'll never catch those sons of bitches. They're to hell and gone."

"How do you know that?" he said.

"I watch Nancy Grace," she said. "It's only those high-profile types that they really go after. The ones that make a good story. The Casey Anthonys and what have you. Those scrappy old nobodies like up there?" She gestured back at the billboard, now fading into the distance. "Nobody cares." She studied Theo. "And you know what else I've learned from Nancy Grace?" she demanded. "Here's the thing: you want to commit a crime, you'd best commit it alone. It's always the accomplice that gets these people in trouble. Go solo, that's what I say."

Her bare foot twitched on the dashboard. She took her sunglasses off and cleaned them on the hem of her skirt, and when she put them back on she was quiet for a few moments.

"You have kids?" she said suddenly.

"A daughter," he said. He didn't offer Ashley's age. "And my mother lives with us," he added. "I got a lot of women in my house."

"Well, maybe that explains it," she said.

"Explains what?"

"You're very kind," she said, "giving a girl a ride."

He shrugged.

"Does your wife know you're buying the Corvair?" she said.

He hesitated. "Now why would you ask that?" he said.

"Just wondering," she said. She rearranged the bun on top of her head and squirmed a bit in the seat, like a child. Then she dug in her handbag for lipstick and painted her lips a bright orange.

"Let me buy you lunch," she said abruptly. "I'm starving." He glanced at her, and her gaze was so openly sexual he almost swerved. "Aren't you?" she said.

He hesitated. "I'm on a timeline," he said.

"Well, that's no fun," she said. She pouted, looked up at him under hooded eyes.

"But I could eat," he said.

They found a TGI Friday's north of Orlando. The inside was forcedly cheerful and smelled like bleach and onions. The waitress showed them to a two-top in the corner, under a fake Tiffany pendant lamp, and they were so grateful for the cool darkness that for a moment neither of them spoke.

"Order up," Stacey said finally. "My treat. The chicken fingers are divine. And they got them appletinis here. You've got to try one. They taste just like Jolly Ranchers."

He tried two. She tried three. Halfway through the second drink he had an out-of-body experience, where he saw himself at the edge of an enormous cavern, a steep precipice before him, beckoning, offering a coolness and a respite he'd never known possible. He tipped his head back and let himself fall.

He wouldn't let her pay for lunch. There was a Ramada Inn next door to the TGI Friday's. He paid for the room too.

When they first got started at it he found himself apologizing quite a bit, but eventually he stopped that and just surrendered to the pure grotty pleasure of it all, the jiggling sticky abandon. With Sherrill sex was always so controlled, procedural. He felt sometimes they could have used a checklist. But this business with Stacey. My God! She was ravenous, greedy, downright riotous. He had no idea such behavior even existed, and he was both appalled and awestruck. He felt a deep recalibration of values.

They reached an intermission of sorts and he got up to use the bathroom. He brought his phone in with him and checked the damage while standing in front of the toilet. A text from Ernie ("kelso a go, bro?") and, from Sherrill, two missed calls and a voicemail.

He stared at the phone for a long moment. The light in the bathroom was overbright, and a web of mildew snaked up the wall behind the toilet. He'd been married to Sherrill for twenty-six years. He'd never been unfaithful to her, not even after she'd confessed her own affair with that thug from the PTA, that snarky single dad working the middle school parents' scene like it was a nightclub. Still—he'd never cheated on her, had never even wanted to. How on earth had this happened? He looked up and saw himself in the bathroom mirror, naked, pale and paunchy. He heard Stacey flick on the TV in the bedroom. He wasn't sure what any of this meant.

A toilet flushed on the other side of the wall. It was the middle of the afternoon! My God, this Ramada was doing some business. He took another long look at himself in the mirror and shook his head. All right. He'd get dressed. He'd call Sherrill. He'd text Ernie. He'd get his goddamn act together, get this girl delivered to Lakeland, get back on the road. He'd forget the Corvair—a penance to Sherrill. He shifted position to flush the toilet, and as he did, his elbow knocked the ceramic towel holder and he watched in slow motion as his phone was jolted from his hand and jumped into a beautiful clear arc toward the toilet bowl, where it plunged into the water and urine in one single, horrifying blip.

Theo stood naked, staring at the phone in the toilet. Then he flushed the toilet once, twice, three times. The phone was lodged in the bottom of the bowl, stubborn.

"You OK, Theo?" Stacey called from the bedroom.

He fished the phone from the bowl; it now featured a strangely beautiful silver bloom across the screen. He punched the on/off button but nothing happened. He wrapped the phone in a towel and threw it in the wastebasket. Then he washed up and walked out of the bathroom and back to the bed. She turned the TV off and opened her arms.

Things were different now. Everything was different.

They took showers and dressed, but the refreshment of the cool hotel and the hot shower was short-lived when they stepped out of the room into the white hot light of afternoon again. Theo looked at his watch: 3:15. Could it be only 3:15? He felt as though a lifetime had elapsed in the space of this one day.

"Hold on," he said to Stacey. He walked thirty yards to the front office, entered, and dropped the room cards on the reception counter, avoiding the clerk's gaze. When he arrived back at the van and approached the driver's door he realized Stacey was bent over near the rear hatch. She straightened as he approached.

"Everything OK?" he said.

"Peachy," she said.

They climbed into the van and headed back to the highway.

"Here," she said. She fished in her bag and pulled out two bottles of water she'd pinched from the room and a packet of ibuprofen. "I think we might need some of this. You front-load, see, and then the hangover is not so bad when the vodka wears off."

"I'm learning all kinds of things from you, Stacey."

"That's right," she said. "And I bet you thought I was just a dumb girl."

He swallowed an ibuprofen and turned on the radio, punching the buttons and then settling on a rock station. AC/DC promised dirty deeds done dirt cheap. God, he'd forgotten about these guys. His heart swelled with love for Angus Young. Stacey tapped her foot on the dash, keeping time. Theo pulled out of the hotel lot and into traffic. He sped forward to stay ahead of the crush, and then he merged cleanly onto the interstate and headed south.

All right, so he'd bag the sales call with Kelso. That was a no-brainer at this point. The loss of the phone had rendered him untethered from reality, it seemed. Plus, he was still a little drunk from the appletinis and the sex, and the result was a welcome bonhomie that was keeping all impending consequences nicely at bay, at least for the moment. He tapped his fingers on the steering wheel and calculated distances again. Take the I-4 south through Orlando, pray they'd beat rush hour, head straight into Lakeland. Straight to the Corvair. Hour and a half, tops, if all went well. He glanced to his right. Stacey had put her hair back up, but she was sweating again.

"I'm sorry there's no air conditioning," he said.

"Air conditioning is overrated," she said. "I like the heat."

They drove for nearly an hour, and she fell asleep for a while and then woke and announced she needed a bathroom.

"We're almost to Lakeland," he said, glancing at his watch. "You can't wait?"

"Theo," she said. "My back teeth are floating."

He pulled over at a Citgo just off the highway.

"Doesn't look too clean," he said. "You want me to find something better?"

"Well, aren't you the gentleman," she said. She bounced up and down on the seat and grimaced. "I gotta pee. I don't care what it looks like."

She left her handbag on the seat and ran inside. He started

to reach for his phone to check messages, then remembered. A shadow fell across the interior of the van and he glanced up to see the beginnings of a thunderhead building in the distant sky. His gaze drifted around the car and fell on the handbag on the seat next to him, where a thick envelope protruded from the open zipper. He glanced up at the Citgo and then slipped the envelope out of the purse and opened it. Inside were several fat bricks of cash, stacks of hundreds in rubber-banded piles two inches thick. He stared at the money, tried a quick calculation. Thousands? At least thousands. Tens of thousands?

The passenger door of the Caravan was yanked open, and Stacey plopped down in the seat and snatched her handbag out of his hands.

"Mind your *own*," she said. A note of fear had crept into her voice.

"How much money is that?" he said.

She hesitated a moment, then turned and looked at him. "Seventy thousand," she said. "It took me eight years."

She held his gaze for a long moment, then pulled at the rearview mirror and leaned forward to apply her orange lipstick. Her hand shook.

"We going?" she said.

"You're scaring the shit out of me, Stacey," he said. He started the van.

"I'm scaring the shit out of myself too," she said.

As he merged back onto the highway she told him how she did it.

"When the patients pay cash, that's easy," she said. "But other times you can record it as a no-charge, or you can give them a discount and pocket the difference. You have to be creative. Not every case is the same."

"And Wainwright had no idea?" he said.

"Pfftt," she said. "He doesn't know his asshole from his elbow." She paused, squinted at the road. "Although now that I'm gone," she said thoughtfully, "he'll probably catch on."

Theo felt a coolness run through his veins, and he processed the implications of the current situation. So far today, he'd initiated (though admittedly had not yet executed) an unapproved expenditure of five thousand dollars from the joint checking account he shared with Sherrill; he'd very likely lost his biggest commission of the month, if not his entire *job,* by blowing off the sales call with Kelso; and he'd committed tawdry and outrageously athletic adultery with a woman half his age. And now, it seemed, he'd also aided and abetted a confessed embezzler. He watched the road. He felt in his pocket again for his phone. He gripped the steering wheel until his knuckles turned white.

"You're wanted," he said.

She rolled her eyes. "Well, how nice of you to say, Theo," she said. "I guess there's a first time for everything."

He adjusted the rearview mirror and drove on.

It was nearly four-thirty. The heat had been dialed back a smidge and Theo watched the thunderheads build in earnest now to the west, the lightning lacing like fingers through the distant clouds. It was hard to tell if they'd drive into the storm or not, but he appreciated the gray cast the sky had taken on and the damp air, merely tepid now, rushing into the Caravan.

He wondered about Sherrill's voicemails, unchecked on the ruined phone, which was probably still sitting on the bottom of the waste pail at the Ramada Inn, steeped in urine. It wasn't like Sherrill to leave voicemails. She was more of a texter. A vague feeling of nausea crept into his abdomen, and he felt the first twinge of regret for the appletinis, for the affair, for the entire afternoon. A fat lovebug hit the windshield and burst, leaving a creamy blob of entrails just at eye level. He turned on the windshield washer, but it was out of fluid, so the wipers simply smeared the bug into an opaque rainbow of whites and yellows, and he had to slouch in his seat in order to see below it. The movement strained his back, and he straightened out and then hunched over the steering wheel. He glanced sidelong at Stacey and tried to muster a bit of the arousal that had so consumed him just a couple of hours ago, but got nothing. Ah, God! Had he ruined everything? He had a vision of himself behaving this way for the rest of his days: a bent, beaten old man, neutered by remorse, driving toward disaster, unable to see.

"No," Stacey said. He looked over at her. "No, no, no, no, no." Her eyes were wide and her gaze was fixed, frightened, on the wing mirror outside her window. He looked in the rearview and saw the blue flashing lights, and his stomach clenched. He glanced at the speedometer and saw he'd inched above eighty.

"Shit," he said. "Holy hell."

"Don't stop, Theo," she said.

He took his foot off the accelerator and scanned the road's shoulder for a place to pull over.

"Don't stop," she said again. Her voice was panicked, desperate.

"I have to stop," he said.

"No, you don't," she said. "Keep going." She reached over and put her hand on the steering wheel, trying to keep the Caravan straight in the lane.

"I have to stop. Are you crazy? It's a cop! I have to stop."

She was wiggling over the center console now, trying to put her own foot on the accelerator, trying to keep the steering wheel straight. Her weight tipped over the console and she fell into him; the Caravan swerved crazily into the next lane. He shoved her roughly back into her own seat and started to pull to the side of the road. A quarter-mile ahead, an exit ramp yawned down a narrow slope. Stacey clutched at his arm and started to cry, and when he looked at her, her eyes wide and terrified, her lips pulled back in a grimace so fraught it was almost beautiful, something shifted. He'd never seen anyone so alive.

"Oh, Jesus," he said. "Oh, Jesus, help me now."

He pulled the Caravan back into the lane, steadied the wheel, and stomped on the accelerator. He pushed it up to ninety, then bulleted down the exit ramp. The cop evidently had a delayed reaction to the pursuit, and Theo imagined him startled, fumbling with the radio, calling for help. But then he obviously floored it and Theo watched in the rearview as the gap dwindled and the police car followed them down the ramp. The light was red at the bottom, and a solid line of traffic rushed across the road perpendicular to the exit. He glanced at the speedometer. They were approaching the intersection and still doing fifty. In the rearview, the reflection of the cop's blue lights ricocheted against the black wall of thunderheads.

"Do it," Stacey said.

At the crossroads, he took his foot off the accelerator for only the barest instant, tapping the brakes just long enough to dodge a semi, and then another. The two trucks closed behind the Caravan like curtains and the truck drivers immediately slowed from the shock of the near miss, effectively blocking both the cop's trajectory and his vision for a good ten seconds, at least. And then—my God! They were still alive, and Theo was piloting the shaking, rattling Caravan straight back up the next ramp to reenter the interstate. He was Burt stinking *Reynolds* now, and he let out a yelp when he realized they were going to make it. In a Caravan! He pounded the accelerator and pulled straight up the ramp, reentering the same stretch of highway they'd just exited and leaving the dumb cop in the distance sniffing around the exit ramp like a geriatric bloodhound.

He accelerated to a sensible sixty and then hung there, panting. He edged into a clump of traffic, alongside a silver Toyota minivan, and they hawked the rearview, silent and sober, but the cop was gone.

Stacey clapped her hands, gleeful.

"You did it!" she said. "You lost him!"

The adrenaline drained as quickly as it had arrived. Theo felt like he was going to be sick. The first fat drops of rain spattered the windshield.

"He's going to have every cop in Lakeland looking for my tag," he said.

She laughed and reached down for her handbag, and then she pulled out the Caravan's license tag. "You mean this old thing?" she said.

They pulled off at the next exit, and she sat in the van in the pouring rain while he stole a license tag off a Honda Odyssey parked at a Waffle House. They moved to park behind a BP, where he bolted the stolen tag onto the Caravan. For once, he was glad it was a Caravan, a million others just like it between here and Lakeland. Then he climbed into the van, wiped the water off his face with an old paper towel he found in the back seat, and got back on the road. With the windows up in the rain, the inside of the van was steamy and dank. He put the vents on full blast. They gasped hot air into the front seat. Stacey clutched her handbag to her chest and held his hand while he drove. Theo felt her trembling slow, then stop.

In Lakeland, they exited the interstate and headed north on a county road slick with rain, the steam rising like ghosts in the distance.

The Corvair wasn't at the auction. It was parked in a chain-link yard behind a garage two blocks away. THE KAR KORRAL, the sign over the garage said, and the man inside explained: "This here is direct sales. These cars won't sell at auction," he said. He was terribly thin, cancer-thin, with sunken eyes and yellowed fingers. He sucked on a cigarette. His name, Rick, was stitched above his pocket. "They're not competitive enough," he said. "Auction is for the cars everybody wants. Not like these here."

He gestured to the lot, and Theo approached the fence. The rain had stopped and the sun was back, brutal, heating the puddles into vapor. Stacey followed him to the yard, where not one but two Corvairs sat sweltering among a crowd of decrepit, rust-eaten Mustangs and Camaros. Rick unlocked the gate and they walked into the yard. Theo pulled the crumpled ad out of his pocket and showed it to Rick.

"Right here," Rick said. He led them to one of the cars. It was a 1963 Corvair, blue, and it was one of the most depressing things Theo had ever seen. It was a convertible, and the ragtop was tattered beyond repair. The interior was a catastrophe—a cheap velour redo now dirty and damp-looking, with burnt orange foam bulging out from between ripped seams. The dashboard was cracked, the floorboards were rusted, and a hefty dent across two quarter panels kept the passenger door from even opening. The whole car smelled like cat.

"Oh, gawd," Stacey said. "I don't know, Theo. This is *it?*"

"No," Theo said. "That's not the one." He turned to the white Corvair behind him. "This one here."

"That's a good 'un," Rick said. "Better car, all around. After the redesign, you know. This here '66 is a sweet little car." Theo nodded. Indeed it was. Neat as a pin, a clean dry hardtop with a beautiful creamy finish and a red interior. It was the car from the photo. It was even better in person. Stacey opened the passenger door and climbed in, smiled up at him.

Theo stared at the ad in his hand, which was written, he now saw, as ambiguously as possible. "Corvair!" it said. "Two models. $5,000. Call for details."

"So which one is five thousand dollars?" he asked, feeling his heart sink, already knowing the answer.

Rick laughed, a wet jagged chuckle. "The ragtop I can let you have for five," he said. "This little coupe here is almost fully restored. She goes for nine."

"Christ," Theo said. He showed Rick the ad again. "This here is bait and switch."

Rick gazed at him levelly. "You saying I don't have a Corvair here for five thousand dollars?"

Stacey got out of the car.

"It's for your daughter here?" Rick said. "Maybe we can negotiate a little bit. She looks pretty as a picture in that coupe."

This was a lie, of course. Stacey was wet, bedraggled, and road-worn, and she looked worse than she had when she'd slid open the frosted glass window at Wainwright's earlier this morning. All of it was a lie, and Theo was sick and disgusted, suddenly, with everything. He didn't have nine thousand dollars to spend on the white Corvair. He didn't even have five thousand for the blue one, come to think of it; he'd debited ninety-five dollars for the room at the Ramada and seventy-nine dollars for chicken fingers and appletinis at TGI Friday. He'd have to do some negotiating just to win the '63, which was a wanked-out proposition to begin with, the damn thing not even drivable, no way to get it home without a tow. A lemon. A '63 — the year *before* the redesign. The idiot year. What a bust. What a goddamn bust.

He turned and strode back to the Caravan.

"You want to take my card, think it over?" Rick said, but Theo didn't turn around. "I'm staying open late. I'm here till six, you change your mind," Rick called. Theo barely waited for Stacey to get back into the van before he lurched into reverse and turned around in the gravel parking lot. He pulled out onto the highway again, drove north into downtown Lakeland, with no particular destination in mind.

"I'm sorry, Theo," she said, after a minute. She bit her lip. "You want me to help you make up the difference?"

He shook his head.

"I'm not buying a car with stolen money," he said. He stopped at a red light and looked at her hard. "Now where the hell do I let you out?"

She turned away, blinking. He'd stung her. He didn't care. Between the appletinis and the heat and the leftover adrenaline, he was beginning to think he might really be sick, so when he saw a Books-a-Million hulking on the corner of a busy intersection, he pulled in.

"We gotta cool off," he said.

They walked into the bookstore, but the café area was too crowded, so they moved to the back of the store and sat on low

benches in the children's department. A young father was parked
on one of the benches across from them, supervising three tiny
kids, all outfitted in some sort of denim camouflage. He was reading the little girl a book, and his voice had the reading monotone
of a second grader. He stopped when the two little boys started
wrestling over an oversized book shaped like a truck.

"Put that book back," the man said. "And don't get you no
more." He looked at Theo and Stacey and grinned. Theo took
Stacey's elbow and scooted her further down the bench.

"Listen, I've got to go home," he said. "I've got a three-hour
drive."

Stacey clutched her handbag to her chest and watched the little
boys, who had turned their attention to a wooden train set spread
out on a low table.

"How am I going to get to Tampa?" she said.

He snorted. "You're filthy rich," he said. "I think you'll figure
it out."

She started to cry, a silent ugly weeping that made him feel
small and embarrassed. The camouflaged family looked at them.
The young father raised his eyebrows at Theo.

"I'm scared, Theo," Stacey said. "What's going to happen
to me?"

He patted her damp shoulder and smiled grimly at the young
father. Then he took a deep breath.

"I'll get you a coffee, OK?" he said. "Just sit tight."

He left her hunched over her purse on the little wooden bench.
He walked toward the café, and his pace quickened as he moved,
until he walked out the front door of the bookstore and over to
the Caravan. He started the engine, rolled down the windows, and
headed for I-4. Northbound.

The traffic on the interstate was heavy, but he'd driven through
worse. He glanced at his watch. Five-thirty. The afternoon's thun-
derstorm was just a lingering dampness now, and he knew that by
the time he approached Orlando the usual rush hour should have
dissipated. He'd probably be home before nine.

He hunkered down behind a U.S. Mail semi, steadied his speed
at fifty-five, and tried to relax. He pushed the play button of the
CD player. And before Susan Boyle had even reached the chorus
of "Wild Horses," he was back down the exit ramp, retracing his

route and pulling into the still-damp parking lot of the Books-a-Million, where she stood like a statue on a parking island, clutching the handbag.

"I'm sorry," he said to her. He leaned over the seat and opened the passenger door. "I panicked."

"It's OK," she said. "I'm panicking all the time."

They struck a deal. A thirty-five-mile ride to Tampa for $3,174.00. They left Books-a-Million and made it back to the Kar Korral just as Rick was locking up the chain-link fence. He gave them a salute and ushered them into his sales office. They signed over the Caravan for a thousand bucks and Stacey fished the tag out of her purse. Rick raised an eyebrow but offered no comment. When they pulled out of the parking lot in the white Corvair, Theo felt as though he'd been reborn. The afternoon sky was a deeper blue. The trees were a crisper green. In the seat next to him, Stacey was radiant, and he felt blood rushing everywhere in his body. Everywhere.

"You are so sexy in this car," he said.

She smiled. "You're full of shit," she said. "Doesn't this thing go any faster?"

He drove her south to Tampa, and the sun drifted slowly lower until the road was dim, and then dusk. She was quiet, and he rested his hand on her thigh for a little while and then returned it to the steering wheel. In Tampa, he followed her directions and pulled up in front of a neat little cinderblock motel on the south side of the city.

"My mother is staying here," she said. "But we're leaving tonight. She's got a car. We're going back to Texas, where we're from." She sighed, then smiled. "Some girls run away with Prince Charming," she said. "I'm running away with my momma."

"You going to be OK?" Theo said. He touched her face.

"Hell, yes," she said. "Peachy."

She got out of the Corvair and leaned in to look at him through the passenger window.

"The car is beautiful," she said. "And you're a good man, Theo."

He stared at her and had no idea what to say. She laughed.

"Now what?" he said.

"Here's where you go home, Theo. And here's where I just walk away," she said.

"Walk away?"

"Yes," she said. "Walk. Away." And she did. He watched her funny gait, short-stepping on the high heels, the way her backside protruded and her skirt stretched tighter than could possibly be comfortable as she walked up to one of the motel rooms and knocked on the door. A tiny woman answered the door and Stacey turned around, waved to him, and then disappeared into the room.

He pulled a U-turn in the parking lot and felt the Corvair's engine rumbling behind him, and though he knew it was a flat-6, it felt like a locomotive. He flicked on the radio and found another rock station. Zeppelin. Gorgeous. The sky was full dark now, and the air had cooled. He could smell the thick, tangy air of the Gulf off to the west, and he pointed the Corvair northeast, headed back toward the Atlantic, only the thick floating peninsula of La Florida left to cross. He thought about pulling over at a pay phone to call Sherrill, then decided against it. There would be hell to pay when he got home. But the devil was in the back seat, keeping time to the music, and hell was a long way up the road.

Mr. Voice

FROM *Tin House*

MOTHER WAS A STUNNER.

She was so beautiful, men would stop midstep on the street to watch her walk by. When I was little, I'd see them out of the corner of my eye and turn, my hand still in hers. Sometimes I'd wonder if the ogling man was my father. But I don't think the men ever saw me. And my mother didn't notice them, or pretended not to notice, or had stopped noticing. She'd simply pull my hand toward the Crescent, or the Bon Marché, or the fountain at Newberry's, wherever we were going then. "Come on, Tanya, no dawdling."

This could have been my mother's motto in 1974: no dawdling. I was nine then, and Mother thirty-one. She had four or five boyfriends at any given time—she eliminated them like murder suspects. We lived in a small apartment above a jewelry store where Mother worked as a "greeter." I think the owner's theory was that men wouldn't dicker over carats with my tall, striking, miniskirted mother looking over their shoulders. She seemed to have a date whenever she wanted one, at least three or four a week. I knew them by profession: "I'm seeing the pilot tonight," she would say amid a cloud of hair spray, or, with a dismissive roll of her eyes, "The lawyer's taking me to Sea Galley." Mother left me alone in the apartment when she went on these dates and I fed myself and put myself to bed. But she was always there when I woke in the morning, sometimes hurrying the pilot or the lawyer out the door. After one of the men spent the night, I'd wonder if he might stick around for a while, but the next night he was gone and in his place came a fireman or an accountant.

Then, one day, Mother stopped dating entirely. She announced that she was marrying one of the men—a guy she'd been out with only three times by my count—"Mr. Voice." He was a short, intense man with buggy eyes and graying hair that he wore long and mod, framed by two bushy gray sideburns and a thinning swoop across his big forehead.

"You're marrying *him?*" I was confused. Mother always said that one day my father would return, that what they had was "different than other people," that these other boyfriends were just "placeholders" until he came back. I didn't remember my father, and she didn't talk about him much—where he lived or who he was—but she'd get this faraway look and say things about him like "We'll always be together" and "He'll come back." Until then, she was just biding her time—or so I thought—until Mr. Voice came along.

"What about my father?" I asked. We were packing up the apartment into grocery-store boxes.

"Your father?" She smiled gently. "Your father's got nothing to do with it. This is about making a house, and a family for us." Wait. She was doing this for me? I didn't want her to make a family for us; I wanted to wait for my father.

She set down the dishes she was packing and pushed the hair out of my eyes, bent down close. "Listen to me, Tanya. You're a very pretty girl. You're going to be a beautiful woman. This is something you won't understand for a while, but your looks are like a bank account. You can save up your whole life for something, but at some point, you'll have to spend the money. Do you understand?"

It was the only time I ever heard Mother talk about her looks this way. Something about it made me sick. I said I understood. But I didn't.

Or maybe I did.

Mr. Voice was fifty then, almost twenty years older than my mother. Although his name was Claude Almond, everyone knew him—and I mean, *everyone knew him*—as Mr. Voice. This was the name on his business cards, the name in the phone book, the name on the big sign outside the studio he owned, the name people greeted him with on the street, mimicking his basso profundo: *Hey, Mr. Voice.* By the summer of '74, when my mother married him, Claude was on every radio station on the dial, on TV commercials, at civic events, hosting variety shows. Mr. Voice narrated our daily life in Spokane, Washington.

Looking for AM/FM-deluxe-turntable-8-track-stereo-speaker sound with psychedelic lights that rock to the music? Come to Wall of Sound Waterbed on East Sprague, next to the Two Swabbies—

Starlight Stairway is presented once again this week, in vivid color, by Boyle Fuel—if you need coal or oil—call Boyle—

This weekend, at Spokane Raceway Park, we've got the West's best funny cars—Kettleson's Mad-Dog Dodge Dart, Kipp's Killer-Cuda, and the Burns' Aqua Velva Wheelie Truck. Your ears are gonna bleeeed—

That was Mr. Voice.

I remember their wedding more clearly than I remember either of my own: Mother wore a light-purple minidress, and she put me in a dress that matched it—in hindsight, perhaps not something a nine-year-old should wear. "I think people can see my underwear," I said.

"At least you're wearing some," she said, tugging at her own skirt. Our long brown hair was fixed the same too, smooth as liquid behind headbands high on our heads, bangs shiny and combed straight. I got to wear lipstick for the first time: a shiny lacquered coat of pink that made my lips look like two candles. I was Mother's only bridesmaid. Claude had four children from his first marriage, but only his youngest son, Brian, who was seventeen, stood with him, in a brown tux that matched his father's. He had these sleepy brown eyes behind big black-framed glasses and a shock of bushy hair that looked like a wave about to crash.

They were married at the end of the 1974 world's fair in Spokane—such was Claude's celebrity that the TV stations covered it and there was a picture in *The Spokesman-Review:* "Local Radio Host Married at Expo." The wedding was in a little outdoor theater-in-the-round on Canada Island, and a judge friend of Claude's performed the ceremony.

While we waited for the bride to emerge, Claude stood smoking a pipe in his brown tux and ruffled white shirt. He was talking to a couple of businessmen in gray suits when he saw me, walked over, and looked down at me with those buggy eyes of his—"Listen, Tanya, I know this came fast for you. I just want you to know, I'm not trying to replace anyone. You don't have to call me Dad. You can call me Claude if you want. Or Mr. Voice."

This was the first real conversation we'd ever had and it was confusing—that omnipresent radio voice telling me I didn't have to call him Dad. Then Claude kissed the top of my head and returned to the men in suits.

Behind me, someone spoke, mimicking Claude's thundering rumble. "Listen, whatever your name is." I turned. It was Claude's son, Brian, doing what must have been a practiced impersonation of his father. "You can call me Dipshit if you want. Or Dickhead Douchebag." Then he rolled his eyes.

Mom and Claude had written their own vows, New Age gibberish about being "mate and muse" to each other and "sharing soul and sinew," not until death do them part, but "as long as we grow and glow."

The judge pronounced them man and wife; they shared an uncomfortably long kiss and then walked down the aisle, to applause. I tugged at my skirt and followed with my new stepbrother, who gracefully offered his arm. I took it. Brian pursed his lips and covered his mouth. "Don't mind me," he said. "I always puke at weddings."

Claude had a big, sprawling new rancher on the back end of Spokane's old-money South Hill, with an open floor plan and a built-in hi-fi system tied to intercoms in every room. He loved that intercom system. You could hear every word spoken in that thin-walled house, but Claude still insisted on using the intercoms. I'd be reading, or playing dolls, and there would be a hiss of static, and then: "Tanya, have you finished your language arts? . . . Tanya, *Wild Kingdom* is on . . . Tanya, dinner's ready, London broil." We ate in a mauve kitchen overlooking a shag-carpeted sunken living room. On the other end was a hallway with three bedrooms lining it: Mom and Claude's, mine, and, every other weekend, Brian's.

In the A-frame center of the house, the walls didn't go all the way to the ceiling—contributing to the open feel of the house, and to some of the worst memories of my childhood. Such was the combination of Claude's vocal power and 1970s home construction that I could hear every sordid thing that happened in the master bedroom the first year of their marriage. Claude's voice must have been key to their foreplay, because he narrated their sex life the way he did weekend stock-car races.

"Dance those ripe tomatoes over here . . . Ooh, let's get it on, baby . . . Mm, yeah, Mr. Voice digs his little hippie girl . . ."

Claude apparently liked to role-play too, because sometimes I'd hear bits and pieces of various bedroom dramas. Like pirate-and-wench: "Prepare to be boarded, m'lady." Or stern British headmaster: "Someone has *bean* a bloody bad girl." He'd play Tom Jones or Robert Goulet records—miming them, I think—and then pretend Mother was a groupie: "Hello, pretty lady. How'd you like the concert tonight?"

I never heard my mother's voice during these sex games, and based on how quickly Claude emerged from their bedroom in his too-short silk robe afterward, the sex itself was less involved than Claude's narration leading up to it. Sometimes I hid under a pillow to block the actual words, but there was no hiding from the rumble of his voice in that house.

Mr. Voice was everywhere then; in my tenth year I couldn't escape him telling me there was "strawberry shortcake for whoever cleans their plate," or that I should "git on down to Appliance Round Up for the rodeo of savings," or that my mother "put the head in 'head cheerleader.'"

One night they were playing some kind of Egyptian pharaoh game—"Take it all off, slave girl"—when my door flew open. This was Claude's custodial weekend and in the doorway was my stepbrother Brian, looking crazed.

Without a word, he took me by the hand, pulled me into his bedroom, and sat me on the floor in front of his stereo. "Listen," he said, "any time I'm not here and that shit starts up, just come in my room, OK?" Then he put his black stereo headphones on my ears and cranked the music: "Wooden Ships" by Crosby, Stills & Nash.

I closed my eyes and played with the springy cord while I listened. Halfway through the song, two things happened: "Wooden Ships" became, in my mind, the story of Brian and me—*Go, take your sister then, by the hand*—and I fell in love with my stepbrother.

I opened my eyes. Brian was sitting on his bed, cross-legged, filling some kind of little pipe with brownish-green mulch that I intuited must be marijuana. I took the headphones off. Immediately, I could hear Claude's voice, more distant than it had been in my room, but still sonorous and rich. "Pluck a grape from my mouth, slave girl!"

"Honestly, it's not the sex," Brian said, still working on his pipe. "It's the acting that offends me."

Then he looked up at me and cocked his head, smiled a bit. "You really *do* look like her," he said.

Back then, I would sometimes stare at my face in the mirror and think of Mother—did I really look like her? Would my father recognize me if he saw me? Would I have fifty boyfriends and then cash out my looks like a bank account? What made someone beautiful, anyway? Mother and I had two eyes, eyebrows, a nose, a mouth—just like anyone. Beautiful? I felt chubby and had a spray of freckles across my nose. Would I get tall like her? Would the spots on my face go away? Would her face become mine? And what did it even mean, *beautiful*?

But that day, I was never so happy to be told that I looked like her. I put the headphones back on, smiled, and closed my eyes to listen to the song—*And it's a fair wind blowin' warm*—I smelled pot smoke for the first time that afternoon, as Claude finished with his slave girl.

Not long after it started, no more than a year, the sex part seemed to end for Mother and Claude, or at least the overacting before the sex ended. I wondered if my mother had just had enough. Or maybe Brian had said something to them about the thin walls.

Having been married twice myself in the forty years since that time, I now know that a marriage can just settle into a domestic swamp too, and maybe that's what happened with Mother and Mr. Voice. Still, I can't recall a happier, more peaceful time than the second year of my mother's marriage to Claude. Unlike our old routine in the apartment downtown, she was around every day when I got home from school and every night when I went to bed. She quit her jewelry store job and embraced the domestic life, cooking, cleaning, doing laundry; she even dressed like a mother, her skirts moving down her thighs almost to her knees. One day I got dressed for school and asked what had happened to the jumper I was wearing. It was strangely stiff. "Oh, I ironed it," Mother said.

Ironing. Who knew?

Claude seemed happy too, or at least busy. He had just started a brand-new business—"Mr. Voice is going national!"—in which he read and recorded books: Bible stories and thrillers, mostly for long-haul truck drivers. "Every new semi truck has a cassette tape player," he said. "And they all want stories."

Claude worked with a partner named Lowell, a lawyer whose job it was to secure the rights to the books. I loved Claude's new job because it meant I no longer heard him on the radio or TV all the time. He was not Mr. Voice anymore, but my stepfather, helping with my homework and pulling the last of my loose teeth. I don't know if it was the new business, but Claude seemed to age ten years in the year he developed Mr. Voice's Stories on Cassette—his swoop of hair disappeared completely; what was left was long and gray on the sides and in back. With the round glasses he'd begun wearing, Claude looked like a sick Benjamin Franklin. He and my mother began to look more like father and daughter than husband and wife.

That year, Brian spent more time at the house too, which I liked a great deal. He'd started out being pretty cool to Mother, but she was nothing if not persistent and nothing if not charming and she instituted a campaign to get him to like her, complimenting his clothes and his hair and making his favorite food, tacos, at least once a week. She called him "Bri-guy," and ruffled his hair at the dinner table. Brian played guitar in a little two-man band with a high school buddy, a drummer named Clay, and Mother encouraged them to set up a practice space in the garage. Clay was tall and dark-haired, with an intense stare, and something about the attention that Mother showed him made me a little uncomfortable. "Well, if it isn't Clay," she'd gush, or "You get handsomer every time I see you, Clay."

That spring Mother set up guitar lessons for Brian with a guy she knew named Allen, who was the guitarist in a big local band called Treason. I remembered Allen as one of the men she'd dated during her "No dawdling" phase—one of the murder suspects, as I used to think of them—a greasy guy with long blond hair who would come pick up Mother on a motorcycle and take her to some downtown club called Washboard Willie's.

But he must've been a great guitar teacher because Brian really improved. I loved it when Brian got more serious about the guitar. I'd sit on the floor of his bedroom while he played the beginning of "Stairway to Heaven" or the intro to "Layla." Brian's voice was, ironically, thin and reedy, but I still held my breath when he sang, and sometimes he'd sneak my name in there, in the chorus to the Allman Brothers' "Melissa." *But back home he'll always run / To sweet Tanya . . .*

One day, I was in my room doing homework when I heard Mother and Brian come in the door from guitar lessons. I hopped off my bed and ran toward the hall just as the door slammed. Brian stomped past me and threw his guitar in his bedroom closet. Mother went into the kitchen and lit a cigarette. I lingered outside Brian's door, waiting to hear him play whatever song he'd worked on that day with Allen but he just sat on his bed and opened a book. He said he was done with the guitar.

"Why?" I asked.

"Because guitar is for assholes," he said, looking up from his book and glancing past me, toward the kitchen.

"What about Clay?" I asked. "What about the band?"

"There is no band!" he snapped. I backed out of his room.

That night at dinner Brian wouldn't acknowledge Mother and she seemed nervous around him. They both stared at their plates while Claude rambled on about the story he'd taped that day—some Western novel about a sheriff who shoots an outlaw and ends up caring for the dead man's horse. Claude was clueless about whatever was going on in the house that night. Meanwhile, I was furious with Mother. Something had clearly happened, and I sensed it had something to do with her. If she drove Brian away, I would never forgive her.

The next afternoon, while I was at school, Mother searched Brian's room, found his marijuana pipe, and confronted Claude with it when he got home from work. From my room, I could hear them arguing. "I won't have this in my house," she said. "What if he's smoking it around Tanya?"

"I'll talk to him," Claude said. "It's a confusing time for young people."

"Confusing?" Mother scoffed. "Your son is a druggie and all you can say is that it's confusing? I don't want him around Tanya. That's final."

"Linda, be reasonable."

They went back and forth like this. I walked down to Brian's room, ran my hand over his guitar, put on "Wooden Ships," and settled under his headphones.

Sometimes your life changes in big, dramatic ways, as though you've been cast in a play you don't remember auditioning for. Moments have the power of important scenes: being paraded in a tiny purple dress at a wedding, someone putting headphones on you and playing a rock song. But other scenes seem to occur offstage; it's as if you just awake one morning and understand that a certain thing is now something else.

That was how it happened, in the summer of 1976, just before my twelfth birthday, when Mother ran off with Brian's guitar teacher, Allen. I don't recall anyone telling me that it happened, or any great argument or fight between her and Claude. I just recall suddenly understanding why Brian had quit the guitar and knowing that Treason was going on the road to open for a larger band and knowing that Mother was going with the band.

I was furious with her, much angrier—it seems to me now—than Claude was. But there's a fogginess I feel from that period too, a disorientation that makes it hard to remember exactly how things played out. Maybe it was the shock of what ended up happening, or maybe it's just the fog of adolescence. Since that time, I have seen this period in my own daughters—that intense dawning of self-awareness that causes teenagers to tune out the rest of the world. A child's powers of observation must be strongest, I think, between eight and eleven; by thirteen we can't quite see past ourselves.

Whatever the cause, I just remember smoothly going from living with my mother and Claude to living alone with Claude. We developed a quiet, easy relationship. We ate dinner and watched TV together. On Tuesday nights, after I finished my homework, Claude would make popcorn and we'd watch *Happy Days* and *Laverne and Shirley*. When Marshall Harper asked me to "go with him" at school, Claude explained what that meant and gave me the words to tell him no, thank you. When my period arrived, Claude took me to the store for tampons and explained the basics of female reproduction and human sexuality to me, something Mother had failed to do. Thankfully, in his sex talk, he didn't say anything about pirates or slaves or Robert Goulet.

Brian came over a lot that year. He was taking classes at Spokane Falls Community College, and we all had dinner together at least twice a week. I was in middle school and could feel myself coming into my looks. My legs and breasts seemed to grow independently of the rest of me, my shirts becoming too tight, cuffs of my pants rising off the floor. My breasts, especially, were a great mystery and concern to me. I would lock my bedroom door and stand naked in front of the mirror, wondering: Were they too high? Weren't they supposed to hang more? Were the nipples supposed to point out like that? Oh my God, my breasts were deformed, my nipples horribly cockeyed! It was around that time that I also became aware of boys and men watching me more attentively. I felt their heavy gazes first with surprise and with discomfort and then with a kind of familiarity. Right. This was how it felt to be her, to always be on a kind of stage, the eyes in the room drawn your way. I recalled her small mannerisms, the way she managed all that attention, the way she'd feign indifference . . . or shoot a glance at someone . . . this tilt of the head . . . that toss of the hair. In a way, it was all so natural, so easy.

While boys began to notice me, the one boy I most wanted to notice, Brian, seemed to see me only as a little kid. I thought of him as I dressed in the morning—would Brian like this skirt, this blouse, these tight jeans? I started wearing makeup to look older. Tall, intense Clay had started hanging around again too, and if Brian didn't notice me, Clay certainly did. "Man, someone's growing up," he'd say, and Brian would look at me as if noticing for the first time. Then he'd grunt with some unknown meaning: *Yeah, I guess so.* Or *Yuck.*

And that's how I started flirting with Clay, I guess. It was another thing I'd seen mother do—work toward the man she wanted through his friend. I'd hear them setting up Clay's drum kit in the garage and I'd put on a pair of short shorts and go out to the garage, get on my bicycle, and pedal slowly away. "Bye, Brian. Bye, Clay."

Clay would watch me ride away, smiling with just half of his mouth, while Brian tuned his guitar. I could sense the eyes moving, Clay's to me, Brian's to Clay, then Brian's to me. I can't say I was intentional in this; it was not a plan, as such. But I'm sure some part of me knew instinctually, intuitively, that the way to Brian was through jealousy, through his best friend. I also knew it was weird to be in love with your own stepbrother, and I held the secret inside, ashamed and worried that it meant something was wrong with me.

I was usually home alone for a couple of hours after school, and I'd sometimes go into Brian's room and look through his clothes or finger through his albums, imagining him in there. Then, one day I heard the doorbell. I ran to the front door, peered through the window, and saw Clay.

"Hey, Tanya," he said when I opened the door, his eyes traveling up and down me, like he was watching someone yo-yo.

"Brian's not here," I said. "He's at his mom's." I tried to be cooler than usual, since Brian wasn't around to make jealous. But later I would wonder: Did I tilt my head too much, give the slightest shift to my hip? Was it my fault?

"Oh," Clay said. Then, "Shit." He glanced back at his blue Nova, skulking in our driveway. "So you're here alone?"

I stared at my shoes. "Um, yeah . . . But Claude will be home from work pretty soon."

He asked if he could use our phone and when I said yes, he followed me into the house, a bit too close, it seemed, and when we got to the kitchen, I took the phone off the wall, turned, and handed it to him. But he hung the phone up. "I forgot the number." Then he moved closer to me, backing me up until I was against the wall.

"Clay . . ." I put my hand on his chest, the way I remembered Mother doing—a way of touching someone that also kept a bit of distance, I thought.

But he just kept coming closer, pressing me against the wall. He kissed me, not the way boys my age had kissed me, but hungrily, with his tongue, as if he was trying to crawl inside me. I closed my eyes and tried to imagine I was kissing Brian, but it wasn't right. I didn't imagine Brian kissing like this. Clay's hands moved over me.

And I thought: Does he know I'm only thirteen? What boy would want to do *this* with someone who is only thirteen? I pushed a little harder on his chest. "Clay," I said, "I don't . . ."

But he just kissed me harder, mashed my lips against my teeth. He sucked at my neck and said into it, "Don't tell me you don't want it. The way you look?"

The structure of the sentence threw me for a second. *Don't tell? Want what? Look how? What?*

Later, of course, you torture yourself, asking, Was I allowing this? Did I do something? It was all so fast. His hands were insistent, quick, aggressive. It was like fighting a war on two fronts. I would stop his right hand from mashing my left breast and his left hand would be moving up my right inner thigh, the whole time his tongue was stuck deep in my mouth. *Don't tell . . . don't want . . . way you look.* He pulled me to the kitchen floor, his weight on top of me. I tried to stop long enough to think, but there seemed to be no time for thoughts at all, just those hands, the battle of those hands: I stopped the right and the left undid my bra; I stopped the left and the right jammed itself down the front of my jeans. I gripped his right forearm but his fingers moved over my bare pelvis. I gasped. No one had ever touched me there. It was like being jolted with clammy electricity, his strong hand trying to move up and inside me. Thankfully my jeans were very tight, and I squeezed my legs together and that's when a clear thought formed, *I do NOT want this,* but the distance between my mind and my mouth suddenly seemed daunting and his tongue was keeping me from talking and I felt a panic go through me, that he would choke me with that thick tongue, and that's exactly when I heard the voice of God descend from heaven and rain down like fire upon the carpeted floor of that 1970s mauve kitchen.

"You little goddamn shithead creep!" In my memory, the dishes rattled and the windows shook and birds scattered at the very moment Claude came home from work, opened the door from the garage to the kitchen, and saw Clay wrestling with his stepdaughter on the floor. Clay recoiled from the thundering boom of Mr. Voice, his wrist catching on my zipper as he yanked his hand out of my pants: "Get your hands off of her! She's thirteen, for God's sake!"

There was much scrambling, one swift kick (Claude's) and a great deal of apologizing (Clay's) and a bit of crying (mine) and then Claude grabbed Clay by the neck and pushed him out the door. "Don't you ever come to this house again!"

I went to my room and curled up on the bed as the Nova rumbled to life and backed out of our driveway.

I was in there for a long moment alone; I think Claude had a stiff drink to fortify himself—I could smell it on him when he appeared in my doorway. "Are you OK?"

I nodded.

"Look, I didn't . . . I don't know if . . ." He looked pained. "I have to ask . . . is it something . . . you wanted to happen?"

"I don't know." I started crying. "I don't think so."

He nodded. "You do know . . . you don't ever have to do what you don't want to do. With a boy. They can be . . . insistent. You just keep saying 'No,' pushing him away. He doesn't have the right to—"

But before he could finish, I started crying again. "It was confusing. He said . . . I wanted it. The way I looked." I wept into my hands.

Claude came in and sat on the bed.

"He's wrong. You know that, don't you?"

I nodded, but I couldn't stop crying.

"Do you want to know what you look like? To me?" Claude lifted my chin. He ran his index finger around the length of my head. "You look like Tanya. This is *Tanya's* face. Understand? It doesn't belong to some boy. And listen to me: it's not *her* face either."

We both knew who he meant by *her*.

"This is Tanya's face."

I stared up into his bulging eyes, veins running up his balding forehead, gray hair wiring off in all directions. "Claude?"

"Yes?"

"Do we have to tell Brian?" I asked quietly.

"Brian? What's—" He cocked his head, looked at me, and, not for the first time, I could see that Mr. Voice knew a lot more than he ever let on. "Oh," he said. "Oh. Brian."

"I don't want him to think I did something wrong."

He smiled, and if he thought I was a creep for having a crush on my stepbrother, Claude certainly didn't show it. "You didn't do anything wrong. And don't worry about Brian."

Of course, it wasn't long after that day that I came to realize something else, again without much fanfare: Brian was gay. Claude must've already known. He was much more open-minded than many of the men of his age: he accepted this fact as easily as he had once accepted that Brian would like girls. And so, when Brian started bringing boyfriends around the house, Claude welcomed them without so much as a hitch in that deep voice. "More London broil, Kevin?"

We talked about this quality the other day, Brian and I, at Claude's funeral, how Mr. Voice was constantly surprising you, how his goofy looks and odd manner could cause you to miss what a good man he was. There was an obituary in the newspaper about his death, not as big as the story of his wedding, but still nice, talking about the period when he was known as the voice of Spokane. Claude's books-on-tape business turned out to be a big failure, mostly because his lawyer partner hadn't actually secured the rights to the books that he read. Claude settled the lawsuits and spent the next twenty-five years doing voice work, but his heyday was clearly behind him. He got remarried late in life, long after I was gone (college, Denver, two marriages, a career) to a nice woman named Karen, who always talked in a whisper, but who sobbed loudly throughout the funeral.

There was a reception after the service for Claude, and I sat with Brian and his husband, a tall, quiet man named Joey, and their two adopted kids. My second husband, Everett, couldn't make it to the funeral and my older daughter, Brittany, was away at college so I brought Meaghan, who was seventeen, and who did me the favor of taking out her various facial piercings and wearing a dress that covered most of her tattoos.

"What a beautiful girl you are," Joey said to Meaghan. "Like your mother."

I looked at Brian and we smiled at each other. I was filled with nostalgia and warmth for Brian, my first love. I thought too of how many times I'd heard that myself growing up—*you look like your mother*—and how it suddenly stopped.

It's another of those things that I barely recall. I was fourteen and it was not long after the incident with Clay. I remember Claude picking me up from school and taking me home in his Lincoln Continental, but a teacher or my principal must've already broken the news to me because I seemed to know when I got in the car; all I remember is him telling me *how* it happened. She'd been gone two years by then. We'd talked on the phone a few times, and there was some discussion of my going to Los Angeles for the summers, but Treason was doing well in Southern California and it was clear that Mother wasn't coming back to Spokane anytime soon, and the road was no place for a girl.

Allen wasn't driving. Claude thought maybe it was the drummer who fell asleep at the wheel. Whoever was at fault, the Treason tour van crossed the center line and hit another car on the high-way outside some town called Victorville. I used to say the town's name in my head, like an incantation: Victorville. Three people died, the driver of the other car, the bass player, and my mother. "She was killed instantly," Claude said, which, I could tell by the way he said it, was supposed to be good news.

She was cremated. We had a small service in Spokane. Mother's two cruel sisters came up from Oregon. I'd met them only a few times; they hadn't bothered to come for the wedding. They clucked and disapproved and said, "Linda never had her shit together." They stared at me and said, "It's crazy how much you look like her," and "You're the spittin' image," as if this meant I was destined for trouble too. They offered to let me come live with them. I asked Claude if I had to.

"Of course not," he said. "Tell them you have a home."

There's not much else, at least not to Mother's story. My own story isn't hers, just like my daughters' stories aren't mine, just like—as Claude said all those years ago—my face isn't hers, and their faces aren't mine. You make a life for yourself and mine has been a good one—I became a special-ed teacher, then assistant principal, and now am principal of a middle school. I had one good husband, one not so good, lots of friends, good health—what can you say about a decent life? Mother's loss affected me less and less as the years went on and I probably thought of her most when my own daughters got older and came into the family looks—that same thick brown hair, same sharp cheeks, same arched brows, same stares from men. I vowed never to say anything like what Mother had said to me, about their looks being a bank account, especially not to Meaghan, who has the other thing Mother had, a danger, a smokiness, a quality that causes men to stop in their tracks.

When Meaghan got the tattoos and piercings, I was angry at first—I had to be, it's a mother's job—but I can't say that I blamed her. I always wanted my girls to be their own people, not to think their fate was tied to bone structure, or to looking like their mother, or to waiting for some man. Nobody gets to tell you what you look like, or who you are.

But back then, back when I was fourteen, I still wasn't sure. I saw her face in my sleep at night. And then, a few weeks after she died, Allen brought Mother's things over to Claude's house—some clothes, jewelry, a purse, some pictures, a makeup bag. It wasn't much. Allen was wearing a cast with pins through his arm and shoulder, jeans, and a denim vest. One of his eyes was messed up from the wreck, all red and bleary. He kept pushing his shaggy, dirty blond hair out of his eyes and staring at me. "Goddamn, you look like her," he said. "Freaks me out how much. There's maybe a little bit a me in there, but not as much as she always said."

And that was it. Somehow, it didn't really matter, finding out. Two years earlier, it would have changed my life. But on that day, I suppose the only thing I felt was some small measure of contentment for her: that he had, indeed, come back for her, just like she always said he would. They were *different* after all, destined to be together. I thanked Allen for bringing her things, watched him ride away on his motorcycle, and went inside to have dinner with my father.

Contributors' Notes

Other Distinguished Stories of 2014

Editorial Addresses of American and Canadian Magazines Publishing Short Stories

Contributors' Notes

MEGAN MAYHEW BERGMAN was raised in North Carolina and now lives in Vermont. She studied anthropology at Wake Forest University and completed graduate degrees at Duke University and Bennington College. She is the author of *Birds of a Lesser Paradise, Almost Famous Women,* and a forthcoming novel. In 2015, she was awarded the Southern Fellowship of Writers' Garrett Award for Fiction and a fellowship at the American Library in Paris.

• I've always been interested in unusual women with power, and when I first read about Joe Carstairs, I couldn't stop thinking about her: her early days as an ambulance driver and companion of Dolly Wilde, and then her later days as commander in chief of a small island in the Bahamas. I admire islands as settings—they have their own peculiar, highly specific pressures and can function as a character in the narrative. While writing the story, I became obsessed with researching Whale Cay, through Kate Summerscale's excellent biography of Joe (*The Queen of Whale Cay*), and through maps and real estate sites. I wanted its mostly unspoiled and wild character to envelop the reader and provide a lush backdrop for the antics of the passionate women who lived there.

When thinking about Joe Carstairs, an independently wealthy woman who loved to race boats and control others, I wanted to imagine the life of someone in her orbit. I'm fascinated by the way we treat others, and how power dynamics reveal so much about characters and values. I came up with the character of Georgie, a girl from the small-town South who ended up as one of Joe's many girlfriends on Whale Cay. There are islanders in the story who are also at Joe's mercy; it was important to me not to romanticize her actions. She was interesting, but she was also flawed.

After I wrote the first draft of the story, I knew it had many successful elements, but it took three years of revising, and a final rigorous pass with the editors of *The Kenyon Review*, to come to the best draft.

JUSTIN BIGOS was born in New Haven and raised in Bridgeport, Connecticut. His stories have appeared in *McSweeney's Quarterly, Ninth Letter,* and *Memorious,* and his novella, *1982,* appears in *Seattle Review.* He is the author of the poetry chapbook *Twenty Thousand Pigeons* (2014). He cofounded and coedits the literary journal *Waxwing* and teaches creative writing at Northern Arizona University.

· "Fingerprints" began as a memoir. I was finishing my first semester as a fiction student at the MFA program at Warren Wilson College (I dropped out the next semester, then eventually went back and finished in poetry). My adviser, Elizabeth Strout, was willing to look at this "memoir," and I remember her e-mailing me at night to tell me that it was the best thing I'd written all semester, and that whatever it was, fiction, memoir, essay, I needed to keep writing it, no matter what. So, of course, terrified, I put it away, for about ten years. During my two years of doctoral study (I'm really good at dropping out of various levels of higher ed.), I had to take a workshop outside my main focus, which was poetry. I enrolled in a fiction workshop. And I struggled, since I hadn't written short stories for so long. I dug out "Fingerprints," and I looked at it. With nothing much to lose at this point, I shattered it, then put it back together, adding new sections and, ultimately, deleting most of the original. I wanted to write a story about stories, I suppose. Though this story is still, to a large extent, a series of memories of my father, as well as my stepfather and mother and the city I grew up in, I wanted the story to be about storytelling—how we tell the stories of ourselves and, especially, of the people who torture us with their tainted love.

At some point I thought I might as well send the story to some magazines, even if I was really a poet. When *McSweeney's* took the story, over a year after I'd sent it, I'd kind of forgotten it was still out there, as it had been rejected from the dozen or so other places I'd sent it. I was pretty shocked. Then I was thrilled, especially since editor Daniel Gumbiner wanted to chat on the phone about revisions and edits, and we went back and forth over e-mail about ways I could make the story even better. Dan's insights and suggestions were essential to the final version of "Fingerprints." I'm grateful to him and *McSweeney's* for taking a chance on a nobody. "Fingerprints" was my first published story. I doubt I would now still be writing fiction if not for the editors of *McSweeney's,* who gave me a new confidence in my writing. A year later, I now have a collection-in-progress of stories, essays, and a novella, over a hundred pages and growing, titled (yup) *Fingerprints.*

Elizabeth Strout: this story is dedicated to you.

KEVIN CANTY's seventh book, a novel called *Everything,* was published in 2010. He is also the author of three previous collections of short stories

(*Where the Money Went, Honeymoon,* and *A Stranger in This World*) and three novels (*Nine Below Zero, Into the Great Wide Open,* and *Winslow in Love*). His short stories have appeared in *The New Yorker, Granta, Esquire, Tin House, GQ, Glimmer Train, Story, New England Review,* and elsewhere; essays and articles in *Vogue, Details, Playboy,* the *New York Times,* and *Oxford American,* among many others. His work has been translated into French, Dutch, Spanish, German, Polish, Italian, and English. He lives and writes in Missoula, Montana.

• This story arose out of a time in my life when a lot of things that had been fixed in place started to come loose and rattle around. I found myself single for the first time since the Ford administration, for instance. My father had died. My daughter went to college in Oregon, and my son and his girlfriend struck out for California. I found myself largely alone for the first time in a long time, and without anybody to take care of. This felt difficult in the way I remembered adolescence as difficult: no clear path forward, not even sure what I was supposed to want. This was a moment I recognized as having a lot of potential for movement, for change, the things that stories are made out of.

Into this complex and volatile mixture of emotions was injected a scandalous barroom anecdote, and the story precipitated out pretty quickly from there.

DIANE COOK is the author of the story collection *Man v. Nature.* Her fiction has been published in *Harper's Magazine, Granta, Tin House, One Story, Zoetrope: All-Story, Guernica,* and elsewhere. Her nonfiction has appeared in the *New York Times Magazine* and on *This American Life,* where she worked as a radio producer for six years. She won the 2012 Calvino Prize for fabulist fiction, and her story collection was a finalist for the Los Angeles Times Art Seidenbaum Award for First Fiction and received an honorable mention for the PEN/Hemingway Award. She lives in Oakland, California.

• When I sat down to write the first draft of "Moving On" I was thinking about a lot of things. I was thinking about being left behind. I was thinking about all the risks we take when we love someone and all the ways we might try to protect ourselves. I was thinking about my dad, who was trying to move on after my mom died. I worried it was too quick and I wished he'd take more time to grieve. I was thinking about how I was drowning in my own grief and wishing I could move on.

I was thinking about a kind of e-mail I used to get when I lived in Brooklyn. Mass e-mails from friends saying something like "My elderly neighbor has just died and left behind this sweet toy poodle named Angel. Do you know anyone who might want to adopt Angel so she doesn't get sent to a shelter or put down?" I was thinking about how confused that poor poodle must feel to have her whole life altered, possibly ended, and probably not understand why. And I was thinking about the people this happens to. Either because they are removed from the only life they know, or because the life they know is forever changed by the absence of the person who is gone. Their loss is doubled in a way.

All of this thinking led to a very short draft. Really just a setup. I had the situation, the narrator, her loss, the shelter, the women on the floor, the manual. But it was just a place populated by shadows of people. Through revision, more elements came to light. The window friend appeared. Women began running. Bingo was played. These things made the shelter and its inhabitants come alive. It became a place where people were either trying to make the best of a bad situation or fleeing from it. Both were attempts to survive, and survival has always been something I connect back to hope. But still, it didn't feel like a story. Then the narrator began writing the letter that figures in the last third of the piece. And finally I felt like I knew her. She wanted something, even though she knew she couldn't have it, the hallmark of grief. It amazed me that for months all these words had existed together without being able to accomplish much, and that the addition of just one element could bind all this material into a story.

JULIA ELLIOTT's fiction has appeared in *Tin House, Georgia Review, Conjunctions,* and other publications. She has won a Pushcart Prize and a Rona Jaffe Writer's Award. Her debut story collection, *The Wilds,* was chosen by *Kirkus, Publishers Weekly, BuzzFeed,* and *Book Riot* as one of the Best Books of 2014 and was a New York Times Book Review Editors' Choice. Her first novel, *The New and Improved Romie Futch,* will appear in October 2015. She teaches at the University of South Carolina in Columbia. She and her husband, John Dennis, are founding members of the music collective Grey Egg.

· When I was in grad school, I became fascinated by medieval female mystics, particularly those who, like Margery Kempe, wrote about their experiences. My first attempt at a mystic story was too comic and outlandish, incorporating not only an obsession with the "holy prepuce," or foreskin, one of the more eccentric relics that supposedly derived from the body of Jesus Christ, but also the obscure tradition of the "lactating Christ" in late medieval religious iconography. After I abandoned that story, female mystics popped up in the dissertations of at least two of my fictional characters. In one story, which remained unpublished, the mystic's feverish visions appeared in big italicized chunks. In a more successful story, unnamed mystics from the narrator's scholarly research hovered in the background of the narrative, occasionally appearing in brief images or lines of dialogue. When I heard about the *Conjunctions* "Speaking Volumes" theme, I decided to rewrite my mystic story, highlighting the medieval practice of mass-producing volumes in scriptoria. "Bride" also chronicles the private writings and obsessions of a female scribe who records her "visions" on stolen sheets of "uterine vellum," fine parchment made from the skins of unborn calves.

LOUISE ERDRICH owns a small independent bookstore, Birchbark Books, in Minneapolis. Her latest novel, *The Round House,* won the National Book Award. Her next short story collection, *Python's Kiss,* will include "The Big Cat."

• Although I tried to improve the relationship in this story, things just kept getting worse. At last I let go of any hope of redemption and allowed Elida's malevolence to emerge in her husband's dream. People in Minnesota will usually comment on a book or story, but when mentioning this one nobody knew what to say. "I saw your story." Mouths would open, hands flap, an odd laugh. Perhaps as a consequence this became a favorite story of mine—it seems to make people uncomfortable.

BEN FOWLKES is a sports writer who covers professional fighting for *USA Today* and its dedicated mixed martial arts site, MMAJunkie.com. He has covered the sport professionally since 2006 for media outlets including *Sports Illustrated,* AOL Sports, CBS Sports, and others. He has an MFA in creative writing from the University of Montana, and his fiction has appeared in *Crazyhorse, Glimmer Train, Crab Creek Review,* and *Pindeldyboz.* He lives in Missoula, Montana, with his wife and two daughters.

• For most of the fighters I know, the period following a loss is its own little identity crisis. If you're the winner, the fight doesn't tell you anything you didn't already know, which is that you're a great fighter, a fighter of destiny, possibly the best ever. The loser has to choose between finding some way to continue believing those things, or else confronting a reality where those things are not and never will be true. This is a choice that can be put off indefinitely, in one way or another.

There's an added layer of difficulty for fighters who've been knocked out. They often don't remember how the fight ended. Sometimes the whole fight—even that whole day—is wiped from their memory. It's a chunk of time that is incredibly important, that exists for everyone else who saw it and who will treat them with the appropriate amount of sympathy or pity or contempt, and yet for them it's gone, lifted straight out of their brains, retrievable only via video replay. Particularly when it's one single blow that does it, a part of them feels like it didn't really happen. There's this sense of injustice. They know this isn't the right result. It can't be.

For this story, I started with that character in mind—a fighter on the downslope of his career, confronting a changing reality, a changing body, a life where a lot of doors have been closed that can't be reopened. From

there I added the familiar mix of self-pity and self-medication, followed by
a situation that almost invites violence. The awful thing for fighters is that
they're so adept at and familiar with violence, they recognize how unfair
it is for them to use it on regular people. It's like being a wizard, but being forbidden to use your powers to resolve your personal problems. It's
terrible, really. For someone already at a certain point, it might feel like
there's nothing worse.

ARNA BONTEMPS HEMENWAY is the author of *Elegy on Kinderklavier*, win-
ner of the 2015 PEN/Hemingway Award and finalist for the Barnes and
Noble Discover Award. His short fiction has appeared in *A Public Space*,
Ecotone, *Five Chapters*, and *Missouri Review*, among other venues. He's been
the recipient of scholarships and fellowships from the Bread Loaf Writers'
Conference, the Sewanee Writers' Conference, and the Truman Capote
Literary Trust. He holds an MFA from the Iowa Writers' Workshop and is
currently assistant professor of English in creative writing at Baylor Uni-
versity.

• I am a little embarrassed to admit that I don't remember actually writing this story. During the mild and rainy October of 2011, my daughter,
Bluma, was born. For the first month of her life she had extreme difficulty
eating, and I had to wake up every hour and forty-five minutes to feed
her with a syringe. The ensuing sleep deprivation was unlike anything I've
ever experienced. I remember being incapable of contiguous thought. I
remember feeling like, once the border between sleep and waking had
dissolved, time was collapsing into itself, until I was somehow inhabiting
the past and the present at once. Somewhere in there, I knew I had a story
due to my graduate workshop, or I risked failing.

At the time, I was doing intensive primary-source research into the Iraq
War (and specifically, the experiences of those soldiers allegedly involved
in atrocities). In the dissociated hallucinations of my sleepless state, my
research, my memories, dreams, and present reality became somewhat indistinguishable from one another. It was just then that I learned about the
U.S. military's strategy of re-creating whole Iraqi villages in the Mojave and
elsewhere, and hiring real Iraqi expatriates to play out complex psycho-
behavioral profiles faked by various intelligence training units. I started
going on long walks, even as I watched a soldier explain that his memory of
the After Action Report had somehow replaced his memory of the actual
events, even as I was trying to get my daughter to take the syringe. Somewhere in there, I must've been writing too, because on the day it was due, I
showed up to class with this story, more or less in its current form, in hand.

But the deeper truth is that this story exists purely via the superhuman
grace of my wife, the love of my life, Marissa. The real wonder here is of
course her, who managed to juggle a newborn and a husband who was

slowly losing his mind, with enough strength left over to somehow, some-how, in the midst of all this, point to my office and say, *I'll stay up, I know you can do it, I believe in you: now get to work.*

DENIS JOHNSON is the author of several novels and plays, as well as a vol-ume of stories and one of nonfiction articles and two books of verse. He lives in North Idaho.

    • I ran across the phrase "the largesse of the sea maiden" in an English translation of a Persian folktale some years back. The words seemed mys-teriously linked to a moment from my youth, when a woman sang a song to me—just me—in a bar in Seattle. In 2007 I asked a class I was teaching to write a story in two pages or less, and the first section of this tale was my own attempt at the assignment. Over the next several years I tinkered with other such vignettes, and one day they came together in a sort of arrange-ment.

SARAH KOKERNOT was born and raised in Kentucky. Her fiction has ap-peared in *Crazyhorse, Front Porch, West Branch, Lady Churchill's Rosebud Wrist-let, decomP magazinE,* and *PANK.* She lives in Chicago with her husband, the writer Juan Martinez, and their son. Sarah is the program coordinator at 826CHI, a nonprofit writing and tutoring center. She is currently at work on a novel.

    • I was living in rural Pennsylvania, reading a lot of late Chekhov, and I wanted to try my hand at something tender and subtle. I was concerned with the unpredictable and even darkly comical situations that can arise from past trauma. But the story didn't begin there. It began with the end-ing—a man picking up a woman's dress shoes as he followed her into the woods at the edge of a field. I wrote my way backward from those woods. Also, ever since meeting Izzy the camel in Waitsburg, Washington, I was determined to include a camel in a story.

VICTOR LODATO is the author of the novel *Mathilda Savitch* (2010), which won the PEN USA Award for Fiction and the Barnes & Noble Discover Award. His stories and poems have appeared in *The New Yorker, Virginia Quarterly Review,* and *Southern Review.* He is the recipient of fellowships from the Guggenheim Foundation and the National Endowment for the Arts. His new novel, *Edgar and Lucy,* is forthcoming.

    • "Jack, July" started with body language as much as with voice. I could absolutely picture Jack's way of moving down the street—and I realized pretty quickly that I was dealing with a person reeling from some kind of intoxicant. In Tucson, where I lived for many years, you'll often see some-one marching down the road or standing at a bus stop with this very odd, twitchy behavior. Of course, meth is everywhere in Arizona. The neighborhood in which I lived slid quickly from working class to something a little more provisional. Coming from a working-class family, I find myself drawn to these sorts of characters: characters who appear to have less armor and artifice. Somehow their exhaustion seems to unmask them.

I never know where I'm going when I begin a piece, and in this story, since I'd stumbled upon a character who also had no idea where he was going, both physically and mentally, his state perfectly mirrored my own. Because of Jack's heightened state of mind, I felt free to go a little crazy, to edit myself less as I wrote—and in doing so, I ended up in some unlikely places.

The beginning of this piece rides on an absurd, almost comic wave. Then the past enters the picture, and the story opens to its true intentions. Jack's intoxication and eventual crash mirror the story's journey from a kind of aching zaniness to a deeper heartbreak. I always knew that something unhappy was near, but like Jack, I circled it, hovered above it for as long as I could, until the weight of it had to intrude.

COLUM McCANN is the author of six novels and three collections of stories. He was awarded the 2009 National Book Award for his novel *Let the Great World Spin.* "Sh'khol" is featured in his new collection, *Thirteen Ways of Looking.*

• We sometimes forget that the construction of a house, or a cottage, or a hut, or even a cathedral, begins with the smashing up of rocks. There's so much between the original sledge blow and the placement of the very last brick. It's the same with stories, of course. Now that "Sh'khol" is in place, I find it hard to remember when I first started swinging the hammer.

One can find beginnings in numerous places, of course, but I recall being at a reading in 2010 and a woman in the audience asking me why I was so obsessed with parents losing their children. I had no good answer for her. I have never lost a child and, at that stage, never even lost a parent. But it struck me that the language of my attempted reply was hampered by the fact that there was no single word for a parent who had lost a child. Odd, given that the English language has (depending on how you classify a word) anywhere from a quarter-million to a million words, and the fact of losing a child is such a deeply traumatic event. Do we not have a specific word precisely because it is so harrowing? This lack of a proper word seemed like an almost hymn-singing absence.

I began to ask people if they knew of an exact word that might work. Most languages failed. There was a phrase in Sanskrit and I learned later that there were words in Arabic as well, but I thought the Hebrew word *sh'khol* was the closest. It was so deeply onomatopoeic as well, with the *sh* implying silence and the *khol* having a distressing sharpness. I hungered to build a story around it.

There were other things I wanted to explore as well. I have long wanted to write about Ireland's dwindling Jewish community, especially in the context of the collapse of the economy there. Also, I had begun to hear a lot of stories about autistic children and the difficulties parents were having with adopted children. What fascinated me was the unknown history: how whole lives get absorbed into new landscapes and indeed new mythologies. I also wanted to sneak in a few references to other countries, so while the story was to unfold in the West of Ireland, it also takes place in Russia and the Middle East, all stories funneling themselves into one story.

So, all of these things became a collision of obsessions.

Still, the trouble with fiction is that it often makes too much sense, and we allow our obsessions to narrow themselves. Characters with their conscious actions, plotlines unrolling themselves in inexorably stable ways, everything neat, ordered, controlled. You always want to keep the critical heckler alive in yourself. I found myself wanting to write a story that would be grounded in action, but still elusive, tenebrous, and certainly unfilmable. Nothing is ever, eventually, found out.

Funnily enough I think it's one of the first times I've put a mobile phone in a story. I wanted to see how I could get rid of the furniture of the modern world.

ELIZABETH McCRACKEN is the author of five books, the most recent of which, *Thunderstruck & Other Stories,* won the 2014 Story Prize. She teaches at the University of Texas, Austin.

• Years ago, I was noodling around on a novel about a woman who disappeared from a suburban street, and I wondered where she might have gone to. This was the kind of idle wondering that is really procrastination: *maybe I'll come up with something more interesting than the book I'm working on now.* One of the possibilities: a cult in Canada, centered around a girl who'd sustained a traumatic brain injury, whose mother declared her a saint.

That idea stayed in my head, faint but persistent, a song I couldn't quite remember. More than ten years later, I was on leave from my teaching job, trying to finish a collection of stories. I was writing at a great rate, story after story. Not since I'd been in graduate school had I had the thought *Need to work on the next thing, but what, what?* Toward the end of the semester, I remembered the brain-injured girl, but now—having become a parent myself in the years that had passed—I was interested in the parents. Generally I know the shape of a story when I begin it, but this one I didn't, which is possibly why it's so long. It was the last story I wrote in the collection.

Also, I once had a French personal trainer named Didier who did take an inexplicable dislike to me, and I am delighted to have my revenge in these pages.

THOMAS MCGUANE is a member of the American Academy of Arts and letters, a National Book Award finalist, and the recipient of numerous writing awards. His stories and essays have appeared in *The Best American Short Stories, The Best American Essays,* and *The Best American Sports Writing.* The author of fifteen books, he lives with his family on a ranch in Montana.

• I started out with some vague ideas about the energy industry, about a more pastoral version of the West, and about the skills learned through agriculture, and how they would finally clash. This was in danger of remaining pretty abstract, pretty ideological, not to mention uninteresting until occupied by human beings, characters I had on hand; and my feeling for the country I was talking about. The energy industry and its taxation on the earth is concentrated in specific places. The extraction of oil from shale through fracking has befallen parts of North Dakota and Montana. Its profits are astronomical. Few dare to stand up in the face of this tidal wave of money. The arrival of hookers, drug gangs, and gunmen in guileless prairie towns and their credulous boosters has been unspeakable. You need to see such broad things through the eyes of individuals in order to make plausible fiction. As usual, this often calls upon a writer's capacity for finding voices for the voiceless. Nothing new about that, but it can be a challenge when, as in the case of "Motherlode," there is such extraordinary distance between these lives and the forces that rule them.

MAILE MELOY is the author of two novels, two story collections, and a young adult trilogy. Her story collection *Both Ways Is the Only Way I Want It* was one of the *New York Times Book Review*'s Ten Best Books of the year. She has received the PEN/Malamud Award, the E. B. White Award, and a Guggenheim Fellowship, and she was named one of *Granta*'s Best Young American Novelists. Her stories have been published in *The New Yorker, Zoetrope: All-Story,* and *Paris Review.* She grew up in Helena, Montana, and lives in Los Angeles.

• There are sometimes elements floating in the back of my mind that I want to use, long before I ever figure out how to do it. The story from the past in "Madame Lazarus" was one of those: I wanted to write about the strangeness of life in postwar France, where those who survived, whether they had resisted the German occupiers or collaborated, stayed out of the way or hunted the resisters down, were all living alongside one another. But I hadn't found a way in; it was too big and uncontrollable a subject. Then I started writing the story of a man trying to resuscitate a small dog, and I realized that there was space inside it for the other story, and they each made the other possible.

I also learn things about stories after they're finished. As soon as "Madame Lazarus" was published, I started getting letters and e-mails from friends and strangers about the deaths of beloved dogs. They were beautiful, heartbreaking stories, and I hadn't expected them. I thought the story was about human illness and aging, the breakdown and betrayal of the body (and, in the past, of a country). I thought those were the things people would respond to, but I was wrong. In the outpouring of grief, I realized that people's love for their dogs is very pure, when there's little in love that is pure. The responsibility for a dog is total, and the sense of failure when they die is enormous. Other loves are guarded—the character's love for his children, his ex-wife, his partner, the boy in the past, the housekeeper—but the love for the dog isn't, and his inability to save that one pure thing is at the heart of the story. Readers knew it when I didn't.

SHOBHA RAO is the author of the forthcoming collection of short stories *An Unrestored Woman.* Her work has appeared in *Nimrod International Journal, Water~Stone Review, PoemMemoirStory,* and elsewhere. She has been awarded a residency at Hedgebrook and is the winner of the Katherine Anne Porter Prize in Fiction, as well as a grant from the Elizabeth George Foundation. She lives in San Francisco.

· This story is part of a collection that focuses on the Partition of India and Pakistan. I had been working on the collection for some time when I was awarded a residency at Hedgebrook, on Whidbey Island in Puget Sound. While there—housed in a lovely cabin overlooking Useless Bay—I knew I wanted to explore a moment of terrifying conflict, and the choices we are forced to make during such moments. I also knew I wanted to write it in the guise of a relationship between a middle-aged woman and a young boy. I wanted the relationship between them to be platonic, yet intense. While walking along the shores of Useless Bay, the sentence "I was widowed long ago" occurred to me. I'm not sure why, or how, perhaps the wind, the shimmering water, the clouded glimpses of a faraway island. Still, it stayed with me, and I thought of all the marriages I have known, and of how, in so many of them, widowhood comes long before a death. It didn't seem sad to me, certainly not tragic: we mourn the people we have been, we mourn the people we are with, we mourn what the years have made us. It is life; it is the basic machinery of life. Once that aspect was decided, to put the woman and the boy on a train, to have that train attacked, to have the woman choose the boy over the husband, and then to have the train burned to the ground, all came relatively quickly. Violence, after all, is not difficult. Humanizing that violence is what is difficult.

JOAN SILBER is the author of seven books of fiction, including *Fools,* longlisted for the National Book Award and finalist for the PEN/Faulkner Award; *The Size of the World,* finalist for the Los Angeles Times Book Prize in Fiction; and *Ideas of Heaven,* finalist for the National Book Award and the Story Prize. She's also the author of *The Art of Time in Fiction.* She lives

in New York and teaches at Sarah Lawrence College and in the Warren
Wilson College MFA Program.

• When Hurricane Sandy hit New York in 2012, I heard a radio report
about older residents of housing projects who impressed volunteers with
how well they managed without electricity or water. (My neighborhood,
the Lower East Side, was in the dark zone, so I knew what they dealt with.)
I began to think about self-reliance and the situations that call it forth, and
the character of Kiki started to form. I had wanted for a while to get Turkey—a place I've happily visited a few times—into a story. And I wanted
Kiki viewed by a younger female character, with her own ideas about risk
and frontiers. Once I'd given Reyna a boyfriend at Rikers Island, I saw the
story heightening. I wanted the two women to understand each other just
fine but view each other across a great divide, where neither envies the
other. I assumed "About My Aunt" was done when I finished it, but it has
become the first chapter of a novel.

ARIA BETH SLOSS is the author of *Autobiography of Us*, a novel. Her short
fiction has been published in *Glimmer Train, Five Chapters, Harvard Review*,
and *One Story*, and she is the recipient of fellowships from the Iowa Arts
Foundation, the Yaddo Corporation, and the Vermont Studio Center. A
graduate of Yale University and the Iowa Writers' Workshop, she lives in
New York City.

• I am not a natural storyteller. By which I mean narrative—the spine
around which a story is built—does not come easily to me. Construction
is slow, laborious, feasible only after I've scored some image or scrap of
dialogue with a thousand tiny lines, trying to see if it will bleed.

In this case, I got lucky. A few weeks after my daughter was born, I
picked up Alec Wilkinson's *The Ice Balloon*, an account of the nineteenth-
century inventor S. A. Andrée's ill-fated attempt to reach the North Pole
via hot air balloon. I was bone-tired, half-drunk on hormones and joy. In
other words, primed. For days, that image dogged me: a balloon fueled by
ambition, sailing over Arctic tundra.

Not long after, my husband went back to work. My days retained their
strange new softness, the baggy shape of time delineated by feeding, washing, and soothing. Men leave, I told a friend, incredulous. Women can't.
Patently false, but I had my blood. Not long after, I sat down and began to
write.

LAURA LEE SMITH is the author of the novel *Heart of Palm*. Her short fiction has appeared in the anthology *New Stories from the South: The Year's Best*,
as well as *New England Review*, the *Florida Review, Natural Bridge, Bayou*, and
other journals. She lives in Florida and works as an advertising copywriter.

• I really like cars. I don't know much about them, but I grew up in a family where most of the men loved and worked on cars, and I married a man who shares that passion. I wanted to write a story about a car, and I remembered that when I was much younger—twenty-one? twenty-two?—I almost bought a used Corvair. I had money down on it and everything, but my father talked me out of it, citing the instability of the car's rear-engine design. We argued about it. It was a beautiful old car, white with a red-leather interior, and I wanted it even though I knew it might be unsafe. In the end I lost the argument, and the kind lady who had taken my deposit gave me back my $200. I ended up buying a Dodge Challenger (what a name!—another car story one day, perhaps), but I never forgot that Corvair. So when I started playing with ideas for a car story I decided to give that latent desire for a Corvair to a character and see what would happen. Once I had Theo on the road, moving southward through the Florida heat on a quest for this car that he unreasonably, irrationally wants, the story started to tell itself. In reading up on some of the car's details, I stumbled across the infamous Ralph Nader judgment that the Corvair was "unsafe at any speed." I thought it would make a great title.

JESS WALTER is the author of eight books, most recently the novels *Beautiful Ruins* (2012) and *The Financial Lives of the Poets* (2009) and the story collection *We Live in Water* (2013). He was a National Book Award finalist for *The Zero* (2006) and won the Edgar Allan Poe Award for *Citizen Vince* (2005). His fiction has appeared in *The Best American Short Stories 2012*, *The Best American Nonrequired Reading, Harper's Magazine, Tin House, McSweeney's, Esquire,* and many others. He lives with his family in Spokane, Washington.

• "Mr. Voice" grew out of that first line: *Mother was a stunner.* Sometimes a line just pops into your head, like a song lyric. You know it's right, so for once in your life, you don't tinker with it. You stare at it, try different second lines, walk around wondering, *Who said that?* Then the characters start to come into focus: a girl, her beautiful mom, Claude. I'd wanted to write a story for a while set in the early to mid '70s: home intercoms, *Wild Kingdom,* waterbed stores, and the 1974 Spokane World's Fair. It was one of those stories that kept surprising me as I discovered a bit more of it every day— *Oh, so she turns out to be . . . Ah, then he is . . . Right, so they are . . .* I have two daughters and when I got to the end of the first draft and wrote Tanya's line ("Nobody gets to tell you what you look like, or who you are") I realized that's what I wanted to tell my own daughters and, sentimental goof that I am, I started crying.

Other Distinguished Stories
of 2014

Editorial Addresses of American and Canadian Magazines Publishing Short Stories

Able Muse Review
467 Saratoga Avenue, #602
San Jose, CA 95129
$24, Alexander Pepple

African American Review
http://aar.expressacademic.org
$40, Nathan Grant

Agni
Boston University Writing Program
Boston University
236 Bay State Road
Boston, MA 02115
$20, Sven Birkerts

Alaska Quarterly Review
University of Alaska, Anchorage
3211 Providence Drive
Anchorage, AK 99508
$18, Ronald Spatz

Alimentum
www.alimentumjournal.com
$18, Paulette Licitra

Alligator Juniper
http://www.prescott.edu/alligator
_juniper/
$15, Melanie Bishop

American Athenaeum
www.swordandsagapress.com
Hunter Liguore

American Letters and Commentary
Department of English
University of Texas at San Antonio
One UTSA Boulevard
San Antonio, TX 78249
$10, David Ray Vance, Catherine Kasper

American Reader
779 Riverside Drive
New York, NY 10032
$54.99, Jac Mullen

American Short Fiction
P.O. Box 302678
Austin, TX 78703
$25, Rebecca Markovits

Amoskeag
Southern New Hampshire
University
2500 North River Road
Manchester, NH 03106
$7, Michael J. Brien

Antioch Review
Antioch University
P.O. Box 148
Yellow Springs, OH 45387
$40, Robert S. Fogerty

Apalachee Review
P.O. Box 10469
Tallahassee, FL 32302
$15, Michael Trammell

Appalachian Heritage
www.appalachianheritage.submit
table.com
$30, Jason Howard

Apple Valley Review
88 South 3rd Street, Suite 336
San Jose, CA 95113
Arcadia
9616 Nichols Road
Oklahoma City, OK 73120
$13, Benjamin Reed

Arkansas Review
P.O. Box 1890
Arkansas State University
State University, AR 72467
$20, Janelle Collins

Armchair/Shotgun
377 Flatbush Avenue, #3
Brooklyn, NY 11238

Arts and Letters
Campus Box 89
Georgia College and State University
Milledgeville, GA 31061
$15, Martin Lammon

Ascent
English Department
Concordia College
readthebestwriting.com
W. Scott Olsen

The Atlantic
600 NH Avenue NW
Washington, DC 20037
$39.95, C. Michael Curtis

Baltimore Review
P.O. Box 36418
Towson, MD 21286
Barbara Westwood Diehl

Barrelhouse
www.barrelhousemag.com
Dave Housley

Bayou
Department of English
University of New Orleans
2000 Lakeshore Drive
New Orleans, LA 70148
$15, Joanna Leake

The Believer
849 Valencia Street
San Francisco, CA 94110
Heidi Julavits

Bellevue Literary Review
Department of Medicine
New York University School
of Medicine
550 First Avenue
New York, NY 10016
$20, Danielle Ofri

Bellingham Review
MS-9053
Western Washington University
Bellingham, WA 98225
$12, Brenda Miller

Bellowing Ark
P.O. Box 55564
Shoreline, WA 98155
$20, Robert Ward

Blackbird
Department of English
Virginia Commonwealth University
P.O. Box 843082
Richmond, VA 23284-3082
Leia Darwish

Black Clock
California Institute of the Arts
24700 McBean Parkway
Valencia, CA 91355
Steve Erickson

Black Warrior Review
bwr.ua.edu
$20, Brandi Wells

Blue Lyra Review
bluelyrareview@gmail.com
B. Kari Moore

Blue Mesa Review
The Creative Writing Program
University of New Mexico
MSC03-2170
Albuquerque, NM 87131
Samantha Tetangco

Bomb
New Art Publications
80 Hanson Place
Brooklyn, NY 11217
$24, Betsy Sussler

Bosque
http://www.abqwriterscoop.com/
bosque.html
Lisa Lenard-Cook

Boston Review
P.O. Box 425
Cambridge, MA 02142

$25, Joshua Cohen,
Deborah Chasman

Boulevard
PMB 325
6614 Clayton Road
Richmond Heights, MO 63117
$15, Richard Burgin

Brain, Child: The Magazine for
Thinking Mothers
P.O. Box 714
Lexington, VA 24450-0714
$22, Jennifer Niesslein,
Stephanie Wilkinson

Briar Cliff Review
3303 Rebecca Street
P.O. Box 2100
Sioux City, IA 51104-2100
$10, Tricia Currans-Sheehan

Bridge Eight
leftonmallory.com
Jared Rypkema

Byliner
hello@byliner.com
Mark Bryant

Callaloo
Callalloo.tamu.edu
$60, Charles H. Rowell

Calyx
P.O. Box B
Corvallis, OR 097339
$23, the collective

Camera Obscura
obscurajournal.com
M. E. Parker

Carolina Quarterly
Greenlaw Hall
CB #3520
University of North Carolina

Chapel Hill, NC 27599
$24, Lyndsay Starck

Carve Magazine
Carvezine.com
$39.95, Matthew Limpede

Catamaran Literary Reader
www.catamaranliteraryreader.com
$30, Elizabeth McKenzie

Chariton Review
Truman State University
100 East Normal Avenue
Kinesville, MO 63501
$20, James D'Agostino

Chattahoochee Review
thechattahoocheereview.gpe.edu
Anna Schachner

Chautauqua
www.ciweb.org/literary-journal
$14.95, Jill and Philip Gerard

Chicago Quarterly Review
www.chicagoquarterlyreview.com
$17, S. Afzal Haider

Chicago Review
935 East 60th Street
Taft House
University of Chicago
Chicago, IL 60637
$25, Ben Merriman

Cimarron Review
205 Morrill Hall
Oklahoma State University
Stillwater, OK 74078-4069
$32, Toni Graham

Cincinnati Review
Department of English
McMicken Hall, Room 369
P.O. Box 210069
Cincinnati, OH 45221
$15, Michael Griffith

Cleaver Magazine
cleavermagazine.com
Karen Rile

Coe Review
Coe College
1220 First Avenue NE
Cedar Rapids, IA 52402
Emily Weber

Colorado Review
Department of English
Colorado State University
Fort Collins, CO 80523
$24, Stephanie G'Schwind

Columbia
Columbia University Alumni
Center
622 West 113th Street
MC4521
New York, NY 10025
$50, Michael B. Sharleson

Commentary
165 East 56th Street
New York, NY 10022
$45, Neal Kozody

The Common
Thecommononline.org/submit
$30, Jennifer Acker

Confrontation
English Department
LIU Post
Brookville, NY 11548
$15, Jonna G. Semeiks

Conjunctions
21 East 10th Street, Suite 3E
New York, NY 10003
$18, Bradford Morrow

Consequence
consequencemagazine.org
$10, George Kovach

Crab Orchard Review
Department of English
Faner Hall 2380
Southern Illinois University at
Carbondale
1000 Faner Drive
Carbondale, IL 62901
$20, Carolyn Alessio

Crazyhorse
Department of English
College of Charleston
66 George Street
Charleston, SC 29424
$20, Anthony Varallo

Cream City Review
Department of English
University of Wisconsin,
Milwaukee
Box 413
Milwaukee, WI 53201
$22, Ann McBree

Crucible
Barton College
P.O. Box 5000
Wilson, NC 27893
$16, Terrence L. Grimes

CutBank
Department of English
University of Montana
Missoula, MT 59812
$15, Rachel Mindell

Daedalus
136 Irving Street, Suite 100
Cambridge, MA 02138
$41, James Miller

DailyLit
Plympton Inc.
28 Second Street, 3rd Floor
San Francisco, CA 94104
Yael Goldstein Love

December
P.O. Box 16130
St. Louis, MD 63105
$20, Gianna Jacobson

Denver Quarterly
University of Denver
Denver, CO 80208
$25, Laird Hunt

Descant
P.O. Box 314
Station P
Toronto, Ontario M5S 2S8
$28, Karen Mulhallen

descant
Department of English
Texas Christian University
TCU Box 297270
Fort Worth, TX 76129
$15, Dan Williams

Dogwood
Dept. of English
Fairfield University
1073 North Benson Road
Fairfield, CT 06824
$47.94

Ecotone
Department of Creative Writing
University of North Carolina,
Wilmington
601 South College Road
Wilmington, NC 28403
$16.95, David Gessner

Electric Literature
electricliterature.com
Andy Hunter, Scott Lindenbaum

Eleven Eleven
California College of the Arts
1111 Eighth Street
San Francisco, CA 94107
Hugh Behm-Steinberg

En Route
www.enroute.aircanada.com
Ilana Weitzman

Epiphany
www.epiphanyzine.com
$20, Willard Cook

Epoch
251 Goldwin Smith Hall
Cornell University
Ithaca, NY 14853-3201
$11, Michael Koch

Esquire
300 West 57th Street, 21st Floor
New York, NY 10019
$17.94, fiction editor

Event
Douglas College
P.O. Box 2503
New Westminster
British Columbia V3L 5B2
$29.95, Christine Dewar

Fairy Tale Review
digitalcommons.wayne.edu/fairytale
review/
$15, Kate Bernheimer

Fantasy and Science Fiction
P.O. Box 3447
Hoboken, NJ 07030
$39, Gordon Van Gelder

Farallon Review
1017 L Street, #348
Sacramento, CA 95814
$10, the editors

Fiction
Department of English
The City College of New York
Convent Avenue at 138th Street
New York, NY 10031
$38, Mark Jay Mirsky

Fiction Fix
fictionfix.net
April Gray Wilder

Fiction International
Department of English and
Comparative Literature
5500 Campanile Drive
San Diego State University
San Diego, CA 92182
$18, Harold Jaffe

The Fiddlehead
Campus House
11 Garland Court
UNB P.O. Box 4400
Fredericton
New Brunswick E3B 5A3
$30, Ross Leckie

Fifth Wednesday
www.fifthwednesdayjournal.org
$20, Vern Miller

Five Chapters
www.fivechapters.com
Jenny Shank

Five Points
Georgia State University
P.O. Box 3999
Atlanta, GA 30302
$21, David Bottoms and Megan Sexton

Fjords Review
www.fjordsreview.com
$12, John Gosslee

Florida Review
Department of English
P.O. Box 161346
University of Central Florida
Orlando, FL 32816
$15, Jocelyn Bartkevicius

Flyway
206 Ross Hall

Department of English
Iowa State University
Ames, IA 50011
$24, Genevieve DuBois

Fourteen Hills
Department of Creative Writing
San Francisco State University
1600 Halloway Avenue
San Francisco, CA 94132-1722
$15, Kendra Sheynert

Free State Review
3637 Black Rock Road
Upperco, MD 21155
$20, Hal Burdett

Fugue
uidaho.edu/fugue
$18, Warren Bromley-Vogel

Gargoyle
3819 North 13th Street
Arlington, VA 22201
$30, Lucinda Ebersole, Richard Peabody

Gemini
P.O. Box 1485
Onset, MA 02558
David Bright

Georgetown Review
400 E. College Street
Box 227
Georgetown, KY 40324
$5, Steven Carter

Georgia Review
Gilbert Hall
University of Georgia
Athens, GA 30602
$40, Stephen Corey

Gettysburg Review
Gettysburg College
Gettysburg, PA 17325
$28, Peter Stitt

Ghost Town/Pacific Review
Department of English
California State University,
San Bernadino
5500 University Parkway
San Bernadino, CA 92407
Tim Manifesta

Glimmer Train
1211 NW Glisan Street, Suite 207
Portland, OR 97209
$38, Susan Burmeister-Brown,
Linda Swanson-Davies

Gold Man Review
www.goldmanpublishing.com
Heather Cuthbertson

Good Housekeeping
300 West 57th Street
New York, NY 10019
Laura Matthews

Grain
Box 67
Saskatoon, Saskatchewan 57K 3K9
$36.75, Cassidy McFadzean

Granta
841 Broadway, 4th Floor
New York, NY 10019-3780
$48, Sigrid Rausing

Green Mountains Review
www.greenmountainsreview.com
$15, Neil Shepard

Greensboro Review
3302 Hall for Humanities
and Research Administration
University of North Carolina
Greensboro, NC 27402
$14, Jim Clark

Grey Sparrow
P.O. Box 211664
Saint Paul, MN 55121
Diane Smith

Grist
University of Tennessee
English Department
301 McClung Tower
Knoxville, TN 37996
$33, Christian Anton Gerard

Guernica
P.O. Box 219 Cooper Station
New York, NY 10276
Meakin Armstrong

Gulf Coast
Department of English
University of Houston
Houston, TX 77204-3012
$16, Nick Flynn

Hanging Loose
231 Wyckoff Street
Brooklyn, NY 11217
$27, group

Harper's Magazine
666 Broadway
New York, NY 10012
$16.79, Ben Metcalf

Harpur Palate
Department of English
Binghamton University
P.O. Box 6000
Binghamton, NY 13902
$16, Barrett Bowlin

Harvard Review
Lamont Library
Harvard University
Cambridge, MA 02138
$20, Christina Thompson

Hawaii Review
Department of English
University of Hawaii at Manoa
P.O. Box 11674
Honolulu, HI 96828
$12.50, Anjoli Roy

Hayden's Ferry Review
Box 807302
Arizona State University
Tempe, AZ 85287
$25, Sam Martone

High Desert Journal
www.highdesertjournal.com
$16, Jane Carpenter

Hobart
P.O. Box 11658
Ann Arbor, MI 48106
$18, Aaron Burch

Hotel Amerika
Columbia College
English Department
600 South Michigan Avenue
Chicago, IL 60657
$18, David Lazar

Hudson Review
684 Park Avenue
New York, NY 10065
$40, Paula Deitz

Hunger Mountain
www.hungermtn.org
$12, Miciah Bay Gault

Idaho Review
Boise State University
1910 University Drive
Boise, ID 83725
$15, Mitch Wieland

Image
Center for Religious Humanism
3307 Third Avenue West
Seattle, WA 98119
$39.95, Gregory Wolfe

Indiana Review
Ballantine Hall 529
1020 East Kirkwood Avenue
Bloomington, IN 47405-7103
$20, Katie Moutton

Inkwell
Manhattanville College
2900 Purchase Street
Purchase, NY 10577
$10, Todd Bowes

Iowa Review
Department of English
University of Iowa
308 EPB
Iowa City, IA 52242
$25, Harilaos Stecopoulos

Iron Horse Literary Review
www.ironhorse.submish-mash.com/
submit
$18, Leslie Jill Patterson

Isthmus
www.isthmusreview.com/submit
$15, Ann Przyzycki, Randy Devita

Italian Americana
University of Rhode Island
Providence Campus
80 Washington Street
Providence, RI 02903
$20, Carol Bonomo Albright

Jabberwock Review
www.jabberwock.org.msstate.edu
$15, Becky Hagenston

Jelly Bucket
Bluegrass Writers Studio
467 Case Annex
521 Lancaster Avenue
Richmond, KY 40475
F. Travis Roman

Jewish Currents
45 East 33rd Street
New York, NY 10016-5335
$25, editorial board

The Journal
The Ohio State University

Department of English
164 West 17th Avenue
Columbus, OH 43210
$15, Kathy Fagon

Joyland
joylandmagazine.com
Emily Schultz

Juked
220 Atkinson Drive, #B
Tallahassee, FL 32304
$10, J. W. Wang

Kenyon Review
www.kenyonreview.org
$30, David H. Lynn

The Labletter
3712 North Broadway, #241
Chicago, IL 60613
Robert Kotchen

Lady Churchill's Rosebud Wristlet
Small Beer Press
150 Pleasant Street
Easthampton, MA 01027
$20, Kelly Link

Lake Effect
Penn State Erie
4951 College Drive
Erie, PA 16563-1501
$6, George Looney

Lalitamba
P.O. Box 131
Planetarium Station
New York, NY 10024
$12

The Literarian
www.centerforfiction.org
Dawn Raffel

Literary Review
Fairleigh Dickinson University

285 Madison Avenue
Madison, NJ 07940
$32, Minna Proctor

Little Patuxent Review
6012 Jamina Downs
Columbia, MD 21045
Laura Shovan

Little Star
107 Bank Street
New York, NY 10014
$14.95, Ann Kjellberg

Los Angeles Review
redhen.org/losangelesreview
$20, Kate Gale

Louisiana Literature
SLU-10792
Southeastern Louisiana University
Hammond, LA 70402
$12, Jack B. Bedell

Louisville Review
www.louisvillereview.org/submissions
$14, Sena Jeter Naslund

Lumina
Sarah Lawrence College
Slonim House
One Mead Way
Bronxville, NY 10708
Lillian Ho

Madcap Review
www.madcapreview.com
Craig Ledoux

Madison Review
University of Wisconsin
Department of English
H. C. White Hall
600 North Park Street
Madison, WI 53706
$25, Elzbieta Beck

Make
www.makemag.com
Katrina Sogaard Anderson

Mānoa
English Department
University of Hawaii
Honolulu, HI 96822
$30, Frank Stewart

Massachusetts Review
Photo Lab 309
University of Massachusetts
Amherst, MA 01003
$29, Ellen Doré Watson

Masters Review
1824 NW Couch Street
Portland, OR 97209
Kim Winternheimer

McSweeney's Quarterly
826 Valencia Street
San Francisco, CA 94110
$55, Dave Eggers

Memorious
521 Winston Drive
Vestal, NY 13850
Rebecca Morgan Frank

Meridian
www.readmeridian.org
$12, Jocelyn Sears

Michigan Quarterly Review
0576 Rackham Building
915 East Washington Street
University of Michigan
Ann Arbor, MI 48109
$25, Jonathan Freedman

Mid-American Review
Department of English
Bowling Green State University
Bowling Green, OH 43403
$9, Abigail Cloud

Midwestern Gothic
www.midwestgothic.com
$40, Jeff Pfaller

Minnesota Review
ASPECT Virginia Tech
202 Major Williams Hall (0192)
Blacksburg, VA 24061
$30, Jeffrey Williams

Mississippi Review
University of Southern
Mississippi
118 College Drive, #5144
Hattiesburg, MS 39406-5144
$15, Andrew Milan Milward

Missouri Review
357 McReynolds Hall
University of Missouri
Columbia, MO 65211
$30, Speer Morgan

Montana Quarterly
P.O. Box 1900
Bozeman, MT 59771
Scott McMillion

Mount Hope
www.mounthopemagazine.com
$20, Edward J. Delaney

n + 1
68 Jay Street, #405
Brooklyn, NY 11201
$36, Nikil Saval

Narrative Magazine
narrativemagazine.com
The editors

Nashville Review
331 Benson Hall
Vanderbilt University
Nashville, TN 37203
Matthew Maker

Natural Bridge
Department of English
University of Missouri, St. Louis
St. Louis, MO 63121
$10, Mary Troy

New England Review
Middlebury College
Middlebury, VT 05753
$30, Carolyn Kuebler

New Letters
University of Missouri
5101 Rockhill Road
Kansas City, MO 64110
$22, Robert Stewart

New Madrid
www.newmadridjournal.org
$15, Ann Neelon

New Millennium Writings
www.newmillenniumwritings.com
$12, Don Williams

New Ohio Review
English Department
360 Ellis Hall
Ohio University
Athens, OH 45701
$20, Jill Allyn Rosser

New Orphic Review
706 Mill Street
Nelson, British Columbia V1L 4S5
$30, Ernest Hekkanen

New Quarterly
Saint Jerome's University
290 Westmount Road
N. Waterloo, Ontario N2L 3G3
$36, Kim Jernigan

New South
www.newsouthjournal.com
$8, Jenny Mary Brown

The New Yorker
4 Times Square
New York, NY 10036
$46, Deborah Treisman

Nimrod International Journal
Arts and Humanities Council of Tulsa
600 South College Avenue
Tulsa, OK 74104
$17.50, Francine Ringold

Ninth Letter
Department of English
University of Illinois
608 South Wright Street
Urbana, IL 61801
$21.95, Jodee Stanley

Noon
1324 Lexington Avenue
PMB 298
New York, NY 10128
$12, Diane Williams

Normal School
5245 North Backer Avenue
M/S PB 98
California State University
Fresno, CA 93470
$5, Sophie Beck

North American Review
University of Northern Iowa
1222 West 27th Street
Cedar Falls, IA 50614
$22, Grant Tracey

North Carolina Literary Review
Department of English
Mailstop 555 English
East Carolina University
Greenville, NC 27858-4353
$25, Margaret Bauer

North Dakota Quarterly
University of North Dakota
Merrifield Hall, Room 110

276 Centennial Drive Stop 27209
Grand Forks, ND 58202
$25, Robert Lewis

Northern New England Review
Humanities Department
Franklin Pierce University
40 University Drive
Rindge, NH 03461
$5, Edie Clark

Notre Dame Review
B009C McKenna Hall
University of Notre Dame
Notre Dame, IN 46556
$15, John Matthias,
William O'Rourke

One Story
232 Third Street, #A108
Brooklyn, NY 11215
$21, Maribeth Batcha, Hannah Tinti

One Throne Magazine
www.onethrone.com
George Filipovic

Orion
187 Main Street
Great Barrington, MA 01230
$35, the editors

Oxford American
201 Donaghey Avenue, Main 107
Conway, AR 72035
$24.95, Marc Smirnoff

Pak N Treger
National Yiddish Book Center
Harry and Jeanette Weinberg Bldg.
1021 West Street
Amherst, MA 01002
$36, Aaron Lansky

Parcel
parcelmag.org
$20

Paris Review
544 West 27th St.
New York, NY 10001
$34, Lorin Stein

Passages North
Northern Michigan University
Department of English
1401 Presque Isle Avenue
Marquette, MI 49855
$13, Jennifer A. Howard

Pembroke Magazine
pembrokemagazine.com
Jessica Pitchford

PEN America
PEN America Center
588 Broadway, Suite 303
New York, NY 10012
$10, M Mark

Phoebe
MSN 2C5
George Mason University
4400 University Drive
Fairfax, VA 22030
$12, Brian Koen

The Pinch
Department of English
University of Memphis
Memphis, TN 38152
$28, Kristen Iverson

Pleiades
Department of English and
Philosophy
University of Central Missouri
Warrensburg, MO 64093
$16, Wayne Miller

Ploughshares
Emerson College
120 Boylston Street
Boston, MA 02116
$30, Ladette Randolph

PoemMemoirStory
HB 213
1530 Third Avenue South
Birmingham, AL 35294
$10, Kerry Madden

Post Road
postroadmag.com
$18, Rebecca Boyd

Potomac Review
Montgomery College
51 Mannakee Street
Rockville, MD 20850
$24, Julie Wakeman-Linn

Prairie Fire
423-100 Arthur Street
Winnipeg, Manitoba R3B 1H3
$30, Andris Taskans

Prairie Schooner
201 Andrews Hall
University of Nebraska
Lincoln, NE 68588-0334
$28, Kwame Dawes

Prism International
Department of Creative Writing
University of British Columbia
Buchanan E-462
Vancouver, British Columbia V6T 1Z1
$40, Nicole Boyce

Profane
www.profanejournal.com
Jacob Little, Patrick Chambers

Progenitor
595 West Easter Place
Littleton, CO 80120
Kathryn Peterson

Provo Canyon Review
www.theprovocanyonreview.net
Chris and Erin McClelland

A Public Space
323 Dean Street
Brooklyn, NY 11217
$36, Brigid Hughes

Puerto del Sol
MSC 3E
New Mexico State University
P.O. Box 30001
Las Cruces, NM 88003
$20, Evan Lavender-Smith

Pulp Literature
www.pulpliterature.com/submission
-guidelines
Melanie Anastasiou

The Quotable
www.thequotablelit.com
Eimile Denizer

Redivider
Emerson College
120 Boylston Street
Boston, MA 02116
$10, Matt Salesses

Red Rock Review
redrockreview@csn.edu
$9.50, Richard Logsdon

River Styx
3547 Olive Street, Suite 107
St. Louis, MO 63103-1014
$20, Richard Newman

Roanoke Review
221 College Lane
Salem, VA 24153
$5, Paul Hanstedt

Room Magazine
P.O. Box 46160
Station D
Vancouver, British Columbia
V6J 5G5
$10, Rachel Thompson

Ruminate
www.ruminatemagazine.org
$28, Brianna Van Dyke

Salamander
Suffolk University
English Department
41 Temple Street
Boston, MA 02114
$15, Jennifer Barber

Salmagundi
Skidmore College
Saratoga Springs, NY 12866
$20, Robert Boyers

Salt Hill
salthilljournal.com
$15, Kayla Blatchley

Santa Clara Review
Santa Clara University
500 El Camino Road,
Box 3212
Santa Clara, CA 95053
$16, Nick Sanchez

Santa Monica Review
1900 Pico Boulevard
Santa Monica, CA 90405
$12, Andrew Tonkovich

Saranac Review
www.saranacreview.com
J. L. Torres

Seattle Review
P.O. Box 354330
University of Washington
Seattle, WA 98195
$20, Andrew Feld

Sewanee Review
735 University Avenue
Sewanee, TN 37383
$25, George Core

Shenandoah
Mattingly House
2 Lee Avenue
Washington and Lee University
Lexington, VA 24450-2116
$25, R. T. Smith, Lynn Leech

Sierra Nevada Review
www.sierranevada.edu/submissions
Crystal Miller

Slice
www.slicemagazine.org
Elizabeth Blachman

Solstice
www.solsticelitmag.org
Amy Yelin

Sonora Review
Department of English
University of Arizona
Tucson, AZ 85721
$30, Heather Hamilton

So to Speak
George Mason University
4400 University Drive
MSN 2C5
Fairfax, VA 22030
$12, Kate Partridge

South Carolina Review
Center for Electronic and Digital
Publishing
Clemson University
Strode Tower
Box 340522
Clemson, SC 29634
$28, Wayne Chapman

South Dakota Review
http://southdakotareview.com
$40, Lee Ann Roripaugh

Southeast Review
Department of English

Florida State University
Tallahassee, FL 32306
$15, Brandi George

Southern California Review
Master of Professional Writing
3501 Trousdale Parkway
Mark Taper Hall, THH 355J
University of Southern California
Los Angeles, CA 90089
Channing Sargent

Southern Humanities Review
9088 Haley Center
Auburn University
Auburn, AL 36849
$18, Chantal Acevedo

Southern Indiana Review
College of Liberal Arts
University of Southern Indiana
8600 University Boulevard
Evansville, IN 47712
$20, Ron Mitchell

Southern Review
3990 West Lakeshore Drive
Louisiana State University
Baton Rouge, LA 70808
$40, Emily Nemens

Southwest Review
Southern Methodist University
P.O. Box 750374
Dallas, TX 75275
$24, Willard Spiegelman

Sou'wester
Department of English
Box 1438
Southern Illinois University
Edwardsville, IL 62026
Allison Funk

StoryQuarterly
www.storyquarterly.camden.rutgers.edu
Paul Lisicky

Strangelet
30 Newbury Street, 3rd Floor
Boston, MA 02116
Casey Brown

Subtropics
www.subtropics.submittable.com/
submit
$21, David Leavitt

The Sun
107 North Roberson Street
Chapel Hill, NC 27516
$39, Sy Safransky

Sycamore Review
Department of English
500 Oval Drive
Purdue University
West Lafayette, IN 47907
$16, Jessica Jacobs

Tahoma Literary Review
www.tahomaliteraryreview.com
Kelly Davio

Tampa Review
The University of Tampa
401 West Kennedy Boulevard
Tampa, FL 33606
$22, Richard Mathews

Third Coast
Department of English
Western Michigan University
Kalamazoo, MI 49008
$16, Emily J. Stinson

This Land
1208 South Peoria Avenue
Tulsa, OK 74120
$40, Jeff Martin

Thomas Wolfe Review
P.O. Box 1146
Bloomington, IN 47402
David Strange

Threepenny Review
2163 Vine Street
Berkeley, CA 94709
$25, Wendy Lesser

Timber Creek Review
8969 UNCG Station
Greensboro, NC 27413
$17, John Freiermuth

Tin House
P.O. Box 10500
Portland, OR 97296-0500
$50, Rob Spillman

Transition
104 Mount Auburn Street, # 3R
Cambridge, MA 02138
$43.50, Tommy Shelby

TriQuarterly
629 Noyes Street
Evanston, IL 60208
$24, Susan Firestone Hahn

Tweed's Magazine of Literature and Art
www.tweedsmag.org
Laura Mae Isaacman

Unstuck
unstuckbooks.submittable.com
Matt Williamson

Upstreet
P.O. Box 105
Richmond, MA 01254
$10, Vivian Dorsel

Vermont Literary Review
Department of English
Castleton State College
Castleton, VT 05735
Flo Keyes

Virginia Quarterly Review
5 Boar's Head Lane
P.O. Box 400223

Charlottesville, VA 22903
$32, W. Ralph Eubanks

Wag's Revue
www.wagsrevue.com
Sandra Allen

War, Literature, and the Arts
Department of English and Fine Arts
2354 Fairchild Drive, Suite 6D45
USAF Academy, CO 80840-6242
$10, Donald Anderson

Water-Stone Review
Graduate School of Liberal Studies
Hamline University, MS-A1730
1536 Hewitt Avenue
Saint Paul, MN 55104
$32, the editors

Weber Studies
Weber State University
1405 University Circle
Ogden, UT 84408-1214
$20, Michael Wutz

West Branch
www.bucknell.edu/westbranch
$10, G. C. Waldrep

Western Humanities Review
University of Utah
255 South Central Campus Drive
Room 3500
Salt Lake City, UT 84112
$21, Barry Weller

Willow Springs
Eastern Washington University
501 North Riverpoint Boulevard

Spokane, WA 99201
$18, Samuel Ligon

Witness
Black Mountain Institute
University of Nevada
Las Vegas, NV 89154
$12, Maile Chapman

World Literature Today
The University of Oklahoma
630 Parrington Oval, Suite 110
Norman, OK 73019
Michelle Johnson

Yale Review
P.O. Box 208243
New Haven, CT 06520-8243
$39, J. D. McClatchy

Yellow Medicine Review
www.yellowmedicinereview.com
Judy Wilson

Zoetrope: All-Story
www.all-story.com
$24, Michael Ray

Zone 3
APSU
Box 4565
Clarksville, TN 37044
$15, Barry Kitterman

ZYZZYVA
466 Geary Street, #401
San Francisco, CA 94102
$40, Laura Cogan

THE BEST AMERICAN SERIES®

FIRST, BEST, AND BEST-SELLING

The Best American series is the premier annual showcase for the country's finest short fiction and nonfiction. Each volume's series editor selects notable works from hundreds of periodicals. A special guest editor, a leading writer in the field, then chooses the best twenty or so pieces to publish. This unique system has made the Best American series the most respected—and most popular—of its kind.

Look for these best-selling titles in the Best American series:

The Best American Comics

The Best American Essays

The Best American Infographics

The Best American Mystery Stories

The Best American Nonrequired Reading

The Best American Science and Nature Writing

The Best American Science Fiction and Fantasy

The Best American Short Stories

The Best American Sports Writing

The Best American Travel Writing

Available in print and e-book wherever books are sold.
Visit our website: *www.hmhco.com/popular-reading/general-interest-books/by-category/best-american*